The

Omega Formula

PAUL SEKULICH

Novel

OTHER BOOKS BY THE AUTHOR

A Killer Season

Resort Isle

This book is a work of fiction. Names, characters, businesses, organizations, places, events, and incidents either are the product of the author's imagination or are used fictitiously. Any resemblance to actual persons, living or dead, events, or locales is entirely coincidental.

Published by Omnibus Productions
and
Printed in the United States by
CreateSpace,
a DBA On-Demand Publishing, LLC

ISBN-13: 978-0991559404
ISBN-10: 0991559401
BISAC: Fiction / Thrillers

DEDICATION

To my beautiful wife Joyce whose love and patience
exceed all reasonable expectations. A bright spirit
and the light of my life, without whom I would be
forever groping in darkness.

ACKNOWLEDGEMENTS

My thanks to Jessica Page Morrell for her
professional guidance, expert editing, and advice
on fiction writing. And for caring about writers.

A special thanks to Detective Jan Ryan and
Detective Mike Pachkoski of the Criminal
Investigation Division of the Harford County
Sheriff's Department for taking their valuable time
to show me the technical inside to real police and
forensic work.

A grateful thank you to all the members of The
Panera Writers' Group for their diligence, time and
critical comments that make writing so much less a
lonely business, and novels like this one so much better.

A man like John C. Rehmert is the best friend a writer
can have; a person who knows, shares, and guides. I'm
proud to say he's been one of mine since we weren't
tall enough to go on a lot of Disney rides.

Many thanks to Dr. Mark Kane for his expert advice
on complex and mysterious science issues, factual and
theoretical. He's become my personal Mr. Wizard.

"Now, I am become death,

the destroyer of worlds."

— *J. Robert Oppenheimer*

Chapter 1

Frank Dugan opened a book and discovered a message from a dead man.

The book was *Les Miserables,* a birthday gift from his late grandfather, but the note inside was a surprise. Frank stared at the small piece of paper tucked in the novel as the day shift prepared for its morning at the Martin County Sheriff's Department in Stuart, Florida. Frank caught the curiosity in Corporal Greg Martinez's eyes as he looked on from his desk across the aisle.

"A love note, detective?" Greg asked.

"Kinda," Frank said. "From my granddad, William."

"Didn't he pass away?"

"Years ago, but he loved to give me puzzles to solve. That's what this is," Frank said and flashed the note.

"What kind of puzzle?"

Frank read the hand-written note aloud.

"'A famous play contains a reference to this Victor Hugo novel. The main characters in both works are on the run from the authorities. The theatrical character cites this book in a farewell scene with his children. Your challenge: Find that play and take in its beautifully-worded scenes. Its message will help you navigate the uncertain rapids of humanity. I thought this appropriate since it will serve as my farewell to you, my beloved grandson.'"

"Wow, what a tough puzzle," Greg said. "That the last thing you ever got from your grandfather?"

"It is now," Frank said and rose from his desk clutching the book. "When I moved into my new house in Stuart, I found the book in a box I hadn't opened in years. He sent it to me for my birthday when I was in Iraq. I read *Les Miserables* when I was in college, so I never opened this copy."

"He sent it to you without knowing if you'd already read it?"

"Didn't matter. This one's a first edition, a collector's item. He knew he was sending me something special. I'm taking it to the Stuart Library. Maybe someone there can tell me what it's worth."

"Thinking of selling it?" Greg asked.

"Oh, no. Just need to know if I should insure it and put it in a safe deposit box."

"You were in Iraq? Desert Storm?"

Frank nodded.

"Army?"

"Marines."

Frank's eyes searched the busy sheriff's office for his tardy partner, Carl Rumbaugh.

"Think you'll find your mysterious play?" Greg asked.

"I'll find it. William never posed an unsolvable puzzle to me."

"You're going to have a tough time with that one," Greg said. "I go to a lot of plays. There are tons of 'em out there."

Frank stared at the book and brushed a tiny white spider off its cover.

"I'll find it."

Chapter 2

Joe Dugan knew what they wanted, but a few face slaps weren't going to make him give it up. Warm blood trickled from his nose and flowed over his lips.

Four feet away were two 9mm pistols aimed at his chest. The two men holding the guns wore Michael Myers masks with matted shocks of auburn hair draped from the high forehead and down the back. From years of being a Baltimore cop, he knew the guns were Beretta model 92s, with the firepower of 15-round magazines, plus one in the chamber. Funny, he thought, here he was sitting with a glass of Jameson Irish whiskey in front of him and facing death, but all that concerned him was identifying the weapon poised to deliver it. Probably the booze was tunneling his vision. He always knew drinking would kill him, but not like this; not in his own home in the safest suburb in Maryland.

The 75-watt glow from a single lamp lit the seating area of the parlor, but the rest of the room fell off into darkness. Joe studied the men through sore eyes as if he were cramming for a college exam. One of them was huge, making the gun in his yellow-gloved hand appear to be nestled in a bunch of bananas. The other man was slim but well-proportioned like a track athlete and dressed in a black Baltimore Oriole sweatshirt, Nike crossovers, and pre-washed jeans. The big man wore a muslin duster-style overcoat which, on him, looked like a circus tent. The big man was watchful of the shadowed surroundings, while the other man burned his black eyes into Joe Dugan's flushed sweaty face.

"Remembering anything yet, Joseph?" the athletic man said, the measured tempo of his bass voice muffled by the mask's absent mouth hole.

Joe wiped the blood streaming from the corner of his mouth with the back of his hand.

"Remembering … ? Oh, yeah, I think I remember I took a whiz an hour ago and I don't remember where I put my johnson," Joe said and chuckled. "I'm in my seventies, for chrissake. What do you expect?"

"You look pretty good to me, old man."

"Joe."

"Okay, Joe," the man in the Oriole shirt said. "I'm Nick and this big guy is … Bud."

"Yeah, sure," Joe said. "What do you want from me? My head hurts. I'm a retired old drunk and my memory's been shot for years."

Nick reached across the cocktail table and tapped his pistol on Joe's knee.

"That's why we're going to give you more remember medicine, Joe," Nick said and picked up a framed photograph of a young man in a Marine dress uniform from the end table, studied it for a moment, then nodded at his large cohort.

The huge man rose to his nearly seven-foot height, tucked his automatic in his belt, and pulled a maroon clamshell case from his coat pocket. He opened it and withdrew a hypodermic syringe filled with a pale yellow fluid.

"Got tired of banging me around, so now we try more truth serum?" Joe said. "Sonny, we used the same methods in interrogation. Never worked worth a shit. Booze is better."

"We'll see." Nick replaced the photo on the table and glanced at his partner with the needle.

Bud moved behind Joe's chair and yanked up older man's bloody tee shirt sleeve with his free hand. Joe tried to pull away, but the big man clamped a gigantic paw on his thin neck, twisting him so they were face-to-face, then slowly shook his Michael Myers head. Joe knew resistance to the colossus was futile and relaxed as the syringe emptied into his bloodstream.

"Hell, I don't mind," Joe said, exhaling stale whiskey breath, "It's like getting a couple of drinks on the house."

"We came prepared for free drinks too," Nick said as he held up a narrow bag with the neck of a bottle protruding from the top.

"Excellent," Joe said with a hint of a slur. "Party time."

6

Joe polished off the remainder of his Jameson and banged down his empty glass on the mahogany cocktail table.

"First, let's get back to business," Nick said. "Your father, William, worked on the Manhattan Project, didn't he?"

Joe picked up a tinge of an accent from his inquisitor. He figured he might be American-born brought up bi-lingual. Maybe Baltic.

"Could be. I don't remember. Maybe it was the Brooklyn project. Who knows? The old man never said what the hell he was working on."

"He was a physicist, wasn't he?"

"*Nucular* physicist," Joe said, slobbering down his chin.

"Ever hear him speak of a man named Hapburg?"

"Never heard of him."

"Your dad invented new things for the government during the war, didn't he? Weapons. Powerful weapons to keep America safe. He worked right down the road from here in Washington, didn't he?"

"Sometimes. Other times out west, overseas... Hey, I don't feel so good," Joe said, frowning. "I think I need a doctor."

"What do you know about something called the Omega Formula?"

7

know what you're talking about. I need a

᠌ed his abdomen and grimaced.

"Maybe you need another drink," Nick said and handed the bagged bottle to Bud, who filled the Jameson glass with the clear liquid and brought it to Joe's swollen lips.

"What the hell is that?" Joe said, pulling back. "I don't drink that crap."

Bud squeezed Joe's mouth open with one hand under his chin like he was medicating a cat, and forced the liquid down Joe's throat. Joe sputtered and coughed, but the big man kept pouring until Joe swallowed most of the drink. Joe gasped for breath while Bud refilled the glass and returned to Joe's face for round two.

"Let's get out of here," said another man's voice from the blackness behind the two masked men. "He's given us all he's got."

"But there's more in this house," Nick said, standing to face the voice. "I want that information, and I get what I want."

"You worked him over, drugged him, and we searched the joint already," the voice said.

"Then it's someplace we haven't searched. This old fortress is hiding it somewhere."

"I think he's too far gone to give up anything useful," the voice said.

"Forgive the cliché, but I don't pay you to think. I pay you to open doors."

Nick turned back to face Joe.

"You know what I want, you old flatfoot, so you can quit the dummy act," Nick said. "You're going to tell me where it is, or you're having your last drink."

"You go straight to hell," Joe said, spraying saliva and standing.

Nick made a gesture to his large partner to move between Joe and the doorway to the hall. Joe stretched out his arm to reach the phone on the lamp table at the far end of the sofa and tripped onto the Oriental rug like a 180-pound sack of flour. He crawled to the phone and yanked the wired handset toward his head, pulling the clattering phone body to the floor in one jerky move.

"I need a doctor," Joe said and awkwardly punched at the buttons on the phone lying beneath his chin.

"Gonna let him use the phone?" the voice from the darkness said. "He could call the cops."

Nick snatched the phone from Joe, who rolled onto his back on the floor, struggling for breath.

"He's not going to need the cops," Nick said.

"Then why am I standing in the dark while you two play Halloween?"

"These masks are keeping you alive," Nick said.

"Yeah, but you said there'd be no killing."

9

"Sometimes you have to adjust the battle plan," Nick said as he turned back to Joe. "You have a son. A detective in Florida, I believe."

Nick stepped to the end table next to the sofa and snatched up the photo of the Marine.

"This your son?" Nick said, thrusting the photo inches above Joe's face.

Joe looked away, blinked his runny eyes.

"Haven't talked to him in months," Joe said flailing his feeble arms, attempting to sit up. "Not since the Ravens beat the 'Niners in the Super Bowl. Lost my ass on that one."

Joe gave up trying and flopped back, flat on the floor.

"Nice looking fellow. A Marine. You call him for money?" Nick asked.

Joe dismissed the question with a drunk-handed wave.

"Maybe we can arrange for him to come visit you," Nick said. "Ask him some questions."

"Good luck with that. He don't even answer my calls."

Joe saw the giant man catch a sign from his partner, and watched him withdraw a second hypodermic from his maroon case and check its clear contents.

Nick pressed buttons on the phone as Bud stepped to Joe and knelt beside him. Joe glared at the huge man as he aimed the needle at the side of his head.

"I'm not telling you squat," Joe said and closed his eyes.

Chapter 3

The homicide division of the Martin County Sheriff's Department in Stuart, Florida was centered in a large open room with pairs of desks butted-up, face-to-face. A half dozen workers scrolled through information on computer screens and spoke into phones while others entered data that streamed across their monitors.

The aroma of coffee perfumed the cool, air-conditioned space, and palm fronds thrashed against the high tinted windows from the Atlantic's late spring breeze. A young deputy checked the ammo in his Glock G23, then snapped the magazine back into the handgrip.

Detective Frank Dugan took his eyes off the activity of the room, thumbed through a wad of messages on his desk, and took a sip of his second cup of coffee.

His desk phone rang.

"Detective Dugan," Frank said and worked in another sip.

"This is Jennifer Melton at St. Luke's Hospital in Baltimore. Are you Frank Dugan, the son of Joseph W. Dugan residing at 1505 Elm Terrace in Catonsville, Maryland?"

"Yes. What's happened to him?" Frank said and put down his coffee.

"He arrived here at St. Luke's last night. I'm sorry to inform you that he was deceased when they brought him into emergency. We made every attempt to revive him, but he never responded."

Frank placed his elbow on the desk and pressed his palm against his forehead. Seconds passed before he spoke.

"What was the cause of death?"

"Appears to be cardiac arrest. The attending physician's chart cites complications likely brought on by alcohol."

"How did you know to call me?"

"The police gave us your information. Looks like they knew your father and you."

"I see."

"As the next of kin, we'll need you to identify and claim the body. I know you're in Florida, sir, but can you come to Maryland to do that?"

"I'll make arrangements."

"Thank you, Mr. Dugan. My sincerest condolences on your loss," Ms. Melton said and ended the call.

Frank slammed the receiver into the cradle hard enough to turn the heads of several people in the office. He had allowed that one day booze would kill the old man, so the call came as no real shock, but deep in his heart was a gnawing sadness. His father

13

was dead. His only living relative was gone. Albeit not the poster boy for dads, but the only one he'd ever have. And now there would never be any chance to discuss the past with him, or re-enter Joe's world and find ways to diminish the pain of so many years. Frank had let time slip by with almost no interaction with his father. Now the door of opportunity had slammed shut.

On another level, Frank felt sorry for his dad, who was a retired Baltimore beat cop, a widower living alone in a cavernous old house. Most of his friends were dead, and drinking had been a problem for him even when he was active on the job and hanging out regularly with his cop buddies. As a boy, Frank had caught the brunt of Joe's drunken rages painfully and often. There were two Joe Dugans in Frank's life: the surly, abusive drunk, and the contrite sober man who was the Boy Scout leader and baseball coach Frank wanted to love and be proud of. As the years passed, the surly drunk was the only one who ever showed up.

Frank picked up his desk calendar and tilted back in his swivel chair. His desk was situated next to an exterior wall with high windows that offered daylight but, for internal security, were high enough to conceal workers from the outside. A concrete block wall was behind his chair and created the back corner of the large room. A sign on the wall read:

**Be gentle with gentle people.
Be tough with tough people.**

Detective Carl Rumbaugh, a short, overweight man of 35, looked up from his crossword puzzle and glanced at Frank from his side of their partnered desks.

"What's a three-letter word for 'first lady'?" Rumbaugh asked, clawing his red walrus mustache, a size overgrown for his pudgy face. "The president's wife won't fit."

"Eve," Frank said without taking his eyes off the calendar he was studying.

"Eve?"

"From the Bible."

"Oh, *Eve*. Like in the Garden of Eden."

"That'd be the one."

Rumbaugh wrote the entry on his crossword, looked at it for a moment and frowned. He tossed the newspaper aside, took a long swig of his tall orange juice, and stared at Frank.

"I think I'm going to give up crosswords and just do the *Jumble*," Rumbaugh said.

"Why?" Frank said. "Are they scrambling two-letter words now?"

"What's so fascinating about that calendar?" Rumbaugh said.

Frank lifted his eyes just enough from under his dark eyebrows to glare at Rumbaugh.

15

vacation, and a death in the family was certainly reason enough to put in for leave. He figured their homicide division would survive for a week without one of its two detectives, since Martin County wasn't rife with murders. Even Rumbaugh might be able to handle it.

Except for Oliver Smoot, the fifteen-victim serial killer Frank had put away during his first year on the job, less than a three homicides every couple of years was about par for the county; even then, those were usually among the tourists and snowbirds, not the year-round residents.

Frank had transplanted himself five years earlier from the Baltimore City PD where murder had kept him busier—

About a-murder-a-day busier.

Chapter 4

"I need to take some time and go to Maryland," Frank said to Sheriff Roland Brand, who sat behind his desk like a sumo wrestler in a too-tight shirt and choker tie.

"What for?"

"My father died. Back in Baltimore."

"Of what?"

"They said heart failure, but his last physical read like an Astronaut's."

"I'm sorry," Roland said. "You'll need bereavement leave."

"Hardly bereavement."

Roland raised an eyebrow and stared at his detective.

"I hated the sonofabitch," Frank said. "I'm going up there to settle the estate and get the bastard in the ground as fast as I can. Unless there are complications."

"How long will you need?"

"I don't know... a week, maybe two. It'll be one boring trip."

"Don't you have friends in Maryland?"

"Couple old cop buddies."

"I don't want to impose on anyone's time of mourning–"

"I won't be mourning. You can bank on that."

"You're sure you're not covering your grief with anger at your loss?"

"The only thing I'm angry about is wasting time with a bunch of lawyers and funeral people."

"Well, if you're serious about wanting to stave off boredom, I can present an idea you might take to."

"Shoot," Frank said and sat in the one of the chairs in front of Roland's desk.

"Funny you should use that word. While you're up there, maybe you could do the department and me a favor," Roland said and removed his Stetson hat, plopped it on his desk, and wiped his forehead with the back of his hand.

"What kind of favor?"

"I'd like you to compete for us in The National Law Enforcement Marksmanship Tournament next week. It's being held in Maryland near DC."

"How will that do you a favor?" Frank asked.

"You do well, it'll make Martin County look pretty special."

"Every crack shot in the country will be there. What makes you think I have a chance?"

"The contests are part accuracy and part psychology. You have to use your head in the criminal recognition tests, and you have to out-psych your competition."

"I'm not a psychologist."

Roland laughed.

"The hell you're not. I've seen your work with suspects in the box. You can talk salmon into spawning *downstream*."

"I don't know…"

Frank rose and stepped toward the door.

"Look, you're a fantastic shot and you can out-noodle these bozos who think they're Wyatt Earp. Wear your old Marine shooting medals just to piss 'em off."

Frank stared at the door and shook his head.

"I don't expect miracles," Roland said. "Just give it your best."

"I'll think about it."

"I'll register you online and email you the details."

Frank turned back to face Roland, who busied himself with paperwork on his desk.

"It won't be boring," the sheriff said low.

*　*　*　*　*

The plane landed at Baltimore-Washington International-Thurgood Marshal Airport on a sultry, 85-degree afternoon. Frank decided to pull up the nearest bar stool, get a cold beer, and make a call on his cell. He wasn't going to visit his old hometown without contacting his former Baltimore PD partner Alasdair MacGowan.

Alasdair left the force shortly after Frank relocated to Florida. He knew Alasdair had always fantasized about being in the movie business and, while Frank never imagined his friend would become another Steven Spielberg, he'd encouraged him to form his own video production company. Since both men had been long-standing bachelors, Frank slipped in his barbs about Alasdair being in such a lucky profession like video work where he could take part in hundreds of weddings without ever having to marry. Alasdair countered by addressing his letters to Frank in Florida to: *The President of the Lonely Alligator-of-the-Month Club.*

The phone rang three times.

"MacGowan Productions," a familiar voice on the other end said.

"I want to make a porn movie and was told you're the go-to guy in Maryland," Frank said.

"Well, we're kinda busy right now shooting the *Titanic* sequels and *Rocky Meets Bigfoot*," Alasdair said.

"Aw, I hope you can fit me in. Doing this is number three on my bucket list."

"Sorry, mister. You may have to scratch that one off."

Whenever Frank or Alasdair referred to anything on a "bucket list" it was code for being a blatant lie.

"Good to know you're busy, you big Scottish lout."

"Scotto-American, to you."

"They'll give anybody citizenship in this country."

"How ya been, laddie?"

"I'm at BWI. I've inherited a big old barn in Catonsville and thought I might drop over and let you take me to dinner while I'm here. I'm particularly keen on Irish cuisine."

"I can't go spending my hard-earned money taking every annoying Irishman to McDonalds, you know."

"Just took a shot."

"Inherited a house, eh? Who died?"

"The old man."

"Sorry for your loss, but if memory serves, you weren't too fond of him."

"I mostly despised the sonofabitch."

"With that nasty attitude you'll never flummox some blind honey into marrying you."

"There's time," Frank said. "Marriage is for later."

"You're already at later. What are you now, 49? 50?"

"Thirty-eight, and looking twenty-five."

"Do I have to come collect you at the airport?" Alasdair asked.

"Shit, no. I'd probably have to buy you a tank of gas," Frank said. "I'll walk."

"Good. It's been five years, you know. And if you really look twenty-five I'd have a bit of a time sorting you out."

"I need to stop at St. Luke's to identify the body, and I have to see the lawyers. I'll be a couple of days dealing with funeral arrangements and all the legal crap."

"Shout out when you get loose."

Frank ended the call and sipped his drink.

The opening to the bar was the length of the entire business front, allowing patrons to fully see the wide corridor of the airport where crowds of people passed by in all directions. An elderly woman tugged her baggage cart and labored slowly by Frank's view. In her struggle, a wallet fell from the purse she clutched under one arm and skittered behind her. A man, trailing her a few feet back, stooped and snatched the wallet up and stuffed it into his jacket pocket. Frank bolted from his barstool and caught up with the man a few yards down the corridor. He grabbed the man by the arm and spun him to a stop.

"The wallet," Frank said.

"What wallet?" the man said.

Frank reached into the man's jacket and yanked out the wallet, ripping the pocket.

"That would be this one," Frank said and thrust his knee hard into the man's thigh, dropping him painfully to the tiled floor.

"Jesus, man," the thief said, gripping his cramped leg.

"Don't ever steal from my mother."

Frank caught up with the elderly lady and handed her the wallet.

"Oh, my stars, thank you," she said. "My whole life's in that wallet."

Frank smiled and took her cart from her and walked her out to the waiting line of shuttles and taxis. He stayed until she was safely helped into a cab. He backed away to leave, but stopped when he saw the back window of the car roll down.

"You'd make a fine police officer, young man," the old woman said as the cab drove off.

Frank got into an airport shuttle and headed for the car rental agency. He checked the calendar on his cell phone. Today was June 20th, a good time to be up north and avoid southern Florida's steaming heat waves, although Frank remembered summers in Maryland weren't always more merciful.

Frank hoped the next few days would pass without complication. And he hoped no one in Martin County turned up murdered before he returned.

Chapter 5

The morgue at St. Luke's hospital was chilly and smelled of a blend of formaldehyde and pungent disinfectant. Frank followed the on-duty technician to a bank of stainless steel drawers until the young man stopped and consulted a chart in his hand. The technician bent forward and squinted at a label on a drawer's compartment door. He gave Frank a nervous smile and pulled on the handle.

"He came in here on Thursday night from a 9-1-1 call. Arrived DOA according to the EMTs," the young man said as he rolled out the waist-high drawer and removed the plastic sheet covering the body. "He your dad?"

Frank stared at the ashen face and naked body.

"That'd be him," Frank said and noticed there was no traditional "Y" stitching on the body's chest. "Is an autopsy scheduled?"

The young man consulted his chart.

"Let me see ... Joseph William Dugan, age 72, Caucasian ... No autopsy. COD was natural causes. Cardiac arrest."

"How can they be sure?"

"The examining doctor in the ER certified it. It's all right here on the chart."

Frank looked over the pale body and felt his father's thin, wrinkled skin that had lost its elasticity, and now was dotted with freckle-like age spots. Going from head to toe, he saw broken spider veins on his cheeks, hands, and ankles. He studied his father's face for a long moment, then leaned in close to see the sides of the head and neck.

"Does the emergency room give injections behind the ear?" Frank asked.

"No injections are listed. Why? What do you see?"

"There's a red dot behind his right ear. Looks like a needle mark." Frank said and looked at more of the body.

"You a doctor?"

"I'm a cop. But I'm a bit of an expert on needle marks. In homicide, I see them often on dead bodies. Like this other one here on his arm."

The young man leaned over the body to see what Frank was calling attention to.

"My God," the man said under his breath and stood back, staring at Frank.

"I want him autopsied and I want it done now," Frank said with the authority of a field general.

The technician dropped his clipboard and quickly picked it up.

"Yes, sir. I'll notify the ME right away."

*   *   *   *   *

Frank knew autopsies often took days to arrange, and obtaining their results even longer, sometimes weeks. His hope was that he could prevail on an examiner he'd worked with back in his Baltimore PD days to expedite the process. Frank also knew when the Medical Examiner's office was overly busy, the latest arriving dead would be labeled "Not For Cremation," and buried until the examiner had the time to do the examination. Disinterment would delay things even more, and could compromise the accuracy of the examination and test results.

He called the ME's office and crossed his fingers.

"Baltimore Medical Examiner's office," the even-toned voice of a woman said.

"Is Doctor Clement available?" Frank asked.

"He's working in the lab until eleven-thirty. Would you care to get his voice mail?"

"That'll work. Thank you."

Frank left the doctor a lengthy message and his cell number. He ended with telling him his father's body was being sent to his lab with the hope that it could be examined without needing to be temporarily buried.

*   *   *   *   *

While he awaited a reply from Dr. Clement, Frank checked with the 9-1-1 service that had answered the emergency call from Elm Terrace and confirmed what the hospital morgue report had said. Frank's instincts told him his father was likely dead by the time the ambulance arrived at the house in Catonsville. He knew people at the facility and persuaded them to let him hear the 9-1-1 recording as a professional courtesy.

The recording presented a new twist to the story. The terse exchange between the 9-1-1 operator and the caller became dramatically alive and disturbing. The digital file was played for Frank as he paced the office, listening intently.

"9-1-1. What's your emergency?" the female operator said on the playback.

"Send an ambulance," the distressed voice of the caller said. *"I've had a lot to drink. I'm sick and need a doctor. My gut's killing me. Pains in my chest. Please come quick ..."*

The strained voice on the phone cut off there. The rest was the operator trying to reconnect with the caller, then dispatching an ambulance to the address displayed on her caller ID information screen.

As an additional police courtesy, Frank was allowed to take a disk copy of the call transcript. He thanked the service personnel and left their office.

There was one important thing the recording told him.

The caller was not Joe Dugan.

Chapter 6

Certain his father had met with foul play, Frank registered at a local motel in Catonsville, since the house on Elm Terrace would now be a crime scene. He was savvy enough to not enter the house and compromise what might be found there by the CSIs, sure to fine-comb the place for evidence.

A few minutes after noon, Frank's cell rang. He put the phone to his ear.

"Hello."

"Detective Dugan," a man's voice said, "Been a while, but still sending me work, I see."

"Yeah, Doctor Clement, but this one's not off some alley in west Baltimore."

"Sorry about your father. I knew Joe. Used to see him at the PBA functions."

"Can you do anything for me?" Frank asked.

"I got the body today before noon, so I can go to work on him right away. Give you the results as soon as I get them."

"Much obliged, doc."

"Happy to help," Clement said.

Frank knew Clement's work. Thorough was the only word to describe it.

* * * * *

The morning drive into Oak Forest looked like it did when Frank left Maryland five years earlier. The great oaks in full leaf shaded Parkside Drive, which led to Elm Terrace and cooled the large traditional houses spaced widely apart on the rural street. Generous, well-manicured lawns spread for fifty yards or more between the stately, set-back homes, insulating each from its neighbors. Fallen acorns peppered the road and crunched under the tires of the rental as Frank turned onto Elm Terrace. He drove to the curb in front of his newly acquired estate at 1505 and parked.

From the street, Frank saw the old place through a young boy's remembrance and felt the nostalgia. The house and grounds were in need of maintenance, but the magic of long ago summers was still alive in his eyes. His gaze panned across the once-beautiful lawn and stopped at something lying in the grass near the driveway that glinted in the bright sun. Frank slid out of the car and ambled onto the asphalt driveway. Twenty feet up, he stooped to pick up the object that had caught his attention. It was a brass button. A brass button from a Baltimore Police uniform; a breast pocket button. His father had uniforms that used that style of button, but he'd retired more than ten years ago. The button proved nothing. Cops came to see Joe over the years and one of them could've popped loose a button. Frank put the button in his jacket pocket and slow-walked backward to the car, scanning the grounds as he went.

He wanted to move in closer, even go inside the house, but though he'd always possessed keys to the place, he resisted the urge. Right now his instincts spoke to him about murder, and he needed to focus on current events. Frank was convinced, more than ever, that a man had been killed in that house, a man who shared his blood. Frank was now going to find out who did it and why.

*　*　*　*　*

The next morning, Frank watched the Baltimore County Crime Scene Investigation team arrive at Elm Terrace and begin their systematic procedures by gathering their equipment in preparation to examine the house and scour the grounds. A couple of CSIs entered the house while others began taking photographs on the outside. One investigator called out several orders to his team, then approached Frank as he stood next to his car at the curb.

"Are you Detective Frank Dugan?" the CSI asked.

"That'd be me," Frank said.

"I'm Detective Luce from Baltimore County CSI."

33

"Here's your consent to search," Frank said and handed Luce the form and a key. "I dropped off the house keys yesterday at the station, but I forgot to give them the key for the garage. Any chance I can get a look in the house?"

"As a courtesy to a fellow officer, but only as an observer," Luce said. "I know this is your house and it concerns your father, but I hope, as a professional, you understand our position."

"I do."

The two men entered the front door of the house and stopped in the vestibule to observe the activity on the main floor beyond. Men and women wearing surgical gloves, hairnets, and hospital-style shoe covers worked with cameras and fingerprint capture kits down the wide hallway. Detective Luce moved into the hall and beckoned Frank to follow closely behind him to the doorway of the parlor.

Frank watched the CSIs in the parlor examine the few books that had been removed from the shelves and strewn on the floor. The stacks of bookshelves ran from floor to ceiling and almost all the way around the spacious library room where items were being pulled out and dusted for prints. Camera flashes bounced off the walls and bright LED lights swept across the Oriental rug searching for evidence hiding in the wool.

Frank turned to face Detective Luce.

"Thanks for the look, detective, but I think I'm going to come back when I can enjoy this old place. Seeing it dissected isn't how I want to remember her."

"I understand," Luce said. "We'll be out of here today. It would be different if there were a lot of blood spatter or bullet holes. This place looks a little disheveled, a few books piled on the floor, but probably not teeming with evidence we can use. We'll have to take any drugs we find to compare with the ME, but that's SOP. If we do come up with anything, we'll keep you apprised. I'll have the clean-up people come in later to remove the fingerprint dust, and we'll put anything we move back the way it was. I'll lock up and you can pick up your keys at the precinct over on Wilkens Avenue."

"Appreciate that."

"One last thing. If you should happen upon anything you think might have a bearing on this case, be sure to contact me," Luce said and handed Frank a business card.

"Will do," Frank said as he stuck Luce's card in his jacket pocket and fondled the police button he'd put there earlier.

Frank walked directly to his car without looking back. In front of his car was an iron grate over a deep drain at the curb, which recalled the day he'd dropped his scout knife into the blackness below. Frank's grandfather, William, had to come out and pull up the grate to allow Frank to lower himself in and gain access to the knife resting on the bottom of the sewer pipe five feet below. It was dark, slimy, and rank-smelling at the bottom, and he felt a choking sensation that stuttered his breathing. Frank grabbed his knife and shot out of the enclosure like a cheetah scaling a tree.

Now, as he stared at the terrifying drain, he could still feel the chilling fear of that long-ago adventure. The car keys were squeezed tightly in his fist. His mouth was dry and tacky, even after he got into his car and drove away.

Having an eidetic memory isn't always a blessing, he thought.

Chapter 7

Frank got the anticipated call from Ed Clement's secretary and drove to the Medical Examiner's office in the city to discuss Joe's cause of death. Frank stood as a tall, graying man came out from the morgue's laboratory and angled toward him in the waiting area. The man's name badge said "Edward T. Clement, MD."

"You still look the same, detective," the doctor said.

"Florida's been kind to me," Frank said and extended his hand. "A lot kinder than working homicide here."

"You were the primary on the Grandview murder case, weren't you?"

"That's the one that sent me south."

"Why so?"

"I pursued a wrong lead. Took me a full day to run it down," Frank said. "When I finally cornered Grandview the next morning it was too late."

"Your job, like mine, deals in death. Comes with the territory."

"Eight innocent children murdered, and their body parts cut up and labeled in freezers was never mentioned in the manual. When I arrested Raymond Grandview, he had his bloody butcher knife in his hand. I wanted him to attack me with it. I begged him to. It would've saved the state a lot of expense and heartache."

"We had ten medical professionals working 'round the clock. Worst case I ever saw."

"Grandview got life in Clifton T. Perkins. He's still kicking and gets to watch TV all day with his other criminally insane friends."

"I know," Clement said. "It never seems like justice for an animal like him."

"I resigned the day the trial ended."

"You can't blame yourself for the acts of a madman."

"I failed to get to him in time."

"He was a ruthless, cunning young man," Clement said. "We all failed to stop him. Trouble is, you can't stop crazy. I went to see him. They put him in a concrete room in the east wing. Room 264. I wanted to personally make sure the sonofabitch was securely locked up."

"Room 264? You remember details like that? Damn, that was over five years ago. Need to get you on *Jeopardy*."

"You missed your calling too, detective. Your observations were correct. You'd make a good ME," the doctor said and looked at the clipboard in his hand. "We did screens for toxicity, liver damage, and cardio-vascular condition. Your father died of potassium chloride poisoning, complicated by thiopental sodium. Delivered intravenous and enhanced by high amounts of alcohol."

"An anesthetic? Like sodium pentothal?"

"Same thing."

"And the other injection?"

"Potassium chloride. Can be lethal in large enough doses. Stops the heart. In this case, the dosage was plenty."

"Blood alcohol tested?"

"Yes. His BAC was .37. Well beyond simply drunk. I checked the clothes they sent over with the body. There were two large stains on his shirt. The darker one checked out to be ethanol with an odor of smoky peat, and a lighter one was strong with the smell of juniper berry. In plain English: I'd guess scotch or Irish whiskey and gin. There were also bruises on his neck and one of his arms. May have fallen."

"May have been muscled around and held down while gin was poured down his throat."

"You sure he would've had to be forced to drink?"

"He hated gin, especially with a potassium chloride chaser."

*   *   *   *   *

Frank called Alasdair.

"MacGowan Productions," Alasdair said.

39

"Death was not from natural causes," Frank said. "Joe was murdered."

"Ay, sorry, lad."

"I have to clear some extended leave with Martin County. I need to stay here and get to the bottom of this. I moved to Florida to get away from this murder-a-day burg and here I am right back in that same old grease."

"People get murdered plenty in Florida. I watch the news."

"Maybe in Miami, but Stuart's a pretty peaceful resort."

"So you took a cut in pay to live in the tropics?"

"Money was never an issue. I wanted to live someplace safe, uncomplicated. Somewhere that doesn't have so many murders that only 70 percent are ever closed. No murder has ever gone unsolved on my watch in Martin County. Why? Because we don't have 500 assholes every year brandishing guns, acting like king shit, because some hapless dolt dissed them, or stared back at them in a bar. Waving a gun around soon escalates to firing it at someone."

The phone line was quiet for several seconds.

"Where are you going to start?" Alasdair said.

"The house. After the CSIs are done, the house has to talk to us."

"Us?"

"Yeah, us,"

"Now don't you go teasing me, Francis. You know I live for adventure."

"I could sure use my partner back on this one," Frank said. "You in?"

"*All* in, brother."

*　　*　　*　　*　　*

Frank looked across the rolling grave fields of Loudon Park where aging gray stones stood like eternal mourners topped in sooty black veils. It was much the same as he had remembered it, except for the large number of recent residents whose pristine markers contrasted with the ancient ones, long in surrender to pitted erosion and stained in mossy-greens.

He wasn't sure he could find his family's gravesite among all the new additions, which confused the landmarks he once depended on. He gazed long and hard at the section he thought was where his grandparents and mother lay, but they refused to be found. After several minutes, he decided to consult the cemetery office.

The clerk in the office was a congenial man of about forty who pulled the Dugan file from a computer database and printed it out.

"We received your father's body after it was released from the Medical Examiner's office yesterday," the clerk said as he brought over the file to Frank.

"I'd like him buried next to my mother, Cynthia Ann Dugan" Frank said.

"Of course. We already have that plot reserved for him. When would you like to hold the service?"

"As soon as possible," Frank said and jotted phone numbers on a business card. "I'll have the church contact you to make the arrangements with the priest. I'm told our law firm will take care of the expenses. Here are the numbers you'll need."

Frank handed the business card to the clerk, who gave him a map with directions to the Dugan grave section. A short drive to the area and a fifty-yard walk between rows of markers and monuments of varied sizes brought him to the resting place of his grandparents, William and Emily Dugan. Next to them was an empty plot and, to its right, the grave of his mother, Cynthia. Their stones were of simple-cut, gray granite engraved with their names and dates of birth and death.

Frank contrasted this solitary visit with the foggy, damp day nearly twenty years ago when the area was crowded with people. People he didn't know, who had come to honor the passing of their friend William.

He was back home from a lengthy tour in Iraq and stood up front in his Marine dress blues next to his dad Joe, who teetered from side to side as the priest delivered his graveside words. That day, Frank suspended his anger for his drunken father and replaced it with compassion. It was embarrassing that most of the people offering their sympathy came directly up to Frank without giving Joe so much as a courteous nod of acknowledgement.

Frank had observed his grandfather's treatment of Joe, and saw how he pitied what his only child had become, and even regarded him as an outcast; the son who never came up to the high standards and expectations William had set. Frank also believed his father found drinking eased the pain of his failures, which was especially poignant because Joe so often depended on William's largess.

Frank remembered that on that day a man, perhaps in his seventies, withdrew from the crowd of attendees and approached him.

"Your grandfather was the wisest man I ever knew," he said. "He was the last of a group of men who likely saved the world. William was especially proud of you."

The man placed his index finger on the Silver Star nestled in the rows of ribbons on the left side of Frank's chest.

"He would be particularly pleased about that, sergeant," the man said and withdrew his hand.

"Saved the world? You mean his work on the Manhattan Project?" Frank asked.

"Manhattan Project?" the man said and smiled. "His work went well beyond that."

The man turned and walked away.

"I didn't get your name, sir," Frank said.

"Vernon. Vernon Ritter," the man said without looking back, and soon faded into the mist that shrouded the cemetery.

Frank became the son Joe had failed to be, the boy upon whom William could invest his attention, his knowledge, care, and hopes. Frank stared at the oak casket resting atop the bier. The passing of William was the lowest point in Frank's 21-year life.

The only man he ever truly loved was gone.

Chapter 8

The law firm of Crowder & Burns had been the family's legal advisors from back in William's day, and occupied offices in the elegant Carrollton Building in downtown Baltimore. Frank was greeted by Winston Crowder, a man he recognized from years ago when he attended William's funeral. Winston, now in his late fifties, was the son of the founding partner, James Crowder, and escorted Frank into his posh office. He seated him on the opposite side of his executive desk and pushed a button on the intercom.

"Ms. Jackson, please hold my calls and see that we're not disturbed."

Winston folded his hands on top of the desk and looked at Frank.

"Our sincerest condolences on the passing of your father," Winston said, then reached into a drawer and withdrew a large legal envelope.

"Thanks for the good thoughts," Frank said.

"Here are the documents you'll need to process the insurance claims and the ownership of the estate," Winston said and handed Frank the bulky envelope across his desk. "We've done all the necessary prep work. You'll need to sign a few documents, and then it's done. Everything in the estate has been left to you."

Frank took the package and placed it on his lap.

"Your grandfather, a close friend of my parents, retained us many years ago. He was precise in his instruction that when he passed, only a life estate in the real property was to go to your father. So, during Joe's possession he could neither sell nor otherwise alienate that property. The real estate was always destined for you upon Joseph's passing. It was William's most emphatic directive."

"And the payment for your services?"

"We are the executors of Joseph's will and will receive $25,000 for our work on his estate. Taxes, inheritance issues, funeral expenses, and death certification fees will be paid from William's trust, which we've been given the power to draw upon. After that, the rest is yours."

"May I take all this with me to look over?"

"Of course, they're yours to keep. And feel free to call me with any questions or concerns," Winston said and stood.

"Good," Frank said and rose with an extended hand.

Frank left the law offices clutching the legal envelope. He felt he was carrying his entire family history reduced to a stack of 100% rag paper documents that wouldn't even fuel enough fire to warm a pair of winter hands.

*　　*　　*　　*　　*

Back at the motel, Frank sat at the small table in his room. His large hands took turns shuffling around the piles of legal documents, and rubbing the sides of his nose as he stared at the array of papers on the table.

One particular letter from William was mystifying. He scoured it looking for hidden answers amid its puzzling words and cryptic phrases. Nothing made much sense. Stranger still was the old fashioned fountain pen clipped to the letter. After contemplating it for several minutes he set it aside.

Frank scribbled his name on an envelope in the packet with the fountain pen. The bright orange pen was a Parker he'd seen William use often in the past, its familiar blue-black ink matched the writing on his grandfather's letter.

He pored over another document from the lawyers and went down the list of its notations from his father's will. Things cited there conjured up the familiar. The suburban Baltimore house listed in the will was originally built and designed by his grandfather, and was located in an upscale section of Catonsville, Maryland called Oak Forest. Frank played at that house and romped on its spacious grounds over many childhood summers, and he could still recall the pungent smell of the boxwoods that surrounded the front porch. It was an aroma he associated with happiness, but Emily Dugan, his grandmother, despised those dense hedges and described their odor as cat pee. Emily made threats to have them hacked out and burned, but they were never removed and Frank never forgot their distinctive smell.

Frank hadn't seen his father in years and was astounded the bastard had left him anything, other than perhaps the heavy leather belt he liked to whale him with in drunken rages.

Because William had bequeathed Frank's father only a life estate in the Elm Terrace house, Joseph had full use of the property during his own life, but he could not sell, assign, or encumber the property. Frank could see his grandfather's determination to assure that the property was ultimately placed in his grandson's hands. But William's adamancy begged the question: *Why?*

The handwritten letter from William was altogether a different story. More than his father's death, or the inheritance of the house, it was this letter that shifted Frank's curiosity into high gear. He hadn't been able to make much sense of it, but he couldn't deny that its message and short poem intrigued him enough to at least consider a personal investigation. A small piece of a mystery, or a shard of a larger truth, pumped up Frank's gumshoe instincts. He'd never been posed a conundrum he didn't want to solve, but to search for clues he needed to visit the scene where the puzzle pointed. Besides, he yearned to stay at the old place again even if it turned out to be a decrepit, termite repository, falling down from decades of his father's lack of care.

Frank had grown up in a row home in Windsor Heights, a quarter-mile inside the Baltimore City line on the west side of town. Catonsville was only a few miles farther west, but, at that time, a world away in social strata and level of living. Frank hated his home life in Windsor Heights, and longed to be able to leave it. After graduation from high school, he enlisted in the marines and, immediately after basic training, was shipped to Iraq to fight the Republican Guard forces of Saddam Hussein.

When Operation Desert Storm concluded, he was ordered to Camp Pendleton in San Diego. Frank liked the California weather so much he decided to live there. He was discharged at twenty-two and joined the San Diego Police Department, where he worked his way up to detective in only four years. When a personal tragedy struck him in his late twenties, he returned to Maryland, rented a refurbished carriage house in Catonsville to be near his grandparents' estate. The house at Elm Terrace was occupied then by his mother Cynthia and his father Joseph, a sergeant in the Baltimore Police Department, who got Frank a personal interview with his superiors. Frank joined the BPD a week later as a detective.

Frank loved his grandfather, the figure he treated as his true dad, since the man stepped in to rear him while his biological father took off on drinking binges and gambling sprees in Atlantic City. William was a just man, imbued with an inordinately strong sense of fairness. Often, William intervened in Joe's abuse on young Frank when Joe stumbled home broke and drunk, and wanted to take out his bum luck on his young son. Unfortunately, William wasn't always there to intercede. Frank's mother, Cynthia, silently deferred to her husband in all decisions, leaving their boy at Joe's disposal and ill temper.

William had been dead for almost two decades, but Frank thought of him often. His letter vividly brought back William's dignified manner and magnetic voice.

Frank,

I wanted you to have this little puzzle in verse. I could lay things all out for you, but that could include my personal bias in what I might choose to reveal. Uncover things on your own, or leave them to die with us, the choice is yours.

Powerful knowledge awaits, and awesome power requires huge responsibility. Remember, wisdom always trumps riches or political gain in the

hearts of seekers of the truth. What you do with what
you find, expose, ignore, or bury forever, will
determine how history will judge the others and me,
but it was never my wish to be either greater or less
in death than I was in life.

You were always superb at solving puzzles, so
I'm certain you can <u>handle</u> *this one.*

Your loving grandfather,

William

The poem that followed played over and over in
Frank's head like a looped recording.

> *Treasure comes not only from gold,*
> *Nor from chattel stately and old,*
> *Brains on paper and acts preserved,*
> *And still Martian men Are swell served,*
> *As secrets lie dormant, never told.*

There was no way to accurately determine when
the letter had been written, but the once white laid
stationery appeared to be yellowing, and the words
in blue-black ink were made by a broad-nib fountain
pen, both from a long ago era. Frank recognized the
beautiful cursive script of his grandfather who had
the penmanship of John Hancock.

William died and had evidently left the letter and pen with his will, and had instructed his lawyers to pass it on to Frank when the time came. Joseph's death must have meant the time had come — for a lot of things.

Frank stared at the poem for a long moment. He reminded himself that he hadn't begun to solve the *Les Miserables* puzzle and here was yet another one. From the grave, William was challenging his grandson one last time. It was as irresistible to Frank as a "triple dog dare" was to a schoolboy in a Jean Shepherd short story.

There were two flashing neon elements in the letter that keened the detective's interest beyond casual curiosity, and beckoned the adventuresome boy in him to accept the challenge — *treasure* and *secrets*.

Chapter 9

The next day, Frank steered the Hyundai rental into the driveway at Elm Terrace and drove the 80 yards back to the three-car garage behind the Victorian mansion in Oak Forest. He parked and stepped out of the car and paused to take it all in; two acres, three stories, and 85 years of it. Alasdair MacGowan lumbered his 6-foot-5 frame out from the passenger side and leaned back against the car to look up at the towering height of the house.

"Be a bitch to air-condition," Alasdair said.

"CSI guys finished up yesterday and gave me a brief report," Frank said. "Only thing unusual they found were several size 16 footprints in the cellar dust and a couple of reddish fibers in the parlor. The kind used in cheap wigs. Recent impressions in the old rugs indicated there had been three or more people recently in the parlor, where they determined the crime was committed. Found a lot of spillage on the floor. Booze mostly, but trace urine too."

"Fingerprints?" Alasdair asked.

"They're working on it, but so far all they pulled belonged to Joe. Place was pretty clean."

"You want me to go inside with you?"

"Yeah, come on. You'll see how people lived who occasionally spent some of their money," Frank said.

Alasdair followed Frank and they both panned the neglected exterior of the house and overgrown grounds, their eyes moving from the street to the huge oaks that shaded the house to the thick woods surrounding the rear and lateral boundaries of the property.

The natural cedar shingles that Frank remembered from childhood visits covered most of the exterior of the house, but they had since been painted a battleship gray with aging white accents on the busy gingerbread trim. The color seemed fitting since the place looked like a mothballed warship rusting past its prime with her enamel skin cracked and peeling. It saddened him to see the site of so many childhood memories in decay, struggling to fight off the neglect of so many years. It was once a vibrant home, and now it was a dying building trying to hide in the cover of the broadleaf trees and put off the arrival of the formidable bulldozer.

He made his way to the front of the house, rubbed his hand on its weathered shingles, and climbed the nine steps to the porch. A metal glider and table sat to the right of the front door, and a large planter countered it on the left with the dried skeleton of a long-dead fern. The windows seemed mostly intact and the wide oak door looked as sturdy and secure as ever. His father had lived there until a few days ago, so there was no reason to suspect the inside wasn't at least livable. He didn't, however, expect to encounter surgically precise housekeeping from the likes of a career drunk like Joe Dugan.

The heyday of the residence occurred under William's ownership and care. Those were the days Frank happily replayed in his memory as his eyes passed over the grass: chasing and wrestling with Erich, their German shepherd, firing BBs into imaginary bears in the woods, and grabbing garter snakes from crawlspace under the house to use later to terrify his grandparents' maid.

The key fitted the lock in the front door and turned with minimum effort. The door whined as it swung inward on its huge brass hinges reminding Frank of his grandfather's instruction that those hinges were never to be oiled. Frank could hear the exchange as if it took place yesterday.

"If you oil the hinges, Grandpa, the door won't squeak," young Frank said.

"You always want to know," William said, *"when anyone enters your house."*

Frank led Alasdair into the vestibule, which served as a kind of air-lock, keeping out the winters' cold from the rest of the house and providing a separate room where wet or muddy boots could be removed without tromping on the Oriental rugs in the main rooms farther in. Within the vestibule, a bronze umbrella stand in the shape of a hollow elephant's foot held two black umbrellas and a hickory walking cane, an item Frank remembered, which concealed a thin, razor-sharp sword he was warned never to touch. On the right was a small closet for coats. A cherry, demilune table was against the left wall under a tall, gilt-framed mirror. On the table was a large bowl with a small notepad and two pencils. The family called this table "the leaving table" since it was where one put keys, messages, and anything else you didn't want to forget as you left the house. This idea worked so efficiently Frank never failed to install a similar one in every place he'd lived since. When Frank found a system that worked, he stuck with it.

Frank's rubber-soled shoes squeaked on the glazed terra cotta tiles as he crossed to open the inner door of the vestibule, which led to the main hallway of the house. Alasdair followed Frank inside.

"Could use a bit of dusting," Alasdair said.

"Yeah. The old man was no Adrian Monk."

An ornate, cherry grandfather clock drew the eye to the widest area of the hall leading to a staircase clad with an Oriental rug runner. The clock's pendulum was still and the time on the brass and silver clock face was stopped at ten past six. Frank remembered William winding up the three chained weights of the clock every Sunday morning while the mixed aromas of breakfast bacon, maple syrup and coffee drifted from the kitchen throughout the house. The lilt of the Westminster chimes rang out every quarter hour and bonged at the top of the hour like Big Ben. Frank found the absence of the clock's sounds and movement more conspicuous than when it was running.

"Ever notice," Frank said, "how when something's missing you're aware of it more than when it was there?"

"The clock?" Alasdair said and stared at it. "Had an uncle once who lost a finger. Thought about it all the time."

"Yeah, like that."

Frank moved into the parlor and library off the long hall and let his eyes remember the large room. On all but one wall, there were the familiar stacks of bookcases, where William often hid surprises for Frank to find. The deal was, Frank could pull out a book to see what treat might be hidden behind it, but he had to dust the book, even if nothing was found. There was always something delightful planted in the bookcases, but Frank often had to wipe down a hundred books or more to locate it. An added bonus was that William encouraged Frank to read his freshly-dusted collection, which widened his grandson's view of the world and helped him immeasurably in school.

"You have an earthquake here recently?" Frank asked, pointing to the books on the floor.

"In Maryland?" Alasdair said. "You serious?"

"Something sure as shit dumped them off the shelves, but I'm betting that something had two legs. CSI said almost all the books appeared to have been moved. And obviously not all put back."

Between the stacks of bookcases, on a wall by itself, was a wide bay window that looked out over the front lawn and tree-lined driveway. Near the house were overgrown grass plots dotted with dandelions, and forgotten flowerbeds, which once contained purple rows of irises, cerise azaleas, and arrays of pansies of every shade. Wild chicory, that normally adorned roadsides with their periwinkle flowers, had immigrated onto the lawn, spread all the way to the house, and seemed to be applying for domestic status.

"The old man was a regular Luther Burbank in the landscaping department too," Frank said.

"You going to keep the place?"

"I want to get landscaping and home improvement people out here to put this property in shape to go on the market."

"I know a few excellent ones."

"Good. Call them in. Get the joint painted and manicured. Send me their bills."

"What's next?" Alasdair said. "Upstairs?"

"The garage."

*   *   *   *   *

Frank led Alasdair out the back door of the
kitchen to a walkway that ended at the garage. The
two men reached the side door on the three-car
building where Frank jangled through a ring of keys
and plucked the one that opened the door. Inside
they saw three bays containing two vintage cars and
a ten-year-old Ford Explorer. One of the classic
oldies was a white 1959 Corvette; the other was a
Nile green, 1936 Reo Flying Cloud, both in
showroom condition.

The Reo had sweptback, teardrop fenders with
bullet-shaped headlamps mounted on either side of
its narrow hood. White sidewall tires with chrome
hubcaps supported the car's sleek body that ended
with a down-sloping trunk. A small silver rocket
framed in a circle sat atop a shiny chrome grille that
ran down to a wrap-around bumper.

Alasdair slid behind the wheel of the Corvette
and ran his hand over the red leather upholstery as
Frank got in on the passenger side. Frank looked
over the instrument panel and leaned in close to the
odometer.

"This baby only has 35,000 miles on her," Frank
said.

"Barely broken in," Alasdair said. "Give you ten
grand for it. I'll leave you the money in my will."

"Get your cheap ass out of my car."

The back of the garage served as a shop complete with a generous oak workbench, neatly displayed socket wrench sets, hammers, power tools, welding equipment, banks of overhead cabinets spaced on either side of an industrial clock, and a huge bench vise with wide steel jaws. Clenched in the vise was the head of an antique golf club.

A wooden stairway on one side of the garage led up to a spacious overhead loft where boxes, several chairs and a table were stored. Chainfall hoists on large pulleys hung from massive beams and extended down through narrow openings in the loft's floor and dangled over the vehicle bays below.

"This is some shop," Alasdair said.

"William did all his own work on his cars."

Alasdair picked up an ancient golf club with a hickory shaft that leaned against the workbench.

"Now this is more my speed," Alasdair said and made a slow arc with the club as though hitting an imaginary ball. "We Scots invented the game, you know."

Frank took the club from Alasdair and carefully examined it.

"This one's an antique brassie once owned by Bobby Jones, but William made his own clubs; state-of-the-art designs back in the '50s. He could've driven Callaway and Ping out of business if he'd gone industrial, no pun intended."

"What's the green car?" Alasdair said and sauntered over to the car's rear door and peered inside.

"A '36 Reo. My grandfather's favorite. Once owned by Clark Gable."

"Clark didn't take good care of the upholstery."

"What do you mean?" Frank said and stepped over to Alasdair.

"The rear seat is pulled up and is sitting upside down on the floor. I can see into the trunk. Ransacked, I'd say."

Frank moved to the back of the car and opened the trunk. The rubber matting was pulled up and the spare tire lay flat on the trunk floor and not in its recessed pocket.

Frank slammed the trunk lid closed and looked at Alasdair.

"Did CSI do this?" Alasdair asked.

"Their report said the garage was untouched."

"Well, somebody sure as hell touched this car."

Frank stared at the Reo and pondered, *What were they searching for in an antique car?*

Chapter 10

Most of the drive back to Alasdair's was a quiet one. Frank stared straight ahead at the road, his thoughts flying to imagined scenarios surrounding Joe's murder, which included guesses at what his father's killers had come there for. He was certain about *killers*, plural. A single individual would've had a tough time subduing and injecting his father. Even though he was a senior and drunk, Joe was feisty and tough. He would've had to be heavily overpowered to let anyone stick needles in him. Other than that, nothing useful was surfacing. There was so much missing in the case, and so little evidence on which to anchor a starting point.

"Maybe you should stay at my place tonight," Alasdair said.

Frank cast a look at Alasdair, then back at the road.

"What the hell were they trying to get out of Joe?" Frank asked.

"You said he was a big gambler and even called you for money."

"Who uses truth serum to get a gambling debt? No. They wanted something else. Something important enough to kill for."

Silence reigned in the car once again. Ten minutes passed until Alasdair broke the dead air.

"Did I tell you I got married?" Alasdair said.

Frank pulled the car over to the shoulder and stopped.

"You *what?*" Frank said.

"Yeah. Got hitched. Jumped the broom. It was time."

"Who'd be nuts enough to marry you?"

"Ah, she's a lovely lass. Worked for the NSA. You'll love her."

"How did you meet her?"

"She called my production company to solicit a bid on an employment video NSA was promoting. I didn't get the bid, but I got the girl. We got married three months later."

"I have to meet his woman."

"You'll meet her soon enough. She runs our production company now."

Frank rolled down the window, stuck his head outside the car, and looked to the sky.

"What are you looking for out there?" Alasdair asked.

"I'm checking to see if the world has ended."

*   *   *   *   *

Returning to Elm Terrace, Frank drove the rental up the driveway and parked at the rear of the

63

house. He left the vehicle and started to head for the front door, but stopped. He looked back at the garage for a moment, then stepped over to the side door of the building and opened it.

Once inside, he sat in the driver's seat of the Reo and immediately felt like he was in a time machine rolling through the Maryland countryside. He recalled images of his days in that car running errands with his grandfather and going on trips with the family. A small stain on the seat where a chocolate ice cream cone had dripped in the summer heat flashed pictures of the soda counter at the Arbutus Drug Store where old Doc Levering patrolled the aisles and never let anyone read the magazines before paying. Whiffs of aging leather, cigars, and gasoline still resided in the car's upholstery and took Frank's senses on yet another ride.

The scene around him brought back memories of days in that huge garage where he and his grandfather worked on cars, bicycles, skateboards, and model airplanes. Frank also remembered times when he wasn't allowed to be in the garage; times when William had his friends over and met privately with them there. The door was always locked, and little Frank was asked to play outside while his grandfather carried out "grown-up business." It puzzled Frank why those meetings were held in the garage and not in the house. A puzzle still unsolved, like a cold case file.

One day, when he was forbidden to enter the workshop, he had stood on a milk crate and peeked inside through a window at the top of one of the garage doors. William had entered the garage earlier with two other men in business suits. Frank saw them at first, but minutes later he couldn't see anyone. There was a moment when they were partially blocked from view by one of the cars. A moment later they disappeared. He stayed on the crate and peered inside for several minutes, but he never caught even a glimpse of anyone again. *How could they keep from view for so long? Were they in the loft? What were they doing up there?*

For Frank, the schoolboy, it was the one thing about his grandfather he never figured out. But Frank, the grown detective, was determined to now.

* * * * *

A nightlight in the wall outlet put out a dim glow that cast the bedroom in long, exaggerated shadows. Frank scanned the room and studied the mahogany highboy in the corner, the matching dresser and mirror, and a small easy chair covered in a crewel fabric with a cream background. Furnishings he recalled from his stays in that same room as a kid.

He climbed into the bed with its tall, carved mahogany posts and pushed the comforter to the side and lay atop the white sheets. Weary from the day's events, he closed his eyes and fell into a twilight doze. A niggling hunch about something in the house pervaded his uneasy rest. Vague dreamlike images played out in thoughts that haunted him.

A blaring siren grew in intensity outside, interrupting Frank's reverie. A heavy vehicle thundered down Elm Terrace, vibrating the house.

A loud noise from downstairs sprang him upright in the bed. He shot a look out the doorway into the dark hall. Frank swung his feet to the floor, grabbed his Browning Hi-Power automatic from the holster draped over the headboard and switched on the brass lamp on the night table. The eerie moonlight outside the multi-paned window and the unsettling creaking of the house made Frank snick off the safety of the 9mm. He grabbed his watch next to the lamp. It was 3:17 AM. The belief that a man had been killed here, and that the killers may have returned, made the hairs on the back of his neck bristle. He rose, pulled on his trousers, and gripped the gun in his right hand.

Frank crept from the bedroom and made his way to the staircase down the hallway. Every step downward creaked as if the house was sending out an audible acknowledgement of his presence.

A double-globe hurricane lamp connected to a timer sat on a Queen Anne console table next to the stairs. It lit the foyer and the surrounding area on the floor of the long hall.

As he neared the bottom of the stairs, a short second noise came from the parlor. Something fell, hit the floor. Frank aimed the Browning at the parlor doorway and stepped off the last riser and onto the first floor hall. He tiptoed toward the foyer, sidled up to the parlor doorway, and peeked into the moonlit room containing all the books.

He flicked on the wall switch and the lamp next to the sofa went on. His eyes panned the room and soon found the source of the noise. A high bookcase shelf had partially collapsed and had spewed books onto the floor eight feet below. A few more books cascaded down as he watched.

Among the fallen books, an object caught Frank's eye. It was a small metal shelf support. Frank began laying out a possible solution. If the support and the high shelf had been removed during the CSI investigation, and improperly replaced, the shelf could have precariously tilted and dumped the books. The passing truck could have set things into motion. Frank found no better reason to blame it on, but kept his gun at the ready.

His eyes panned the high bookcases that covered three of the room's walls, and took a long look at the oriel window on the remaining wall. His eyes were drawn back to the books and passed along each stack as he thought about what had been nagging at him: *Had William left him one last gem behind one of those old books?*

It certainly was possible since William was known for his inventive nature and his love of a good brainteaser. Even as he faced death, he would have likely been wringing his hands in delight over thoughts of his grandson finding a piece of his final conundrum and searching for its ultimate meaning. Theirs was a symbiotic relationship. Frank was addicted to figuring out the solutions to the puzzles William posed, and William loved doling them out. Frank wondered if there were one or two more waiting for him.

There were twenty, floor-to-ceiling library stacks built into the walls of the parlor. Thousands of volumes teased him by their overt silence, but sent him invitations by a unique telepathy: *Over here. Try me. What you're looking for is behind me. No, not there behind that old Melville, here behind Fielding's first edition of Tom Jones.*

This new challenge was playing games with him, taunting him, like those William engaged him in so many summers ago. It was time to think clearly now and get down to business. *If there is a final puzzle piece hidden within the bookcases, where should I start searching?* He decided to begin with the stack on the far left.

An hour later Frank was pulling out books from the third stack. On the bottom shelf of the bookcase was a volume on genetics by Gregor Mendel. Frank pulled it out. Nothing was behind it. Nor the second, third or fourth book in that row. The fifth book was Charles Darwin's *On the Origin of Species*. Behind it was a barely-visible, folded piece of white paper. Frank's heart raced as he withdrew it from the back of the shelf and hurriedly opened it. The note read:

Are you dusting as you go?

Chapter 11

Frank answered the pounding on the front door to find a long-faced Alasdair dressed in jeans, dock shoes, and a Baltimore Ravens football jersey. His tousled, sandy hair made a sea anemone look neat.

"For the love of God, man," he said, storming into the vestibule. "I agreed to be your partner, but that doesn't include hours a vampire wouldn't keep."

"It's only a little after four. I'm working in the library stacks," Frank said and disappeared into the parlor.

Alasdair followed and stood in the parlor doorway.

"I don't smell coffee?" Alasdair said. "I slept through three beltway exits on the way over."

"We'll make some in a minute," Frank said and climbed high up on one of the two library ladders in the room. "I've worked through one whole wall here and only found one note from my grandfather."

"What'd it say?"

"Asked me if I was dusting as I went. Ol' William was a hoot, eh?"

"Let's have a look at the note," Alasdair said entering the room with his hand extended.

"It's there on the lamp table," Frank said and pointed.

Alasdair examined the note.

"Looks like regular 4-by-6 note paper," Alasdair said squinting. "Kind of old, yellowish. Think it's from your vacation days here?"

"I don't ever remember seeing notes from him like that. He always used classic stationery, letter-size. This is more recent, like the note pad on the leaving table."

"Surely you didn't drag me away from my wife's gorgeous behind to chat about note paper?"

"I need you to help me pull books out and see if there's anything important behind them.

"Didn't the CSI team check all these books?"

"Not all of them. They pulled sample batches for prints. Plus, they put everything back the way they found it."

Alasdair stared at the pile of fallen books on the floor.

"Apparently not everything," Alasdair said.

"Yeah, they *almost* put things back properly."

Alasdair studied the enormous number of volumes in the bookcases.

"There must be a few thousand of them. We'll be here 'til next week."

"Need me to call the little woman?"

"Let's have at it," Alasdair said as he rolled one of the library ladders to a section of the bookcases across from Frank. "Start here?"

Frank nodded, scampered down his ladder, and headed for the hall.

"I knew when you called, this was going to cost me," Alasdair said.

Frank stopped.

"I haven't asked you for a red cent," Frank said.

"It's costing me my sleep and my domestic tranquility."

"Sleep's overrated. I'll fire up the coffee pot ... if I can find some coffee," Frank said and left the parlor.

"If you can't, you get your Mick hide down to the 7-Eleven and don't skimp on the donuts."

*   *   *   *   *

The sun had barely peeked above the trees in the front yard when Frank and Alasdair pulled out the last book. They sat facing each other, slumped down in two of the wing chairs in the center of the parlor. A quartet of 7-Eleven coffee cups and an empty donut box cluttered the cocktail table in front of them.

"You know," Frank said, "I hate what they say about cops on TV and in the movies."

"Yeah, what's that?"

"The donut thing."

"Well, we'll have to start snacking on bear claws. Come back to donuts when it's safe."

Frank picked up the four notes on the lamp table next to his chair and sorted them.

"Let's review. This one says: *Don't give up. It's here someplace.* The next one we found says: *Are you sure you're dusting these books?* And this one says: *Your reward is under* a *Detroit wonder.* You already know what the first one said."

"We now have to go to Detroit? What's a wonder there besides the Silverdome."

"That's in Pontiac."

"Pontiac. Maybe it's a car. Hell if I know."

Frank's tired eyes widened and he sat up in the chair like somebody had plugged him in to a 220 outlet.

"You hit it. It's under a Detroit wonder," Frank said and leapt to his feet. "The 1936 Reo Flying Cloud was touted to be the wonder car of the era."

"Isn't that what's in the garage?" Alasdair asked.

But Frank was already gone.

*   *   *   *   *

Frank was standing at the rear of the Reo when Alasdair entered the garage. He gestured for Alasdair to join him and turned his attention to the floor near the car's rear bumper.

"How can we get a look under the car?" Alasdair asked.

"Like this," Frank said as he reached down and pulled open a metal door in the floor and let it rest on the gray concrete, revealing a set of steps leading under the Reo. "It's a mechanic's trench. A pit that lets you work on the underside of the car without needing a lift."

Frank descended the eight narrow steps on the right side of the concrete trench and looked around the 12-by-4-foot rectangular space. There was barely enough headroom for a six-foot person to stand, but the shallow overhead space made the undercarriage of the car fully accessible. A metal utility cart with large rubber wheels was parked against one of the vertical walls. A wired light in a small protective cage hung from its hook on the cart's push handle. Frank picked up the light, switched it on and hung it from the Reo's chassis.

"Is there room for two down there?" Alasdair asked.

"Yeah, but watch your head."

Alasdair descended the steps and kept his big frame hunkered over.

"Nothing much exciting under here," Frank said scanning the car's underside.

"Maybe it's not on the car." Alasdair said looking around at the walls of the trench.

"Four concrete walls painted gray, a parts cart and a 100-watt light bulb," Frank said. "Where's the reward?"

"Beats me. I can't even stand up straight. Like a grave in here."

"There must be something under this car. My grandfather wouldn't disappoint me."

Frank grabbed the light and inspected the walls of the trench. He went down on his hands and knees and crawled around inspecting the floor for any sign of a significant opening or secret compartment. A 2-foot-wide recess next to the narrow steps caught his eye. He crawled over to it for a closer look.

Frank knocked on the small wall with his knuckles. "It's not masonry. It's steel, painted gray to look like the concrete."

Frank felt around the wall to find a possible handle or latch, but came up with nothing. Alasdair joined him by kneeling on the steps and tried his hand at getting the steel wall to budge, but to no avail. Frank sat back against the adjacent wall and again looked around the small enclosure, slowly checking out each wall and corner. His eyes finally came to rest on the tool cart.

"Move that cart," Frank said.

Alasdair rolled the cart down to the end of the longer wall. The part of the wall concealed by the cart contained a duplex electric outlet with nothing plugged into it.

"Notice anything out of place?" Frank asked.

"You mean like the light being plugged into an outlet way across the upper garage while this more convenient outlet is down here unused?"

"Bazinga," Frank said and moved over to the duplex. He stared at it for a moment then pushed on it. It moved into the wall for about half an inch and then sprang back to its original flush position.

A low rasping sound came from the area beside the steps. Both men looked toward the narrow steel panel as Frank held up the light.

The gray wall there creaked open about five inches.

Chapter 12

Frank tugged on the steel door and swung it fully open. Beyond the wall's 2-by-5-foot opening, a ramp revealed a tunnel leading downward into blackness. Frank washed the narrow walls with the light, scrunched down, and held the bulb up to cut into the black space ten feet away. Musty air wafted out from the darkness and filled the tunnel with odors of aging wood and mildewed masonry.

"I'm betting your reward's in there," Alasdair said.

Frank led the way with the light and emerged in a large room. Alasdair scuffed along behind. Frank's free hand groped around the interior walls for a possible light switch and found one a foot from the end of the tunnel. He flicked it and the room and its contents became visible from a bare bulb hanging from the low ceiling.

"It looks like a safe room," Alasdair said.

"It's what people built in the '50s. A fallout shelter. William told me all about them and the paranoia of post war America."

"Thought the Russians were going to start the unthinkable?"

"Yeah, and believed these little caves would allow them to survive a nuclear war."

Two folded-up cots leaned against the back corners of the 12-by-18-foot room, and several five-gallon glass jugs filled with water lined the wall on the right. Four wooden folding chairs were arranged evenly around a rectangular utility table. An oak kneehole desk and swivel chair sat against one long wall on the left. The upper wall behind the desk displayed a 1945 calendar with a photo of the Statue of Liberty above an ad that encouraged buying liberty bonds. A multi-band radio sat on the desk next to a lantern flashlight and a wind-up alarm clock. A Baltimore Sun newspaper lay on the middle of the desk dated August 15, 1945. Its huge headline read:

JAPAN SURRENDERS

"Wonder how they pulled fresh air in here," Alasdair said. "Could use a wee bit now."

"My grandfather mentioned that most fallout shelters used an underground pipe that extended a distance away and came up in a remote place so no one could monkey with the air supply."

"Monkey with the air?" Alasdair said and leaned his weight on the utility table, testing its strength.

"People who didn't have shelters might sabotage them. They were not going to allow selfish shelter owners to lock them out and live while they died outside in the radiation."

"Nice Christian philosophy all-round," Alasdair said as Frank pulled open a large file drawer in the desk.

"William never admitted he had one. Told me doomsday projects like this were useless and ridiculous."

Frank fingered through several manila file folders and stopped at one labeled *The Omega Formula.* The file was wrinkled with age and smelled like a wet dog. He took the folder out of the drawer and spread it open on the desktop. One document inside drew his attention enough for him to pick it up and strain to read it in the poor light. It was a printed sheet containing what appeared to be a poem stapled to a photo of his grandfather and another man.

Alasdair moved over to Frank and looked in the open file drawer where Frank had removed the folder. Frank stuffed the photo back into the folder and watched as Alasdair reached into the drawer and removed a metal film reel can covered with an amber-brown, waxy substance.

"In the '40s not many people had TV," Frank said, "but they had movies."

"Looks like it's been coated with Cosmoline," Alasdair said.

"Old military stuff, but a good sealer." Frank said, taking the can.

Frank peeled the rubbery Cosmoline off the can and lifted out a 6-inch movie reel nearly full with 16-millimeter film. He unwound out about a yard of the black and white footage and held it up to the light.

"See what you can make of it," Frank said and handed the film to Alasdair.

"Time for some spectacles, eh?"

"Just see what you can see," Frank said.

"Ay, nothing in this light."

"We need a projector."

*　　*　　*　　*　　*

Frank dug around in the closets of the house and found a 16mm movie projector in a cupboard under the staircase. It was a 1940s vintage Keystone model William had used to show Tom Mix westerns, cartoons, old movies starring Laurel & Hardy and Buster Keaton. Frank set up the projector in the dining room, but the first flip of its chrome toggle switch proved to be the end of movie night. The bulb gave out a burst of light, popped like a muffled gunshot, and went out.

"I guess 'that's all folks,'" Frank said.

"You know, in a way, this could be a blessing," Alasdair said. "We could burn up this old film on that dinosaur, or even chew it to pieces in those pointy sprockets."

"I'm open to suggestions."

"I suggest we visit my wife, whom I haven't seen for more than eight hours in the past two days."

"Your answer to watching this film is to go pester your wife?"

"Celine is an expert on converting old film media to a digital format. She worked for over 10 years for NSA's video department, and now she's my right arm at the production company which, by the way, she's been operating by herself since her husband's off chasing flying clouds under old Detroit wonders."

"Well, let's go find Celine."

"It's about time you met her," Alasdair said. "Been married for almost eight months now. Come over for dinner. Around seven."

"How'd you con somebody to marry you? Mail order? Tell her you owned Warner Brothers?"

"Told her I was great company in the tub, and I could hold my breath for over three minutes."

"Good God, you Scots throw more bullshit than Texans," Frank said and removed the film from the projector.

"We come by it honest. Sam Houston, don't you know, was a one of our own."

Chapter 13

Celine MacGowan was everything Alasdair had advertised her to be: charming and intelligent, a dark-haired beauty with hazel eyes who could cook like a master chef. She also was reputed to be able to operate computer equipment with the best IT experts.

After dinner, Celine sat at her desk in their home office and adjusted a gooseneck lamp for optimum light. Frank handed the reel to Celine who examined the first few frames over the bright bulb with a jeweler's loupe.

"Looks like early stages of nitrate deterioration," Celine said. "It progresses to cellulose triacetate degradation, and from there it's usually game over for the film. Lucky you showed this to me before we ended up with a can of powder."

"Any clue what's on the film?" Frank asked.

"First frames say something about being property of the Department of War. Have to see more to know more."

"You can convert this to a viewable video format?"

"Not a problem. Maybe take a couple of days," Celine said and placed the film back in its metal case.

"Excellent," Frank said and gave Alasdair a thumbs-up.

* * * * *

Frank sipped the last dram from his glass of 15-year-old Laphroaig scotch while Alasdair and Celine sat together on the sofa in the den.

"Celine, that was perhaps the best dinner I've ever eaten," Frank said and flopped in a leather recliner.

"Glad to have someone over who appreciates good home cooking," Celine said.

"Frank gets Christmas cards from Pizza Hut," Alasdair said.

"How did you two meet?" Celine asked Alasdair.

"In an all-star baseball game. Semi-pro league," Alasdair said. "He did something the baseball world has never seen before or since."

"For God's sake, Al, is nothing sacred?" Frank said and got up and poured himself another scotch.

"Tell, tell," Celine said tugging Alasdair's arm.

"In the eighth inning, the star pitcher of the other team threw a fastball directly at Frank's head," Alasdair said. "A rocket-fast fastball."

"What happened?" Celine said. "Wait. Frank was knocked out and you gave him mouth-to-mouth."

"Not hardly," Alasdair said and sipped his drink.

"Well, what then?" Celine said.

"In a nanosecond, Frank caught that baseball in his bare hand and fired it back at the pitcher. Now Frank was our center fielder and he could really throw a ball far and hard. That ball hit that pitcher square on his beltline and dropped him like a stone. He had to be taken off the field on a stretcher. It was like something supernatural."

"Served him right, I'd say," Celine said and winked at Frank.

"Well, the umpire thought different and ejected Frank from the game. However, the crowd cheered and applauded his departure like he was a rock star. They carried on for twenty minutes and later booed every call made by the ump."

"Who won the game?" Celine said.

"We did, 9 to 3," Alasdair said. "Frank was voted the game's MVP."

"If story-telling is over, who gave you the pricey scotch?" Frank said to Alasdair.

"Gave me?" Alasdair said. "You miserable Irish boor. It's my favorite libation. I bought that with my income tax refund just for you on this visit, since I haven't laid eyes on you for five long years. And without so much as a Christmas card, mind you."

"Really?" Frank said and downed his drink.

"A client gave it to him for Christmas last year," Celine said grinning at the stern look from her husband. "But it is his favorite, when he'll part with the money for a bottle."

"I knew it," Frank said and placed his empty glass on the nearby side table.

"You going back to that old place with the creepy fallout shelter?" Alasdair said.

"It's my house now," Frank said. "I need to reacquaint myself with it."

"You're welcome to stay here, Frank. Anytime," Celine said.

"Thanks, Celine, but would we have to keep him?"

"Did you know he can hold his breath for over three minutes?" Celine said.

"I've often wished he'd hold his breath a lot longer," Frank said. "Goodnight, you two. Celine, you're way too beautiful and too good for an oaf like him."

Frank strode for the door.

"I'll have Alasdair call you when the video's ready," Celine said.

"Later," Frank said and made his way outside to the rented Hyundai and climbed behind the wheel.

William had left a puzzle, a poem, papers, a photograph, and an old film. Frank pondered their meaning.

What else has William planted, and where are these discoveries leading?

*   *   *   *   *

Frank spent hours going through the house on Elm Terrace, again searching for any clues that might shed light on his father's murder or anything to help him understand his grandfather's puzzling last words. He struggled for a connection between the two mysteries.

The house displayed all the signs he expected regarding his father's living habits. The master bathroom looked like a gorilla had lost a bout with a ten-gallon bottle of depilatory. Frank remembered Joe had always been doubly bedeviled with hair problems. He'd lost most of the hair on his scalp, while having more body hair than a sasquatch. The hair and floor grime gave Frank an indication that Joe apparently never found the vacuum a useful appliance.

Frank gathered up an array of cleaning items and began the task of getting the house in a semblance of hygienic order. He inspected each room, pulled from it what information he could, then cleaned it. He doubted he'd find anything useful that the CSIs had missed, but the items he might uncover didn't have to be crime-related. William was providing him with plenty of other clues to unravel.

The master bedroom had not been touched in years. The bedclothes were wrinkled and stained with everything from slopped booze to pizza sauce. The white sheets had become giant napkins. The kitchen displayed food-crusted china and cookware stacked on the counter tops. Pots lay coated with molded food in the sink and dishwasher, with the added joy of stinking beer bottles overflowing the trash receptacle beneath the counter. It was a career slob's man cave.

Nothing turned up on the other floors of the house. The third floor looked like it hadn't been used since the Eisenhower administration, but the basement held a minor surprise or two. The stacks of labeled cardboard boxes lining the rear wall had been ripped open, their contents scattered on the floor. Old rugs, oil paintings, and outdoor tables and chairs were jumbled in an adjoining section six feet from the oil furnace. The entire basement appeared to be recently visited from the fresh footprints in the dust that covered the floor. Some, Frank knew, belonged to the CSI team and they had recorded the suspicious ones, especially a size 16 group.

Frank again mulled over why the killers had been there in the first place. *If they wanted something, what had they taken? Or was the mission simply to kill Joe? For gambling money? Then why use truth serum?* Joe had called him asking for money last winter and Frank had refused. The hypothetical answer was that someone wanted something from Joe Dugan and murdered him for it, but Joe had no real money, so what was it? *And if it was money, why kill him? Dead men seldom pay off debts.*

It was time to switch focus and head for the other mystery lying under the garage. Instinct told Frank there was a connection there to his father's fate. Exhibit A: There was an old secret room underground on the property built to appear to be a fallout shelter. Frank knew William didn't believe in fallout shelters, and often spoke of the folly of constructing one. The question was then, why was it there? Frank realized the answer had to be in the secret room itself. Exhibit B: The tipoff was the table and chairs. William had held his clandestine meetings in there. And it was where William's grown-up business took place, and where everyone mysteriously disappeared from view.

But what were they meeting in there about?

Chapter 14

Frank returned to the garage and entered the fallout shelter. He went straight to the desk, gathered up the Omega Formula folder and returned to the house.

He sat on the sofa in the parlor and placed the folder on the cocktail table, opened it, and began to examine its papers one by one. There was printed matter typed by an old typewriter using an archaic font. Many of the typed characters were uneven in their leading lines, kerning, and density of ink, the latter likely from a ribbon in need of replacement or a worn typewriter platen. Several papers were handwritten in blue-black ink while others contained sketched diagrams and scrawled chemical equations. The papers and inks showed extensive age and their information was faded and, in some cases, barely readable.

Frank adjusted the floor lamp to focus the maximum light on the documents. Many of the pages contained equations and scientific notations that ended with the words: "Failed" or "Ineffective," which he set aside. The pile contained dated memos, typewritten with more misaligned letters and partial impressions. He stacked these in chronological order and pulled the first one out and read it.

June 5, 1945

To all concerned:

 The pair of bombs may not be enough to effect a surrender, and we certainly have to come up with something better than the invasion alternative. If they discover that we only have the two, they may not even entertain giving up. They are a proud people who are not afraid of death, only ridicule and losing face. Therefore, I will be testing something I have been working on for months that may be our salvation.

 I have proposed a meeting for 8 PM this week to discuss my new plan. I can't stress enough the need for absolute secrecy concerning our meetings and our decisions. No politicians, including Truman, should be privy to the course we take, lest it be bogged down in bureaucratic wrangling. We'll need every moment we have left to put what we decide into action.

 The clock is ticking, gentlemen.

W

He flipped through to another memo written on July 1, 1945:

To all concerned:

I have completed the lab experiments on the formula and the results are encouraging. Tomorrow three of us will be flying west to perform the practical, outdoor tests. Everything will hinge on the outcome of those few days. Aerial filming will accompany the tests. V will lead with his air group.

I will meet with you all on the 7th with my report.

W

Frank skimmed through the rest of the notes and placed them neatly back into the file folder along with the photo stapled to the poem. He stood up slowly, like a defendant about to hear a jury's verdict.

What the hell was William into?

Frank piled the chemistry papers into a separate stack and replaced them in the file folder with all the other documents. He tucked the folder under his arm and went out to the rental car.

*   *   *   *   *

Frank drove to the local Kinkos and made copies of all the documents in the Omega file folder. He also had the photo scanned and had it transferred to a thumb drive he carried with him. He thought about scanning the poem too, but that might chance leaving it on a Kinkos' hard drive. The photo alone, he hoped, wasn't essential to solve the Omega formula, and even he didn't know who the second person was in the picture. He was certain he'd need to have a digitally transmittable copy of the photo to later get it identified, so he had little choice but to risk that no one would be interested in an uncaptioned, black-and-white photo from the past.

When Frank returned from the copy store he separated all the documents into two piles. One set contained copies of everything in the Omega Formula file found in the fallout shelter, minus William's memos and the photo with the attached poem. This amended set he replaced in the original manila folder and put it on the sofa beside him. The next pile contained copies of everything in the original Omega file, plus the original memos from William, and the photo with the poem. This set he put into a new manila folder and placed it on top of the original Omega set. Frank took all the files back into the fallout shelter and replaced the yellowing manila Omega Formula file back in the oak desk.

Frank slid his new Omega file under his arm and stepped over to the light switch. For a moment he stood there staring back at the room, considering whether he'd made the right decision to withhold some of the documents. He knew from William's notations of failure that the chemical formulas were worthless and would lead nowhere in explaining how the Omega formula weapon could be devised, if there ever was such weapon.

The memos could have backup substantiation for the entire hoax, but also lent credence to the reality of the weapon by their mention of its encouraging testing. The fact that they were shared by only the few involved with the plot, and never part of what the Japanese might ultimately view, made the weapon seem real. But the poem attached to the photo presented another matter. Frank knew the poem and photo were classic William Dugan *modus operandi*: cryptic, nearly impossible to decipher, and usable only by the sacred few who could fathom how a man like his grandfather thought out and processed his puzzles. Would the explication of the poem prove the Omega formula a hoax or a reality? Frank had no idea which was true.

The fact that the unviewed film had so easily slipped from the trusted safety of its inheritor, and could possibly open a 21st Century Pandora's box, confirmed his resolve. He had acted foolishly before. He wouldn't chance a repeat performance. No one would ever see the memos, nor the photo and poem document. That was certain.

Frank switched off the light and left the shelter. He pushed the secret door closed until it latched.

He stepped outside into the thick, warm air of the back yard and sat on a teak bench near an ornate, alabaster birdbath. He put his Omega folder in his lap, pressed his hands down on the bench on either side of his legs to steady himself and stared straight out, focusing on nothing.

After a few moments, he opened the folder and studied the photo. It was an 8-by-10 glossy of his grandfather standing next to another man, both wearing lab coats with the National Aeronautics and Space Agency's embroidered logo over the right breast. William looked to be about sixty, but his strong chin, chiseled features and full head of graying hair gave Frank a future peek at himself. It was obvious he shared most of his grandfather's traits and few of his father's.

The men were working at a laboratory table with a partial view of a metal object before them that looked like a space-age garden hoe. William was smiling at the other man who was handling the object. The attached paper contained a poem signed by his grandfather.

Frank turned the photo over and skimmed over the poem's four verses and swiped his sweaty face with his hand.

Men wish to swing in their seventies and fly with eagles,
   like boys who dream of playing on the moon.
   Find someone to recount the sheep, avoid the deep six
      that rusts plain iron, and keep a tool as a rune.

If need be loosed this awful power,
it lies asleep until that hour.
Sealed in a pipe all eyes can see,
but blind to all, save you and me.

His eyes stung from the perspiration, causing him to squeeze them shut and blink several times. He replaced the photo, rolled up the folder and went back into the garage.

Frank made his way over to the Reo, sat in the driver's seat and studied the simple dashboard and gauges. His eyes fell to the keys hanging from the ignition switch. He removed them, noting the familiar leather pouch they folded into that he'd so often seen in his grandfather's hand and on the leaving table.

He moved to the rear of the car and opened the trunk. He put the rolled folder down on the left side of the trunk, straightened out the pulled-up matting and replaced the tire in its recessed well and bolted it securely. Inside were the usual tire changing tools and a Mason jar box containing quarts of Quaker State motor oil and an old license plate. It was a 1938 California plate with lettering and numbers painted in gold on a black background. Frank remembered William had told him that the car once belonged to Clark Gable, who drove it during the production of *Gone With the Wind*. He smiled at the thought, thankful for a moment of pleasant diversion from the heaviness of the Omega files. He put the license plate in the box and closed the trunk. He inserted the key back in the ignition, left the garage, and locked the door.

He wended his way through the high grass and weeds to the backyard bench and plopped down. He bent forward, placed his head in his hands and mulled over all the events of the day.

Frank's quiet moment with his thoughts was short-lived.

Shuffling footsteps approached from the driveway.

Chapter 15

A woman and a man appeared around the corner of the house and made their way toward Frank. They brushed through the thick grass and stopped fifteen feet away.

"Are you Frank Dugan?" the pretty thirty-something woman asked.

Frank stared at her, then stood up.

"That'd be me."

"You're Alasdair MacGowan's detective friend from Florida."

"Right again," Frank said and wondered how she knew that. He noticed her comfort-fitting attire was losing its battle to conceal her shapely build. "I'm going to say something now that , in my line of work, people often say to me: What's this all about?"

"I'm FBI Special Agent Braewyn Joyce, a friend of Celine MacGowan," she said and showed Frank her identification. "This is my partner, Special Agent Tom Gardner."

Tom said nothing and hung back while Braewyn moved in closer to Frank.

Frank studied her intently. The woman had a sensual mouth and her beautiful face conflicted with her strictly-business air. His eyes washed her body down to her stylish pumps.

"Again, what's this about?" Frank said.

"It's about your film." Braewyn said. "The NSA called us in to have a look."

Frank immediately felt at a disadvantage.

"You saw the film?" he said. "Anyone else see it?"

"My partner and Celine, and possibly her former supervisor at NSA. It has ramifications we need to discuss with you."

"I haven't seen the film. When do *I* get to see it?"

"It's under government scrutiny, at present. You never saw the film?"

"Not a frame."

"We thought you'd seen it since it came from you."

"It was too fragile to run through a projector. Celine was going to make me a digital copy."

"You're going to be asked a lot of questions, detective. Your film has caused quite a stir in Washington."

"It's from World War Two, I believe. What does an old film stir up over half a century later?"

"Do you have any other information about this Omega formula?"

My God, how did she find out about that?

"Omega formula?" Frank said. "Something in the film?"

"You know nothing of this weapon?"

"I came here to bury my father. I found the film on the property and gave it to Celine MacGowan. I haven't seen the film, and anything about it is all news to me."

Braewyn studied Frank's face for several seconds. Frank recognized the ploy to see if he blinked or showed any tacit evidence of deception. He stared unflinchingly back at her.

"We'll be in touch, sir," Braewyn said and nodded to Tom.

The FBI agents turned and headed back to the street.

"That's it?" Frank said, following them down the driveway. "'We'll be in touch'?"

The agents continued walking to their car without looking back. Frank yanked his cell from his belt and punched in a number. Seconds passed as Frank paced across the lawn.

"Alasdair, I need to talk to you."

*   *   *   *   *

When Alasdair arrived at Elm Terrace, Frank was rocking in the porch glider. Two empty beer bottles sat on the table next to him.

"Drinking alone is a sure sign of a problem," Alasdair said as he ascended the porch steps holding a spiral notepad.

Frank noticed the pad.

"Taking notes?"

"Got something I want to show you," Alasdair said, patting the pad.

"Show me this: Why has everyone seen my film except me? Show me how that happened?"

"It's the government, Frank. Federal agencies. You know how they are. Full of themselves. Slinging their power everywhere they might to validate their self importance."

"I gave you that film and trusted you to make sure it didn't get into the hands of those power slingers."

"Celine had to use her former contacts at NSA to get the film converted to a digital format. Her supervisor took it on himself to call in the feds when he saw it. But not before Celine got a copy and brought it home."

"So, where's the copy?"

"The FBI found out about her copy and made her hand it over."

"To this Braewyn agent?"

"Yeah, Braewyn's an old acquaintance of Celine's. Made PR and training videos with our company for the Bureau."

"So you charged over here to comment on my drinking and tell me I'm sucking eggs."

"I can't say I haven't enjoyed that part of my trip, but if you'll lose the snitty attitude, I'll make your day."

Alasdair looked back toward the street and panned his eyes in a wide arc. He then pulled a DVD from inside his notepad.

"Made a copy of Celine's copy," Alasdair said and extended the disk to Frank. "Before Ms. FBI got hold of it."

"Laptop's inside," Frank said and strode to the front door.

*   *   *   *   *

Frank led Alasdair into the parlor where the laptop was set up on the cocktail table in front of the sofa.

"Got any idea how long this is?" Frank asked.

"Celine's copy said six minutes."

"Have you seen it?"

"Nope."

Frank inserted the disk into the laptop's DVD tray and activated the video. The first few frames credited the film as being the property of the United States Department of War. Next, Frank heard the familiar voice of William Dugan as he narrated the

101

opening scenes, taken from several World War II battle films in the Pacific:

"Four trying years have passed and our nation is weary of war. American families, who have sacrificed so much, want victory at the earliest possible opportunity."

William's articulate voice sounded similar to Franklin Delano Roosevelt's in its precision, pace, and timbre. Frank smiled at his remembrance of the narrator.

On the laptop screen: A kamikaze dove into an American aircraft carrier, exploding into a fiery horror on the vessel's deck. The narration continued over more battle scenes:

"We are now faced with the final days of a long, costly campaign to preserve the liberty of America and many of her sister nations that have fought so valiantly by our side. Conventional bombs have had an effect, but not enough to achieve an end to the war."

Next came scenes of the U.S. Marine assault on the beaches of Iwo Jima with American soldiers being cut down by heavy Japanese gunfire, again and again.

"The final days confront us with options to either fight on conventionally, or resort to the deadliest means we have at our disposal to shorten

the strife and save many thousands of lives, even those of the enemy."

Footage of an atomic bomb test explosion in the desert burst onto the screen with mock buildings and mannequins being evaporated by the bomb's shock wave, and the following all-consuming fires and devastating winds.

"We intend to embark on the latter option. The invasion of mainland Japan will lengthen the war interminably and add tens of thousands of Allied lives to the terrible price that has already been paid."

A U.S. Army corpsman on the screen carried an unconscious soldier through mortar blasts and heavy machine gun fire.

"Our first tactic will be to use our weapons of atomic force. These will cause incredible damage and heavy losses of enemy lives, and should bring about the unconditional surrender of Japan. We have enough of these to wipe out multiple major cities in Japan, but our hope is that she will capitulate early in this campaign and save her citizens. These weapons leave behind the destruction of infrastructure, as well as humanity, but because of problems associated with radiation, they will make our occupation and provision of medical aid complicated and greatly delayed."

More scenes rolled by on the screen of large American ships at sea being torpedoed, crippled and sinking, while U.S. Navy sailors abandoned them, diving into the flaming, oil-slicked water.

"The Japanese are a proud, resourceful, and determined people. Should we not obtain the unconditional surrender we demand, we will be forced to use our weapon of last resort: The Omega Formula, a weapon of unbelievably selective devastation. The following scenes show the incredible lethality of this device, but with one remarkable new feature."

The screen showed a large flat expanse with hundreds of prairie dogs shot from a high angle. A baseball-size pellet was shown in a close-up on a plane, then dropped and activated a moment before contacting the ground. A rippling wave distorted the air below the plane for a split-second, and when it cleared, the entire prairie dog population lay dead, but not one burrow, bush, or stone on the surrounding plain had been affected.

"It kills all animal life without radioactive fallout, fire, or damage to inanimate objects. The humans will die without bloodshed, and the buildings and infrastructure of the targets will remain intact. The kill range of a small amount of this weapon is its most powerful feature. The weapons will contain thousands of these pellets and will be dropped from a low altitude all across the island of Honshu where they will be activated by atmospheric pressure as they near the earth. This

aggregate weapon is lethal for a radius of several miles at ground level, while below ground and the overhead atmosphere will be equally affected for several hundred feet. Our aircraft can accurately drop these pellet packages with complete safety at moderate altitudes and return home safely with their crews.

"Please note the following demonstration:"

A scene depicted more than five hundred adults, mostly men, in a huge circle in a vast desert, like the ones shown in documentaries of the Mojave or Death Valley. A close-up inside a small plane showed a baseball-size pellet being dropped from its open door. A close-up of the plane's altimeter showed a steady altitude of three thousand feet. The pellet was set off when it reached near-ground level, creating an almost invisible wave, which resembled a heat mirage. The wave expanded rapidly across the ground, well beyond the people as every person in the circle crumpled and fell, lifeless.

"We can have ready the number of weapons needed within the next few days. If our atomic attacks don't quicken the surrender of Imperial Japan, we will deploy the Omega Formula.

"May God forgive us for having to unleash this deadly device and its awesome power."

The screen faded to black.

"Those people looked real," Frank said, his head bowed.

"Aye."

Frank shut down the laptop and closed the lid.

"You think your grandfather's having us on?" Alasdair asked.

"There's one thing I know about William. He never lied."

"I think we need to keep this between us as best we can," Frank said. "Answer no questions for anyone. We know nothing."

"Done," Alasdair said as he left the house. "Even if the PETA people contact me about the prairie dogs."

Frank had little interest in prairie dogs, but he was concerned about his grandfather's role as a mass murderer, and he felt a great pillar of his life was about to be toppled. And he knew something else: this latest window into his grandfather's past would force him to solve the mystery, and not relent until he answered all the questions posed by the film he'd just seen.

Was this something William could've been a party to? How could he kill innocent people in cold blood? For all these past years, have I revered a monster?"

Frank planned to pursue the clues left by William to the end. He would dig in and find meaning in all the hidden mysteries surrounding his grandfather, and either exonerate him or condemn him. Frank was a detective. He had to know the truth. He had to accept the commitment.

Frank Dugan squared his shoulders and crossed the Rubicon of his life.

Chapter 16

The late afternoon air outside the house was warm but fresh, and carried the mixed aroma of lawn tractor exhaust and newly-cut grass. Frank returned to the garage to retrieve the Omega folder from the trunk of the Reo.

Frank wished he was still a young boy who wasn't allowed to know what transpired in the garage. His father often said, in his unvarnished street vernacular, *"Information gives monkeys the shits."* A phrase Frank never understood until he was in his teens. It meant knowing too much can create fear. Some things, he agreed, were better left unknown.

He was on the verge of the shits, but he sat in the Reo and continued to read the memos. His grandfather's words gained intensity as the messages approached August of 1945. But it was the last one, written in 1995, that had his head reeling.

August 14, 1995

Gentlemen,

On this auspicious 50th anniversary of our victory over the tyranny of the Empire of Japan, I call us to assemble for what may be our last time

*together. For this meeting, I have asked my son
Joseph, a police officer of whom I am very proud, to
witness our discussion, our re-telling of the events
that led to our victory, and our admission to our
complicity in the making of the Omega Formula
film. Someday the world may need to know what we
accomplished, but perhaps never how we did it. I
have also left clues for my beloved grandson, who
now fights terrorism and tyranny overseas, to learn
the facts about our deeds.*

*The judgment of the world upon us may rest in
their hands and, most importantly, the secret of the
Omega Formula will forever be preserved, or
revealed, as these modern times move these two men
to do so. May God guide their hearts.*

*You are the finest of what freedom has to offer
on a planet steeped in strife, oppression, and human
suffering. I salute you for your service and courage
in the face of a most challenging history.*

*When MacArthur accepted the surrender of
Japan on the battleship* Missouri, *and every soldier
and sailor came to attention, it was a tribute to you.*

Your constant friend and servant,

W

Frank gripped the wheel of the car and closed
his eyes. After a moment, he rolled the folder back

up and went to the trunk and opened it. He carefully tucked the folder behind the spare and wedged it down into the tire well. He closed the trunk and laced his fingers on top of his head. His eyes glistened.

My God, my father knew everything about the Omega formula. Was that what his killers wanted?

* * * * *

Frank watched Alasdair gaze at the bubbles rising in his beer glass as they sat at the bar at Alfredo's Lounge in Catonsville. A day had passed since the visit from the FBI and Frank was not getting anywhere solving his father's murder. He looked at himself in the mirror behind the bar. His face was unshaven and his thick chestnut hair looked like he'd driven in the Indy 500 with no helmet in a convertible with the top down.

"I told Celine I saw the film," Alasdair said.

"I wish we'd left it in the fallout shelter."

"I'm sorry for the trouble this has caused you. Celine couldn't use the film editing equipment at NSA without clearing it with her boss who oversees those sorts of things. They're a tight-ass bunch. He felt obligated to inform the government and pressured Celine to turn over the film."

"It's okay. This Omega thing has blindsided me. I knew my grandfather worked on the Manhattan

Project and had been a consultant for the Army Air Force in World War Two, but I never suspected he was into this James Bond stuff."

The bartender moved toward Frank and Alasdair.

"Get you fellas anything else?" she asked.

"I think we're good," Alasdair said.

"Two's my limit. He'll take the check," Frank said.

The bartender placed the check in front of Alasdair who tossed a twenty-dollar bill down and shot Frank a glare. He waited until the bartender was at the cash register before he spoke.

"That Omega film deals with issues of national defense," Alasdair said. "Celine learned of things at the NSA she could never discuss with me, and I'm her friggin' man. With a grandfather and a grandson? Probably a wider discussion gap."

"I loved the man. I tried to keep in touch with him almost every day before I was sent overseas. I was with him at the end, right up until his last breath," Frank said.

"What's on that film was way before our time, lad," Alasdair said. "But I can't bring myself to believe your grandfather would kill people to make a scare film."

Frank stared at himself in the mirror behind the bar.

"Maybe it wasn't just a scare film."

"You think it was for real? An Omega formula exists? Then why are we only finding out about it now?"

"Same reason: my grandfather. He helped invent it, made sure the Japanese had a gander at it, then covered it up like it was rotten fish."

"William created the damn thing, sent it on its mission, and then destroyed every trace?"

"Well, not *every* trace," Frank said low and scanned the room for nearby ears. "I found chemical compounds and formulas in a file folder in the shelter."

"Good grief, man, then all we have to do is whip up a batch of that stuff, rustle up a bunch of homeless people, and find a passel of prairie dogs."

"I would, but I chucked my chemistry set when I was fourteen. Are you nuts?"

The bartender returned and placed Alasdair's change on the bar and left.

"If the damn thing works we can charge the government a pretty penny for it," Alasdair said poking Frank's arm. "My video business could sure use a boost."

"They'd simply take it and not pay us an honorable mention," Frank said. "Or toss us in jail and throw away the jail. You know how those dot-gov bastards operate."

"Okay, then we'll peddle it to the Vatican. They have tons of money, and they're bound by the peace of the Lord not to use weapons to harm anyone. They'll stick it in one of their secret vaults under St. Peter's. It's a win-win," Alasdair said and laughed.

"You make jokes, but if word of this leaks out, there'll be a lot people after it. If that formula works, North Korea could wipe out South Korea in a day. Iran could rule the world. Israel could be gone. That's one scary-ass movie. A reel of wicked shit, brother."

"Bury what you have and play dumb," Alasdair said. "Put everything back in the fallout shelter and seal up the lot."

"Truman had to know after Nagasaki we'd need to go in on foot."

"Yeah, after two A-bombs we were done," Alasdair said.

"Like us here," Frank said, lifting his beer. "Two and through."

Frank slugged down the last of his beer, then moved his face closer to Alasdair's.

"Here's the big question: Did Japan give up because of the Omega formula film?"

Here's a bigger question," Alasdair said. "Where's the Omega formula now?"

Chapter 17

Frank left Alasdair at Alfredo's parking lot and returned to Elm Terrace by 10:30. He wheeled the car up the long driveway, shut down the engine, and turned off the headlights. When he glanced through the windshield he spotted light spilling out onto the walkway from the side door of the garage.

Frank instinctively reached for the Browning in his shoulder holster, but then realized it wasn't there because he didn't yet have a concealed carry permit for Maryland. He debated whether to charge for the house for his gun, or crank the engine and get the hell out of there. Good sense won out. He cranked and ripped out of the driveway in reverse, bounced the hefty SUV onto the street, and sped away. Half a block later, he U-turned, aimed the truck toward the house, and called Alasdair on his cell.

"Didn't we just have a few pints together?" Alasdair asked.

"I have company. Trouble is, they weren't invited. My piece is in the house, so I'd appreciate if you'd drop by for a quick visit with some ordnance."

"Jesus, it's like having Mel Gibson for a partner."

"Come. *Now*."

*　*　*　*　*

Frank watched the house and kept the motor running. Fifteen long minutes passed and no one showed themselves at his house or on the surrounding grounds. *Did they see me drive in and beat it out through the back yard?* There was no car in the driveway and those parked on the street he could plainly see, should anyone have come or gone.

A big white GMC Denali pulled up behind Frank's car and doused its lights. Seconds later, Alasdair slid into the Santa Fe next to Frank. He was carrying two pistols; a snub-nose Smith & Wesson .38 revolver and a .357 Colt Python.

"I keep the little guy as an extra kicker in the truck," Alasdair said. "Got a permit for anything I carry, including a flame thrower."

He handed Frank the S&W.

"Haven't spotted anyone, but the garage lights are on and the door's open. Not how I left it."

"What's the plan?" Alasdair asked.

"My favorite one is where I sit here and you go in and shoot whoever's there."

"Let's go with the one where we both go in and try not to shoot each another."

Frank opened the SUV door and eased it closed. He scuttled toward the garage while Alasdair skirted around the house to approach the property from the

115

rear. Both men converged on the garage, creeping soundlessly until they were next to the open door. Frank carefully peered inside.

"Don't see anyone," Frank whispered, "but I can't cover every angle from here. Cover the door. I'm going inside."

Frank, gun at the ready, slipped inside the garage and scuttled around the Explorer. He ducked down and peeked across the truck's hood, then dropped lower to view the rest of the garage from floor level.

"See anything?" Alasdair said low as he entered and positioned himself at the rear of the Explorer.

"What I see is not what's *in* here, but what's *not* in here."

Frank straightened up and stepped around the Explorer. Alasdair circled the truck and joined Frank in the middle of the garage. They both stared across the top of the Corvette at the open bay where the Reo had been.

Chapter 18

Frank and Alasdair examined the garage searching for any evidence left by the car thieves.

"The door was picked by a pro. Not a lot of scratches on the lock," Frank said.

"They had to open this third bay door to move the car out," Alasdair said. "We might find a print. Should we call in the locals?"

"Hell, no. We have to keep this our own gig. I've had enough with CSIs traipsing all over this place."

"Got it."

"I'll find some graphite and tape," Frank said and opened the workbench cabinet, searched through the shelves, and retrieved bottle of powdered graphite and some clear packaging tape.

Frank dusted the bay door handle and other likely places for fingerprints, while Alasdair followed with the tape.

"I pulled a few prints, full and partials," Alasdair said, peeling off the tape. He scrutinized his work against the overhead lighting.

"Let's hope they don't all belong to my relatives," Frank said.

Frank held back telling Alasdair about the recent bits of information he'd taken from the safe room. He sensed that William's notes, the poem, and the photo could each play a vital part in this Omega business. At the moment, one thought gave him chills: The rolled-up file folder with a lot of untold secrets was lying in the trunk of the Reo.

*   *   *   *   *

The following morning, Frank drove to his former precinct on Font Hill Avenue in Southwest Baltimore. The station was a square brick building built in the late 1950s with tall, multi-paned windows and a large, overhanging roof high above the entrance. Inside, steel desks with Formica tops now supported computers, which had replaced most of the upright manual typewriters and IBM Selectrics Frank remembered. A few vintage models stubbornly sat in protest on a desk or two.

The watch captain, John Dellarue, a friend and former boss Frank had worked with a decade earlier, sat at a desk covered with papers. The heavy-set man was dressed in a white uniform shirt and plain black tie held in place with a Baltimore PD tie clasp. He was a burly six-foot fellow with gray hair, unruly Andy Rooney eyebrows, and projected old cop toughness. Frank knew when the captain had worked out of the main station at Fayette and Fallsway in the center of town he had not been opposed to an occasional, friendly shakedown of the illegal

118

gamblers in the city, and often took a cut from the prostitution ring centered on Baltimore's infamous Block District. Later, he rolled over his ill-gotten cash into a profitable bookmaking operation. Supplementing a paltry police salary with money from shady operations was generally overlooked and, in those days, not cause for any strict disciplinary action.

Dellarue had been Joe Dugan's superior in the western district, and Frank knew he maintained valuable contacts all over the state. He also knew Dellarue had handled all of Joe's local betting. When Frank made detective, he left Dellarue's purview and lost his ability to keep close tabs on Joe's gambling.

"Holy crap, you leave the front door open and look who drags his ass in," Dellarue said and stood as Frank entered the office.

"Good seeing you too, Johnny," Frank said and held out his hand.

"Sit down, fella. I never thought I'd ever lay eyes on you again. What, did the governor of Florida ask you to leave?"

"The old man died and left me a property in Oak Forest."

"Joe lived in Oak Forest? Pretty snooty area for cops like us. What happened to Windsor Heights?"

Frank noted Dellarue's indication that he hadn't been aware of where Joe lived. Oak Forest had been his father's home since William died, and he was certain Dellarue knew the address well.

"Had a snooty grandfather with money. Left him a better address than Windsor Heights," Frank said.

"Well, what's up? Want your old job back?"

"Got a few minutes?" Frank said. "I'll fill you in."

The captain and Frank spent the better part of a half-hour behind the closed doors of the captain's office. Afterward, Dellarue accompanied Frank to the forensics lab and had the garage prints run against the Integrated Automated Fingerprint Identification System, better known as IAFIS. They scored a positive hit on a career thug named Richard Jason Korbel, AKA Dickie K. He had a nice curriculum vitae: armed robbery, attempted murder, aggravated assault, extortion, breaking and entering, and attempted rape. A speck of good news came at the end of the dismal report. He'd been released from prison only three weeks ago and was likely still in town.

"Korbel just finished a year at Patuxent for check fraud," Dellarue said. "I'll get his parole officer to check on his whereabouts and we'll bring him in. I put out an APB for the Reo. Now go meet my buddy at the state police, Major Mark Hollenbeck, and get a carry permit. He's at the Waterloo barracks. I'll call him, and take this."

Dellarue extended a business card.

"Don't know how to thank you," Frank said.

"Try visiting Charles Street Liquors. Maybe you'll think of something."

Frank saluted John goodbye and stepped to the door where he noticed the captain's blue uniform coat hung neatly on a hanger on a coat tree as he left the room.

The left breast button was a shade brighter than all the others on the coat.

Chapter 19

The theft of the Reo had Frank chewing his lip in thought as he drove south on U.S. 1 toward Jessup.

Eliminate all the scenarios that don't make sense; what's left likely contains the truth. Who would want to steal a vintage auto? A collector? Not probable, or wise, since it's too big and too rare. Someone willing to fence it for half its collector value? Still not smart, but possible. Maybe sell to a foreign buyer? Too much red tape with shipping and customs. Gambling debts? Again, possibly. A better motive? The Reo theft was made to throw me off the real reason for killing Joe.

That last one made the most sense.

A showroom-condition 1936 Reo Flying Cloud was worth about thirty grand, but the Dugans' perfectly restored Reo had been owned by Clark Gable, and driven by him during the months of shooting one of the most famous movies of all time, which premiered in 1939. That would enhance its value significantly. It even had its 1938 license plate for added value and provenance. The question remained: who knew the car was there? It had to be someone familiar with the estate and its residents.

Joe Dugan's past gambling habits crowded into Frank's thoughts. He knew his father was addicted to gambling and bet on horses, blackjack, and sports, and he was particularly fond of Atlantic City. He worked with bookies who would take wagers by phone, but they expected to be paid when you lost. Credit was not something they extended to the average player, and Joe was no Las Vegas "whale." Joe owed money, probably a lot of it, but Frank was certain he wasn't murdered for it, and the car got confiscated strictly to cover up the true reason. Joe knew about the Omega formula and someone killed him trying to pull that knowledge out of him. It was a connection that made cop sense, one which could explain the use of truth serum. The truth serum angle didn't fit with the gambling debt motive, no matter how hard he tried to justify it.

My father took what he knew to the grave with him, bloodied but unbowed.

In the end, the good dad Frank always wanted finally showed up.

*   *   *   *   *

The Waterloo barracks of the Maryland State Police was a dated brick building situated among newer ones, with a multi-bay maintenance garage in the rear. The desk sergeant was military official, but cordial in his greeting and rang up the major for Frank. Minutes later Frank was led down a hall to a modest office. Mark Hollenbeck rose from his desk and smiled as Frank entered. He was in his late fifties, tall and fit-looking in his dark brown uniform. He wore rimless glasses and sported a well-trimmed, dark pencil mustache, which contrasted with his silver hair.

"John Dellarue says you're one of his former all-stars who left the fold," the major said and extended his hand. "Mark Hollenbeck."

"Frank Dugan," Frank said and shook the major's hand. "Yeah, got tired of scraping ice off my car and decided to head south."

"You know, they say if we men paid more attention to our testicles, we'd start fewer wars and live in a warmer climate," Hollenbeck said, grinning.

"I'm going to have to write that one down."

"Said you need an accommodation," the major said and gestured for Frank to sit in the wooden office chair next to the oak desk.

"I came up to check on the property left to me when my father died and became a crime victim."

"John says they stole an antique car."

"That, and I discovered my father was murdered."

"You have proof of that?" Hollenbeck said and sat down at the desk.

"The ME report and the 9-1-1 call tell the story."

"I got your temporary carry permit okayed from Pikesville, but you might want to let the county boys go primary on the felonies. We'll step in if anything occurs outside of their jurisdiction. I've managed to cultivate an ensemble of key people in high places over the years. We'll get your crimes solved."

"I just want to wrap this up and get back to Florida."

"Where are you in Florida?"

"Martin County. Stuart. A nice resort town on the Atlantic side."

"Stuart? Sheriff there still Roland Brand?"

"You know him?"

"He and I attended Florida Southern in Tampa, more years ago than I care to admit. We were frat brothers. Pi Kappa Phi. A good guy. Please give him my best regards."

Hollenbeck handed Frank a business card from a holder on the desk.

"Will do," Frank said, took the card, and stood.

"I've already signed your courtesy permit. Pick it up from the desk sergeant on your way out."

"Thank you, sir. If you ever come down to Stuart, look up Roland and me for a free beach tour and dinner," Frank said and left the office.

Frank picked up his permit and drove back northeast toward the Baltimore Beltway.

His grandfather's words haunted him.

"Powerful knowledge awaits, and awesome power requires huge responsibility."

125

Frank wasn't sure he wanted that powerful knowledge and awesome power. He just wanted to be a cop. But now he'd been challenged. An ace pitcher had fired a 95-mile-an-hour heater at his head and he wasn't about to merely duck and set up for the next pitch.

He headed to Elm Terrace to rethink his day and categorize his options.

*　　*　　*　　*　　*

The Baltimore Sun headlined more tax increases and budget deficit problems from Congress. Frank long held that no matter what the average American citizen wanted, it rarely swayed the government to actually do something on their behalf. Government news only affirmed his feeling of helplessness regarding the passage of bills that negatively affected the nation's middle class, who seemed to carry the burden of paying for everyone else. That same government, paid by taxpayers like him, had its mightiest police force pestering him with questions as though he were a terrorism suspect. He went straight to the comic page, read his favorites, and studied the crossword.

Frank and William loved to do crosswords together, especially the big one on Sunday. The puzzle in front of him now was medium-hard and he jumped around the clues trying to find ones he could

126

easily answer first. Midway through, one clue in particular stopped him cold.

"Omega to a physicist" required a three-letter answer. The intersecting spaces put an "o" in the first space and an "m" in the last. Frank concluded that the word the puzzle sought was "ohm."

The Greek character Ω, which stood for the spelled-out word "Omega," was also the electrical symbol for the word "ohm." Frank knew that, and originally imagined William had named the formula Omega because it was a term synonymous with final or "end" things. *Could the word "ohm" be the true reason William had named his device the Omega Formula?*

Frank needed to learn some scientific facts about the physics of electricity. He thought of the Internet, but Wikipedia and other encyclopedic sites weren't always reliable. However, Frank knew one resource that was extremely reliable.

*   *   *   *   *

The physics department at the University of Maryland at Baltimore County was highly regarded by everyone in national academia. Its department chairman was Dr. Marvin Dekler, a man with more awards, publications, and titles after his name than any professor in the discipline. He was also an old classmate of Frank's from high school.

127

Frank had called on Dekler's advice and expertise in past criminal cases in Baltimore and, as a result, his testimony had helped keep several thoroughly bad people out of free society for good. If anyone could show a connection between an ohm and a ray-borne death weapon, it would be Dr. D of UMBC.

Frank walked into the office where Dekler sat at a desk piled high with science journals, textbooks, and papers. The professor's eyes peered over the top of the stacks.

"Uh-oh. Detective Frank Dugan is here. Who's been murdered now?" Dekler said.

"The spirit of sensibility, professor."

Dekler rose and came around the desk and took Frank's hand.

"Good to see you," Dekler said. "Get tired of life among the coconut palms?"

"Just visiting. But I find myself needing a little help with physics, especially as it applies to electricity."

"Well, lay it on me."

"If you were going to create a powerful ray, say, like a laser, what would *ohms* have to do with its construction or use?"

"Boy, you don't beat around the bush, do you?" Dekler said and stepped over to a rolling Melamine whiteboard. "Would this ray be used for manufacturing or in the field of medicine?"

"Killing."

Dekler stared at Frank, narrowed his eyes.

"Like small varmints, insects, bacteria?" Dekler asked.

"Let's say more like bears, or gorillas."

"Hmm…and this has to employ the use of ohms…Well, ohms, as I'm sure you're aware, are units of electrical resistance," Dekler said and began scribbling symbols, letters, and numbers with a dry-erase marker on the whiteboard. "And if we were to create a powerful electrical charge, and resist it with equal force, it will build, like a compressed spring or a pressurized gas. Assuming the potential speed of the resisted charge is *phenomenal*, like that of the speed of light, or 186,000 miles per second, upon release it could produce a powerful current, or perhaps a ray, at any desired frequency. The possibilities are shaky but infinite."

Frank took a photo of Dekler's whiteboard notes with his cell phone.

"Could the released wave made by your equation kill?"

"This equation is merely a guide. Like $E=MC^2$. Actual quantitative values would have to be introduced for it to make sense and actually work. Probably other elements as well. Actually, an EMP would make a better weapon."

Frank's eyes widened.

"An EMP?" Frank said.

"An Electro-Magnetic Pulse. It's been experimented with for years. Properly administered, it could deliver lethal damage to a an animal's nervous system."

"So, it could kill?"

"It could kill anything with a cerebral ganglia or a brain."

"Could anyone in World War Two have manufactured such a weapon?"

"Without using laser technology and transistors, which weren't discovered and refined until much later? I don't see how."

"How about this EMP's effect on other objects?"

"The pulse would likely pass through inanimate matter, like most radio waves and x-rays do. Ohms deal with electricity. And brains and hearts need electricity produced in the body to function. If you can block that electrical current, you can easily stop oxygen-bearing blood flow to the brain, a condition called global cerebral ischemia. Or interrupt oxygen directly from *getting* to the brain, called massive cerebral infarction. In either case, death would occur rather instantly. Lack of oxygen to the brain is ultimately the reason all animals die, including us invincible *homo sapiens*."

"You're a physicist. How'd you end up end up with so much medical savvy?"

"My father was a neurosurgeon at Hopkins. Was what I said helpful?"

"It's all I needed to know. You are still the Solomon of science."

"Look, let's get something straight. This idea you have may be possible, in theory, but implementing it is quite another matter. It would require incredible knowledge, astronomical resources, and a lot of luck to effectively produce. Archimedes, back around 230 B.C., posed that he could lift the moon if he had a long enough and strong enough lever. A theory yet to be tested."

"I have no intention of trying to lift the moon or make such a device."

Dekler pursed his lips.

"You're not going terrorist on us, are you, Frank?" Dekler said.

"A hundred-and-eighty degrees the opposite, doc."

"It's illegal and immoral to kill gorillas, you know."

Chapter 20

Frank exited UMBC's Loop, turned onto Route 195, which led to Interstate 95 south. He drove 25 minutes to the Maryland State Police facility in Beltsville where their annual marksmanship tournament was being hosted. The last thing he wanted was to take hours away from his father's homicide investigation, and now the Omega mystery had added to the compromise of his available time. But Roland wanted Frank to compete for the coveted National Police Marksman of the Year Award, the trophy which he believed would bolster his upcoming re-election campaign for sheriff. Frank had never worked for a person he respected or liked more than Roland Brand, ergo, a lower priority or not, he was going shooting.

One stroke of luck was on his side. When Roland emailed Frank his registration information, it included his starting position at the tournament. Frank would compete in the number three slot, allowing him to leave the field early and get on with more urgent matters.

Frank had no delusions about winning the tournament. It was going to be tough, and every hotshot and deadeye in America would be there.

Events there would include slow, timed, and rapid fire aggregates, plus the obstacle course which led contestants down a simulated street where plywood cut-outs of bad guys would pop out from around corners, while similar depictions of innocent bystanders would intermittently appear from out of nowhere. The trick was to plug the baddies and not the bystanders.

Now that he'd secured his carry permit, he holstered his Browning in his shoulder rig and prepared to blast away several mags of 9mm ammo, and try not to embarrass himself by blowing away a plywood old lady who pointed an umbrella at him.

*　　*　　*　　*　　*

When Frank got back to the house, the sight of Braewyn Joyce leaning on her car at the curb on Elm Terrace had him torn by two emotions: dread and lust. Braewyn nodded at Frank's arrival and walked up the driveway toward the house. It was after eight PM, but there was plenty of daylight left to see her as she moved in fluid strides ahead of his car.

Frank pulled the rented Santa Fe parallel to her, Braewyn's perfect body, now better revealed in her tailored navy pants suit and a white blouse than in her former roomy attire. He was attracted to women who dressed conservatively, even preppy, and found tasteful fashion every bit as sexy as any bikini or

133

thong. Especially since Roland, on a trip with Frank to the Stuart beach one day, described the array of thongs within sight as "Florida fanny floss."

Frank killed the engine and slid out of the car.

"If I were a doomsayer, I'd think, 'What new hell is this?'" Frank said.

"You have good instincts for not-so-good news," she said.

"My crap meter has been going off full time lately," Frank said and bounded up the steps to the front door of the house and opened it. "Welcome back, Agent Joyce."

Braewyn followed Frank onto the porch.

"Should we invite your partner Tom to join us?" Frank said and tilted his head toward the FBI car.

"He'll be fine."

"Come in? Have a drink?"

"No, thank you. Let's just talk out here."

Frank stepped over to the rail where Braewyn stood.

"You said you'd have questions," Frank said.

"We have a *lot* of questions," Braewyn said. "Since you are William Dugan's grandson, we thought you might know something about this Omega formula. Number one: Have you seen the film yet?"

"Yes."

"I thought you'd get a hold of a copy somehow."

"No thanks to you."

"I have my orders. So what did you make of the film?"

"I'm a homicide cop from Florida. What makes you think I'd know about some freaky, sci-fi weapon from World War Two?"

"It's a matter of national security," Braewyn said. "If such a device exists, this country certainly doesn't want a foreign power to have it."

"Foreign *power*? Hell, if Latvia had something like that there'd be a world of trouble."

"I agree," Braewyn said. "So, can you help us?"

"If I think of a way, I'll contact you. Leave me your card."

"Just so we're clear, my visit today will be, in your jargon, the good cop version. What follows me may not be so friendly," she said.

"Going to waterboard me?"

She reached into her pocket and pulled out a business card.

"Call me if you come up with even the smallest shred, okay?" she said.

"The FBI, with all its resources, needs me? And here I grew up thinking the FBI was invincible... infallible."

"Sometimes the best laid plans come up short."

"Like in that little incident in Waco with David Koresh? Or that pesky Al Capone, who had to be left to the IRS to obtain a conviction? That's not reassuring."

"Look, detective, you don't have a lot of options here."

Frank stared at Braewyn for a long moment, then shifted his eyes toward the garage.

"The question is, how are you going to act on it?" Braewyn said. "Homeland Security, the CIA, the NSA, and others are going to want answers. And trust me, they won't go away until they get them."

"I don't know anything about what's on that film."

"This is where *my* crap meter goes off," Braewyn said. "I think you know more, maybe a lot more. And I can't, for the life of me, understand why you're hiding it."

Frank respected people with good instincts, especially smart people. Braewyn had both attributes and beauty as well, a combination which tended to weaken his resolve. He was tempted to tell her everything he knew, but William's oft-quoted Ben Franklin warning from long ago played in his head: *"Three may keep a secret if two of are dead."*

"And I thought we were going to be friends," Frank said.

"Be a friend to yourself, detective. Be truthful and tell us what you know. I came back here today because it will be a lot easier to tell me what you know now than to have to face what's coming."

"What's coming?"

Braewyn descended the porch steps and turned back to Frank.

"One more thing," she said. "The government people who will be coming at you from Washington will not be the only ones. The film, if it ever gets into the wrong hands, will stir up every power-seeking faction on the planet. You're going to be asked a lot of questions, detective. Your film has caused quite a stir in Washington. Brace yourself for those who may not stop at only asking questions. If there actually is a formula for that weapon, you'd better be the one to find it and hand it over to your country. We're in a race to prove or disprove the validity of the Omega formula. And time may not be on our side."

Braewyn strode over to the driveway and headed for the street. Frank watched her get into her car and drive away. Tom Gardner stared back at him from the passenger side.

Frank's world had zoomed from complicated to chaotic in a matter of minutes. He jumped from the porch and started for the garage when something in the street caught his attention.

Television and radio news vehicles were arriving in a caravan and lining up in front of the house.

* * * * *

The writing on the vehicles ranged from the call letters of radio and television news channels to the names of newspapers, and even talk shows.

Frank wasn't sure why the media was there. His father's murder wouldn't have generated a buzz on this scale. *The Omega Formula film? How did it get leaked to the press? And so soon?* He thought of fleeing into the house and barring the door, but past experience told him that evading the media was as impossible as running from the flu.

Fending off the media always proved to be exhausting. Frank had been interviewed with television coverage in high-profile cases he'd handled in the past, but the prospect of a full frontal assault by the paparazzi, news people, and talk show preppers was overwhelming. Frank felt himself being sucked under in an emotional whirlpool. He was swimming for his life and now had to fight to make every stroke count.

Frank defiantly stood his ground and glowered at the encroaching mob.

"All of you get off my property and move back to the street," Frank yelled. "I'll join you there in a moment."

The dozens of media reporters and cameramen retreated to the curb where neighbors were now pouring out of their homes and flowing in among the news cars and vans. Frank wiped the sweat from his face with his shirtsleeve and joined the crowd at the end of the driveway. Boomed microphones came at Frank from every direction and hovered over his head like venomous snakes. Video cams pointed at him as their red tally lights blinked away, reminding him of the eyes on *The Terminator* cyborg.

"Why are you here?" Frank asked.

"The Omega Formula film," a reporter said.

"How did you hear about it?"

"We have our sources," another reporter said. "Bernstein and Woodward aren't the only people who have resources."

"What's that got to do with me?"

"Come on, detective," a woman in the front row said. "Give us more credit for uncovering facts."

Ben Franklin was so right, Frank thought.

Frank knew the mantra of the press: Get the five Ws at all costs. He was certain these sensation hunters had at least rudimentary ideas about the What, the Why, the When, and some of the Who. They now were digging hard for the Where and the How.

"What you may have heard about was an old film made by men during the Second World War who wanted Japan to believe we had a super weapon that could annihilate their population," Frank said. "They thought it might end World War Two without further Allied bloodshed. Turns out, they were right, and it did persuade the Japanese to surrender, but it

139

was all a hoax, a clever deceit. There is no such thing as the Omega formula or an Omega weapon, and there never has been."

"We were told people and animals were shown being killed in that film. Said it didn't look like trick photography," one reporter said from the back of the cluster of media people.

"It had to look good," Frank said. "It had to look real. The Japanese hierarchy was not composed of fools. They had to believe in its authenticity. The men who fabricated the film were betting everything on its effectiveness."

"We know the idea of a 'death ray' has been explored in the past. Could this be a refinement of earlier efforts?" a woman on the left asked.

Frank reached deep into his interrogation and rebuttal skills, including those that employed partial truths.

"Research has come up with nothing but failed attempts to make such a device, going back to scientists like Tesla and Edison. I'm sure you realize that fantasy comic books and science fiction movies depicting such technology aren't based in reality. Even recently, our modern military has tried to develop such weapons with no success."

"What about the Omega formula plans?" another reporter asked.

"Omega plans? I know of none. There was nothing whatsoever found with the film that could create such a weapon," Frank said. "Now, all of you kindly leave. I've told you what I know. I've told you the truth."

Frank turned back toward the house and hiked up the driveway. He was weary of deflecting interest away from something he believed to be plausible. Gamesmanship and subterfuge layered lies in the mind of a man whose profession demanded the truth.

One thought chanted in his head.

Grandpa, what impossible test have you laid on me?

Chapter 21

The following day Frank called to make arrangements with Martin County to extend his leave while Roland Brand groused about the problems his absence was causing the sheriff's department. Frank assured him he would return as soon as possible and urged Roland to rely on his partner, Carl Rumbaugh, to take up any pressing homicide matters. The suggestion amped up Roland's railing to another level. Frank ended the call mid-tirade.

He dialed Braewyn Joyce's cell number.

"Special Agent Joyce."

"Frank Dugan."

"Detective Dugan. What can I do for you?"

"I have something I want to discuss with you. In person."

"Omega something?"

"Yeah."

"I can be there in an hour."

"With... Chatty Tom?"

"It's bureau policy."

"See you in an hour."

Frank contacted Alasdair and asked him to join the group for what he believed would be a pivotal moment in the Omega film issue with all of its dangling question marks.

"They'll be here in an hour," Frank said. "Think you can get here before they arrive?"

"I'm out the door," Alasdair said.

*   *   *   *   *

When Alasdair pulled up at Elm Terrace, Frank met him in the driveway.

"I think I may have to give what I have to the FBI," Frank said. "Everything's in the Omega file in the fallout shelter, but it's all about failed experiments and other nonsense. Nothing worth crap about any super weapon. What do you think?"

"I agree," Alasdair said. "They're a bad bunch to have on your back."

"Good. I wanted your take on that before I spill what I know to the government."

"Let them have it all. It'll take you out of the picture."

"Not sure of that, but it could relieve some pressure. Last thing I need is the FBI complicating my life. I've got a murder to solve."

Minutes later, Braewyn and Tom arrived, and the current situation brought on by the leaked video information was discussed. Afterward, everyone moved into the garage and shut the door. Frank pulled Alasdair away from the FBI pair and stopped in front of the grille of the Corvette.

"You still think we should go ahead with this?" Frank asked Alasdair low.

Braewyn casually sidled to within earshot. Tom Gardner followed.

"I don't think you have much choice," Alasdair said. "The whole world's going to converge on you soon and you may need help defending yourself. Be better to turn it all over to the American pros than let it land in the wrong hands."

"Okay," Frank said and stepped over to Braewyn and Tom. "I've had a night to think things over. I'm placing everything I have with you."

Frank led the group into the shelter and switched on the light. He noted the amazement on Braewyn's face, her eyes darting to everything in the secret room.

Frank sat at the desk and retrieved the Omega Formula file folder and handed it to Braewyn.

"The film and what's in this folder is everything I know," Frank said.

"You're sure?" Braewyn said.

"Yes. You'll need to scan these privately and make copies. Give the originals back to me and a keep what you need for yourselves," Frank said, knowing full well he'd never see any originals or copies coming back from the FBI, ever.

Braewyn sat at the utility table and fingered through the papers in the file while Tom looked over her shoulder. She looked quickly at each page then closed the file.

"We're going to need help with the chemistry," Braewyn said to Tom.

"Celine's offered to help," Alasdair said. "She knows how the NSA operates and she knows top people on the outside."

"We have our own experts," Braewyn said.

"We done here?" Frank asked.

"Alasdair's right," Braewyn said to Frank. "The world's going to come calling. And I'm betting they won't all be good cops."

"I'm betting they won't be cops at all," Frank said.

*　　*　　*　　*　　*

The FBI agents and Alasdair left and Frank went into the house, got himself a beer, and sat on the sofa in the parlor. A minute later, his cell rang. The displayed number was unfamiliar, but showed the call was from a Maryland exchange.

"Hello," Frank said.

"We located the halfway house where Dickie K is staying and found him MIA," said the voice of John Dellarue. "People there say he's been gone for days. Pulled a job and booked, my guess."

"Thanks, John," Frank said.

"No word on the Reo yet. We'll keep the bulletins running."

"Can't ask for more."

"Part of the job. Take care," Dellarue said and hung up.

Frank suspected Dellarue was somehow involved in more than just a stolen Reo, but he needed proof before he could press harder on the captain. *For now, play nice, play dumb, and see what develops.*

Frank called the Martin County Sheriff's Office. It was 9:45 AM. They would've already studied their assignments and slugged down the first few cups of coffee for the morning. Frank trusted that Roland would be at his most receptive after his second cup and third cruller.

"It's Frank again."

"Well, spank the baby, if it isn't our wandering detective. Get tired of solving all the cases in Maryland?"

"Not yet, but I'll be back soon to solve some of yours," Frank said. "Wanted to give you a heads-up."

"I'll alert the day watch, the *Enquirer* and the *Miami Herald*."

"Anything earthshaking going on?"

"Yeah, I need to go over a couple of things with you."

"Job things?" Frank asked.

"National Security Agency things."

Sonofabitch. The bastards are already on a background check, and the Omega film was revealed only two days ago.

"NSA? Why the hell are they hounding me?" Frank asked.

"Don't know, but they had a lot of questions. Call 'em up and get these guys off our necks. I got better things to do than screw with the NSA."

"They leave a number?"

"I don't know what you've got yourself into up there in Maryland, but these guys mean business. They're down here digging into your background like genealogy scouts."

"I found a Second World War film and some military documents left by my grandfather and—"

"Listen, Frank, I want these monkeys off my back. They have questions and you answer them, understand? Here's the man you need to talk to: Anton Chernac, *Colonel* Anton Chernac, who left a goddamn million-digit international phone number. I'll text it to your phone.

"I'll take care of this."

"And when you get that done, how about hauling your ass back down here and doing a day's worth of hometown police work?" Roland said. "I kinda like a full staff on the job down here, detective."

147

"Rumbaugh isn't picking up the slack?"

"Rumbaugh couldn't pick bowling balls out of celery seed down at the spice company," Roland said.

"His father thought this was the perfect job for him," Frank said, knowing he was pushing a hot button.

"Mayor Rumbaugh is the result of a stupid and uninformed electorate. It's what's wrong with this country. I can't wait until the next election to get his ass out and send him back where he belongs: back working at his brother's funeral home. He can only screw up a dead body up so much."

"I'll get this Chernac guy squared away, chief."

*   *   *   *   *

Frank leapt to his feet and hurled an accent pillow from the sofa against a wall of books across the parlor. It hit so hard it stuck in the space between the volumes and the shelf above.

His cell phone rang. Frank clicked the receive button and put the phone to his ear but said nothing.

"I got this idea," Alasdair said.

"You've discovered fire?"

"You going to be nasty or would you like to hear it?"

"Ah, I'm pissed about the heat I'm getting from the office. Shoot."

"What's going on in Stuart?"

"NSA's already picking my life apart."

"In Florida? Come on."

"What's your idea. Cheer me up," Frank said.

"How about if I place an ad in the paper and online as a collector looking to pay top dollar for vintage Reos?"

"I like it. Put it out there."

"Think our perps will bite?"

"No, but worth a shot."

"That's pretty negative."

"Do it," Frank said. "I'll be in Bermuda."

"Bermuda?" Alasdair said.

"It's on my bucket list."

"Aye, Bermuda. You'll love Hamilton this time of year."

If the intel the press got came by way of cell phone hacking, Frank would do his best to throw them off in his phone conversations with those he trusted. Information coming from other quarters was out of his control. It was a troubling fact that made him wonder if the media didn't have better detective techniques than those used by law enforcement.

It was time to stop being the prey and become the hunter.

Chapter 22

Talking to Colonel Chernac, even on the phone, was like going to the principal's office in grade school. Frank was antsy about unsecured phone conversations anyway, and this one was likely to be one-sided and demeaning. But Frank made it clear, early into it, that he was not a scoldable child and turned on the toughness he was known for.

"We looked at the film," Colonel Chernac said. "The actual 16mm film, not the digitized version."

He saw the original film? How? Through the FBI?

"And you deduced what?" Frank said.

"It looked real to us."

Frank tried to identify Chernac's accent. Maybe eastern European.

"People in the film looked like they died?"

"They looked quite dead."

"Maybe they were actors. I see actors killed in movies all the time. They look quite dead too."

"And the prairie dogs?" Chernac said. "Were they merely acting?"

"Got me there," Frank said.

"Our chemists are working on the experiments. That may tell us more."

He's seen the file?

Frank had another reason he didn't like these phone conversations with strangers, especially strangers with international phone numbers: he couldn't see their faces and body language, something he was expert at interpreting. There was also the question of identification. He wanted to see Chernac's credentials.

"I think we need to meet face-to-face," Frank said.

"Maybe play some chess?"

"I'm better at that than trying to unravel ridiculous chemistry."

"Are you a student of the Sicilian Defense?"

"The Dragon variation or the Najdorf?" Frank asked.

"Oh, my. You *do* know your chess."

"Let's meet, Colonel."

"We shall, soon enough," Chernac said.

"Contact me with the time and place."

"You'll be well-informed, I assure you."

"Good."

Frank ended the call and pulled a business card from his pocket.

*   *   *   *   *

"I don't know a Colonel Anton Chernac," Braewyn said on the phone. "If he's NSA, as you say, we don't cross paths often."

"He claims to have seen the original film. He get his info from the FBI? And has he seen anything in the Omega files?"

"I seriously doubt that any single individual would be asking such intimidating questions at this stage of the game," Braewyn said. "Copies were made and distributed only to a handful of specialists and higher-ups on a need-to-know basis. But it's possible. NSA's specialty is code-breaking, you know."

"The government hires people from overseas with accents?"

"We hire people from all over. We need and use folks who can speak and understand more than one language. Did you think all our enemies only speak English?"

"All right, all right. I found the bastard sneaky, …rude,… arrogant."

"Part of the job. They're not Welcome Wagon, they're the National Security Agency."

"Got it."

"Our agency tested everything we were given on this Omega weapon. The results were not what people expected. My superiors think you know more than you're telling."

"And you?" Frank said.

"If I were implicated in a murder, you'd have to do your job and suspect me until you could eliminate me from any complicity, wouldn't you?"

"I understand. I don't have to like it. By the way, the media have already paid me a visit. A whole boatload of them. Security on this apparently sucks."

"Be careful, Detective Dugan. Remember, if the press obtained information about this, it's not only our government you have to worry about."

Frank hung up and his gut told him she was right.

*   *   *   *   *

Frank trudged into the hot stuffy hallway, where drawing a breath was a chore, and cranked the thermostat down to 68 degrees. The kitchen had the only cool thing in the house and Frank headed straight for it and stuck his head in the open door of the 25-cubic foot Kenmore refrigerator. He stayed there ahhhing for a full minute before taking out a cold beer and his head and closing the fridge.

It was then that he looked out the kitchen window and noticed two men in business suits standing in the back yard. He adjusted his pistol in the back of his waistband and opened the back door.

"Get you guys a beer?" Frank asked as he strolled outside and set his beer down on the back porch railing with his left hand. His right hand fondled the grip of his 9mm.

"Are you Frank Dugan?" the shorter of the two men asked.

"I am."

"We're from the Department of Homeland Security," the larger man said. "We need to ask you a couple of questions about this Omega Formula film."

"And I need to ask you one. Got some ID?"

The two men pulled out their bi-fold wallets and held them out for Frank's inspection.

"Okay, ask away, but I don't know much more than you do," Frank said.

The large man wiped his sweaty face with a handkerchief.

"You fellas need a beer?" Frank asked.

"No, thank you," the big man said. "You think this Omega weapon exists?"

Frank released the pistol grip and picked up his beer.

"I think it was all a big ruse to make the Japanese think it was real," Frank said and took a long sip.

"The killing depicted in the film looked pretty convincing," the smaller man said.

"That was the whole point, wasn't it?" Frank said.

"Could be," the smaller man said. "The secretary has set up a meeting in DC to discuss the film with other agencies along with the military chiefs."

The larger man reached into his suit jacket and took out a folded paper.

"This is a subpoena to appear at that meeting, Detective Dugan," the man said and handed the paper to Frank. "This has become a matter of national security. That film of yours has caused a lot of concern in Washington, especially with the president."

Frank opened the paper and noted the date.

"Day after tomorrow?" Frank said.

"The director wants to resolve this immediately," the large man said.

"I want this thing cleared up as much as the government does, gentlemen," Frank said. "I'll be there."

"You know," the smaller man said, "if there's something you feel like telling us right now..."

"See you at the meeting," Frank said and swept his arm toward the driveway.

"We understand how hard it can be to discuss things about family business, but–"

Frank raised his hand to cut off the good cop routine being played by the larger man. He was a pretty fair interrogator himself and knew how to play the game with tight-lipped perps. Frank stepped to the men and stared directly at them without a blink.

"I have told you the truth," Frank said.

155

The men nodded, filed down the driveway, and disappeared around the corner of the house.

Frank went back inside and picked up a bottle of Jameson Irish Whiskey from the bar in the dining room and took a huge belt of it, followed by chugging his beer until the can nearly collapsed.

The air conditioning at last began to make its welcome presence felt as Frank sat on the sofa. He pulled his pistol from inside his belt, gripped the piece firmly and cradled it in his lap. He put his head back on the sofa cushion and closed his eyes.

What the hell was he going to say to a room full of the nation's top military chiefs and defense agencies when they asked him about the Omega formula?

Frank despised government bureaucracy. Collectively it was like dealing with a huge animal with a tiny brain, centered in its id. It only did what it perceived as necessary to thrive, and preserve its power. Like lawyers who perpetuated senseless and costly litigations to keep their billable hours ringing on their registers, he distrusted any group that voted on behalf of themselves and their own interests. Lawyers became judges who interpreted the laws and benefits approved by politicians who often started their careers as lawyers. It was an out-of-balance continuum. Congress voted on its own absurd salaries, and even more absurd lifetime pensions and perquisites, ad nauseam. Frank knew it wasn't right nor fair to the American taxpayer. He became a cop to protect the righteous and enforce fairness. His decision about what he'd say at the meeting would be easy.

He would to tell the government as little as possible.

Chapter 23

The Pentagon was everything Frank had imagined it would be: enormous, severe, and immovable. He was met at the gate to the North Parking Visitor Screening Facility by a marine master sergeant who studied his subpoena and then provided him with a Department of Defense "Red Badge" building pass attached to a lanyard he was instructed to wear around his neck. It was required to be worn in plain view so everyone could see he did not have a security clearance, and that his presence in the building required an escort. The marine led Frank to a visitor's parking area where he left the rental car and plodded the hot hundred yards to the main entrance of the building.

Once inside, Frank used his visitor badge in a turnstile and entered the four digit PIN code he'd been given by the security officer. Once he gained access to the lobby, the personnel at the Pentagon Force Protection Agency desk determined his business, scanned him for weapons, and checked for cell phones, cameras or any other suspicious or disallowed items. They looked over his subpoena and called the contact name on the document. A DD Form 1466 was issued to him, which allowed him further access into the building, but required an escort at all times.

Minutes later, the larger of the two men who had visited him at Elm Terrace appeared and led Frank to the elevators.

The meeting room was located several levels down and guarded by two marines. The spacious area was alive with more than thirty people who began to turn their attention Frank's way as soon as he entered the door. He was seated at the center of a long conference table. The room was filled with several high-ranking military officers, high-profile politicians, cabinet heads, and other men and women in conservative business attire. A female stenographer sat near the conference table ready to record the proceeding.

Overnight Internet research had informed Frank that there were more than 15 U.S. organizations involved with intelligence and national security. He would be meeting with several of the more well known ones today. The subject of the meeting would center around the Omega film, the rumor of which was bouncing all over cyberspace. Leaked information such as that shown in the film would be classified as "open source" information, now public and impossible to withdraw or label as secret or even classified in the military sense of the terms. But the Omega files, now in the hands of the FBI and other security agencies, would be put in a cool, dark place and tightly closed with a classified level of secrecy stamped all over them. The last thing the government wanted was for those files to make their way to the Internet.

Frank recognized Mary Allcott, the Secretary of Homeland Security, and the Secretary of Defense, Van Jeffries, plus a few of the familiar politicians from their TV news interviews. Braewyn Joyce, with Tom Gardner, nodded at Frank from across the room. The rest of the attendees were new to Frank, although one heavily decorated army general stood out as someone he'd seen recently in the news.

Secretary Allcott called for everyone to take their assigned places around the table and brought the meeting to order.

"Please, be seated," the secretary said and took her place directly across the wide table from Frank.

"I have called this meeting and have asked the CIA, the FBI, the NSA, Homeland Security directors, scientific specialists, and the joint chiefs of the armed forces to attend. I thank all of you for coming. We are here to discuss a film and certain documents, which are making a lot of buzz in the media lately. A buzz that may involve the security of this nation. Detective Frank Dugan, has kindly agreed to come here today, from some distance, to answer a few questions about these recent events, since he's close to the source of this rather intriguing discovery from the Second World War."

Frank mused that he had "kindly agreed" to attend like Nathan Hale had kindly agreed to go to the gallows.

"I have placed copies of the documents found with the film before you for discussion," Secretary Allcott went on. "But before we begin, I want you to watch the entire film, snippets and talk of which seem to be making the rounds on the Internet, rumor mills, and every media outlet and publication in our country and beyond. This explosion of publicity is the reason I have called this rather impromptu meeting."

The secretary nodded to a man operating a computer, which projected DVD media onto a large screen at one end of the room. The lights in the room dimmed and Frank's grandfather began his narration of the Omega film as everyone in the room glued their attention to the movie. Faces in the room grimaced and contorted as the film demonstrated the horror of war and the killing power of the baseball-size Omega bombs. The film ended, the lights came back up, and most of the people in the room seemed to relax from the tension the film had evoked.

"The narrator of the film was William Dugan, Detective Dugan's grandfather, a nuclear physicist and Army Air Force consultant during the Second World War," Allcott said. "Recently, Detective Dugan inherited the house and property formerly owned by his grandfather, and discovered this film and several files pertaining to the film. We think the movie was used to convince Japan to surrender in August of 1945, after we had used up our only two atomic bombs on Hiroshima and Nagasaki. The question that remains is this: is the Omega formula a real weapon capable of the incredible killing power depicted in the movie, or was it only a clever fabrication produced by talented film makers in the 1940s? Detective Dugan, can you address this question?"

Frank looked around the table and then looked straight across at the secretary.

"Madam Secretary, you know about as much as I know regarding this," Frank said. "I discovered the Omega files and the film mere days ago."

Frank reached for the manila folder on the table in front of him. He opened the folder, shuffled through several of its papers, and removed a few sheets.

"The originals of these papers were in a file folder I discovered at my grandfather's home in Catonsville, Maryland," Frank said. "I shared them with the FBI to find out if any sense of danger or validity could be obtained by examining them and perhaps testing the chemical formulas in the files. As far as I know, no one's come up with a weapon like the one demonstrated in the film. My own conclusion is that the Omega formula was a clever ruse leaked to Japan to hasten the end of the war, and nothing more. My thoughts about it? There's no such thing as an actual Omega formula weapon; never was, and never will be."

An army general raised his hand and looked toward the secretary.

"General DeBaker," the secretary said.

"Those scenes showing the killing of those animals and people looked awfully real, in my estimation. And I've observed plenty of that first hand," the general said.

"I believe that's the basic concern here, detective," the secretary said.

"Precisely the reason the film would've worked," Frank said.

"Do we believe this film is the reason why they surrendered?" the secretary said. "Japan was a country of people dedicated to fighting to the bitter end. Men in the know at the time laid odds against a surrender after the two atomic bombings, especially since we opted to hit targets that were not strategically the most important. We decided to stay away from religious areas and places where American prisoners were being held, a decision leaving us almost no high-impact choices."

"Why are we just finding out about this weapon now?" a man at the far end of the table asked.

The secretary looked at Frank.

"I discovered a secret room at my grandfather's estate. A room I never knew existed. A fallout shelter containing the documents we have here."

"What caused you to find it now?" another man said.

"I was examining one of the antique cars in the garage and accidentally pushed a button that opened a hidden door to the shelter."

"You never knew about it before then?" a woman to Frank's left asked.

"I was never allowed in the garage unsupervised as a kid. I never got a chance to explore it as I did recently."

A woman to Frank's right raised her hand.

"Senator Cranston," the secretary said.

"I think this thing is still a weapon, whether it works or not," the senator said. "You leak this to an enemy, he has to seriously consider its reality. He has to think his army, or his countrymen, could possibly be wiped out in a single stroke. He's back on his heels and concerned that he's up against something he can't defeat, counter, nor survive."

"I like that aspect of it, senator," the secretary said, "but if they called our bluff, what then?"

"Then we'd have to kick their ass the old fashioned way," General DeBaker said.

The room filled with polite smiles. The secretary stood.

"Any further questions?" the secretary asked.

No one volunteered.

"I thank all of you for coming today and apologize for the brevity of this meeting, but time is of the essence. And a special thanks to you, Detective Dugan," the secretary said. "I have authorized each of your departments to have copies of what we have. I can't stress enough the need for Top Secret confidentiality regarding what these documents contain. I want those chemical equations and formulations checked out thoroughly by the best military and scientific resources at our disposal. And I want it done under the utmost secrecy. If such a weapon is possible, God help us if it should find its way into the possession of terrorists, unfriendly politicos, or power-seeking countries. We all have a lot to think about. Please contact my office if you come up with anything pertinent to this; anything whatsoever. Detective Dugan, you contact my office post haste if you discover any further Omega formula information."

"Absolutely," Frank said as he rose, followed by everyone in the room.

One of the marine guards opened the door for Secretary Allcott as she exited the room, followed closely by the other ranking attendees. Braewyn Joyce and Tom Gardner were in the last group to leave and kept their attention on Frank until they disappeared into the hall. Senator Cranston stayed back and confronted Frank.

"Gloria Cranston, Detective Dugan," she said and extended her hand.

"Honored to meet you, senator," Frank said and took her hand briefly.

The senator and Frank were the last to leave the room. While Frank mulled over that almost anyone else would've pawned their mother's silverware for a personal audience with an assembly of so many powerful people sworn to defend the security of the United States, he hoped to heaven he'd never have to see any of them ever again.

Frank's waiting escort approached him and the senator.

"Just a little tip for you," the senator said, stopping Frank in the hallway. "Your house in Catonsville will be examined down to its last plank. If you think the Department of Defense is going to rely on you coming forward with any new information on this, you'd better prepare yourself for stark governmental reality. Frankly, their procedures run against my Constitutional grain."

"Thanks for the heads-up," Frank said and tightened his jaw.

"You were brought here for two reasons. One, to put you on the hotseat about what you know. And two, to get you out of the way."

"Get me out of the way?"

"This very minute, the government is tearing through your house."

166

Chapter 24

Frank's rental car was blocked in its parking space by a black SUV. Frank could see no one inside through its dark-tinted windows. He jogged fifty yards to the entrance gate to get a guard to help him get the SUV moved. The guard made a two-minute call from the guard booth and returned to Frank.

"They're coming to move the vehicle, sir," the guard said.

Frank shrugged off his sport coat and quick-stepped it back to his car, his sweat-soaked shirt clinging to his body. When he got there, the black SUV was gone.

An hour later, as Frank pulled up to 1505 Elm Terrace, the house and grounds were crawling with people and government cars lined the street.

Braewyn Joyce approached Frank's rental as he motored to the end of the driveway and parked. Frank glared at her as he jumped out of the car.

"How did you get here so fast?" Frank asked.

"We know shortcuts."

"Is this place going to be salable when they finish?"

"They're being careful, detective," she said. "I told them to only search for things relating to the Omega weapon."

"Good of you," Frank said and strode past her to the front steps of the house.

"I pulled everyone out of the house," Braewyn said. "They're all in the garage."

Frank spun off the porch steps and ran past Braewyn and into the garage. Inside, he saw the concentration of the investigators in the mechanic's pit and in the safe room beyond. He leaned back against the side of the Corvette and folded his arms.

"There is some good news," Braewyn said from the garage door.

"I should never have let you and Tommy boy in this place."

"You did the right thing."

"I have people crawling like army ants over private and personal things. I should've closed up that room and never taken a single thing out of it."

"Having your life turned inside out is never pleasant, but I have sworn an oath to protect this country. If anyone's going to have a superior defense weapon it's going to be America."

"If you're through with reciting the bullshit Bureau line, what could possibly be good news?"

"Well, we found this Japanese-American gentleman whose father was in the Imperial leadership of Japan during the war. I had a chat with him by phone."

"Interesting," Frank said and steered Braewyn out of the garage.

"He was only a boy then, but he remembers his father, a high Imperial Council member, discussing Japan's options with his family after the two A-bomb attacks."

"Where is this guy?" Frank said ambling over to the backyard bench as Braewyn followed and stood nearby.

"He's in a senior facility in Manhattan Beach, California. The man's in his eighties, but still sharp."

"He said his father agreed with the Emperor and the other elder statesmen about surrendering, but the military and others wanted to fight on, even to the death, if it would preserve their honor. And they didn't agree with Truman's terms of the surrender, especially the part about the removal of their Emperor."

"But they still surrendered."

"Yes. But only after they viewed the Omega film."

"Holy crap, the trick actually worked," Frank said and pumped both fists.

"They didn't think it was a trick," Braewyn said and sat next to Frank. "There were two reasons they quit. First, the fear that the Omega weapon would eliminate the entire population of Japan, and second, they beheld, for the first time, a side of the United States they'd never witnessed before, our willingness to kill our own people to test the weapon and demonstrate its power. Seeing we were willing to sacrifice American citizens convinced them that fighting on would be futile."

"Did he say how they came by the film?'

"Many years after the war, his father told him about that. Coastal defenders found it in an American observation plane that had crashed on the beach in Tokyo Bay. They turned what they pulled from the wreckage over to the authorities."

"Any survivors of the crash?"

"He didn't say."

"Amazing," Frank said and smiled, but he wondered why Braewyn was buying the Japanese informant's story. *Why is an FBI agent sharing this information with me? Is she trying to draw more out of me by showing her trust?*

Frank's smile faded and he turned to Braewyn.

"Anything on Colonel Chernac?"

"Celine found out he works in NSA's cryptography division. A code and language expert. No one admits he's a spy, naturally, and no one would divulge his whereabouts. If he uses unorthodox means to obtain information, NSA likes the results."

"Any chance you can get these coyotes out of my hen house soon?" Frank asked.

"I'll round 'em up," Braewyn said and stood.

Braewyn hurried to the garage and Frank watched her shapely hips roll from side to side until she was out of sight. He gazed at the ground and shook his head.

How could someone so sexy and beautiful be such a colossal pain in the ass?

*　　*　　*　　*　　*

Frank's cell phone rang and he brought it to his ear.

"They picked up Dickie K near Sandy Point on the bay," Alasdair said.

"The bastard was having a day at the beach?" Frank said climbing the central staircase at Elm Terrace.

"Not exactly out for a dip in the Chesapeake. He was floating in the bay face down. It'll be on the news."

"There's justice for you."

"The barracks commander down that way tried to get hold of you but didn't have a number, so he called me. Knew him from the old days. He showed me a business card they found in Dickie's pocket. Came from one of those storage places."

"Which one?"

"Not sure yet. The water blurred a lot of the writing on it. State police are working on recovering the name of the business."

"We'll need to bring them in on this investigation," Frank said as he reached the top of the stairs.

"I know. Even if we find the storage company they may want an authorized signature and ID to allow access to the unit. The state lads'll know how to get around that. I can wangle us a search warrant, or something that looks like one."

"Business card have a number on it?"

"No phone number you can read."

"Any other numbers?"

"Matter of fact, it does, four digits. And that part's large and readable, handwritten with a marking pen. Could be a PIN used to open a gate to the facility. Storage units are all padlocked by their owners. Management can help us get access, though. They also found an old set of lock needles on Dickie. Might explain how he got in your garage."

"I'd like to verify that," Frank said. "Have them bring them with the business card."

"Will do," Alasdair said.

"Keep me posted and let's have dinner tonight," Frank said and waited several seconds for a response, but none came. "Okay, okay, I'm buying."

"Well, why didn't you say so," Alasdair said. "I'll pick us out a nice place."

"You make sure it's in the continental United States."

*   *   *   *   *

By 6 PM, the state police lab had recovered the name, address and phone number of the storage facility on Dickie K's business card and shared their findings with Alasdair. It was *U-Stor-It* facility in Parkville, a suburb north of the Baltimore city line.

Frank, Alasdair, and two state police officers met at the storage facility two hours later. The four men assembled in front of the company's office window and peered inside.

"Dark in there, but it looks like they're open," one of the troopers said.

Alasdair reached into his jacket pocket, took out a leather pouch and handed it to Frank.

"Take these before I forget, or they find out I boosted them," Alasdair said.

Frank pulled out a couple of the lock needles from the pouch and examined them.

"These are magical keys to just about any standard lock."

"They look like miniature harpoons with wooden handles," Alasdair said.

"Yeah, I've seen antique sets like these before," Frank said and slid the 6-inch needles back into the pouch and tucked it in the breast pocket of his jacket.

They entered the storage facility office and Alasdair presented the tattered business card to the elderly man at the counter, plus a photo of Dickie K.

173

"I'm the man who called earlier," Alasdair said. "You the man I spoke to?"

"Had to be," the man said. "Only fella here."

The man, who identified himself as the manager, was a small, skinny fellow with a New England accent and a sour demeanor. The presence of the policemen seemed to instill a grudging cooperation in the old man as he looked over the photo and studied the business card, then referred to a computer screen on his desk. A moment later, he retrieved a paper from his printer.

"Can't do anything with this PIN number. No, sir. Only the renter uses that. Only opens the gate anyways. Ay-ah, but this fella in the picture took one of our largest units," the manager said. "Said he was an antique collector. Said his name was Korbel, like the wine. Like it says here on his file. Offered him our fire and theft insurance, but, says here, he declined."

One of the state troopers placed a typed document on the counter, which the manager glossed over like a speed reader and tucked into the file drawer.

"Did you understand the search warrant?" Frank asked.

"Get to see plenty of them in this business. Usually come from spouses, but they all look pretty much the same. Always cooperate with the police."

The manager ducked behind the counter and picked up a heavy-duty pair of bolt cutters, then led the group out of the office and down the gated drive to the rows of storage units.

"How long has he rented the unit?" Frank said as they walked.

"'Bout best part of three years now. Pays on time. Check's always good," the manager said.

"Whose name is on the checks?" Frank said.

"Hm... an antique company out of Ellicott City. *Main Street Antiques*, ay-ah, that's the name," the manager said.

"Do you remember the last time you saw the guy?" Frank said.

"The last time I saw him was the first time I laid eyes on him."

"Doesn't he bring things to his unit once in a while?"

"Mister, he can come and go as he pleases here. He don't need to check in with us to use the facility like you do. He can come any time, day or night. He knows how to use the keypad that opens the gate out there," the manager said and stopped at a large unit the size of a double garage. "Here 'tis."

The manager moved to a personnel door next to two roll-up garage doors. He placed the jaws of the bolt cutter on one side of the padlock shackle and squeezed the handles together with noticeable effort. A couple of grunts from the old man and the lock

175

jangled to the ground in two pieces. The manager opened the door fully so everyone could step inside.

One side of the space was crowded with old pottery, brass lamps, mahogany furniture from the days of Hepplewhite and Chippendale, oil paintings and lithographs, and glass-doored cabinets, stacked high with china and crystal. A plywood and exposed-stud partition separated the two large bays, but left an opening at the rear to allow passage between the two spaces. The second bay contained a solitary object.

It was a Nile green 1936 Reo Flying Cloud that had once belonged to Clark Gable.

*   *   *   *   *

Frank found the keys for the Reo in the glove box and immediately stepped to the back of the car and opened the trunk. He glanced behind the spare tire. The rolled-up folder was still there, seemingly untouched, and Frank exhaled the breath he'd been holding. He decided to leave the folder in the trunk. No one with him should know about the secret documents he'd withheld from the FBI, including Alasdair. Alasdair was a trusted friend, but he was another set of eyes, another mouth, beyond Frank's control. Ben Franklin again recited his timeless axiom in Frank's head.

Alasdair and the two state troopers were talking with the manager as Frank returned to the other bay.

"Looks like everything's still there," Frank said. "I was concerned about losing that 1938 license plate."

"We can get the forensic team to check the car for evidence, detective," one of the state troopers said.

The last thing Frank wanted was people going over the Reo, especially police people.

"I'm certain I know who stole the car. We won't need to prosecute a dead man."

"Okay. If you're satisfied, we'll leave it at that," the trooper said.

The state troopers filed outside, followed by the manager. Frank signaled Alasdair to meet him at the rear of the Reo.

"The state boys are leaving," Alasdair said. "I thanked them for obtaining the warrant and for their help getting old Ebenezer out there to work with us."

"They say anything about the lock needles?"

"Nope. Musta slipped their mind."

Frank now wanted to drive the Reo somewhere safe, but he didn't know where safe might be. If he took it back to Elm Terrace there could be a repeat of the robbery since he wasn't there much of the time to keep an eye on it. He could install a surveillance system, but why sink that kind of money into a house he intended to sell? Besides, it would take too much time, a commodity he presently had too little of.

Frank stared at the car from the side. He stroked the roof line like it was a cherished pet.

"I know what you're thinking," Alasdair said. "Take the damn car to my place. I'll keep it in my garage and park my clunker in the driveway in front of the garage door."

"You sure?" Frank said and slipped into the driver's seat.

"No one's going to bother it there. Monkton is not like Catonsville. We don't allow thieves to even come into town. Besides, I have a full video system and alarms all over the property," Alasdair said. "After all, I own a video production company, don't I?"

"God, this is going to cost me a buttload of dinners and drinks," Frank said and cranked the Reo to life, while Alasdair rolled up the storage unit's garage door.

Frank switched on the headlights, even though half a ball of sun was still above the horizon.

"Good God, it runs, it lights up, *it's alive*." Alasdair said.

"Tomorrow we pay a visit to Main Street Antiques," Frank said.

"The manager here says he copies all the checks he receives for this unit," Alasdair said. "I'll make a copy of one of his before I leave and meet you at my house. It's pretty warm out, partner. Better put the A/C on high in that old buggy."

"Go stuff a caber up your kilt," Frank said and roared out of the storage unit.

*   *   *   *   *

A few blocks from the storage facility Frank pulled the Reo over to the side of the secondary road he'd taken and shut down the engine. Something kept troubling him, something he needed to confirm. He looked up and down the road for any activity. Satisfied that no cars were approaching in the fading light, he hopped out of the driver's seat and lifted the trunk lid. He retrieved the folder from behind the spare and unrolled it. The paper stapled to the back of the photo was the object of Frank's interest.

Frank was relieved when he saw the words:

Men wish to swing in their seventies and fly with eagles.

Chapter 25

Main Street in Ellicott City was officially Old Frederick Road, but for the five blocks of the antique shops, specialty stores, and restaurants it was known by its simpler name. Funny thing was, Frank and Alasdair discovered there was no such place as Main Street Antiques, and the address shown on the storage rental check belonged to a bakery. That left them with one final thing to look into: the bank that issued the check.

The Madison Park Bank was a state employee credit union with branches just about everywhere except in Ellicott City. The nearest one was off Route 70 in nearby Marriottsville. The signature on the check was made by the same guy who taught doctors how to write prescriptions. It consisted of a curlicue and a wavy line, like a hieroglyph for a tadpole. Even if Frank had access to the Rosetta Stone, he wouldn't have been able to decipher the name.

The young teller at the credit union looked up the account on a computer screen and knitted her eyebrows as if something displayed on her monitor appeared unusual.

"This is a special account," the teller said. "It's locked for privacy."

"We are police officers and we can get warrants to inspect this account," Frank said and side-glanced at Alasdair. "We don't allow accounts to be locked to government authorities here in America. You want that level of privacy, go to Switzerland."

"I'll speak to my supervisor," the teller said, and left her station to talk to a woman overseeing a young woman working the drive-thru window.

"Where do you come up with such bullshit?" Alasdair said low.

"*Law & Order.*"

The teller returned with the supervisor, an older woman with steeply arched eyebrows, which gave her a hard, angry appearance. Anticipating resistance, Frank held up his Florida police badge.

"What is it about this account you require, officer?" the woman asked.

"All I want is the name of the account's owner," Frank said. "We have this check, but we can't make out the name from this signature."

Frank showed the woman the copy of the check. She tightened her lips and shook her head.

"This account is involved in a homicide," Frank said. "Where we got the information will never come back to you. You have my word."

The tellers in the bank watched the confrontation with keen interest.

"I can't tell you that information on a private account such as this," the woman said as she scribbled something briefly on a slip of paper, folded it, and slid it across to Frank, "but you can take it up with the bank's vice-president if you like."

"I'll do that," Frank said and nodded at the two women as he and Alasdair left the bank.

"Going to call the number she gave you?" Alasdair said when they reached their car.

Frank opened the piece of paper and read it.

"Probably not."

He showed the paper to Alasdair.

"Sweet baby Jesus," Alasdair said.

The name on the paper was John D. Dellarue.

* * * * *

Frank and Alasdair sat in the car and stared out the windshield.

"Let's figure out the logic in all this," Alasdair said. "Dellarue hires a career thug, with a rap sheet from here to Tasmania, to steal antiques and store them in a rented garage to cool off and sell later. A pretty stupid hobby, I'd say, for a high ranking cop near retirement."

"Maybe he bought the stuff legit. Could be he's into something bigger than boosting antiques. Maybe drugs. Putting treasure away to augment his pension," Frank said.

"Or gambling. Grabbing your Reo makes sense, if your theory about Joe's gambling is stirred into the mix. Why else would he steal something from you, of all people?"

"I'm no longer buying that theory." Frank said.

"Even so, we're going to need more proof than Dellarue allowing an ex-con to use his storage facility," Alasdair said.

"When we came up with Dickie's prints in my garage, I had them processed through Dellarue's lab, and he went right to work and implicated his own accomplice. Then he has him eliminated?"

"The only real mistake he made was in leaving the storage company's business card in Dickie K's pocket," Alasdair said. "Might've been rushed. Didn't take the time to search him. Probably figured no one would ever find the body."

"Little things like that trip up the smartest criminals," Frank said. "And trust me, Dellarue's got more mistakes in his past."

"Always follow the money, Alasdair said."

"And always follow the power."

*   *   *   *   *

Frank heard Celine calling out to the garage where he and Alasdair were sitting in the Reo.

"Last chance for a fine Italian dinner," Celine called from the house. "The caterer just left."

"Be right there," Alasdair said. "What are we having?"

"Pizza," Celine said.

"Ah, the world's most perfect food," Frank said, climbing out from behind the steering wheel. He reached back into the car and pulled out and pocketed the key from the ignition.

A minute later, the two men came out of the garage and entered Alasdair's house. Frank carried the rolled-up folder with the photo and poem from the Reo's trunk in his hand.

"Ever see this Colonel Chernac?" Frank asked Celine as he pulled the photo from the folder.

"Is he one of the men in that photo?" Celine asked.

"No," Frank said. "Someone else."

Frank placed the folder on the cocktail table in the den and with the curled photo on top.

"I've never actually met him," Celine said and placed the pizza box on the dining table. "He's always on remote assignments, foreign hot spots, I imagine. I worked in a different department."

"I talked to him on the phone," Frank said. "Weird guy, annoying."

"I got the meat lovers' special," Celine said and handed out paper plates. "Dig in."

*   *   *   *   *

After eating, everyone went into the den. Frank took out a letter from his jacket pocket and sat on the sofa in front of the cocktail table where the file folder lay with the rolled-up photo. He opened the letter and looked at it for a moment.

"This is a poem from my grandfather," Frank said. "He loved to create puzzles, like the one we had to solve to find the fallout shelter."

Frank read the first stanza of the poem.

"Treasure comes not only from gold,
Nor from chattel stately and old,"

"What does that mean?" Celine said.

"I guess there's something at Elm Terrace more valuable than money," Frank said and read more.

"Brains on paper and acts preserved,
And still Martian men Are swell served,"

"He found a UFO alien?" Alasdair said.

"The 'brains on paper' has to be what's in the file folder, maybe the chemical equations, and the "acts preserved" must be the Omega film," Frank said.

"What about the 'Martian' part?" Celine said. "Men are from Mars. Hmm, I guess that's true."

"Mars is the Roman god of war," Frank said. " *'Martian men'* are warring men ... wait a minute ... I just picked up on something here for the first time.

'Martian men Are swell served' with the word *'Are'* capitalized mid-sentence.

"A typo?" Celine asked.

"Not likely from a scholar and perfectionist like William," Frank said.

"Let me have a go at the line," Alasdair said reaching for the letter.

Alasdair looked carefully at the poem then looked up and smiled.

"How about if we read it as: 'Martian men *Ares well* served' instead?" Alasdair said.

"Of course," Frank said. "Ares was the *Greek* god of war. William was covering all of his war gods, for sure. And who are war gods? The leaders of nations, the heads of governments, kings, dictators, and emperors, that's who."

"You've nailed it, man," Alasdair said.

"Good eye, Alasdair," Frank said, then read the final line.

"As secrets lie dormant, never told."

"Well, we certainly know what *that* means," Celine said. "How long has that secret room been down there unopened? Since World War Two?"

Frank knew the room had been used since then, but he was sure the dormant secrets started there.

"Actually," Alasdair said, "that poem was pretty easy to figure out. I'd've thought your grandfather's clues would be more challenging. At least up to the caliber of the 'Detroit wonder' one."

"I agree. It was way too easy," Frank said. "The poem makes sense, but what's with this picture?"

Frank picked up the photo and its attached paper. He stretched the picture and paper over the edge of the cocktail table to take the persistent curl out of it so it would lie flat on the table. He placed it picture-side up.

"The only thing I can be sure of is that William put this photo in the Omega file folder for a reason."

Frank hesitated at showing the photo and the poem to his friends, but reasoned he had to trust some people to help him, and who better than his best friend and his wife. He was careful not to reveal the stack of memos inside the folder. There were things they contained needing no interpretation, things his instincts warned him not to share with anyone. He pointed to the photo on the cocktail table.

"What do you make of it?" Frank said.

Alasdair and Celine sat on either side of Frank on the sofa and studied the photograph.

"Looks like two men... possibly in a laboratory," Celine said.

"Two men in lab coats who work for NASA in front of a little shovel on a metal rod with a handle," Alasdair said.

"The man on the left is my grandfather. I have no idea who the other guy is," Frank said. "William was a consultant to NASA in the '70s and '80s."

"What's on the other side?" Celine said.

"Just another stupid poem," Frank said.

Frank flipped over the photo to briefly give them a flash shot of the poem. Alasdair and Celine had no time to scan it before Frank slid it back into the folder.

"Any thoughts?" Frank asked.

"Your grandfather was a strange fellow," Celine said.

"But once you got to know him," Frank said, "he was even stranger. He took me to Washington late one night and we drove to the Capitol and sat on the steps until midnight. At the stroke of twelve he looked at me and said, 'Where else in the world can you sit in your nation's capital on its most important government building at midnight? This is freedom, Frankie. And it's never ever free.'"

Frank stuffed the letter in his jacket pocket, picked up the folder and stood.

"Thanks for indulging me," Frank said. "I'm going to head home and try to grab a little sleep."

"Tomorrow I may set up a video camera in your garage," Alasdair said. "We'll see then who comes and goes. I don't want you to lose that gorgeous 'Vette as well."

"You're worth every burger I force you to eat."

Frank left the MacGowans knowing poems could be explicated, even cryptic poems like William's. And even by less than scholarly people. Frank would keep the poem attached to the NASA photo out of anyone's reach. And he knew precisely how to do that.

He would memorize the poem and destroy the document.

*   *   *   *   *

He was comforted by the fact that only three people had ever seen the poem and attached photo. Plus, Alasdair and Celine had so briefly been shown the poem they wouldn't be able to even make a guess at a word it contained, and certainly not a hint of its interpretation. On the possible downside, they both knew it existed.

Frank drove back to Elm Terrace and popped the cap on a St. Pauli Girl. He sat in the recliner in the parlor and reviewed his intense day. One notion kept surfacing: *How would anyone gain the information necessary to build a device of such devastation as the Omega weapon?* Even he couldn't make any sense of it, and he was intimately acquainted with its author.

Frank began to allow that William was having the last laugh on everyone… and probably nothing more.

189

Chapter 26

Frank drove up close to the garage at Elm Terrace. He was curious. Would Dickie K's lock needles match up with the tool marks on the garage lock? He knew even tiny scratches like these were as reliable as fingerprints when it came to identifying and comparing tools and instruments with the scars they left on other objects. He went into the garage and found a magnifying glass and stepped over to the door. He took the lock needle case from his breast pocket and examined the garage lock.

There weren't many scratches, but there was one small gouge, readable under the ten-power glass. Three of the needles didn't match the mark, but the fourth, a large pointy one, was spot on; a marriage of tool and tool mark. Without question, Dickie K's tools were used to open the Dugan garage. The question was, had he acted alone?

Frank re-entered the house, ascended the staircase and went into the master bedroom. Alasdair's call came in while he was sifting through William's things in the armoire's lower drawers, where nothing there, thus far, had jumped out as useful.

"A pleasant surprise," Alasdair said. "Ebenezer at the storage company just called me as I instructed him to if there were any further visits to the space where we found the Reo. A man came in to get the key to the new lock the old man put on the unit. He made him identify himself. It was Dellarue."

"His lackey is dead. Has to run his own errands."

Frank swept his hand through the clothes hanging in the armoire's upper wardrobe and encountered nothing significant.

"What can we use against him from these visits?" Frank said. "Opening a storage unit isn't against the law, and it won't convict the bastard of murder."

"Patience, laddie," Alasdair said. "He'll trip up sooner or later. Remember all those stakeout nights we spent? Pays off in the end."

"My time's limited here."

"I can keep after him even when you're away, you know. I can nail him."

"You're not a cop anymore. Where's your authority?"

"Where's *yours*, Florida copper?"

"He murdered my father."

"You *think* he murdered your father, and your opinion alone is not going to hold up in court."

Frank drifted over to a mahogany triple dresser.

"You're taking all the fun out of this," Frank said, picking up the King James Bible on the dresser.

"Patience. Things will fall into place in time."

"I'll try," Frank said.

"Celine's making stuffed pork chops from a recipe she conned from the chef at *La Brasserie*. You won't want to miss it."

"I have to beg off. If I eat one more of Celine's dinners, I'll be a stuffed pork chop."

Frank ended the call and opened the Bible to a place marked by a red ribbon sewn onto the leather binding. It held a place in the New Testament's Book of Hebrews. There was a verse, high-lighted in bright yellow in Chapter 11. It read:

"Now faith is the assurance of things hoped for, the conviction of things not seen."

Frank studied the verse and considered its simple message. It was a favorite line of his grandfather's from the scriptures. Frank felt William was, once again, speaking to him from the great beyond.

The leather binding on the Bible was well-worn, its edges tattered in places. Frank set the book upright and held out the cover and the back like the wings of a bird as he attempted to shake out any loose material that might be tucked in the pages. He immediately noticed the back cover was thicker than the front. It felt like something was inside between the leather back and the glued inner lining. Frank found a starting point and began peeling the inside material from the outer leather. It soon became evident what was in the category of "things not seen."

Frank pulled a folded cloth from inside the binding and opened it fully, revealing a full-color map printed on the sheerest silk.

It was a detailed map of the coastal area around Tokyo, Japan.

*   *   *   *   *

Frank took the mysterious silk map to the Dewey Loman Veterans of Foreign Wars Post in Arbutus, a community southwest of Baltimore. He asked some of the older war vets what it was. The consensus of the group believed it was a map used by airmen in World War II if they had to bail out and needed to determine their geographic position. Unlike paper, the silk was relatively impervious to water damage and could depict the area of a bombing run or mission destination, often including important landmarks. A parachuting soldier might save his life, or elude capture, if he could guesstimate where he was and find a way to safety. Frank also learned that the skill required to manufacture and print these specialized maps was top secret and expensive. Many in the group knew about the maps, but only one veteran at the post had ever seen one in person.

The fact that Frank's map covered the central coast of the main island of Honshu and, in particular, a specific section of Japan's Tokyo Bay coastline, had Frank's synapses making strobe light connections. His mind immediately locked on the conversation he'd had with Braewyn Joyce; the conversation about an American observation plane that had crashed on Tokyo Bay late in World War II.

Chapter 27

As Frank sat in the parlor with his morning coffee, he began reviewing the past few days. There were so many loose ends and unanswered questions he hardly knew where to begin. Frank decided to start with his father's death, the event that had put everything else into motion.

It was known that Joe had gambling debts and dealings with characters who likely weren't the most upstanding citizens. If the money he owed was big enough, someone might kill him for his default on payment, but that would've been a stupid thing to do. A murder rap on your head and no chance to ever get paid? All that to make a statement to other offenders? It made no sense when he'd considered it earlier, and still didn't. Maybe Joe's death was an accident, an intimidation attempt carried too far. Still, a dumb move, even for an angry bookie, but Frank never met a truly smart criminal.

Recently something else had come to light. Joe had known about the Omega formula. He had to have. William's memo put his son smack in the middle of his conspiracy. That being the case, someone might have wanted information about the alleged Omega weapon.

But where would they have obtained any knowledge about it in the first place?

The fallout shelter appeared undisturbed until he and Alasdair had entered it. The film was still encased in Cosmoline. And if anyone should have known about the activities at Elm Terrace, it should have been Frank, the only living heir, but he knew nothing of it up until the last few days.

One thing was certain. Joe knew about the Omega Formula and never divulged a word about it, or else the fallout shelter would've been ravaged and everything inside would now be in the hands of his killers. That hadn't happened. This new motive for Joe's murder dimmed the spotlight on Dellarue.

What the hell would a cop near retirement want with a weapon of massive killing power?

Frank refined his thinking to the only scenario that made sense to him: Joe had known everything about the Omega Formula and died without giving it up.

Maybe my father was a man deserving of my respect after all.

So many Christmases had passed without seeing Joe, and Frank's insides churned from the awful pride he'd harbored. A pride which hardened him from making contact throughout those wasted years and allowed for so many missed opportunities. Frank made no attempts to contact Joe on birthdays, holidays, or Father's Days. Now he discovered his father had been heroic in the face of death. Frank had failed to keep in touch with the one hero every son wants in his life.

Frank also knew out there were murderers who needed to be found for the sake of justice, his personal satisfaction, and for what they might actually know about the Omega Formula. If they knew enough to come looking for it, and kill for it, they had to know *something*.

Frank may have wasted time in his past life regarding his father, but, for his sake, he couldn't squander a moment more from here on.

William's portent applied, now more than ever: *"The clock is ticking, gentlemen."*

*   *   *   *   *

That night, Frank returned to the house from his search of what remained in the fallout shelter. The FBI hadn't left a lot, but Frank wanted to be sure they both hadn't missed something... *anything*. After an intense re-investigation of the shelter, he discovered that, in fact, they had. The back of the oak desk displayed a sticker with the name of a furniture store where it apparently had been purchased. The name of the store was Hapburg's Home Interiors in Lancaster, Pennsylvania. It wasn't much, but Frank wasn't going to disregard the find.

Frank returned to the house, tossed his keys in the bowl on the leaving table, and looked at his face in the vestibule mirror. He saw lines around his eyes that hadn't been there a month ago and his mouth was uncharacteristically down-turned. He hung his jacket on a coat hook, took off his shoulder rig and draped it over the Newel post at the bottom of the stairs.

The kitchen air was warm and humid. He turned on the noisy exhaust fan over the range, poured himself a neat scotch and tossed it down. He refilled the glass and plodded into the parlor. He pressed a button on the remote and the TV came to life. The late news was on with the anchor introducing the lead story of the day.

"Three more bodies have been recovered from the collapse of the schoolhouse in Cairo," the news anchor said, "bringing the total to ninety-seven children and five teachers. The cause of the disaster—"

Frank switched channels. A popular talk show, *Tell It Like It Is*, filled the screen.

"Our investigative team's diligence has been rewarded by getting a clip from the Omega Formula film from the 1940s that has the media buzzing," the show's host said as a brief portion of the film played on the screen and faded out. "There's much more to the film, but it may be disturbing to some viewers, so we're going to leave it for you to watch, at your own discretion, on our late edition at eleven."

Frank sipped his Johnnie Walker Black Label and dropped onto the sofa.

"There has been so much buzz over this item that even the president weighed in today after a closed door meeting this week at the White House," the anchor said. "Did this movie cause Japan to surrender in World War Two, or is it a hoax like the famous Orson Welles radio show in 1938, which had a lot of people panicking about the world being attacked by Martians? I suppose the answer is: Who knows? And who knows if we'll ever know?"

Frank pressed a button on the remote and the stern face of the talk show host was replaced by a military documentary. Artillery barrages boomed throughout the room. The scotch was having its effect and he placed his glass on the cocktail table, relaxed his tense, upright posture and slouched on the sofa, resting his head on the back cushion. His eyelids drooped. The drone of the noisy kitchen fan and the monotonous warfare sounds on the TV combined with a drowsiness that began to shut down Frank's typically sharp perception.

Frank slipped into a pleasant, restful state that weighted his eyelids and dulled his senses from interpreting extraneous sounds...

Like the squeaking of door hinges from the vestibule.

Chapter 28

"Can I join the party?" a man's voice said from behind the sofa.

Frank leapt to his feet.

Staring at him from the parlor doorway was a man with a revolver aimed at him. Frank recognized it as a Charter Arms .38, a gun the cops back in the day called "a throw-down piece." The man holding it was John Dellarue.

"So you confiscated my collateral on your deadbeat old man's gambling debts."

"The Reo?" Frank said picking up his drink and moving away from the sofa. "The car belongs to me. You'll have to deal with my father for your money. Oh, that's right, you offed him. Collecting debts from a stiff's a bitch."

"You can't prove any of that and you know it."

"I do, but I know what I know."

"That's precisely why I'm here," Dellarue said moving into the room and nearer to Frank. "I want my money—"

"And me dead."

"Doesn't have to be that way," Dellarue said.

"That would explain the gun aimed at me."

"Would you cooperate without it?"

"May not with it."

"I know you're a tough sonofabitch, Dugan," Dellarue said moving closer. "I pinned a lot of those commendations on your uniform back in the day, but this is business, not personal."

"I'm willing to bet if I handed you the money right now my life wouldn't be worth using for a doorstop."

"You're wrong, Frank. I just want what's due me and I walk away. You've got nothing you can use against me, and if you try to squeeze me, I'll be back."

"Okay then, let's talk business," Frank said then raised his glass of scotch. "Get you a drink?"

"Gin, neat," Dellarue said and lowered the pistol.

Frank started for the kitchen by walking past Dellarue, but, as he passed close to him, he threw his remaining scotch in the captain's face. The momentarily blinded Dellarue reflexively fired the .38 at the floor, then reeled into the arm of the recliner. Frank snatched the brass lamp from the end table and attacked Dellarue with it, bashing him on the side of his neck with a respectable swat. The force of the hit knocked Dellarue across both arms of the recliner and rolled him onto the floor. Dellarue dropped the gun, trying to cushion his falling bulk with his hands, while Frank scooped it up and held the barrel to the back of Dellarue's head.

"You twitch an eyebrow and I'll send you to straight to Hell," Frank said.

"You kill me, you'll go up for murder. Then we'll see who's in Hell."

"Get up."

Dellarue struggled to lift his oversize frame back to its feet. He rubbed the bright red side of his neck and clenched his teeth in pain.

"What now, detective?" Dellarue asked, huffing for breath.

"Not sure, but the offer of a drink's out. We're all out of *gin*."

Frank maneuvered a safe distance from Dellarue's reach and kept the gun on him.

"I'm going to give you my one time get-out-of-jail-free pass. After that, if I have to tangle with you again, I put you in the dirt. You understand me, captain?"

"Couldn't be clearer."

"Now get out of my house and off my property."

Dellarue hesitated a moment and looked at Frank.

"Forget how to find your way out?" Frank said.

"Naw, I know my way around this joint."

"How's come?"

Dellarue about-faced toward the door without responding and hobbled out of the room with Frank a few feet behind him.

"You knew your way around here when you killed my father," Frank said.

"I didn't kill him."

"Who did?"

"I don't suppose you'd have the integrity to work out a payment plan for the twenty grand Joe Dugan beat me out of?"

"You know, John, you should try stand-up."

"I'm only trying for fairness," Dellarue said and turned back to Frank.

"Quit trying," Frank said moving close.

Dellarue swiped at Frank's gun hand and knocked the .38 to the floor where it skidded down the hallway. The captain fell to one knee and snatched at his pant leg to grab a pistol from an ankle holster, but fumbled at retrieving it. Frank pulled the walking cane from the umbrella stand, withdrew its concealed rapier, and rammed it into Dellarue's gun hand. The big man screamed, the pain forcing him to drop the pistol. Frank yanked out the blade from Dellarue's hand and kicked the ankle pistol away. Blood dripped from the wound onto the hardwood floor.

"Jesus Christ, man," Dellarue said in agony and clutched his bleeding hand. "What the hell is this place? A medieval armory?"

"Never know when a piece of shit cop may come visit," Frank said as Dellarue stumbled to stand and trudged out the front door and onto the porch. He pivoted back and made a hand gesture of firing a pistol at Frank's head, then turned away to go down the steps.

"Hey, Dellarue," Frank said. "You want your money?"

Dellarue stopped in his tracks and slowly turned to face Frank.

"Come on back inside."

"What the hell for? Last time I went in there I got beat up, stabbed, and threatened."

"Good times, eh, cap?" Frank said.

"If this is your idea of making nice so you can talk to me, your approach needs work."

"I want to make a deal with you," Frank said and leaned on the porch railing.

"If this includes money coming my way, I'm listening."

Dellarue took a handkerchief from his back pocket and pressed it on his bloody hand.

"Could be," Frank said. "Here's the thing. I know you had something to do with my father's death."

"See ya, asshole," Dellarue said and trudged for the steps.

"Hear me out."

"You got ten seconds."

"I can place you at Elm Terrace on the night Joe died. The gin bottle tagged you."

Frank waited for the lie to sink in. Dellarue faced Frank, disbelief on his face.

"What gin bottle?"

"The one we found in the kitchen with your fingerprint on it."

"Bullshit."

"Okay, John, play it any way you want, but I'm going to make enough stink about this with your department the Grand Jury will have to indict you. Even if you get off, the stigma will follow you forever. You could lose your pension. The one you're only weeks away from claiming."

"I can beat any rap you lay on me, bub."

"I got storage units with a stolen Reo, money motives, bank accounts, Dicky K's murdered body, my father's forensic results. It's enough to get you charged big time and dragged into a long public trial. You'll be the darling of the media. Damning stuff, and I'm not the only one who knows all this."

"Circumstantial, all circumstantial."

"You and I both know enough circumstantial evidence can convict. Look, I personally don't give shit-one how you spend your retirement: a publicly-tormented ex-cop accused of the murder of one of his own, the inmate ex-cop in Patuxent's max security with a lot of cop-hating unfriendlies with shanks, or a respectable man enjoying a well-earned retirement fishing off the Outer Banks. The choice is yours."

"What's your deal?"

"Tell me the truth and I go away for good. Were you there when Joe Dugan was killed? And who killed him?"

"I give it to you straight, all I know, and you walk away from this for good?"

"For good."

Dellarue lumbered to the glider and dropped hard onto the seat. He wound the bloody handkerchief on his wound.

"I didn't kill Joe, but I was in the room when he got the hypo that did him in. I didn't want any part of it, but it was out of my control. They called me on the phone. Threatened my wife and family. I believed them and took them to Joe that night. They came to my home. Two of them stayed with my family, and I was told to go with the other two in the car. One of the men that stayed at my house called the main guy Caesar, like Julius Caesar, I guess. They all wore disguises. Masks, like that big asshole Michael in them Jamie Lee Curtis *Halloween* movies. Said if I knew who they were, they'd have to kill everybody."

"What did they want?'

"Some fucking sci-fi weapon, a bomb maybe. They thought Joe knew about it and knew how to make it. Your granddad was in the picture too. They worked Joe over. Rough stuff at first, then later with drugs and booze. But Joe wouldn't tell them anything. He showed guts, and call it cop instinct, but I think he knew what they wanted. I tried to get them to stop leaning on him, but in the end they finished him off. That wasn't the original plan, the lead guy told me, but it's how it ended up. I still remember his words. Told me, 'Sometimes you have to adjust the battle plan.'"

"Who were these guys?"

"One was a big fella, never spoke, huge bastard. Got no real name on him. They gave Joe bullshit names. Nick and maybe Bubba, Buddy, something like that. I don't remember exactly. I was in the back of the room out of sight. Couldn't hear every word they said. Like I said, the main one, the brains of the outfit, was called Caesar. Maybe they called him that 'cause he was the boss. He ran the whole damn show. Intelligent bastard. And let me tell you, he was one cool and scary sonofabitch. The scariest. And I've run up against some frightening people in my line of work. I'd sooner deal with Hannibal Lecter."

"Anything else?"

"As I said, I was in the background the whole time. I don't think Joe knew I was even there. That's the straight story. I swear it."

"I believe you. And I won't bother you again unless I find out you've lied to me."

"It's the God's truth, Frank."

"So long, John."

"Wait a minute. No money?"

"No money from me," Frank said. "I'm not paying you to bring killers to my family's home. But you enjoy your pension."

Dellarue hung his head, strained to rise, and shuffled down the porch steps. Frank waited until he made it to his car and drove away before he went back in the house. He locked and chained the front door and decided to use the adrenalin rush he was experiencing to clean up the mess in the parlor.

The smell of spent gunpowder hung in the still air of the room. He wiped up the whiskey and noted the small hole in the Persian rug made by the .38 bullet. He retrieved the lampshade from where it had been flung. When the lamp was rejoined with the shade, Frank noticed something on the lamp's bulb socket. It was a bug, and not the kind you'd study in an entomology class.

The rest of the house needed a thorough search for more bugs. Frank started by checking everywhere one could be concealed in the parlor. He examined the rest of the house from ceiling fixtures down to the floorboards. Any room where conversation might take place, especially telephone conversation, had to be scrutinized, particularly the telephones themselves, but he discovered no other eavesdropping devices.

The next step was to find out who might've planted the bug in the parlor. And whether it was placed there before Frank arrived in Maryland. Someone may have wanted to listen in on Joe's conversations too. That may have been the case, but Frank concentrated on more recent events. *Who had been in the house? Alasdair, The CSI team, the FBI, John Dellarue?* Dellarue could've planted the bug on a past visit to see Joe, but the FBI angle made the most sense. They had recently stormed the house when Frank wasn't there and had ample time to install the tiny device. They also had the most to gain by eavesdropping. The government was erupting over this Omega weapon issue, and pressure was coming from high up to get answers. America's leaders were consumed by the fear that any individual or foreign faction could become the world's new superpower. The U.S. government would spare nothing to obtain the answers they craved.

Frank had lost something because of the bug's discovery: the assumption of privacy. But he had gained a little extra at the same time. The killer's name was Caesar, or maybe Nick. And he had a big helper who likely had size 16 feet.

Not a lot, but something.

Chapter 29

It was time to get his facts straight about the end of World War II, in particular, the history concerning the surrender of Japan. He couldn't be in a better place to do his research. He was an hour's drive away from the greatest collection of knowledge in the universe: the Library of Congress.

The address of 101 Independence Avenue in Washington, DC consisted primarily of a group of three capacious buildings named for American forefathers Jefferson, Adams, and Madison. After Frank registered and was photographed at the Madison Building, he was directed to the Jefferson Building where colonial America, and later, the United States, kept most of the accounts of her history, especially the eras of wartime.

After all these years, Frank believed the ultimate truths about the final chapter of World War II would be in print. If such information existed, it would most certainly be in the most renowned repository of world history.

He pulled out every book he could find on Japan's last days of the war, and there were plenty of them. While minor variations in the accounts existed, undeniable consistencies dominated that era of history. Almost every authority on the subject concurred on two major points. One: Japan's military believed it could win a war of invasion if the Allies came onto their shores. Two: They believed Japan could get help from Russia in the end because they believed their countries shared a possible kinship in their mutual hatred for China, and the Reds harbored great distrust of the United States. The Japanese had erred on both counts.

Frank read further and discovered that the factions that controlled the government of Japan were split and deadlocked about the surrender because of the terms outlined by president Truman and the U.S. Congress, which specified *unconditional* surrender plus the removal of Japan's emperor, demands they couldn't bring themselves to accept. Of the fourteen entities that were assembled to make decisions on their country's fate, the three votes of the Japanese military were for fighting on, five votes hung undecided, and the remaining six were for surrender, *if* the terms were modified. But Frank had uncovered another factor that few ever learned was in place: the Omega Formula film. He found it ironic that it was perhaps the simplest element, and one that practically no one on the American side knew about or paid much, if any, attention to.

Frank's history lesson went on: The island of Tinian, situated in the Marianas chain in the south Pacific, a hundred miles north of Guam, was assaulted by U.S. Marines on July 24, 1945. Nine days later, they took control of the island after killing over 8,000 Japanese and capturing another 313. The island was destined to be one of the most strategic in the history of modern warfare. More than a thousand Navy Seabees quickly made it into a workable airbase able to accommodate American bombers, in particular, the B-29 "Silverplate" superfortresses, the only ones specially modified to carry and deliver the 10,000-pound atomic bombs. The location was perfect for staging the atomic attacks on Japan only 1,500 miles away, and backup bombers were positioned on another island a few miles away en route in case the initial bomber ran into trouble early on.

The books unfolded history stories which read like a great novel, but Frank knew everything he was taking in was something that had actually happened, something too big, too photographed, reported on, and participated in to be fabricated. Reading further, his eyes danced across the pages of text and pictures. Colonel Paul Tibbets entered the stage and took command of the first B-29, the *Enola Gay*. He led her crew of 12 in the attack on Hiroshima on August 6, 1945 and carried out the first ever atomic bombing in the history of the world. Frank read how secrecy was paramount. Only Paul Tibbets and two others on the plane knew the mission's actual intent.

A day before the *Enola Gay* was to takeoff, the insignia on her tail was changed from a depiction of a stone-hewn arrowhead to a large Helvetica "R" in a circle. One book cited that Japanese mainlanders knew about the change mere minutes from when it occurred, even sooner than Americans on the backup island only a few miles away. The amazing thing was, the message to Japan came from the island of Tinian itself.

What no one knew until well after the war was that there remained a surviving squad of Japanese soldiers hidden in an outpost in the hills of Tinian with a radio. They transmitted intelligence information to their homeland daily and were privy to practically everything about the planned missions. They knew something else that had Frank reeling in his library chair: They knew the United States only had two A-bombs, and more would not be coming for months, if ever.

The targets of Hiroshima and Nagasaki, and other alternates, were chosen for many reasons, the accounts said. Prevailing weather conditions ultimately dictated which cities would be bombed, but Hiroshima and Nagasaki topped the list. They were cities which contained few, if any, allied prisoner of war camps. They weren't of great religious, military, or strategic significance, and acceptable weather conditions had been predicted for August. Frank now gleaned from this retrospective history lesson that the atomic bombings would not have brought about the surrender the United States so desperately wanted. It would've taken something else, something more fearsome.

Frank was now certain the work of his grandfather and his colleagues was instrumental in bringing about the unconditional surrender of Japan. He also realized it was of the utmost urgency that he, and he alone, find the solution to the Omega formula's enigma.

The possible outcome of his failure was unimaginable.

Chapter 30

The picture of William and the other man in the NASA lab was troubling. Frank needed to know who this unnamed person was. He now began to believe the unknown man might be key to every fact he was scrambling to gather. He knew NASA had a website which provided an email response form he could use to contact the agency for general questions, but he discovered they would not respond to questions concerning photographs. He decided to contact NASA directly in Houston, Texas. He would use his grandfather's name to gain access to what he wanted. It had been decades since William worked there, but Frank hoped someone would remember him. Frank dialed their number knowing the odds were against him.

After being transferred to four different departments, Frank connected with a man in the engineering division.

"Dan Balfour," the man said. "How can I help you?"

"I'm the grandson of William Dugan, a physicist who worked for NASA in the '70s and '80s," Frank said.

"Ah. What did he do for us?"

"He helped design implements used in space, tools for the moon missions."

"I see. That was quite a while back. Before my time here. So what can I do for you?"

"I have a photo of my grandfather standing with another man in a NASA laboratory. They both are wearing NASA lab coats. I'd like to know who the other man is."

"From more than thirty years ago? I'm not sure—"

"How about if I email the photo to you and you can ask around?"

"I don't know, sir…"

"I'm a police officer and this is very important."

"Oh, man, this sounds like something out of my hands."

"No one's going to subpoena you, Mr. Balfour. I just need to ID the man in the photo. Simple as that. There's no crime involved here. It only concerns my own family history."

"Nothing criminal?"

"Nothing. What's your email address?"

Frank emailed Balfour and attached his scan of the photo.

*   *   *   *   *

It was time to head south and return to his day job. Frank was weary of the calls from the *Today*

Show, *Good Morning America*, Fox News, and every talk show from Bill O'Reilly to Rush Limbaugh. *What had happened to the expectation of privacy? Could anyone at all get your non-published home phone number? Even your cell?* And now William's house had been bugged. He'd done all he could in Maryland. It was time to button up Elm Terrace and get out of there.

Frank carefully tucked the folder with the copies of the Omega files, William's memos, and the NASA photo inside the lining of his suitcase and re-glued it in place. He memorized the poem and burned the original.

Frank left Catonsville feeling he'd done all he could to "sanitize" the house for the time being. He knew he'd need to come back to sell the estate and make decisions about the three vehicles.

*   *   *   *   *

Frank got into his unmarked cruiser at the Orlando airport and drove the 95 miles south to Martin County. After two hours he was crossing the Roosevelt Bridge and wending his way down U.S. 1 toward Colorado Avenue. It was Sunday night and Stuart, Florida had never looked so good as Frank motored under the street lights of Ocean Boulevard and headed east toward the sea. A right on Krueger Parkway, a right on Stafford Drive, and he'd be home. His house was near the Indian River, the last body of water between Stuart proper and the beautiful Hutchinson Island beaches on the Atlantic. Frank was glad to be back in Paradise.

He pulled into the driveway in front of the white stucco and Spanish tile bungalow and parked. The sun had set in the west hours ago, but its 90-degree heat was still toasting the air.

Frank called Roland before he went into the house. He wanted to get police business out of the way before he flopped on the sofa to watch some TV and tapped into a cold beer.

"I'm back. See you first thing in the morning," Frank said.

"I want you to work nights this week," Roland said.

"Good. I like nights."

"I'll be here when you check in and we can catch up."

"Any more from the NSA?"

"Been quiet."

"No murders?"

"That's implied in the phrase 'been quiet.' Save the stupid questions until tomorrow night," Roland said and hung up.

*   *   *   *   *

He climbed out of the cruiser and started to go to the front door, but stopped short. He pulled the pistol from his holster and took a small LED flashlight from his pocket, skirted around the house to the back yard and checked the doors and windows where he'd placed paper matches, poised to drop if anyone opened them. The matches were all in place, so he returned to the front of the house and checked the matches above the door. Many of his neighbors could view the front of his house, and while he didn't think any suspicious entry would go unnoticed, he wasn't going to place complete trust in that. Vigilant neighbors or not, Frank wasn't about to get caught flatfooted again by the government or anyone else in or around his home.

The inside of the house harbored hot, musty air from the July sun that beat down on the roof by day, unaided by air conditioning. He turned the thermostat on the A/C down to 68 degrees, opened the fridge and let the coolness inside wash over his face for a few seconds, then opened a beer.

Frank toured the rooms, turning on ceiling fans. He figured the house would be tolerable in an hour. What he didn't figure on were the jalousie window slats lying broken on the terrazzo floor of the bathroom.

*   *   *   *   *

Frank hadn't placed his matchstick tells in his bathroom window because it was high up on the wall and not a likely entrance to the house. The screen was missing and there were enough glass slats removed to allow a Cape buffalo entry. The question was: w*hat had been taken?*

Frank searched the rooms like he would any other crime scene. He found the most evidence in the office he'd transformed out of the second bedroom. There were desk drawers pulled out and papers strewn everywhere, but the real loss was at his computer. The cover was off and the hard drive was missing from its slot. Practically every business and personal detail relating to his life was on that drive.

"Roland, someone's been in my house," Frank said on his cell. "Looks like they got into my computer. Send the forensic techs out to my place to check it out."

"I told you to install security cams at your house. I could be sitting here in my office right now looking at the perps' kissers on my machine."

"And I told you, cut back on the subs and pizzas and you might live to make sixty. We're both wasting our breath. Now can you get me a couple of techs or will I have to dig up David Caruso at *CSI Miami*?"

* * * * *

"Nothing yet from forensics, detective," Corporal Greg Martinez said. "It's only been two days. They may come up with something."

Frank nodded his thanks and headed for Roland Brand's office.

Frank framed himself in the office doorway. The sheriff was looking at a small box sealed with tape.

"This came for you an hour ago," Roland said, pushing the box toward Frank. "No return address."

Frank cut open the box with a pocket knife and looked inside.

"It's my hard drive."

"Do you know more than you let on about this Omega thing?"

"Don't go there, Roland."

"Maybe I can help."

"I wish you could, but I don't want anyone else involved in this mess."

"Who would want your computer data?" Roland asked.

"Everyone in the government down to the congressional pages."

"The government sends back things they steal? Not in my experience with the bastards."

"Maybe because there's nothing on that drive about the Omega weapon," Frank said. "And maybe I have a friend somewhere in the government."

"I'm putting an unmarked car on your house."

"I know you don't have unlimited resources here, but it'd be appreciated."

"I had the state guys alerted. They'll do their best to cover your back. What's going on in Maryland with your dad's murder?

"I got a name. Now I have to find him."

"That's something," Roland said.

Frank strode for the door and stopped.

"You think forensics can get something off this disk drive?" Frank asked.

"You might want to rethink that if you've been surfing *'Girls Gone Wild in Daytona'*" and the like."

"Bad thought. Never mind."

* * * * *

Frank called Alasdair from his backyard tiki bar and sipped on a scotch. While he wasn't comfortable making an appearance back in Maryland at the moment, he wasn't going to stop gathering all the intelligence he could. Alasdair could be the ally he needed to do precisely that.

"Hey, partner," Frank said. "It's not a lot safer here than up there. My house got ransacked. They got the hard drive off my computer."

"Oh, man, that's rough. You have to back your data up. My whole life's on mine."

"Ditto. No usable evidence at the scene, but here's the good part. The hard drive was sent back."

"If they read or copied your hard drive they've got information that could hurt you. Probably things they can use to implicate me as well."

"Yeah, they'll know about everyone I know. Comforting."

"Suspects?"

"The Russians, the Germans, the U.S. government, people I haven't even encountered yet. Shit, Maltese terrorists, disgruntled pygmies, who knows?"

"Power has its allure."

"But this is merely the *possibility* of power," Frank said. "No one knows for sure it works. I sure as hell don't."

"A lot of people think it may. And they think you know how it works."

"To make it even more fun, Dellarue thinks I should pay him what my old man owed him."

"Like him for the one who bugged your house?"

"Maybe, but if he did, the bug was there to monitor Joe, not me. Keep tabs on his gambling."

"What's the plan?"

"First, I want to get Elm Terrace in salable condition. Get some contractors to pretty-up the grounds, paint the exterior and clean the inside ceilings to floors."

"I'll get you the best people I know."

"You've got keys to everything. Call me with estimates and I'll send you the money. I received

Joe's insurance money last week. William bought him a policy and a half. Joe may not have been able to pay his bookies when he was alive, but someone sure insured his dead body for plenty."

"Sounds like William was protecting his grandson," Alasdair said.

"Or his legacy."

"By the way, I'm coming down Saturday to right up the road from you. Going to maybe shoot some video and make a bit of money."

"Who's getting married?"

"No one. The folks at Cape Canaveral want to discuss making a documentary, and I'm going to be shooting on an ancient Spanish shipwreck off Vero Beach."

"Like underwater?" Frank said.

"A whole lot like underwater and I'd love for you to go with me."

"Underwater?"

"That's where they keep old sunken Spanish galleons. Arghh. Ya hardly ever find 'em up on the beach, laddie. I've got plenty of equipment and the wreck site is only about eighty feet down."

"When did you take up this crap?" Frank said.

"A year or two ago. I'll have you know I'm a U.S. certified scuba diver."

"You're a U.S. certified lunatic."

"When I was on sub tenders in the navy I got the bug to get into more than fixing bent rudders."

"I jumped in the water a couple of times in the marines. Demolition experts get wet too."

"So you'll go, then?"

"Let me put some new colors in your paint box, Allie. Indiana Jones hates snakes, and I hate close, tight places and deep water. What you propose has all those scary things, plus a few hungry barracudas thrown in for laughs."

"That would be a no, then?"

"That would be a no, no, oh, hell no," Frank said. "I'm a terra firma, sea level kinda guy. Nothing too high or too deep.

"At least come up to Vero and watch me feed the makos."

"Email me the details and I'll try to work it in between robberies, assaults, and government subpoenas."

"Let me know if you change your mind about diving."

"There's only one kind of diving I do."

"That can be dangerous too, you know. You should open your vistas a wee bit and test the water."

"When I grow gills. Later, brother."

Frank ended the call and downed the remainder of the scotch. He smiled at the thought of Alasdair going all Jacques Cousteau with a garish, DayGlo yellow wetsuit and enormous flappy fins. He also thought about the offer to go wreck diving and shuddered. Deep diving was merely delayed drowning to him. The closest he was going to get to eighty feet of ocean water was on a cruise ship to the Bahamas.

Chapter 31

The air conditioning had lowered Frank's small house to a chilling level when he woke from a long doze on the sofa. The drawn curtains in the house kept it cooler in the early morning sun, but a lot darker as he fumbled for the lamp on the end table. The light popped on at the same moment his cell rang.

"Dugan," Frank answered.

"We're going to need you down at the station, Frank," the familiar morning growl of Roland's voice said.

"I'm on nights this week."

"Carl Rumbaugh is missing."

"Did anyone check the swing sets at the elementary school?" Frank said.

"Damn it, Frank, something for real's happened to the stupid sonofabitch. He never misses his shift, and there's no answer on his cell or radio."

"All right, be there in two shakes. This isn't my week to work mornings, you know."

"Extend yourself. And bring a gallon of real coffee and a buttload of pastries on your way. Could be a long day."

Frank ended the call then plodded into the bathroom to throw water on his face. He checked his repair on the jalousie window and closed the slats extra snug with the hand crank.

Rumbaugh is missing? Coffee and baked goods, my ass. Rumbaugh's gone? Shouldn't we be breaking out the Dom Perignon?

*   *   *   *   *

Frank nursed the last drop from his Dunkin' Donuts cup and traipsed into the small conference room where Corporal Greg Martinez, Sheriff Roland Brand, and Janis Geller, the unit's administrative assistant, were assembled. The group looked intense, their faces somber.

Frank liked Greg and saw the young man as a potential detective. Roland also had seen promise in his young officer and often brought him into meetings like this one to build his experience. Frank knew Janis was an efficient worker and regarded the slim, forty-something woman as a police secretary who carried herself like a runway model. Roland held few meetings without her involvement.

"Where was Rumbaugh the last time we were in contact?" Frank asked, moving to a large map covering almost one entire wall of the room.

"I saw him last night when he finished his shift at four PM," Greg said. "He checked in by phone a few minutes later. Said he was on a pull-over on 5th

Street. He should've checked back afterward and been here for his shift by eight this morning."

"It's not like Carl to miss checking in," Janis said.

"Got anything more precise on his 20 when he called in last night?" Frank asked Greg.

"On 5th Street, off Colorado. Said he was a block from Confusion Corner," Greg said.

Confusion Corner was a well-known location to residents of Stuart where the confluence of six streets and a set of railroad tracks existed near the center of the town's business district. It was a location where accidents happened with the regularity of the tide.

"From there he could've headed anywhere," Frank said.

"I called the state boys to help out," Roland said. "They gave me that 'wait 24-hours' crap because right now he's technically not missing. If I have to, I'll call in the damn state militia."

The main line lit up on the conference phone in the center of the table, and Janis Geller picked up the receiver. A long moment passed while she listened and everyone in the room watched her in silence. She reached for the speaker button on the phone, then withdrew her hand without activating it. Janis scribbled something on a piece of notepaper, her writing hand unsteady.

"I'll tell him," Janis said and hung up the phone.

Everyone stared at Janis.

"They have Rumbaugh," she said, her voice quavering. "Sounded like a Russian talking. Carl's their hostage. They said they nabbed the wrong detective. They want Frank and want to make a trade."

"Carl's not just missing anymore," Greg said.

"Anything else?" Roland asked.

"He gave me a cell number to negotiate the trade, then hung up," Janis said and pushed the paper to Roland. "I was going to put the call on speaker, but he told me not to."

"Trade Frank for Rumbaugh?" Roland said. "Dugan's worth at least fifty Rumbaughs, plus two draft picks."

"He sounded serious," Janis said.

Everyone scrambled from their seats and looked at Roland.

"I'm not trading shit with any goddamn Ruskies," Roland said. "Greg, see if you can get a location on that call and set up a perimeter. Janis, call the state police and tell them we've upgraded our missing person to a kidnapping. I'll get a SWAT team ready to get in the air as soon as we know where to send 'em. I want these jokers hemmed in *now*."

"Put out an APB for Carl's car," Frank said to Greg. "And get the guys to warm up the chopper."

"Wonder where they have him," Janis said.

230

"Could be in Cuba by now, for all we know," Roland said.

Chapter 32

The triangulation method used in cell tower communications to determine where a cell call originated placed the kidnapper's phone somewhere on the west side of U.S. 1, a roadway known by locals as Dixie Highway, and a few miles out on Route 76, the old Indiantown Road. Frank knew the sparsely populated area well.

"Greg," Frank said into his radio mike, "call the kidnappers with the cell number they gave you and ask them where they want to meet to make the hostage swap. Then get a new fix on their location and radio me back."

"Roger that," Greg said and clicked off.

The baking heat on the road ahead rippled the rising air, making it look like wide puddles of water lying in the path of Frank's cruiser. He passed several roadside vendors selling everything from chenille blankets to carved coconut heads, but as he approached an upcoming fruit stand he noticed something out of place. A tall man wearing a sweatshirt was picking out oranges and mangos. It was strange enough he was wearing a long-sleeve sweatshirt in 90-degree heat, but there was something else that had Frank's curiosity piqued. On the sweatshirt was a faint printed image. It was a faded logo of the long-gone Brooklyn Dodgers.

*   *   *   *   *

The sweatshirt man paid for his fruit and lumbered for a black Nissan SUV parked a few yards away from the vendor's stand. Frank watched him from across the road as the man stopped to answer his cell phone.

"Greg, are you in contact now with the kidnappers?" Frank said into the radio mike.

"Roger, that," Greg Martinez whispered. "Can't talk right now."

"Don't talk. Listen. Have the guy you're talking to look up and ask him if he sees a helicopter."

A moment later the sweatshirt man gazed up and panned the sky, shielding his eyes from the sun with his bag of fruit.

"Got him," Frank said and hung up the mike.

Sweatshirt climbed into his car and drove west with Frank on his trail, but well behind. The road was nearly bee-line straight and the visibility was excellent, so Frank slowed to allow a car to pass him and pull in between Sweatshirt's vehicle and his unmarked car. He decided a little extra cover couldn't hurt.

Two miles later, Sweatshirt steered left onto a dirt road, which disappeared into a copse of thick cabbage palms, brush, and banyan trees. Frank followed and slowed, unsure as to how far to push his luck. He pulled to the side and parked. He slid out, stepped to the front of the car, and raised the hood. He fiddled with the engine's wiring as he gazed down the road where Sweatshirt had driven from sight. Frank knew it was a dicey move, and he should call for backup, but that could take time and he was not about to let up on his pursuit of this likely kidnapper. Problem was, he had no idea of the size of the opposing force. Only an idiot would charge blindly into opposition which might be overwhelming. He decided to play it smart and called for backup and gave the station his position.

The walk to the thick flora was about twenty yards, but after that, he hadn't a clue to what awaited him. He pulled out his Browning and crept slowly through the shaded tunnel of trees until he spotted a clearing ahead. From the cover of the brush, he surveyed a long-abandoned farmhouse and cattle barn with barely any paint left on their scorched wood exteriors. He studied the weather-worn doors and windows for any signs of life or movement. Nothing stirred.

Then voices carried from the farmhouse.

"What do you expect? I've told you a hundred times, I know nothing about any bombs."

Frank recognized the strained voice of Carl Rumbaugh.

"Quiet. Don't make me want to shoot you," a heavily-accented voice said.

Frank believed the accent might be Russian.

"Let me out of—"

The up-pitched voice of Carl Rumbaugh instantly went silent.

Frank needed to determine how many Russians, terrorists, or whatever they claimed to be, occupied the house, and pinpoint any other accomplices within range. He calculated he could safely make it to the nearby barn and set up closer surveillance. It was thirty yards to the left of the house and about the same distance from where he was hiding. He certainly wasn't going to wait until the cover of night, hours away.

The far left side of the thick brush would provide Frank with concealment from the farmhouse and, from there, he could come in from the back side of the barn. He plowed through the foliage toward the decrepit building. The bootjack spikes on the trunks of the sabal palmettos scratched and cut his face and hands as he waded low through the dense undergrowth, but he eventually made it to an open area facing the barn's back wall, now only fifteen open yards away. Frank gave one last look around and sprinted for the barn.

He came to within ten feet of the building when the sandy soil violently erupted around his feet and spewed hot grit onto his pants, stinging his calves.

He was taking automatic gunfire.

*　　*　　*　　*　　*

In spite of the pelting of bullets striking around him, Frank made it to the rear of the barn and dove inside through an opening between the dry-rotted boards. He took cover behind an ancient tractor, a mass of rusted cast iron with giant, cracked and rotted rubber tires. Once there, he caught his breath and checked himself for wounds. His legs smarted, and his side burned from a rasping on the splintered barn boards, but nothing was flowing blood.

Frank heard a voice speaking a foreign language outside the front of the barn.

"He says not to shoot him," a different voice said with authority.

There were two, maybe three, of them approaching the barn's main doors from the side of the building, now open wide enough to allow a hay wagon to pass easily in and out. The space where such a hay wagon could fit was currently occupied by the black Nissan SUV. The opening was also large enough to allow entrance to men moving closer with weapons; weapons Frank could hear being loaded, their breech slides activated with unmistakable metallic clinks, as they neared the gaping doorway.

236

Frank took aim at the opening and felt for the two extra magazines hanging below his shoulder holster. He had 43 bullets available to dissuade the converging squad, but he could only lay down fire one round at a time. His adversaries, who wielded automatic weapons, could spray lead like water from a fire hose.

"We have Detective Rumballs with us, and he says you could be man we want to talk to. Are you Detective Frank Doggon?" the foreign voice asked.

That dumb shit "Rumballs" gave me up without a moment's hesitation.

Frank stayed silent and kept his pistol leveled on the doorway. He looked around to locate other access points his adversaries might use, and for escape holes when the time came.

"Detective Doggon, we only want to talk. Please make dis easy. No problems for all of us. Afterward, we go our own ways," said the accented voice.

Then Frank heard more excited, foreign jabber he loosely interpreted to mean: "Go in there and pull this Amerikanski pig out here."

Two men peeked around either side of the barn entrance. Frank waited until he could glimpse a little more enemy flesh before he squeezed the trigger of the Browning. He had been an expert marksman in the marines, but at better than sixty feet in a combat situation he opted for patience, and waited for the biggest possible target.

A short, heavy man, wearing military battle gear, tiptoed into the barn with his AK-47 assault rifle pointed close to where Frank crouched. In a blink, he expected a volley of 7.62mm rounds would be rocketing his way at over 2,300 feet per second.

Frank took the offensive. A single bullet from his pistol hit the intruder an inch above the bridge of his nose. The overweight man tilted backward and sprawled out onto the barn floor. If his enemy was wearing body armor, Frank's head shot made certain it was unable to save him.

The talkative one outside yanked his head away from the open door, then yelled and carried on in his native tongue. Frank couldn't interpret the words, but understood that angry cursing in almost any language came out with a similar meaning.

"You are moddafucker!" Mr. Heavy Accent screamed. "My cousin only come in dere to talk to you. Think, detective. What good are you dead to us when we need you for information?"

A sensible point, but Frank didn't trust a word he said. He knew he'd blown his concealment in the barn. It was time to find new cover. *Hell, if these turkeys wanted me dead, all they'd have to do is set a match to this bone-dry tinderbox. It'd burn to the ground in minutes.* Frank knew revealing his position put him at a tactical disadvantage. Never a good thing.

He looked around for options and spied something that gave him a lift. *The dumb ass outside is moving back and forth near the door, revealing himself through the open gaps between the boards.* Frank took careful aim and squeezed off a single round. A board at the front of the barn moved slightly and the silhouette behind it crumpled. Frank was two for two. Now it was probably time to pull Carl from the farmhouse and get him a Valium.

That would've been the plan were it not for the annoying cold steel pressing against the nape of his neck.

Chapter 33

Frank dropped his Browning on the hay-strewn floor and raised his hands.

"Good at chess and good at combat too," the familiar voice behind him said.

"The mysterious Colonel Chernac, I presume," Frank said.

"A good ear for voices and a good eye for targets," Chernac said. "Even under threat of automatic gunfire."

"You know, the best gunfighters in history never discounted the value of a single, well-placed shot over a scattering of many," Frank said.

Chernac's gun stopped pressing on Frank's neck. Without waiting for permission, Frank wheeled around and faced the colonel.

"FBI catch you spying on them, Chernac?" Frank asked and lowered his hands.

"Not yet, detective, not yet," Chernac said and patted down his black mustache with his free hand.

"Playing chess is a hell of a lot more fun than this killing-dying thing."

"Let's go up to the house and have a talk," Chernac said as he waved his pistol toward the front door of the barn.

Both men walked outside, Frank in the lead. A breeze kicked up, stirring the scrub palms and cooling the air a degree or two. When they reached the farmhouse, Chernac stopped and touched Frank's shoulder. Frank turned to face him.

"It's nice outside. We can talk on the porch. I like it warm and balmy, don't you?" Chernac said as he took the porch steps two at a time and sat on a rustic, mission-style bench.

"It's hardly 'balmy,' but it beats living in Quebec."

"Too cold there for your taste?"

"I don't care for the French."

"Come sit here, detective," Chernac gestured with a latex-gloved hand.

Chernac's high-cheekboned face was pale, but covered in perspiration that dripped down his forehead, around his thick dark brows, and into his black eyes, causing him to blink. When Frank hesitated, Chernac managed a brief smile, moved over on the wide bench allowing ample space for Frank. He patted the empty seat like he was summoning a trusty hunting dog.

"If this is about any goofy bomb shit, I'm kinda tapped out," Frank said as he stepped up and lowered himself onto the far side of the bench.

"When I examined the papers in the Omega file folder," Chernac said, keeping his pistol trained on

Frank, "I couldn't help but think a page or two was missing."

"And you think I have these imaginary pages?"

Chernac wiped his face with a handkerchief from his pants pocket.

"You're my best choice. I watched as my people scanned them, so I'm skeptical that we have all there is. I compared what we have to the files of the other agencies and found our pages to be identical to theirs. Which leaves yours."

"And suppose my documents are the same as yours?"

"Then one might conclude that you removed some before anyone else saw the complete set."

Frank shrugged.

"Why did your men kidnap Detective Rumbaugh?" Frank asked.

"Same reason those men are dead. Stupidity. What makes you think they are *my* men?"

"You're their leader aren't you? And I'm sure you already knew what I looked like."

"I hadn't arrived yet. These men are communists who want the same thing I want. They are in competition with me. So I baited them into coming and used them. I sent them ahead to bring you here under the pretext that they could share in what we discovered about the Omega weapon. They had a fifty-fifty chance of getting it right and they failed. But they were going to die one way or the other. I don't tolerate competition."

"So you let me execute them for you," Frank said.

"A lot of people do things for me. A good leader delegates and expands his base. I send out a bunch of spaniels and reward the one that comes back with the pheasant."

"So what's the point of this field exercise?"

"I want you to know I can get to you anytime I wish. One way or another, I'll get to you. Even in your own police jurisdiction. Even where you live, I can get to you, and all your cops can't stop me nor protect you. I think you'll find it far easier to give me what I want rather than persist in stubbornness."

"Good to know."

"I want those missing pages, detective."

"And I want a cure for cancer and an ocean villa in Palm Beach, so where does that leave us?"

"At an impasse, I'm afraid," Chernac said and stood with his automatic pointed at Frank's midsection. "For now."

"You know," Frank said, "for a guy of means I'd think you could afford better than a 200-buck Makarov."

"It's cheap and untraceable, like those I hire. Personally, I prefer a revolver. Revolvers are more dependable, but, you know, less firepower," Chernac said and combed his black hair back out of his face with his splayed fingers, then cocked his head skyward.

The staccato whups of a helicopter could be heard approaching in the distance. Frank's eyes searched the sky. The sound steadily increased. Chernac rushed to the rail of the porch to find its source, his head scanning the low clouds. Frank stood and could see the 'copter coming from the east, heading straight for the farmhouse and closing fast.

"By the way, where is old 'Rumballs'?" Frank asked.

"You'll find him. He's with another of my hunting dogs. Sorry I can't stay, detective, but we'll renew our revels soon," Chernac said and vaulted over the porch railing and sprinted for the thick brush.

Frank scurried to the edge of the porch just as Chernac vanished into the green and brown overgrowth. Amid a whirlwind of dust and weed shrapnel, the helicopter descended onto a parched area near the farmhouse. Four state policemen jumped out with assault rifles at the ready and headed for Frank.

"He ran into the brush," Frank shouted and pointed where Chernac had fled. "He's armed."

Three of the officers charged to where Frank indicated, spread out, and disappeared into the heavy foliage. The fourth officer hung back and ran for Frank.

Frank marched to the front door of the farmhouse and kicked it open. The sweat-soaked Brooklyn Dodger fan bolted from the house, knocking Frank to the weathered boards of the porch, then dashed for the thick foliage. Three rifle bursts cracked and the Dodger fan stumbled for a few tripping strides and collapsed onto the bone-dry grass. Frank sprang to his feet and shot into the farmhouse. Musty smells of rotten wood attacked his nose. Inside was Carl Rumbaugh, gagged, blindfolded, and strapped with duct tape to a rickety kitchen chair that swayed and racked under his weight.

"It's time for a diet, Carl," Frank said. "You've practically destroyed this nice Shaker chair."

Carl tried to say something, but the tape only allowed him muffled grunts. Frank yanked off Rumbaugh's adhesive blindfold and ripped the tape from his mouth.

"*Damn*, Frank," Rumbaugh howled with tears in his eyes. "I think my eyebrows are on that tape."

"The state police are here to take you to the hospital. You lucky dog. You get to ride in the helicopter."

Rumbaugh's face went from ruddy to ashen.

"Take me in your car, Frank. You know how I feel about flying."

"I would, but you ratted me out, Rumby, and you know how I feel about stoolies," Frank said as two state troopers entered the farmhouse.

"Frank, for God's sake, take me in the car," Rumbaugh yelled and squirmed violently in the chair, which collapsed and discharged his corpulent frame onto the filthy floor.

Frank hefted Rumbaugh to his feet and looked him over.

"You look okay," Frank said.

"My mouth hurts."

"You shouldn't use it so much," Frank said and hurried out the door to retrieve his Browning from the barn.

*   *   *   *   *

Two state police investigators intercepted Frank at his cruiser and began their questions concerning the kidnapping incident, especially the shooting of the three dead perpetrators. The pair of big men looked like a wrestling tag team. They grilled Frank for almost an hour and had him walk them through the entire scenario step by step. They took Frank's firearm and told him to report to Sheriff Brand.

"How long will I be on administrative leave?" Frank asked.

"That will depend on the findings of this investigation and the judgment of the DA," the lead officer said.

"It was self defense," Frank said.

"Could be. But when two men armed with automatic weapons are found dead from single shots from a lone man with nothing but a pistol, it raises questions."

"Shit," Frank said and pounded on the trunk of the cruiser.

"Just doing our job, detective," the second investigator said. "Nothing personal."

"I'm getting screwed for doing *my* job," Frank said.

"It's policy, Dugan," the lead investigator said. "And this isn't your first experience with this procedure."

Frank knew they were right, but he didn't have to like it. He puzzled over how an NSA agent like this Chernac character could get away with masterminding a kidnapping.

Did the NSA have that kind of power?

Maybe, but Frank doubted it.

Chapter 34

"You made that fat tub go in the chopper?" Roland said, laughed and tilted his desk chair back until his cowboy boots came off the floor. "Woo, Jesus, we'll be able to bury Rumbaugh in a Tic Tac box with all that crap scared out of him."

"He'll survive," Frank said.

"Speaking of survive, what the hell were you thinking going in on those bastards without waiting for backup?"

"Seemed like the best way to handle it."

"Horseshit. You're always charging into snake pits before you pull on your boots. You follow protocol from now on. Who do you think you are? Bruce Willis?"

"I have more hair."

"Go screw yourself *and* your hair. We've got two of your dead men out there to deal with. You're off active duty until the DA finalizes his report on your self-defense statement."

"I'll be on administrative leave for God knows how long and I've got to settle a few things."

"What kind of things?"

"I want to find out more about this Chernac bastard."

"Let NSA handle him. Better yet, why don't I call your FBI buddies to nail him?"

"Let me deal with him. If you call in the FBI he'll bust ass for overseas. Then we'll never get him."

"You're a knucklehead."

"He came down here to get at me and almost pulled it off," Frank said. "He may not even be going back to the NSA. I think he's gone rogue, playing the field, independent. Maybe working for foreign money."

"You making any progress with this Omega stuff?"

"NASA in Houston refused to give me any information on a photo I found of William and another guy dressed in NASA attire. So I looked up a man named Vernon Ritter. He attended my grandfather's funeral. The army found him for me in Omaha. A retired lieutenant general, no less."

"He was still alive?"

"Barely. But he was able to tell me a lot. He commanded training for part of the 6th Bomber Group based in Nebraska during the war. To be more specific, he trained men to fly the Silverplate B-29 superfortresses that dropped the atomic bombs on Japan. He worked with William on the Omega project and named a third man. An ordnance expert named Simon Hapburg. Same fella worked with William at NASA."

"The mystery man in the photo."

"Bingo."

"What does that do for you?"

"Simon Hapburg has relatives. I looked up a furniture store owned by a couple of them in Pennsylvania. That got me another one living in Michigan, a grandson of Simon's. Name's David. I need to talk to him."

Roland rose from his desk chair and stepped over to a picture on the wall opposite his desk. The color photo was of his younger self dressed like a cowboy and wearing a ten-gallon Stetson. He was perched on a cattle yard's rail fence with Florida Cracker cows all around him, a rare breed specially-suited for the tropical climate of the Sunshine State. On the fence in the photo was a sign that read: *The Brand Beef Company*. Roland delicately straightened the cocked picture.

"How long you gonna need? All I got in homicide without you is Carl the mayor's moron. And now you've got him scared to go near an airport."

"In drama class, they said if you don't know what you're supposed to do on stage, ad lib your part. Get Rumbaugh to ad lib that he's a detective."

"Rumbaugh couldn't ad lib a fart at a Texas chili cookoff."

"Stop worrying. I'll see if I can get David down here. Providing the department can cough up a few bucks for airfare."

"All right, we'll label it an out-of-state investigation," Roland said and returned to his desk chair. "Tie it in with this Chernac kidnapping."

*   *   *   *   *

David Hapburg sat in his Jeep Cherokee in front of the Martin County Sheriff's Department and cut the engine. He pressed the window buttons down and took in the warm Stuart air. More than twenty hot minutes passed while he decided whether to go inside or not. He had never been so torn about anything as much as this seemingly simple decision, but there could be consequences, consequences that might end his 32-year life.

His rimless glasses fogged up in the humid air that drifted into the car from the open windows. He wiped them with a tissue from the dispenser in the armrest between the seats. The long drive from Michigan had started with resolve and positive action, but now that he'd arrived, he felt uncertain about his decision. His stomach churned and he could taste a sourness from the orange juice he'd had for breakfast.

A sheriff's department SUV pulled into the lot and parked a few yards in front of him in one of the

251

spaces marked for official vehicles. Two men stepped from the truck and headed for the entrance to the building. One of the men was in a police uniform. The taller one, dressed in khakis and a white golf shirt, stopped and stared toward the Jeep. David found himself locking eyes with a man who studied him with interest from thirty feet away.

David made up his mind and stepped out of his car. The man in plain clothes ambled cautiously toward him.

"Need some help, sir?" the tall man said.

"Are you Frank Dugan?" David asked.

"Who wants to know?"

"I'm David Hapburg. I drove here from Michigan to talk to him."

"Come inside," the tall man said. "I think he'll want to see you."

*　*　*　*　*

David Hapburg passed through the metal detector escorted by the tall man, who introduced himself as Frank and directed him to the department's conference room. Frank closed the door and gestured to a chair on the far side of rectangular table. David lowered himself into the seat.

Frank sat facing David and folded his arms. As was his habit in this room, Frank waited for the guest to speak first. Most of his guests here were people you wouldn't let in your yard, let alone your house. He didn't regard David as a suspect, but old routines in the box died hard.

"I met your grandfather when I was a kid," David said. "He came to Detroit to visit my granddad and watch a Tiger's game. They were playing the Orioles that day. He was a nice man. Gave me a dollar. A silver certificate. I still have it tucked inside the baseball cap I was wearing that day."

"William was a special man," Frank said. "We didn't ask you to come all this way to tell us that. Why did you drive? We told you we'd pay for airfare."

"I know. The offer was more than generous. Truth is, I hate flying. And I wanted to visit my sister in Pennsylvania on the way back."

"In Lancaster? The one with the furniture store?"

"Yeah. She said she talked with you. Said you were nice."

"I asked you to come here to talk to me about your grandfather," Frank said. "I thought it was important that we meet. What can you tell me about him?"

"Yeah. It actually felt good to know someone else knew about this," David said. "Best I can remember from what my dad told me, was that in the

253

'40s, my grandfather worked with your grandfather on several government programs. The Manhattan Project and others. One of the projects was top secret and named the Omega Formula."

Frank leaned closer to David and placed his elbows on the table.

"I don't know much about it," David said. "Just what my dad told me. And when he died, he left me a weird letter, and a poem that had some connection to it. My grandfather was an explosives expert on the highest military level."

David removed an envelope from his jacket's inside pocket.

"He left me this," David said and pushed the envelope across to Frank.

"How did your dad die?" Frank said, opening the envelope.

"He was allergic to bee stings. He apparently got stung by one and died of anaphylactic shock."

"When did that happen?"

"In February. He'd just turned 60."

Bees sting people in February? In Michigan?

"Sorry for your loss."

Frank read the contents of David's envelope. The letter from Simon was strikingly similar to the one he'd received from William after Joe died. The attached poem was identical to the one stapled to the photo Frank had. He glanced at the first stanza.

Men wish to swing in their seventies and fly with eagles,
  like boys who dream of playing on the moon.

The bottom of the letter showed Hapburg's Detroit address, as well as William's at Elm Terrace.

"I had this same poem," Frank said.

"I saw you on TV. Heard what they said."

"What's your take on it?" Frank asked.

"I never saw the film those reporters asked you about. So I'm not sure about that, but my father told me the formula was for real. That it exists."

"How'd he know for sure?"

"My granddad told him so. Why would he lie about something that'd already done its job? I mean, the Japanese surrendered, didn't they? The war was over."

"Where does that leave us?" Frank said.

"I don't know about you and me, but there's a guy who's pretty interested in finding out about this Omega Formula. It's the reason I agreed to come here. He's paid me visits. Asked a lot of questions."

"A lot of people want to know about it. They'll come after you. I got people dogging me about it too. The *Today Show* and *Good Morning America* wanted to interview me. I'm plastered all over the supermarket checkout rags. Every agency that viewed the film has interrogated me. The military, of course, then Homeland Security, NSA, CIA, FBI, even the ATF. I thought it best to tell them the truth. I know nothing, and I think the Omega Formula film was invented as a hoax, an elaborate trick."

"Some folks aren't buying that," David said. "Especially this guy who's bugging me."

"You know this guy?"

"From the old neighborhood. Went to the same school until tenth grade when his folks moved. He used to hang out with me and the kids I knew."

"What's he like?" Frank asked.

"The school bullies picked on him a lot, pushed him around. He was kinda easy to make fun of. Little weird, but a nice guy, smart, good in sports, but his old man embezzled money where he worked and served jail time. Got him razzed and beat on by the school toughs, and left the family bad off. Got so bad they had to move away. He came by the old neighborhood a few years later. He was in med school on a scholarship. The kid was no dummy. But I think he had to drop out before he finished his residency when the money ran out. I hadn't seen him in years, but lately he's been back. He's changed. Not the fella I knew in school. Now the guy kinda gives me the creeps."

"What's his name?"

"Cezar Nicolai. American, but his parents were Romanians, I think. He did a stint in the navy, and for a while I got postcards from him. From all over. Cool places like Greece, Saudi Arabia, and

Denmark. Then I lost track of him. Last I heard he landed a job with the government."

"What does he know about the Omega Formula?"

"Probably not much more than I do, and I don't know diddley about it. The poem makes absolutely no sense to me. Truth be known, I have trouble figuring out my phone bill."

"Listen to me," Frank said. "Don't give this guy the time of day. Nothing. If this thing is for real, imagine it getting into the hands of a foreign government, or a terrorist group, or a maniac with a hard-on about America. Jesus."

"Well, … I'm afraid it's a little late to bolt that barn door."

"What's that mean?"

"I gave Cezar Nicolai a copy of the letter… and the poem."

Chapter 35

After an exchange of contact information, Frank walked David out to his Jeep.

"Sorry I blew up in there. Feel up to going someplace for a drink?" Frank said.

"Thanks, but I don't drink, and I need to see my sister and get back to Detroit."

"Look, I want you to have this," Frank said and handed David a DVD. "It's a copy of the Omega film. Everybody else in the universe has seen this, so I figure you should too."

"Be nice to finally get to see it."

"Have a safe trip, and watch out for the speed trap out on Route 76 right before you hit the interstate."

"I will, thanks," David said and slid into the Jeep. "By the way, I just remembered something else my dad said about the Omega thing."

Frank moved close to the car.

"The formula is written on a piece of parchment-kinda paper and rolled up and tied with a red ribbon, like a little tiny diploma," David said. "A roll maybe five, six inches long."

"I'll remember that," Frank said and closed the driver's side door. "Can I give you money for gas?"

"No, I'm good."

"Take this anyway," Frank said and tossed three twenties onto David's lap. "I appreciated you sharing your knowledge with me."

"Even the bad news?"

"Bad news is why I have this job."

*　　*　　*　　*　　*

Back in the building, Frank banged his way into the men's room and splashed cold water in his face like it was on fire. He tried to imagine the implications of yet another hunter having clues to the possible reality of the Omega Formula. He placed his hands on the sink, leaned toward the mirror, and gazed at his drawn face.

The men's room door swung open and Greg Martinez barged in.

"Roland's asking for you," Greg said. "Could be something serious. He never even touched the calzone I brought him from Scaldetti's."

Frank plodded to Roland's office and stood in the doorway, his tight lips and lowered eyebrows telegraphed his discontent as he glared at Roland.

"Close the door," Roland said.

Frank closed the door and plopped into the chair in front of Roland's desk.

"What's up?" Frank said.

259

"Got a call back from Mark Hollenbeck in Maryland. Had a team of his insiders gather us some information," Roland said and paused.

"And…"

"Your boy Chernac can't be Anton Chernac of the National Security Agency."

"Why so?"

"'Cause Anton Chernac's been dead for over three years."

Frank stared blankly at the ceiling, then closed his eyes.

"Died in the Middle East, maybe Iran," Roland said, "During some covert, black ops shit. They even held a retirement party for the guy, then sent him on the mission. The idea was that no one would suspect him to still be active. He could be a ghost operative with a new identity, and get into places the old Chernac couldn't. Turns out, he got into pretty sensitive quarters, and started sending the NSA some sweet intel, but then his encrypted messages stopped. They never recovered his body, but Mark Hollenbeck says the CIA has a film of him being shot, execution style. NSA's kept the whole thing under wraps, like everything else they do."

"Then who's the guy who's been bulldogging me?"

"'That,' said the elephant as he shat in the road, 'remains to be seen.'"

Frank moved to the window and stared out at the tops of the palms surrounding the parking area.

"In your encounter with this guy, did he ever leave any prints, any DNA?" Roland asked.

"I didn't sleep with the bastard. I don't know—"

"Think, damn it," Roland said and pounded on his desk so hard the calzone jumped off its paper plate.

"He wore gloves, wrapped around a Makarov. I wasn't gathering evidence. I was trying to survive him."

"By the way," Roland said, reaching into a desk drawer. "Your precious Browning's back from the Internal Affairs' dry cleaners."

Roland handed Frank the gun.

"Been two long weeks without her," Frank said and took the piece. "I don't understand why these things take so long to sort out."

"I want you back on days," Roland said. "Only thing lately that happens at night is it gets dark."

Roland pressed a button on his phone.

"Janis, send Rumbaugh in here when he gets back."

"Will do, sir," the pleasant voice of Janis said.

Frank rubbed his face with his hands.

"It's a long shot, but maybe he'll remember something," Roland said.

"He's lucky to remember where he lives," Frank said.

Roland glared at Frank.
"I said it was a long shot."

Chapter 36

The blare of Frank's desk phone speaker jarred his morning coffee time and peaceful thoughts.

"Dugan," Roland growled over the intercom. "I need a word."

Frank tramped to Roland's office and stood in the door.

"We got a call from an old codger in Jensen Beach. Says his neighbor just tried to kill his wife with a baseball bat."

"The old codger's wife? Or the baseball bat's wife?

"The batter's old lady," Roland said and handed Frank the address. "Take a drive and find out what's going on with these lovebirds."

"Sensitive as usual about serving and protecting, I see," Frank said.

"You know, police work ain't always them nice shoot-'em-ups you're so fond of."

"Why did I think I was a homicide cop. Must've been dreaming."

"Hear of anybody getting killed today?"

"Day's not over yet."

"No homicides, you take what comes up."

Frank bunched his lips and stared at Roland.

"Sounded like a he-slap-she-slap to me," Roland said, "but there may be some merit to the complaint. I'd send a couple of uniforms over there, but the guy who called said you know these people. Mentioned you by name."

"I'll check it out," Frank said.

"You look like two cents waiting for change. How 'bout some backup?"

"Who're you going to give me? Rumbaugh?" Frank said. "I can handle a couple of locals having a dust-up."

"Domestics can turn out bad as shootouts."

"They're overrated."

"Take the rookie, Burnett. He can use the experience."

"Watching me work is always edifying."

"God, it's nice to have you back," Roland said. "Try sleep tonight. Did I mention you look like shit?"

*   *   *   *   *

At 11:55 AM, Frank and 22-year-old Hollis Burnett arrived at the Perkins home just off NE Skyline Drive in Jensen Beach. The new officer drove his own cruiser and parked behind Frank's. Frank slid out of his car and stepped back to Burnett's.

264

"Stay put," Frank said to the young officer and walked up to the front door on the Perkins' portico. The Sandra Drive residence was quiet; no sounds from TV or radio, conversations, or fighting. He rang the bell and heard muted chimes inside the house. A pot-bellied man dressed in a dirty tee shirt and boxer shorts opened the door. The pungent aroma of fried country ham wafted out from inside.

"Good morning. Are you Albert Perkins?" Frank asked.

"I am. What can I do for you?" the sixty-plus man said scratching his three-day stubble.

"I'm Detective Frank Dugan from the sheriff's office. We received a complaint about an assault at this address."

"An assault? Who told you that?"

"Apparently one of your neighbors."

"Aggie," Albert yelled. "There's a police fella out here who says someone reported an assault. Know anything about that?"

A 250-pound woman dressed in a skimpy nightgown appeared in the doorway and looked at Frank.

"Only thing been assaulted here is a cured ham and a stack of pancakes," Aggie said and cracked a broad smile revealing a mouthful of wide-spaced, yellow teeth.

"Did Albert here hit you?" Frank asked Aggie.

"G'wan with you. Aw, hell no. This tub o' guts hits me, I send him to intensive care," the woman said and elbowed Albert's ribs.

"You mind if I come inside?" Frank said.

"Come on in, officer" Albert said. "We got nothing to hide."

The gauzy nightgown confirmed a lot of that statement, although Frank wished Aggie would've kept some things out of sight. Inside, Frank panned the living room. It was messy, but he saw no signs of a struggle. He glanced over at Aggie and noted her lack of any evidence of abuse.

"I guess someone is pulling a fast one on us," Frank said. "I don't see a problem here."

"Got plenty more ham and pancakes, if you'd like some," Aggie said.

"Oh, no thanks. I appreciate the offer, but I need to get back to the office," Frank said and sidled to the front door. "I stay here you'll make me fatter than I am."

"Who're you kiddin'? You look better than that Pierce Brogan feller in that *Thomas Crown Affair* movie," Aggie said and cackled.

"Who you think made that call?" Albert asked, opening the door for Frank.

"Don't know, but we'll figure it out," Frank said. "Sorry to bother you folks."

Frank left the house and crossed the street to his unmarked car parked a few yards down Sandra

Drive. As he stepped up to the driver's side to open the door, Frank saw people approaching in the reflection of his car window. In a second, he was surrounded by four buff-looking men dressed in sport jackets.

He knew immediately they weren't from Jehovah's Witnesses.

Chapter 37

Hollis Burnett tried to get out of his cruiser, but two of the men hurried over from Frank's cruiser and aimed guns his way. They forced him back into the car and took his service pistol before he could draw it. They got into the back seat of Burnett's car and closed the door.

A tall man wearing a Devil Ray baseball cap removed Frank's Browning from his shoulder holster and patted him down. The small revolver in Frank's ankle holster was found and taken. He also snatched Frank's cell phone from his waist clip and slid it into his breast pocket.

"Get in," he said as he nodded toward Frank's car.

"I was intending to," Frank said and climbed behind the wheel.

"And don't touch that radio," Devil Ray said, pointing with a gloved hand.

Devil Ray slid into the front seat beside Frank and pulled out a pocket-size Beretta and nestled it in his lap. A second man with sunglasses climbed into the back seat from the passenger's side. A fifth man approached Frank's window and stood outside the door. He was lean and wore his black hair slicked back straight without a hint of a wave. His matching black eyes bore in on Frank. It was the man who called himself Colonel Anton Chernac.

Frank rolled the driver's side window down.

"Detective," Chernac said.

"I was worried I wouldn't ever see you again," Frank said. "You never write."

"You'll need to follow the blue Mercedes up the street. My two friends in your car will help you to comply without straying far from our rear bumper. Clear?"

"What about my partner?"

"He'll be fine as long as you follow directions," Chernac said.

"I heard you died."

"An unfounded rumor, I'm sure."

"I'm betting this has nothing to do with this domestic call," Frank said and ran up his window.

Chernac walked several yards ahead of Frank's car and got into the blue Mercedes. A moment later the car pulled out and drove away. Frank started his engine and followed three car lengths back as they turned onto Skyline Drive and headed south.

* * * * *

The two-car caravan made its way down a dirt road into a forest thickly populated with Australian pines and stopped where the two tire-width ruts in the sandy soil ended. The men who rode in the cruiser stood by Frank as he got out and escorted him past a large abandoned house set back from the rutted road, almost hidden by overgrown hedges. They scuffed and waded their way through weedy grounds to a clearing deeper within the trees. A 40-foot recreational vehicle was parked at the center of the clearing. Chernac approached from the Mercedes with two of his men close behind. Devil Ray handed over Frank's cell phone and pistol. Chernac dropped the cell into his jacket pocket and tucked the Browning under his belt.

"I know you must regard these little meetings as tiresome, detective," Chernac said, "but I intend to obtain answers."

"You know as much as I know," Frank said. "How often do I need to say that?"

"Until I get the truth," Chernac said. "What you've given me so far does not add up."

Frank wanted to confront his captor about the death of his namesake and find out the real name of the impostor, but he knew coming from a position of weakness was not a good interrogation tack. He decided to play along with the charade for the time being.

"Look, Chernac, you work for the NSA, the U.S.A., right?" Frank said. "Let's say I knew how to make this Omega thing. Shouldn't that information be given to our government? To America's Defense

Department? What difference does it make who hands it over?"

"Therein is where we differ. I don't *give* anything away anymore. I sell things. I am at a point where I want financial security and the power to maintain it. I'd sell the weapon to the highest bidder."

"Okay, now that we've established what an unscrupulous mercenary you are, what do you want with me?"

"You're holding out. I strongly suspect you know exactly how to make this Omega formula work."

"What makes you think I have the scientific knowledge to put something like this together? I'm just a county cop."

"You grew up with a deeply involved, brilliant scientist. Some of his knowledge had to rub off."

"I had a grandfather who knew things, and died with them locked in his brain. You're pissing in the wind."

Chernac stared at Frank and gently shook his head.

Frank drifted over to the RV and leaned on its side. Chernac's men followed him and stood nearby. Chernac looked over at Devil Ray and nodded. The armed henchmen moved in on Frank and forced him into the RV.

"We going to Disneyworld, Anton?" Frank asked.

The inside of the RV was appointed like a suite at the LAs Vegas Bellagio. A big screen TV, a full bar, and beautiful wood décor revealed the handiwork of a high-end designer. The space smelled of fine leather in the cool air conditioning, and the reclining chair where Frank was deposited was baby's bum soft, buttery to the touch.

"We want what you know," Chernac said after he entered the RV and stood in front of Frank.

"Going to work me over?" Frank asked.

"Too primitive," Chernac said. "Modern interrogators use drugs."

A huge man entered the room from the rear of the trailer. He opened what appeared to be an eyeglass case and stepped behind Frank's chair.

The prick of a needle being plunged into Frank's neck made him twitch and soon his bright, Technicolor world faded to black.

*   *   *   *   *

The sandy ground was damp under the pine needles where Frank lay. His head was spinning. He tried to determine where he was, but his vision was not returning in hi-def, in fact, it wasn't returning much at all. His eyes were dilated to the point he could only perceive harsh, blurry glows, even in what he thought were night conditions. He couldn't make out distinct shapes and the gauzy brightness hurt his eyes. The light normally needed to clearly see objects worked against his perception. He was actually blinded by nebulous light.

Frank's hearing was fine, even sharper than usual. He heard men talking in the distance.

"What does the colonel want us to do with him?" a baritone voice said.

"He's done with him," a gravelly voice said. "He said to let him go and help him back to his cop car, but I think he can finger us. Look, the way I see it, the colonel took off and left us with this mook, so I figure it's up to us to dispose of any evidence."

"Where you want to do him?" baritone asked.

"Over that-a-way, off the road, in those high weeds," gravelly said. "Let's get to it. It's getting dark."

"I got trash bags in the RV," baritone said.

"I'll go get the car. Meet me here in five," gravelly said.

Frank started a desperate crawl in a direction he believed was away from the voices. He slithered for what he judged was about forty yards, then sensed salvation in the air. It was coming by way of his grandmother Emily.

He smelled cat pee.

Chapter 38

Frank felt his head bump the wooden steps and realized he'd made it to the front porch of the abandoned house, but he knew better than to try to hide inside. It would be the first place the killers would look. The smell of the box hedges reminded him how densely they grew. He scrabbled his way in between the thick bushes and the latticed crawlspace under the house. There were only a few inches of space, and forcing his body in tight behind the prickly hedge row gouged his face and hands. He pulled his body farther inward and upward until he was suspended off the ground between the thick wiry branches of the hedges and the front of the porch below the decking. Exhausted, he stopped moving and hoped it was concealment enough. He concentrated on controlling his heavy panting down to shallow puffs and waited. Perspiration flowed from his scalp and stung his scratched face.

Minutes later Frank heard the men again. They were hollering at each other.

"Why didn't you watch the guy?" gravelly said.

"I had to get them bags, moron," baritone said. "So don't be givin' me the red ass."

"I had to go get the goddamn car," gravelly said, "Where were the bags at? New Mexico?"

"Kiss my Alabama ass," baritone said. "Let's find this muvva."

Frank could hear rustling through the dry grass. The men's voices got louder, closer.

"Shit, he couldn't have gone far," baritone said. "The sonofabitch was loaded with drugs, and his cop car's still here."

"Yeah, but by the time we got back he could've hauled ass anywhere," gravelly said. "Maybe he caught a cab."

Both men laughed.

"What the hell, let's look in the house and around back," baritone said. "If he ain't there, fuck it, we go. If ole Chernac wanted him dead, he woulda done 'im hisself. He ain't payin' us extra to babysit his leftovers."

"Good enough," gravelly said.

The men clomped up the porch steps and later slammed doors inside the house. A minute later their voices were barely audible, maybe around the back of the house, Frank figured. A moment later the voices seemed to be coming from the left side of the house, moving toward the front.

"You look in the hedge?" gravelly said.

"Man, them bushes stink like panther piss," baritone said. "I ain't going in there."

The nearby weeds whisked under their passing steps. Frank held his breath until their sounds moved away and faded out completely.

275

Fifteen long minutes passed and Frank heard a car's engine start and drive away down the rutted road. When he no longer could hear the car, he clawed his way out from behind the pungent shrubs that had saved his life.

Vision was returning, not perfect, but enough to see where he was walking without ramming into objects. Now he had to find his cruiser, if he still had one.

* * * * *

The radio in Frank's cruiser was spitting static and confusing phrases as Frank came to. His tongue felt like a cat had been grafted to it, but his vision was returning in longer flashes of sharpness with only an occasional blur. The involuntary nap had helped.

On the seat next to him were his cell phone and his Browning 9mm.

"Frank, answer your damn radio," the voice of Roland Brand demanded.

Frank fumbled with the microphone and pressed it against his mouth. "I'm here, Chief."

"You don't sound good. You okay? We locate you somewhere five miles west of Jensen Beach."

"I'm okay. I'm in a woods. Lots of pine trees. Pretty place."

"A bunch of pine trees are pretty. You okay to drive? Sounds like you tied one on."

"I'm not drunk, damnit. Where's Burnett?"

"He's not here. Thought he was with you."

"He's not, but I'm okay. I'll be there. Give me a few minutes. I'll be there."

Frank started the car and followed the road. He traveled for more than a mile and came out on a road announcing he was in St. Lucie County. He headed southeast, crossed the Martin County boundary, picked up U.S. 1 and rolled toward Stuart, shoulder gravel stinging the undercarriage regularly as he struggled to stay alert and pilot the car between the lines.

He spotted a convenience store off the highway, pulled into a parking spot in front of the entrance, and banged his car hard into a guard post. He called in his location to the station and clambered out of the cruiser. He was desperate for water as he galumphed into the store in a fog, but awake enough to realize that back on the road he'd be no better than the worst drunk he'd ever pulled over.

He'd get water and some coffee and soon feel like his old self. Cops were on the way.

My guys are coming to get me. I'll be okay. I'll be oh-kay.

Frank collapsed on top of the ice cream box and slid down its stainless steel side. He never felt the floor that rose to accept him.

*   *   *   *   *

Roland was talking on the phone when he saw Frank stumble into his office, followed by the two deputies. Frank caromed off the wall and bumbled his way toward Roland's desk.

The deputies rushed to Frank and steadied him.

"I'll call you back," Roland said and hung up.

Frank swayed in front of Roland's desk.

"I send you out on a domestic and you stroll back nine hours later," Roland said. "You look like shit. You get laid? I hope so. In nine hours you could've knocked off a piece in Key West."

Roland grabbed his Stetson and jammed it on his head.

"And you two," Roland said glaring at his officers. "Why the hell wouldn't you take him directly to the hospital? You bring him here to give him a sobriety test?"

Frank grinned and his eyelids blinked like slow caution lights. A second later, he crumbled into the arms of the two deputies.

Chapter 39

Roland and Greg stared at Frank's unconscious body on the hospital bed.

"He's been drugged," the young doctor at Martin County General said. "He's resting now. His vitals are good."

"Drugged?" Roland said. "With what?"

"Lab results will tell us for sure," the doctor said, "but it looks like a strong sedative or even an anesthetic. His eyes looked like they may have been dosed with a mydriatic."

"What the hell's that?" Roland said.

"Dilating drops the ophthalmologists used to put in patients' eyes to check for glaucoma. They use a puff of air now."

"They kidnap him and then give him an eye exam?"

"Probably used it to impair his vision. Marijuana can create a similar symptom. Even Viagra, but then you get a very different side effect. He take any drugs to your knowledge?"

"Only drugs Frank takes is scotch with a beer back."

"They probably used it so he couldn't give chase when they left," Greg said.

"You're awfully goddamned smart. You pushing for detective, Martinez?" Roland said.

Greg smiled.

"Look at his face," Roland said. "Looks like country roads on MapQuest."

"A few scratches and bruises, nothing serious. His body seems to be in good shape. We'll keep him here tonight for observation. I think he'll be okay to go home tomorrow. You can come back later to talk to him, if you like."

"Much obliged, doc," Roland said.

The doctor left and Roland and Greg moved into the corridor outside Frank's private room on the second floor.

"You stay here and keep an eye on him," Roland said. "If you see anyone suspicious snooping around, haul 'em in. If you can't hook 'em up, shoot 'em."

"Right, sheriff," Greg said and took a seat on a bench in the hall near Frank's door.

"You need anything to eat, send out for it and tell them to bill the sheriff's office. They give you any shit, tell 'em we may be a mite slow responding to their next emergency."

"I should tell them that?"

"Hell, no. I'm just shooting off my mouth 'cause I'm pissed."

"Go on home, sheriff. I'll be here for him."

"I'll be back around eight."

Roland walked to his cruiser in the parking lot and sat behind the wheel. He moved the car where he could spot anyone entering the lot from the street, as well as anyone going into the main entrance of the hospital. He rolled down the windows and slid down on the seat and pulled his Stetson down low on his eyes.

Hours later, the thick perfume of the night blooming jasmines enveloped the car. It was going to be a long wait. He studied the hospital doors and the lighted windows and tightened his lips. An occasional nurse or orderly passed by the glass. If anyone entered that hospital intent on harming Frank, Roland Brand would make sure he left in a body bag.

*　　*　　*　　*　　*

At 9 o'clock the next morning, Frank protested being wheel-chaired out of Martin County General, but gave in to hospital policy and let Greg Martinez roll him to the department SUV. Frank felt tired as he climbed in, half-dressed with wild hair. Greg drove out onto Ocean Boulevard and continued east toward Frank's house on Stafford Drive, while Frank rummaged through the bag containing his jacket, shoulder rig, and other items he'd opted not to wear home.

281

"I wonder who took my clothes off when they brought me in?" Frank said.

"The nurses," Greg said.

"God, I hope I hadn't crapped myself."

"If you had, wouldn't your dirty shorts be on you now?"

"Good point. Nope, I did not crap myself."

"I'll turn the A/C up a notch, just in case."

"What happened after I left Skyline Drive with Chernac?" Frank asked.

"One of the jackoffs in Burnett's car took his cruiser keys and threw them into a neighbor's back yard, across from the Perkin's house. The neighbor said he got a fair look at him, for what it's worth."

"You won't ever see those men again. Protected by the government, anyway."

"The government authorizes kidnapping?" Greg said. *"Our government?"*

"Yeah, our government's perfect, all right," Frank said.

"How about murder?"

"What do you mean, murder?"

"Roland didn't want to tell you this at the hospital, but Burnett's dead."

"The new kid?"

"They shot him. We found his body in his cruiser."

"Good God almighty."

They spent the rest of the ride in silence until the SUV came to a stop in front of Frank's driveway.

"Roland wants me to stick around and keep an eye on you," Greg said.

"I'll clean up and we can get to the office," Frank said and stepped out of the SUV. "By the way, where's my car?"

"The boys found it in the hibiscus bushes behind the department parking lot."

"I gotta have those brakes checked at the motor pool."

"You were out of it, Frank. Your car only needs a couple of headlights. And we'll plant new bushes," Greg said as he adjusted his rear view mirrors and checked the street behind him.

"Rats," Frank said.

"Your cruiser's fine," Greg said. "I'm just messin' with you. Trying to cheer you up. The deputies drove your cruiser back. They weren't going to let you near a steering wheel last night."

Frank dug out his keys, opened the door, and entered the house. Thirty minutes later he came out dressed in khaki slacks, a red golf shirt, and Nike cross-training shoes. His gun and phone were clipped to his belt.

"Remember that stage play my grandfather challenged me to find?" Frank said as he climbed into the SUV. "The one with *Les Miserables* in it?"

"Oh, yeah?" Greg said. "Don't tell me you found it."

"Not exactly. It's in a movie I saw on TV. *Watch on the Rhine,* based on the play by Lillian Hellman."

"So who says anything about *Les Miserables* in the movie?"

"Paul Lukas, the actor. Won an Academy Award in 1944 for his performance as the Kurt Muller character, the father of the kids he says goodnight to. You have to watch it yourself. The scene is a piece of pure art, poetry."

"I will. I'll search it on Netflix."

"By the way," Frank said, "the Stuart Playhouse is putting on Hellman's play next month. I plan to go see the stage version."

"*You* are a theatre buff?"

"I'll have you know I was one of the better actors in my class at USC. Played lead in a bunch of plays. Should've stayed at it. Gone to Hollywood."

"Roland is always saying you're a heck of an actor. Um … or was that *bad* actor?"

"Maybe a little of both. Now, fire this mother up," Frank said as he shut the car door and locked on his seat belt. "I need to find me a whole cast of *bad* actors."

*   *   *   *   *

Roland Brand waited for the phone to ring on the other end of his call then hit the speaker button. He tilted back in his leather desk chair.

"Hollenbeck," said a business-like male voice.

"Mark? It's Roland."

"Roland who?"

"Roland Brand. How many damn Rolands do you know, boy?"

"Roland. How the hell are you, brother?"

"Here's the deal. We got us an a-hole from NSA thinks he's God almighty and can ride rough-shod over one of my detectives, and now the bastard's killed one of my young deputies."

"My God, Roland, what can I do to help?"

"One of my top detectives is in this guy's crosshairs."

"Would that be Detective Dugan?" Mark asked.

"Yeah, you met him. The guy we want is in deep shit up to his eyeballs for kidnapping, and now murder, among other charges. Just killed my unarmed young lad while he sat in his cruiser. Sonofabitch claims the name Chernac, Colonel Anton Chernac. But we both know the real Chernac is dead. This guy says he's in an upper echelon with NSA. Maybe a covert operative. I personally don't care who the hell he says he is, but I know he can't pull the crap he's been pulling. False imprisonment, harassment, battery, torture, illegal drug use, on top of the kidnapping and murder. So would you kindly dig me up some intel on this dingleberry so I can formally charge him and put him away?"

"We'll get you whatever we can. Got a picture of him?"

"No. Black hair, dark eyes, black mustache, tall, athletic, mean as a cross-eyed badger. Works with a huge bastard about six-eight, 350. May be a free rover, off the grid."

"Not a lot to go on, but I'll do what I can."

"Sorry to blow off this way without so much as a howdy-do, but this phony's come into my house and is messin' with my family. Let's have us a nicer chat soon."

"Look forward to it."

Roland hung up the phone and looked out his open door and into the outer office. Everyone in sight was staring back at him in total silence.

Chapter 40

Frank scrolled through data from the National Crime Information Center as Roland walked up to his desk and leaned in close.

"FYI, Oliver Smoot gets his ticket punched tomorrow."

"Tomorrow? He hasn't been scheduled," Frank said.

"Yeah, well, he passed on any further appeals and wants to get on with it."

"Damn. I need to talk to him. I thought I could see him next week."

"Well, you'd better update your plans if you want to see him while he's above room temperature."

"I'll call Union Correctional today. Maybe I can get to see him today."

"What's with wanting to see that murdering sonofabitch?" Roland said.

"He was also a college professor. A bright teacher, but he had another talent."

"Like what? Mayhem?"

"Forgery."

"I don't get it."

"I need him to do a piece of creative writing for me," Frank said as Roland pulled out a department business card from his wallet.

"Use this. Ask for Walt Peddicord," Roland said and flipped the card on Frank's desk. "Tell him you work for me. He's the new warden."

*   *   *   *   *

Frank wasn't looking forward to the nearly five-hour drive north to the Florida State Prison, a sprawling complex, which covered over fifty acres across Union and Bradford Counties. The former FSP-East Unit was originally part of the state prison in Raiford, now known as Union Correctional Institution. Regardless of what they called it, Frank knew it was no Grand Hotel.

Frank had wanted to talk to Oliver Smoot ever since his second encounter with Chernac, and figured he could stop to see him on his next trip to Maryland. In about 24 hours that would be way too late.

Smoot had been a college drama teacher, in fact, a professional stage director with a PhD from Carnegie Mellon, who enjoyed wielding power over people. He rose to chairman of the drama department at the University of Florida in Gainesville, but he soon tired of telling actors what to do on stage and evolved his talents into a second occupation. He opened a private office away from the college and offered discreet counseling to people who wanted to learn to be more assertive and more in control of their lives. In truth, he was only interested in killing his clients to observe their mental condition as he administered his custom brands of death.

While he was extremely careful about covering up his connections with his victims, when several people disappeared in Martin County, he drew the attention of the local police. Roland Brand assigned Frank to investigate their suspicions.

Smoot had repeated his grisly experiments on more than 15 victims before Frank volunteered to be one of his subjects, and quickly became one of Oliver's favorites. Smoot made the mistake of trusting Frank, and proudly showed him photos of his former handiwork moments before he planned to add him to his growing toll of bodies. Frank, who had been stripped of any weapons, was led into one of Smoot's private chambers where the doctor tried to put restraints on him so he could experiment on his predictably unwilling patient. Frank was not only unwilling, he resorted to a primitive defense technique and knocked Smoot out cold with a solid right cross to the unwilling side of the doctor's head.

Smoot was similar in many ways to Chernac's imposter, and Frank believed he might be able to shed light on complicated personality aberrations, and even motivations used by actors. But that was not the only reason Frank wanted to see him, even though he'd be happy to accept any bonus help the diabolical killer could provide. Frank knew Smoot had a special talent; a talent he needed. The question was: *Will he agree to share his talent with the man who'd put him away?*

In a few hours Frank would know.

*   *   *   *   *

The Union Correctional Institution loomed up ahead as Frank drove toward the gate. It was the only maximum security lockup in Florida and it housed most of the death row inmates for the state. Even in daylight it was a scary place to imagine taking up residency.

Officials met and processed Frank for entry into the highly secure section of the men's death row, and soon he was led into the austere cellblock that contained inmates awaiting the final resolution to their sentences. Frank was escorted by two linebacker-size guards past several over-built steel doors before they stopped at a cell about midway down the row.

"I know you got this visit cleared with Warden Peddicord, but are you sure you prefer to meet with this man in his cell instead of in the visiting room?" the ranking guard said and motioned toward Smoot's door.

"I'll be fine, officer," Frank said.

The guard opened the door of Oliver Smoot's cell, checked out the inside carefully, and bid Frank to enter.

"We're required to be present, detective," the guard said. "We'll be right outside the door keeping an eye."

"I understand," Frank said and stepped into the cell.

Oliver Smoot was a small man with thin gray hair that barely covered his scalp. His true age was exaggerated by his ashen skin and sunken eyes, and his prominent cheekbones made him look more like a concentration camp survivor than a prison inmate. He looked up from his bunk where he lay, staring at Frank through his horn rim glasses.

Frank stood in front of Oliver while the guard retreated, secured the door, and joined his fellow officer in the corridor. Even though Smoot was not being interrogated like one of Frank's typical suspects, he waited for the inmate to speak first.

"Detective Dugan," Smoot said and sat up.

"Doctor Smoot."

"Come to see the fruits of your work?" Smoot said.

"No. Came to pick that warehouse of horror you call a brain."

"Haven't lost your gift of charm, I see," Smoot said. "So you want to give a final exam to the professor. That may take some doing."

"I could use your help with a case I'm working. Involves a man not unlike you. Smart, crafty, an alpha type with an inordinate desire for power and control."

"Ah, I like him already."

"You'd need to fight him to be the lead dog."

"If you'll remember, I killed all the other lead dogs I knew. Then I took their followers."

"All but one."

"All but one," Smoot said. "But I reigned as king for quite a time."

"And here you sit."

"An undeniable point. What do you want to know about this man?" Smoot said, rose, and walked the two steps to the stainless steel toilet and peed. The smell of urine wafted to Frank's nostrils as he leaned on the wall near the cell door.

"Seems he's bent on great power and limitless money. Strange thing is, this guy's almost personable."

Smoot buttoned up and sat back down on his bunk across from Frank.

"Sounds like a sociopath," Smoot said. "Personable? Napoleon and Hitler had their personable sides. Many people loved and adored them. Does your man seem to have any compassion for those he targets?"

"None I can see. I doubt he's a stranger to using whatever it takes to get what he wants."

"Sociopaths and psychopaths are almost identical. They have no moral compass, never feel remorse for their acts. Products of a deprived or abused childhood perhaps. Whatever the psychopath wants, he feels he has a right to, regardless of who gets hurt in the process. He almost never accepts blame for his actions, and never apologizes. A few of these types are relatively harmless, but a true psychopath, driven with a need to control and wield power, is another story altogether."

"And murder?" Frank said.

"If he finds that killing will work to his advantage, he'll murder without regret or afterthought."

"Is that a force that drove you?" Frank asked.

"To be a good theatre director one must be a student of psychology. A director armed with knowledge of one's inner thoughts and private desires could gain control over the mind. Trouble was, I also wanted the power. Not simply power over actors in plays, but over lives on the stage of life. I'm sure you know the timeless cliché: money corrupts, but *power* corrupts absolutely."

"What do you think about tomorrow?"

"Death? It's over-feared. It's an eternal sleep. Peaceful. Painless. Shakespeare said: 'That which is so universal as death must be a blessing.'"

"I commend your courage."

"Life's a long process of getting tired. Tomorrow, I'm going back to the timeless nap I was taking before I was born."

"No belief in God, heaven?" Frank said.

"Detective, where I'm going tomorrow *is* heaven."

"I realize this is the eleventh hour to ask, but is there anything I can do for you?"

Oliver placed a finger on his lip and gazed at a photo of a young girl taped on the wall.

"As a matter of fact, you can," Oliver said and stood. "Incredible as it may sound, I have a daughter. Helen Darby. She lives in Salerno, near you in Stuart. Perhaps you could stop by and tell her I always loved her. She won't be here tomorrow. She hates me for what I did, especially since I came to Martin County to do my work and be near her."

Smoot paused and peeled the photo off the wall and handed it to Frank.

"I always called her Hellie when she was a little girl. She liked that. It was something special between us, back when she called me Papa and kissed me goodnight. Back before I went... amoral."

"I'll find her," Frank said and tucked the photo into his jacket.

"Exquisite," Oliver said and, for the first time in his visit, Frank saw the condemned man's bright white teeth.

"There's one more thing I'd like to ask of you," Frank said.

"Name it."

Frank reached into his back pocket and withdrew several pieces of paper and unfolded them on the bunk. One was the letter Frank had received from the law firm, the one written in William's classic handwriting.

"I remember you were a superb forger in your heyday."

"Yes. Loved graphology. I once penned a copy of the Declaration of Independence. It could well be the one on display in Washington," Smoot said.

"Well, I need you to write one more of your lovely deceptions."

"Ah, to be useful one last time," Smoot said and smiled.

"Here's the handwriting I need copied and here's what I need it to say."

Frank took two more letter-size papers from under William's letter and handed them to Oliver. Smoot studied the genuine letter, then read the words Frank wanted transcribed.

"Piece of cake," Smoot said and picked up a clipboard from under his bunk. He made a few practice strokes on a note pad clipped to the board then went to work on the blank piece of aged paper with the fountain pen Frank had given him. The pen flowed out its words in wet, royal blue strokes, and Frank marveled at the precision of Oliver's easy and perfect penmanship. It was as though William himself were guiding the nib.

The sun was setting on the prison as Frank left the complex. It was also setting on Oliver Smoot's life.

How could the man I just left be so evil?

When Frank was ten years old, his mother told him something about evil he never forgot.

"The devil is not a red man with horns, a pitchfork, and a pointy tail. He is one of the most attractive persons you'll ever meet. He'll be the best liar you'll ever encounter, and you'll want to believe every word he says."

His mother's words had aptly described Oliver Smoot…and another man. An attractive man with an *ad hoc* army of believers; a man who called himself Colonel Anton Chernac.

Chapter 41

Cezar Nicolai sat in the Tresor Penthouse in the Fontainebleau Hotel, studying a paper lying before him on an elegant cocktail table. After a few minutes he gazed out the eastern windows of the sumptuous suite. His view from the 37th floor overlooked the blue-green Atlantic Ocean and a transverse view of Miami Beach and beyond.

"This Omega riddle is not an easy one, Vladimar," Cezar said. "What does 'Men wish to swing in their seventies and fly with eagles' mean to you?"

The huge body of Vlad Torok lounged on the white leather sofa in the great room. His eyes followed a biplane, a few hundred feet above the beach, towing an ad banner past the hotel.

"Men in their seventies...flying with eagles...? Maybe it has to do with older men getting pilot licenses and flying their own planes."

"What would that have to do with a weapon? The way it could be delivered? You may be on to something. Small deadly aircraft... Although that plane outside, with its unsolicited , annoying commercial, is not one of them."

"It's for the new country club in Key Largo. I thought you liked golf."

"This week, if all goes well, we may be taking out the boats for their test runs," Cezar said. "Do we have the personnel we need?"

"We do, sir," Vlad said. "Standing by."

"Good. You will captain both boats and manage the crew on the larger vessel. I'll be a passenger onboard, nothing more. No one should know who I am or what I'm doing there. All purchases will go in the name on the passport I had made up for you. Understood?"

"Yes, sir. Understood."

"Excellent," Cezar said and brushed back his straight black hair as he stood before a floor-to-ceiling mirror. "We meet with the sellers on Wednesday. Crude bunch, but what are you going to do?"

"I'll keep them in line, sir."

"I know you will."

Vlad's cell rang and he plucked it from his jacket pocket. Cezar stared at Vlad as he studied the phone's screen.

"The plane's ready. We can leave within an hour," Vlad said and returned the cell to his pocket.

"Tools onboard?"

"Tools are onboard, sir."

╫ ╫ ╫ ⚔ ⚔

Janis Geller strode into Roland's office and placed two papers on the desk in front of the sheriff, who held a phone to his ear. Roland casually glanced at the papers, acknowledged them as a portion of the many emails sent daily to his department, and nodded a dismissive thank you to Janis, who smiled and left the office. He was on hold in his call and began to scrutinize the email as he waited. The top page was from his friend Mark Hollenbeck in Maryland. The message portion read:

Roland,

Thought you might like to have a picture of the man you inquired about. It was in the Washington Post three years ago.

Best,

Mark

The email attachment was a copy of a newspaper article and photo showing several smiling people in an office setting. A middle-aged man in a business suit was centered in the picture with a small group surrounding him. The caption over the article stated:

**Anton Chernac retires from
the NSA after 20 years**

Beneath the photo were the names of the others in the picture.

Roland finally gave up on his phone call and hung up. He pressed a button on the intercom.

"Greg, come see me for a second."

In less than a minute Greg Martinez was standing in front of Roland's desk.

"Give this to Frank as soon as he gets in," Roland said, handing Greg the email from Hollenbeck. "I can't imagine it doing him any good, but give it to him anyway. You know what an info sponge he is."

"He does things his own way," Greg said with a smile and took the email from Roland.

"Do you know why killer bees, fire ants, and pit bulls are so dangerous?"

Greg shrugged.

"You can't reason with 'em. They do what they do no matter what. They're actions are automatic, instinctive. Frank Dugan's a lot like 'em."

"Amen to that," Greg said and left the office.

Roland knew that Frank's instincts had built up an arrest and conviction record for his department that had helped him win a landslide victory in the last sheriff's election. He also knew those same instincts had often put his detective in tight situations, like the one he was in now.

Helen Darby was watering her baked lawn when Frank drove up her gravel driveway in Salerno. The smell of the nearby fisheries filled the warm air, but not in an unpleasant way. It was almost inviting, like the aroma of a fresh catch displayed in the Publix supermarkets. It had you thinking of flounder or red snapper for dinner.

Helen was in her twenties with green eyes and flaming red hair. She shut off the water and put down the hose when she saw Frank step out of the cruiser. She waited for him to approach like she expected to be handed a summons or a warrant for her arrest.

"Hi," Frank said. "You must be Helen."

"I am," Helen said. "Is something wrong?"

"If you mean am I here on official business, no. I met with your dad yesterday."

"I saw on the news. He's finally paid for his crimes. About time, I'd say."

"I'm Frank Dugan."

"I know who you are. You're the man who arrested my father, and none too soon."

"He asked me to give you a message," Frank said.

"Yeah?"

"He said to tell you he always loved you."

"Little late for that."

301

"I sat with him for a while. We had time to talk. He smiled when he talked about you."

"He tell you why he did those awful things, and screwed up our lives, and murdered all those poor people?"

"Yes, and he owned up to his deeds, and wished he'd been a different man, and a better father to you," Frank said and forgave himself for the embellishment.

"He said that?"

"He did."

"Thanks for that. And for taking the trouble to come by," Helen said.

"He said he liked to call you Hellie."

Helen dropped her head down and stared at her feet.

"Call me if you need anything," Frank said and handed her his card. "Anything."

Helen stared at Frank, then at the ground.

"Thank you," Helen said and turned her back on Frank and strode into the house.

Frank sensed her abruptness wasn't meant as an affront. He watched her display of hardness dissolve, and he felt certain she just didn't want the detective to see her tears.

His promise to Smoot kept, Frank ambled back to the street.

The radio squawked as he neared his cruiser.

"Frank," Greg's voice said from the speaker, "Roland needs to see you. It's important."

Chapter 42

Frank arrived at the station and was surprised to see Special Agent Braewyn Joyce standing in the lobby.

"Getting anywhere with your grandfather's files?" Braewyn asked.

"No."

"Still think it was all a clever deception?"

"Yep. More than ever."

"Does that mean you're giving up on it?"

"It's a game. My grandfather never posed a puzzle to me that wasn't solvable."

"Suppose you discover there actually is a useful Omega formula?"

Frank stared at her in silence.

"Detective, if you think people are after you now, wait 'til they believe you're holding the secret to the greatest killing weapon on earth."

"Can't imagine it'd be a whole lot different."

"Who would be more important to an ancient warring nation?" Braewyn said. "The guy who has the ingredients to make gunpowder, but can't figure out how, or the guy who doesn't have all the ingredients, but knows how?"

"What would you do?"

"Hand off the knowledge to someone who can secure that kind of information. Someone who'll keep it safely in the hands of trustworthy people and a nation with moral integrity."

"Like the nation that dropped those atomic bombs?" Frank said.

"Better us than a faction governed by twisted fanatics."

"Well, this is all academic. I don't have the foggiest notion what William was pointing to in his files. Maybe he had Alzheimer's, or slipped into a psychotic state at the end of his life."

"Weren't you with him until he died?" Braewyn asked.

"Not every day. I checked on him once or twice a week. He was becoming more and more distant and introverted in his last months. He often wasn't the same man I knew as a kid growing up."

"Age snares us all in the end."

"What are you doing here, besides pumping me for info I don't have?"

"We're chasing down a lead we got on a foreign arms deal. May connect with your Omega weapon."

"In Stuart?"

"Miami."

"Who knows anything about the Omega formula in Miami?"

"I can't discuss this with you, Frank."

"Why the hell not?" Frank said. "I'm in the middle of this. Maybe I can help. Throw me a bone."

"I'll tell you this much," Braewyn said. "We got an anonymous call from a public phone we traced to Michigan. The caller said there was a man, besides you, who had information on the Omega weapon. Recommended we check him out."

"A man named Cezar Nicolai?"

Braewyn looked away.

"I have to go."

"The caller in Michigan was a fella named David Hapburg. He sound scared?"

"Please thank your sheriff for trying to get you in here to see me, and for his kind offer to lend me an office."

"And you chose our elegant lobby?"

"I was getting ready to leave when you showed up. You have my number should anything new come to light," Braewyn said and placed her hand on the door to leave.

"Yeah, I've got your number," Frank said.

Greg Martinez stepped into the lobby and handed Frank a sheet of paper.

"Roland said you might find this interesting," Greg said and left.

Frank looked at the paper and twisted his lips to one side. Braewyn took her hand off the door's panic bar and stepped back toward Frank.

"What's the paper?" Braewyn asked.

"Email from the office. Picture of Chernac at his retirement party. The *real* Chernac," Frank said and handed Braewyn the paper.

Braewyn looked over the copy and studied the photo.

"So that's Anton Chernac," Braewyn said. "Back when he was alive… with all his office buddies…and uh-oh… what have we here?"

Braewyn lifted the paper closer to her face and stared intently at the photo.

"What do you see?" Frank said.

"The woman standing at the right of Chernac, the one holding his arm. Caption says here her name is Ross… C. Ross."

"C. Ross? So what?" Frank said.

"Her hair is lighter and longer here, but…"

"What are you saying?"

"I knew a gal named Ross a while back who looked a whole lot like this one."

"So?"

"Her married name is Celine MacGowan."

Chapter 43

Long after Braewyn left, her words clawed at
Frank's insides. He'd have to delve into Celine's
past and find out who she actually was before
Alasdair came into her life. *My God, does Alasdair
know about her past?* Frank would start with
Celine's NSA years. *Why did she pretend she didn't
know Chernac? If she knew him, she had to know he
was dead. Why did she leave the NSA?*

Frank would need to call upon Roland's friend,
Mark Hollenbeck, to dig up more answers.

Frank didn't have a lot to go on regarding the
Celine Ross investigation, but his instincts told him
to lay out what he knew to Alasdair, in person, while
he had the chance. He didn't like going in with thin
suspicions based on even thinner information, but he
had to know what Alasdair knew, and his friend was
only a few miles north of Stuart.

*   *   *   *   *

Vero Beach was windy and cloudy when Frank
drove up to meet Alasdair after his dive. Gusts
hitting 30 miles per hour turned gentle waves into
churning whitecaps, still prominent even at twilight.

When Frank arrived, Alasdair was seated on a bench on the dock, a pile of equipment surrounded his feet.

"Well, where's all the treasure?" Frank said.

"No treasure yet," Alasdair said and stood. "But we verified the wreck site."

Alasdair began picking up his equipment.

"I'm amazed you guys go in the water in this weather," Frank said, hoisting up duffel bags of the dive gear.

"It's calmer down deep," Alasdair said, shifting the weighty duffle bag's strap, slipping off his shoulder. "It's a wee windy, not a big electric blow. Long as we can hook up a safe anchor line to guide us, we dive."

"You're a wee maniacal."

"That Chernac character still on your case?" Alasdair said as he plodded beside Frank down the concrete pier at the Vero Beach Marina.

"That Chernac character ain't Chernac. He's some other character who's still on my case."

"You're kidding," Alasdair said and shifted the hefty gear bag to his other shoulder.

"Celine ever talk about him?"

"She never discussed anything about her job with me. She was about to leave the NSA when I met her."

"And after she left?"

"She was still forbidden to discuss anything about her NSA work. What's with all the questions?"

"Fill you in later," Frank said. "I want to hear about the dive."

Frank felt his jacket pocket to make sure he still had the email photo of Chernac and Celine. He found it hard to believe that Alasdair could be involved in anything underhanded, and espionage had to be out of the question. He decided that the upcoming marina bar, after a couple of drinks, might be the best place to reveal his recent findings.

The two men trekked across the windblown parking lot toward the restaurant and bar that served the ocean-side marina and resort. A page from a tumbling newspaper whapped against Alasdair's leg and the strong wind held it there for several strides. Frank bent forward and low to protect his face from the biting, sand-laden gusts, which jostled his cell phone out of his shirt pocket. He fumbled the cell and watched it fly from his free hand and smash on the asphalt.

"Shit," Frank said as he bent over to pick up the plastic components of the phone skittering and blowing about in a six-foot radius. "The one time I forget my belt clip ..."

Alasdair clunked down his diving bags and helped Frank retrieve the scattered parts. He picked up a rectangular case piece and the phone's battery.

Frank gathered the rest and examined the pieces closely in the bluish, mercury vapor lighting of the parking lot. One of the pieces, a small round object, brought a frown to Frank's face.

"Since when has Verizon included bugs in their smart phones?" Frank said.

"What?" Alasdair said.

"A bug was in my phone," Frank said low, holding up the tiny bit of electronic technology for Alasdair to examine.

"A high tech one, at that. You've got to be kidding me."

"High tech?" Frank said. "You recognize this?"

"They're fairly common. Got over a mile range," Alasdair said. "I've used them in surveillance jobs. Someone could track your conversations almost anywhere. Who had a chance to plant that?"

Frank dropped the tiny transmitter on the asphalt and stomped it twice.

"God, anybody. When I was in the hospital, after I left my desk at the office, when…wait a minute. When Chernac, or whoever he is, drugged me in Jensen Beach. He kept asking me the same questions he had asked me before. Then I got popped with a knockout needle. It made no sense. But what does make sense is that he needed a chance to bug my phone. It was the perfect opportunity."

"There is one question that needs to be answered then," Alasdair said as Frank began re-assembling the phone on the bumper ledge of a pickup truck.

"What's that?"

"What's been said since the bug's been in your phone?"

"I don't know. A lot."

"Think, man. It could be important."

Frank snapped the halves of the phone case together and pressed a button to activate it. Miraculously, it came back to life with a melodious measure of digital tones.

Frank scrolled through his call log. He could see there were many conversations going back to his abduction, conversations he wouldn't want any third party to hear, nevermind an enemy.

*   *   *   *   *

Frank knew Alasdair needed to be told about Celine, even if it didn't turn out all rosy or productive. He sat his beer on the bar and took the email photo from his back pocket, unfolded it, and placed it in front of Alasdair. At first, Alasdair appeared to be puzzled about the significance of the picture, then he read its caption.

312

"What the hell," Alasdair said and jumped up from his stool knocking it backward. "You think my wife's in on your Omega hunt?"

"She knew Chernac. The real one. She told me, right in your house, that she never met him, But who's the woman in the photo holding his arm? She knew him all along."

"So what? Alasdair said. "That doesn't make her Mata Hari."

"It sure doesn't make her Mother Teresa either."

"I think you're jealous I found someone."

"Where's that coming from? You mean to marry? Hell, you fell in love with every woman who let you get to second base."

"It's better than your life, chasing one-night broads, or sitting home all alone having a wank."

"You know damn well why I haven't run to marry. I'm surprised you'd play that low card."

The bartender approached and eyed the two men.

"Everything okay, gents?" the bartender asked.

"Everything's fine," Frank said, never taking his eyes off Alasdair who stood tight-jawed and glaring at him.

"Put yourself in my place for a minute," Frank said. "How would you explain the problem I have with this?"

"I don't know. Maybe she forgot she met him. Even though she's in that photograph, she still might not know him. You've had your picture taken with people you didn't know. So have I. Proves nothing."

"I hope you're right and I'm wrong. The last thing I want is for this Omega crap to come between us. But he was the guest of honor at his retirement."

"I'll ask Celine about it."

The two men sipped their beers.

"I think that jealousy comment was out of line," Frank said.

Alasdair nodded. "Sorry for that. Anger talking."

"After Amy and the kids were murdered," Frank said, "the thought of another wife has never entered my head."

"It's been over ten years, lad."

"I'm not dead. I have desires. They just haven't pushed me to that first big move."

"You mean like asking a gal out?"

"Kissing a woman again. Really kissing her, like it means something."

Frank slapped a twenty on the bar and strode out of the marina restaurant and into the parking lot.

The one person in the world he could trust may now be involved with a person of interest. Frank felt Alasdair was wrong to misplace so much anger on the implications of the photo, but he also knew his friend was right about one thing.

Frank was alone now.

Chapter 44

Frank entered the sheriff's station and went straight to his desk. He stood near the back wall and let his eyes wash over the latest wanted posters.

"It's Saturday night, Frank," Carl Rumbaugh said. "You forget to stay home?"

"Crime's an eight-day-a-week job, in case that fact's eluded you," Frank said without facing Carl.

"You got a call from some guy in Michigan. Memo's on your desk."

Frank gathered up the stack of pink phone messages and thumbed through them until he came to the one from David Hapburg. He looked at his watch, then picked up the phone and dialed the number on the slip. The phone picked up in one ring.

"Hello," David said, caution in his voice.

"It's Frank Dugan. Are you all right?"

"Right now I'm okay. Not sure about later."

"What do you mean?" Frank said and sank slowly onto his desk chair.

"That guy I was telling you about. Cezar Nicolai. He just called me. Wants to come by, look for more of Simon's files. I found some new stuff you might find useful. I don't want him to get it."

"This guy been to your house?"

"A while back...he—"

"He ... *what*?" Frank asked.

"I don't know…maybe…there's no time—"

"Your message said you called the FBI."

"I'm scared this guy is going to kill me."

"He's not going to kill you. He thinks you have something he wants. Tell him you've given him all you have. Then tell him to hit the road."

"I'd like to, but he's—"

"He's what?"

"He's got some video tapes."

"Of what?" Frank said and wiped his forehead.

"We were stupid kids, you know, messing around."

"What's on those tapes?"

"Me and a couple of guys, you know, *experimenting*."

"You mean with each other? Sex stuff?"

"Uh, yeah, like that."

"Bad stuff?"

"A lot of stuff. Stuff you wouldn't want your mother to see…or your wife…or especially not your employer. Not anybody, really."

"So he's threatening to blackmail you. Have you seen them yourself? Are you sure he has them?"

"Oh, I'm pretty sure, 'cause he emailed me a little sample."

"Why didn't you destroy those things?"

"I totally forgot about them. It was years ago. We were watching the tapes along with other porn.

316

We were drinking and smoking weed. I don't even remember all we did. Screwing around like teenage idiots. Looks like he took the bad ones with him."

"How can I help?" Frank said.

"I'm leaving as soon as possible," David said. "Going away for a while. Took leave from work. Didn't tell anyone where. I want you to get these files and not Cezar. It's important that he never sees them, but I won't have time to send them to you. The tape sample came from Miami, but I think he's coming here to see me *tonight*. I think he's close to figuring out something. As I told you before, I don't know anything about this Omega thing, and I don't want to. But I know if there's anything to it, I sure as shootin' don't want this nutjob Nicolai to get his hands on it."

"I'll second that," Frank said. "You taking family?"

"The wife and I are separated. No kids. She lives in Lansing with her boyfriend."

"So what's the plan?"

"I don't trust this phone line, so let's just say I want to stick the files someplace safe. I'll leave you something to direct you to where they are. Remember our first conversation? I told you I was given something by a relative of yours, and where I put it?"

The phone was silent for a moment.

"Yeah...yeah, I do," Frank said.

317

"Find it."

"It's almost eight here. Nine where you are, right?"

"Right."

"I'll be there as soon as I can grab a flight. Probably tomorrow morning before I can get there."

"You still have my address?"

"I do. How will I get into the house?"

"Go to my neighbor to the right as you face my house. Red brick place. Tell her who you are. I gave her a description. She'll give you a key. Her name's Etta Nelson."

"Call me when you get settled."

"I will. Listen, Frank, I gotta fly. A car's pulling up near the curb. Not sure who it might be. I'm going to beat it out the back. Take care."

David hung up and Frank dialed the airport in Orlando. With luck, he might be able to catch a redeye, grab a nap on the plane, and make it to David's house by morning.

With luck, by morning David Hapburg might still be alive.

*   *   *   *   *

Frank would've given anything to have Alasdair with him on the trip to Michigan, for lots of reasons. To fill the empty hole in his stomach for one, and to have the best backup man in the business at his side should the going get unstable. But Alasdair was diving in Florida. This time he would have to handle things alone. His thoughts shifted to Braewyn Joyce and the FBI. Would they be able to pinpoint this arms deal in Miami? At least if they were working another angle on the case maybe they'd be staying off him and the Omega issue. He'd take any relief he could get.

At Orlando International, Frank identified himself and secured permission to carry his pistol in the suitcase stowed in the baggage section of the plane. He wasn't certain of what he was in for in Detroit. Having an "equalizer" would certainly be a comfort.

Frank caught a business charter and landed at Detroit Metro Airport before sunrise. He flagged a cab and headed out Route 94 to the city. Thirty miles and an hour later the cab drove down Lakewood Street where Lake St. Clair's narrowest neck meets the Detroit River. Hapburg's house had a partial view of the lake, but Frank could barely make out the mist-covered water at the pre-dawn hour. As the cab passed by Hapburg's house it was completely dark, not even a porch light was on. Frank retrieved his gun and an LED flashlight from his suitcase and asked the driver to park well past the house and hang close while he finished his business.

Daybreak darkness or not, Frank needed the key to Hapburg's house, so he light-footed up the steps of the red brick house next door, reached the door, but hesitated to ring the bell. The dead quiet made him want to hold down his breathing. *Maybe if I at least wait until the sun is up a little more it won't seem so damn early.* He leaned on the side porch railing and, to kill a few minutes, shined his flashlight over at David's front porch. He spotted something there that told him he wouldn't have to bother Mrs. Nelson.

The front door of the Hapburg house was wide open.

Chapter 45

David's front door had been pried open, the frame was splintered, and Frank's flashlight revealed deep gouge marks consistent with the uncaring use of a crowbar or a claw hammer. Frank double-checked his Browning to make sure a cartridge was in battery and held his 9mm ready. His heart rate moved into the nineties and adrenalin charged his muscles. He eased his right index finger onto the trigger and stepped through the dark doorway.

The interior of the house looked like a tank division had driven through it with winter treads. The place had been thoroughly ransacked. Drawers pulled out and thrown to the floor, sofa and chairs ripped open and flipped upside down, and rugs dragged to one side, baring the unscuffed hardwood beneath. The kitchen fared worse. The refrigerator was gutted, and every drawer and cabinet lay open with its contents dumped on the floor and in the sink. David might've been right about fearing the car that had pulled up to his curb.

The rest of the house was more of the same, but Frank wanted to find a single item, which, on its face, would not be a target for Omega formula hunters. He looked in the hall closet. Nothing. He checked the other rooms' closets and eventually came to a sparsely furnished upstairs room Frank thought might've once been a guest room. It was as austere as a monk's quarters, and had been hardly molested by the wrecking crew. The closet door was open, but inside there were only a few metal coat hangers dangling from a sagging wooden dowel, and the stifling smell of mothballs.

A banging noise had Frank peeking out from the closet, his gun up and aimed into the room. Nothing there looked out of place, nothing stirred. The banging noise returned, louder than before. This time he caught a glimpse of a shutter swinging outside the room's only window as it slammed into the frame and swung out of view. He took a deep breath and lowered the Browning.

Frank cursed at the possibility that the only clue to the whereabouts of Simon's files had already been taken. He started to leave when he noticed the door to the room slowly closing as he trod on one of the creaking floorboards on his way out. When the pivoting door revealed its interior side, Frank found what he'd been looking for. There, hanging by itself on a coat hook, was a Detroit Tiger baseball cap. He took it down and looked inside the crown. In the lining was a small envelope. In the envelope were two things: A note from David and a crisp, one-dollar silver certificate. A long ago piece of William's generosity had found its way home to his grandson.

David's directions in the note were terse. Apparently he had rushed to compose it before he fled from the house, but there was enough there for Frank to decipher its intent.

The cab parked directly in front of Saint Mary's church on Jefferson Avenue near Chalmers Street. Frank jumped out, hiked up the steps, and made his way into the main sanctuary of the cathedral. Inside, he looked for the stairway to the organ loft David had written was off the vestibule. He opened a door on the far side of the room and found the steeply ascending stairs and climbed them to the humid, musty room above.

David's note said the files would be in the organist's bench where sheet music was kept, and would be at the bottom of everything else in the compartment. Frank pulled up on the heavy walnut seat and opened it fully. There were stacks of sheet music, mostly hymns and Christmas carols. He dug down deep to the bottom and found a large manila envelope and took it out. He opened its metal clasp and found a single, letter-size sheet inside. Frank removed the paper and read its brief message.

Late again, detective. Too late to save your reputation, and too late to save the world.

* * * * *

Heading south was a Learjet 24 carrying Cezar Nicolai, Vlad Torok, and a manila file folder marked "Top Secret." The plane was descending from ten thousand feet above I-95 when it zipped past West Palm Beach, powering back to under 200 knots on a final heading to Miami International.

"Please buckle up, gentlemen," the pilot said over the plane's intercom. "We'll be on final approach to MIA in about two minutes."

"What time are we scheduled to meet Cardoza?" Cezar said as he secured his seat belt.

"One this afternoon, at the church," Vlad said. "He's bringing pictures of the properties."

"I hope they're each worth their reputed thousand words."

"I'll check the goods out in person if the photos pass your approval."

"And vet the crew," Cezar said.

"I'll see to it, sir."

"It's only one mission, but I want it to go off without any problems."

"Was the file of any use?" Vlad said and glanced at the manila folder between them.

"Perhaps in time," Cezar said, staring out at the approaching signs of civilization on the ground. "Cryptic. It's going to take work to unravel any meaning."

The beaches of Miami came into view outside Cezar's window. He took a notepad and a pen from the breast pocket of his Savile Row suit jacket and jotted a few lines.

"We're going to need more of those yellow nitrile gloves," Cezar said and handed Vlad a page from the notepad. "In both of our sizes."

*   *   *   *   *

"He knows who I am, goddamnit." Frank said. "And I don't know anything about him."

"Well, you've sure been visible enough," Roland said. "I bet people in Tasmania know who you are."

"How did this Nicolai connect the dots with me and Hapburg?"

"Hapburg could've told him. You said he was scared skinny of the guy."

"I doubt that Hapburg conceded that. He didn't want to help the bastard with any information he didn't have to."

"You said Hapburg was afraid his phone was bugged."

"I don't remember ever saying who I was in our conversation,…oh, wait a sec. Yes, I did. At the first part of the conversation I said, 'It's Frank Dugan, David.' Gave him all you'd need to find out the rest."

"He doesn't seem like your garden variety criminal, does he? Kinda smart."

"Cunning," Frank said and wandered over to the window and gazed outside. "Do I have any leave left."

"Here we go," Roland said. "Gonna leave us shorthanded again. It's like you work somewhere else and only drop in to visit us from time to time when you need to make a few long distance calls."

"Any comp time?"

"You've used your comp time up for the next decade. You've got a couple of vacation days left."

"I may need to go to Miami."

"Wonder why Hapburg didn't bring the files with him when he came down here to see you." Roland said.

"Well, unlike Mr. Nicolai, Hapburg's not the quickest rabbit in the warren."

"Speak English."

"I may no longer be the lead dog in this race."

Chapter 46

"No murders again today," Carl Rumbaugh said across the desk from Frank.

"You want murders?" Frank said. "Move to Chicago."

"Shift's not over for six more hours. Still time," Rumbaugh said and yawned.

Frank needed to talk to someone, and it wasn't Carl Rumbaugh. He needed to talk to someone he could trust about the latest findings on the Omega formula. Alasdair was out. Maybe it was time to reveal things to Braewyn Joyce. He'd promised her he'd convey any new information about Omega, but he hadn't intended to follow through on that. But now might be the time to at least toss her something. He needed advice from someone who wasn't part of the Dugan history, someone who could offer him an impartial opinion. He regarded the agent as a person posing a lot of negatives for his life, but he never thought of her as anything but honest. It was time for him to call the FBI for help, as strange as that would feel.

At noon Frank called Braewyn's cell.

"Special Agent Joyce," the familiar voice said.

"We need to talk," Frank said.

"Detective Dugan, what a nice surprise."

"I went to see Alasdair in Vero Beach and showed him the picture of Celine with Chernac. Didn't go so well."

"Alasdair is in Florida?"

"He's treasure diving in Vero Beach."

"You sure you want to talk to me?" Braewyn said. "I think you need a friend, not an FBI agent who's investigating you."

"I want to talk about Alasdair and Celine, and the Omega files. Can I meet with you somewhere?"

"I've got to stick around Miami. Know any place down here?"

"There's a bar on Biscayne in Lemon City. Blarney's."

"I'll find it. When?"

"Anytime after two hours from now."

"I've got an appointment around lunchtime this afternoon, but—"

"Afterward then. Two o'clock work?"

"See you there," Braewyn said and hung up.

Frank pulled himself together and prepared to seize what was left of the day. As soon as the cruiser was loaded and gassed up, Frank headed south on the Ronald Reagan Turnpike to Miami almost two hours away. His anticipation of talking with Braewyn was mixed. And that stone-faced Tom Gardner was likely going to be there, which added to his apprehension.

The small Catholic church was nearly empty of parishioners, and library-quiet, except for the occasional creaking of the few occupied ancient pews. Cezar and Vlad took seats in the back row of the left section near the center aisle and studied their surroundings. A couple of women prayed in the front rows in the right half of the sanctuary; a woman in black emerged from one of the two confessionals on the far right wall. A waiting woman on the right aisle rose from her pew and entered the vacated confessional. The place smelled of melted candle wax, and dust motes drifted weightlessly in the rays of sunlight penetrating stained glass panels depicting the Stations of the Cross.

"Where are they?" Cezar said, barely moving his lips. "It's one o'clock."

"I'm sure they'll be here, sir," Vlad said. "They were enthusiastic about the deal."

"I like people who keep their commitments. Like being punctual for appointments."

Cezar waved a finger at the disorganized missals and hymnals in the holders attached to the pew in front of him. Vlad immediately neated them up and glanced back toward the church entrance. Ten more minutes passed. Cezar looked sternly at Vlad, who rose and marched into the vestibule of the church. A few seconds later he returned, followed by three men dressed like extras from Al Pacino's version of *Scarface*. One of the men held a Panama hat in his hand and wore a tan sport coat with a loud floral shirt underneath. He carried an envelope tucked under his sweat-stained armpit. The other two men tagged along behind and carried baseball caps. Vlad led the trio to Cezar, who remained seated in the pew, staring ahead at the Corpus Christi above the altar.

"I am Miguel Cardoza, *senor*. I'm sorry we're late," Cardoza said to the profile of Czar's head, and sat down in the pew. "The midday traffic is brutal out there today. Must be the heat."

"Interesting. We had no trouble getting here at all," Cezar said and glanced at his Rolex.

Cardoza looked at Cezar and shrugged.

"You have photographs for me?" Cezar asked.

"*Si*, uh, yes, right here in this envelope," Cardoza said and opened the clasp envelope and handed it to Cezar.

Cezar looked through the 8-by-10 photos and stopped at one.

"This is the item from Cuba?" Cezar said.

"Yes," Cardoza said. "It's right off our coast as we speak."

"And the Viking yacht?"

"In the marina where I first talked with your man, Mr. T, here," Cardoza said. "*Your* Mr. T, the

330

one here with you, not the man on the television show. The slip number is written on the picture."

"And the papers?" Cezar said.

"On the boat in the marina," Cardoza said.

"We'll meet you at the boat later today, say five PM," Cezar said. "Will that time be convenient for you with all that pesky traffic?"

"We'll be there, sir," Cardoza said rising and backing out of the pew. "Five o'clock sharp."

Cardoza turned to his two associates.

"Cinco anoche, y en punto," Cardoza said with glaring eyes.

"If everything looks all right, we'll trade you bills for your boats," Cezar said. "*Mucho* bills."

"I'm sure you'll be happy, sir. You have the word of Miguel Cardoza. I selected these items myself. Top quality, I guarantee it."

Cardoza gave final bows and nods to Cezar and Vlad, and ushered his men out of the church.

"Like what you saw, sir?" Vlad asked.

"I did," Cezar said and shuffled the photos to one in particular. "Especially this one."

He displayed the photo to Vlad.

"If it sails as well as it looks, it'll be perfect, sir."

"I'll teach the crew how to man it, but they are only to know me as...let's use Grainger. My man in Amsterdam did such a lovely passport for me as a Mr. Leonard Grainger. After their lesson, I'll go over the offshore plan. Are all these men qualified divers?"

"Every one. I'll assemble the crews tomorrow if all goes well tonight."

"I sometimes wonder why I go in for these bizarre and expensive pastimes, but, then again, what's money for except to enjoy it? And right now I'd like to enjoy a Patron margarita."

"I know the perfect place," Vlad said.

"I knew you would, my friend," Cezar said sliding to the end of the pew and rising. "Afterward, we have to decide how we want to deal with the United States Coast Guard."

*   *   *   *   *

Moments after Cezar and Vlad left the church, Braewyn Joyce, wearing sunglasses, with a black scarf covering her head and most of her face, stepped out of a confessional on the right aisle. She checked her cell phone, pressed a few buttons, and placed it in her purse.

Braewyn left the church by the large double doors facing the street and descended the granite steps. She reached her Chevy Traverse parked a few yards down the street and bent slightly to retrieve her car keys from her purse. She opened the door with the keyless entry remote and felt something hard being jammed against the small of her back.

"Get in the car," the masculine voice said.

Braewyn slid behind the wheel. The man got into the back seat.

"Hand me your purse and gun," the man said. "Carefully."

Braewyn complied and swung her arm slowly into the back of the car and handed the man her purse and her Glock.

"Drive where I tell you and you'll be okay," the man said. "You need to talk to someone. Remember I have my gun at your back, and I also have your gun and cell phone. I'm not afraid of being in an accident, should you attempt that silly ploy. If you do, you'll die and I'll walk away. Not a smart strategy for a bright lady from the FBI."

"I'm doing whatever you say, mister," Braewyn said with robotic calm and started the car.

The man said, "Do you know how to get to the Fontainebleau?"

Chapter 47

Blarney's Irish Pub had a large rectangular bar with turned, dark wood posts at each of its corners running from the top surface of the bar to the ceiling. Numerous beer and ale taps ran in a line at one end of the bar, and a center island of liquor bottles displayed an assortment of libations set on three levels of shelves. Posters were framed and mounted on the walls all around the room's pub-height tables which boldly announced Guinness, Harp, and Jameson brands in colorful artwork. The place smelled of many mop-ups of spilled brews, with an occasional whiff of more pleasant aromas drifting out from the kitchen. Whenever Frank thought of his perfect setting for a bar, Blarney's always came to mind.

It was a minute before two and the pub was nearly full of late-lunchers, drinkers, and tourists, but Braewyn was nowhere to be seen. He allowed that he had arrived early and forgave her for being fashionably late. A pretty woman popping in early and alone at a touristy bar was often looked upon with wishful possibilities among men already there, lying in wait, and on their third drink. A smart woman who planned her lateness was an aware woman deserving of Frank's respect.

Forty minutes passed.

"Another Guinness," Frank said to the auburn-bearded bartender.

Frank took a Prince Albert tobacco tin from his jacket pocket and opened it. Inside was a folded piece of paper. He spread it out on the bar and stared at the strange mathematic symbols written on it. It was the equation Doctor Dekler had written on the college blackboard. Understandably, Frank could make no sense of it, and returned it to the tin box and put it back in his pocket.

As he had every day, Frank recited, in his head, the four-stanza poem from William.

Men wish to swing in their seventies and fly with eagles,
    like boys who dream of playing on the moon.
    Find someone to recount the sheep, avoid the deep six
    that rusts plain iron, and keep a tool as a rune.
    If need be loosed this awful power,
    it lies asleep until that hour.
    Sealed in a pipe all eyes can see,
    but blind to all, save you and me.

Frank deliberated over it every day. And he was sure he understood what part of it meant. He knew time was running short and struggled to grasp its larger meaning, the full solution to the Omega formula puzzle.

Frank's cell rang. He brought it straight to his ear.

"Well, it's about time," Frank said into the phone.

"Detective Dugan? It's Special Agent Tom Gardner."

"Agent Gardner. What's up?"

"Agent Joyce was supposed to pick me up at the office and take us to meet with you. That was over an hour ago. I've tried several times to get her on her cell, but it goes immediately to voice mail."

"She was supposed to meet me at two," Frank said. "I was about to call her myself."

"I had to work at the North Miami field office today. She told me she planned to follow a tip she got about some people we've been watching. I didn't want her to go without me, but I was needed here at the office, so she went by herself. That was around twelve-thirty. She sent me pictures from her cell phone at 1:18. That's the last I heard from her."

"How about I come get you and we devise a plan?"

"Let's do it."

Frank got directions to the FBI field office from Gardner and settled up his tab at the bar. He looked at his watch as he hurried to the door. It was five minutes after three.

Braewyn Joyce was no longer fashionably late.
She was missing.

Chapter 48

Frank picked up Tom Gardner at the North Miami field office and they drove south on 79th Street.

"What's shaking here in Miami?" Frank asked.

"Some guys are buying and selling war surplus," Tom said. "Boats, naval ordnance, stuff like that. Throws up red flags at the bureau."

"The terrorists used planes once, so now it's boats?"

"The ports are vulnerable. A nuclear weapon set off in Miami, Baltimore, New York, anyplace like that, could be another 9/11."

"These guys look capable of nuclear stuff?"

"One of them has deep pockets. Knows his way around the arms dealers overseas. He's a concern."

"Cezar Nicolai?"

Tom fell silent.

"That where Agent Joyce went today?" Frank asked.

"Yes," Tom said. "And I should've been there."

Tom and Frank arrived at the Mershon Hotel and pulled up to the entrance to their private garage. The lot attendant stopped Frank's car and requested the guest ID. Tom Gardner leaned across Frank and displayed his plastic room key.

"I'm registered here. My partner has our car."

The attendant checked the key code and returned it.

"Use any space on the third level," the attendant said.

Frank drove up into the multi-story garage and parked near the elevator.

"Braewyn had to register our car's license plate number and registration with the front desk when we arrived," Tom said. "I need to get that vehicle ID number from the concierge."

"Putting out an APB for the car?" Frank asked.

"I've already called every law enforcement agency I could think of with descriptions of the car and Braewyn. We need that VIN for another reason."

"What make is the car?"

"Chevrolet."

"Has OnStar."

"You got it."

*　*　*　*　*

Thirty minutes later, Frank and Tom took seats at a table in the hotel lounge. Tom waved off the waiter who approached. He checked for any messages on his cell, then placed it on the table.

"I reported the car stolen to Miami-Dade police," Tom said.

"What about your partner?"

339

"Find the car, find the partner."

"I've had to use the OnStar program in the past," Frank said and pulled out his cell phone. "I have their number in my contacts."

"We need a location asap," Tom said.

Frank rang OnStar and had them start a trace on Braewyn's Traverse. When he ended the call he stared at Tom's phone.

"You mentioned Braewyn sent you some photos. Of your suspects?"

"She did."

"Mind if I see them?" Frank said.

"Why?" Tom said. "They're FBI business."

"I live here and I know a lot of bad boys who also live here. Couldn't hurt for me to see if I can ID any in your photos."

Tom stared at Frank for several seconds.

"Maybe you're right. Couldn't hurt."

Tom brought up the photos on his cell and handed the phone to Frank. Frank scrolled through the pictures and frowned.

"These were shot from a distance," Frank said. "Features…not so clear…"

Frank stopped at the photo of two men sitting together, both facing the camera. His mouth twitched.

"See something?" Tom asked

"This guy on the right. He's a man I know as Anton Chernac."

"That's great. What do you know about him?"

"I know Anton Chernac's dead."

"Then who's the man in the photo?"

"Good question," Frank said. "Send these photos to my phone. You have my cell number."

"Those photos are part of an FBI investigation."

"That man has all but killed me. He's part of *my* investigation too, so send 'em."

Frank handed back Tom's phone. Tom tapped and swiped the screen of the cell a few times and glared at Frank.

"I better not have a reason to regret this," Tom said and pressed a final icon on the cell.

Frank checked his phone to see if the photos were received and nodded.

"Good. We may have to join forces against this prick."

Frank started to slip his phone in his jacket when it rang.

"Yes," Frank said.

"This is OnStar," a woman's voice said.

Frank switched the phone to speaker mode.

"We found the car, sir."

"Where is it?" Tom asked.

"It's in the valet parking area of the Fontainbleau Hotel."

"Thank you," Frank said.

"The hotel's in the 4400 block of Collins Avenue," the lady said.

"I know where it is," Frank said and ended the call. "Everybody in the western hemisphere knows where the damn Fontainebleau is," he muttered as he charged out of the bar, chased closely by Tom Gardner.

"Call for back-up," Frank yelled back to Tom. "Get some of your agents on this."

Chapter 49

The computer in Frank's cruiser cut back on the interior air conditioning in favor of controlling the temperature of the more important cooling system for the engine. Idling along in the sluggish afternoon traffic in the Miami summer heat had the A/C blowing air only a few degrees cooler than the 95-degree, humid air outside. Tom Gardner wiped his face with a handkerchief and scowled at Frank.

"Should've taken one of the FBI cars," Tom said. "Their air actually works."

The Fontainebleau Hotel towered fifteen stories up. Frank parked in the hotel lot, killed the engine, and started to open the car door when his cell rang. He looked at its display in relief. The caller ID showed Braewyn Joyce's cell number.

"Are you okay, *Ms.* Joyce?" Frank said, with his phone on speaker.

"I'm fine, but I seldom get called Ms. Joyce," a man's voice said.

Frank immediately recognized the responder.

"Maybe you could give us a name. A *real* name." Frank said smearing the sweat around on his face.

"I would have wagered you'd have figured that out by now, detective."

"Well, we sure as hell know you're not Anton Chernac," Frank said. "So my next guess would be Cezar Nicolai, the guy who's been hounding David Hapburg."

"'Hounding?' Why David's an old friend."

Tom Gardner squirmed in his seat and reached over to take the phone. Frank raised his free hand, blocking him.

"Knock off the bullshit. Where's Agent Joyce?"

"She's right here with me and she's fine, I assure you."

"Let me speak to her," Frank said.

"All in good time," Nicolai said. "We need to have a chat, you and I."

"What are we having now? And how do you know Agent Joyce knows me?"

"Do I have to educate you on having sources?"

"Answer the question."

"Since you have me on speaker, I imagine there are other ears there."

Tom again reached for the phone. Frank shook his head at him.

"I want a private chat, face to face," Nicolai said.

"Again?"

"I'm afraid so."

"About what?"

"Don't be coy, detective."

344

"I told you before. I don't know anything about this Omega thing," Frank said. "Nothing's changed. You need to bug my phone again?"

"Perhaps you have some ideas, and I have some ideas, and we could combine them and arrive at the answers we both want. How does that sound?"

"Okay. Let's meet and discuss it."

"Excellent," Cezar said. "I can't today, I'm afraid. I have appointments to keep, but I'll contact you soon. By the way, I'm ecstatic that you kept your old phone."

"Now, may I speak to Agent Joyce?"

A moment passed before the Nicolai's voice returned.

"*C'est dommage*. I'm afraid she's taking an afternoon nap and has asked not to be disturbed. We'll meet soon, detective."

The connection ended abruptly. Frank pounded on the partition between the seats with his fist.

"Why didn't you let me talk to him?" Tom said.

"What were you going to say? Hi, I'm an FBI agent so let me come pick up my partner, okay? Jesus, Tom, the last person in the world a guy like this wants to talk to is Braewyn's Fibbie partner."

"Might scare the bastard."

"This guy scares like a wolverine scares. Forget it."

Perspiration dripped onto Frank's lap. He breathed deeply and options raced through his brain like a psychedelic slide show. He knew he might be able to find out where Braewyn's cell phone was by using cell tower triangulation, but it would only show a general area. He was already certain she was somewhere nearby. His mental slide show stopped on one particular architectural image.

"It's big hotel," Frank said. "But we have to get in there and find her."

"Okay, we'll play it your way. What's next?"

"Get Miami-Dade in the hunt."

Frank called the Miami-Dade PD, identified himself, and informed them of the abduction details. He emailed them the photos he had of Braewyn and Nicolai for their APB and made sure the rented Chevy Traverse would be under police surveillance at the Fontainebleau's parking facility. Tom did the same with the local FBI office in North Miami Beach to prepare the incoming agents.

Frank and Tom scurried the fifty sizzling yards to the hotel entrance and wended their way to the main lobby's reception desk.

"May I help you, gentlemen?" a clerk behind the counter said.

"I'm looking for a friend of mine," Frank said, breathing hard. "I have a picture of him here."

Frank extended his cell phone and showed the clerk the picture of Nicolai that Braewyn had sent

"Ah, Mr. Grainger," the clerk said and moved to a computer for a moment. "Was in the Tresor

Penthouse. Looks like he checked out this afternoon."

Mr. Grainger, Anton Chernac, Cezar Nicolai. The man's got more names than the census bureau.

"Oh, no. He said if he was gone when I arrived that he was going to leave something for me. My name's Dugan, Frank Dugan."

The clerk searched the area around the desk and counter and opened a couple of drawers.

"He didn't leave anything here, sir."

"Could I possibly look in his room? He's forgetful at times. May have left it there."

"Uh, I don't know about that ..."

Frank showed the clerk his ID.

"It'll be okay. I'm a Florida cop. I'll take full responsibility. Shouldn't take but a minute."

The clerk made a phone call and hung up.

"I'm sorry, sir, but the manager says we'll need a search warrant to allow you access to any of our private rooms."

Frank glared at the clerk and considered going "tough cop" on the guy, but figured it would be a waste of time, something he had too little of. He also thought about sicking Tom and the FBI on the hotel management, but that would not only slow their progress, but might also bring in the media, neither of which they needed.

There was another way.

*   *   *   *   *

Frank and Tom cornered one of the bellmen near the wall of elevators.

"We need to go up to the Tresor Penthouse," Frank said to the young bellman and flashed a hundred dollar bill.

"I'd love to take you up there, sir, but I have no access to that suite."

"You don't carry pass keys?" Tom asked.

"I do for most of the rooms, but that suite gets its code changed after every occupancy. Only the daily room service people have the master keys."

"Are there service people up there now?" Frank asked.

"Probably," the bellman said.

"Take me up to them and the hundred is yours," Frank said.

The bellman looked around to see who might be watching, then pushed a button on the express elevator. The door opened and all three men stepped inside. The doors closed.

"Cops down here have hundred dollar bills to throw around?" Tom said low.

"I'm on a road trip expense account," Frank said.

"The Tresor Suite has a private elevator. I can only take you to the floor below the Tresor," the

348

bellman said. "From there, you'll have to take the service stairway up a flight."

"The Tresor just got vacated," Frank said. "Any chance the service people are in the room?"

"Maybe," the bellman said as the elevator slowed to a stop and opened its doors.

The bellman led the two men up the service stairs and arrived at the hallway of the Tresor Suite. A woman pushed a service cart with towels, soap, and other hotel accommodations in their direction. The bottom section of the cart contained a large, bulging trash bag tied with a plastic zip-tie.

"We're too late," the bellman said. "She's already done the room."

"Crap," Frank said and watched the housekeeping woman push her cart toward a service elevator at the far end of the corridor.

"Ask her where she got that trash," Frank said.

"Had to come from the Tresor," the bellman said. "There's nothing else occupied on this level."

"We'll take it."

"You want the trash?"

"It may contain something our friend meant to leave us," Frank said.

"Absent-minded as he is, he could've dropped it in a trash can," Tom said. "I wouldn't put anything past him."

"Something important, huh?" the bellman said.

"I'll level with you," Frank said. "An FBI woman's been kidnapped and could be in great danger. What's in that trash could help save her life."

Tom held up his FBI credentials to the bellman.

"My God. I'll get you that trash bag."

The bellman sprinted down the corridor to the work cart the moment the maid rolled it into the service elevator. He jammed his arm between the closing doors, forced them open, and pulled the cart back into the hall. The maid followed the cart, bewildered.

"Que pasa?" she asked.

"Need your trash from the Tresor. *Su basura,*" the bellman said, snatching the big plastic bag.

The bellman handed Frank the trash bag and showed the two men the back way out of the hotel. Frank gave the bellman the hundred-dollar bill and thanked him. He and Tom then slogged their way to Frank's car and alternated carrying the bulky trash bag over their shoulders.

Miami-Dade police vehicles poured into the parking lot. Tom waved his arms above his head to get their attention. Four cruisers and an SUV surrounded Frank's car and their officers converged on Frank and Tom, who held up their IDs.

"Bring us up to speed, detective," a Miami-Dade sergeant said.

"In this bag there may be evidence from the hotel room of the suspect, Cezar Nicolai," Frank said to the cops nearest him. "See if you can get me any usable prints, DNA, anything to help us identify who we're dealing with."

Frank opened the bag and carefully sorted through its contents with a ball-point pen. Inside he found tissues, plastic cups, snack wrappers, and coffee filters. A heavier object, a whiskey bottle, rested on the bottom of the bag, which Frank fished it out by inserting his pen into its neck. He brought it up into the daylight revealing a Laphroaig scotch bottle. He replaced the bottle and the rest of the bag's contents and handed over the bag and his card to the Miami-Dade officers.

"See what turns up in the lab. Special Agent Braewyn Joyce has been kidnapped by the man we're seeking and he should still be in the area. We have sent photos of him and Agent Joyce to all FBI and police in the region. I know it's going to be nearly impossible, but we'll need to check all modes of travel leaving the city: marinas, airports, toll booths, and train stations, the works. Video surveillance may help. He's likely traveling with a big man, a bodyguard-type, maybe six-eight and over three-fifty."

The police carried the Tresor's trash to the SUV and pulled back vehicles to allow Frank to drive out of the lot. He headed back to the Mershon Hotel to drop off Tom Gardner and discussed with him what the FBI would do to make sure Braewyn's room at the Mershon would be secured until she returned...*if she returned.*

There was only one thing he wanted out of that bag, and he hoped mightily it was in there. A fingerprint, a discarded drinking cup, a cigar stub, a cigarette butt, a disposable toothbrush, a hair with an attached follicle, anything that might contain a tiny trace of DNA. A shred of evidence that would accurately identify this man who haunted his life.

Chapter 50

Frank's cell pinged. He scrolled to his emails and read the message on the screen. It was from Roland Brand.

"Celine Ross worked in NSA's public affairs department. Sex-tangled with Chernac who'd been planted in overseas ops and got her ass fired. She learned about arms dealer Cezar Nicolai and his connection with Chernac later. All I have so far from Hollenbeck."

Frank called Roland, unsure of his next move. He was tired, hot, and assailed by factions coming from all directions.

He could almost make out vultures circling overhead.

*   *   *   *   *

"I need to go back to Maryland," Frank said into his cell, "but I can't go now."

"And you would be *who*?" Roland said.

Frank hung his head for a moment.

"I have a lot to tell you."

"So talk," Roland said.

Frank gave Roland the whole story of the past days and waited for his reaction.

"So this bad guy, Nicolai, has got the FBI gal, and he's obtained new stuff on this Omega shit?" Roland said. "So what's in Maryland?"

"I need to look harder into the things I found in my grandfather's house. I have to figure out this formula before this Cezar Nicolai character does."

"I'll call the feds and the boys at Miami-Dade, and relay you anything new that comes up. Go. Do what you have to do."

Frank didn't respond. Several seconds of "dead air" passed.

"There's more?" Roland asked.

"I need to find the proof regarding who killed my father."

"Well, son, looks like you've got yourself a full plate. But saving people, solving crime, and protecting the public: Isn't that what folks pay you to do?"

"Yep, it is."

"Well, unless you think there are clues in this telephone conversation, I suggest you get your ass out in the action, set your priorities in order, and start scratching things off your list."

Frank ended the call knowing the old man was right — Prioritize. Nicolai would have to be dealt with head-on. Unraveling the Omega Formula mystery would be priority one.

* * * * *

354

Cezar Nicolai steered the ocean-going Viking yacht due east out of the marina. Once in the open Atlantic, her modified twin engines planed the boat and throbbed through the dusk at full throttle. Vlad Torok sat next to Cezar on the enclosed bridge, while Miguel Cardoza and his two associates squatted against the transom and gripped the gunwales on the lower aft deck.

"She responds well and can make over 40 knots," Cezar said, his voice topping the roar of the powerful engines.

"The shakedown cruise of the other vessel went well according to the man I hired to captain her," Vlad said. "Looks like we made a good deal and we have an able crew."

Cezar nodded approvingly.

The Viking reached 15 miles out from Miami when Cezar idled down the engines to barely making headway.

Cezar patted Vlad's arm and said, "Let's go pay the dealer and get back to the marina."

Vlad stepped down to the aft deck while Cezar stood looking on at the top of the stairway. Cardoza and his men stood as Vlad approached.

"Payday, gentlemen," Vlad said. "Mr. Grainger loves his purchases and we have a deal."

"*Bueno*," Cardoza said, displaying almost all of his incredibly white teeth.

When Vlad pulled the Beretta 9mm from the shoulder holster under his jacket, Cardoza and his men shuffled back against the starboard side of the stern.

That was exactly where Cezar wanted them.

Three shots flashed and boomed into the black of the moonless night, followed by three nearly silent splashes.

For a moment, the low gurgle of the Viking's exhaust was all that broke the quiet of the open sea. Then another tiny splash followed. Cezar knew it was the sound of a pistol piercing the surface and sinking into the depths of the Atlantic's continental shelf.

*   *   *   *   *

Frank drove north to Stuart. He needed to pack a suitcase with fresh clothes and get back to Miami as soon as possible. All creation was going to break loose in the search for Braewyn Joyce. Every law enforcement agency would be double-timing it to rescue a kidnapped FBI agent. Frank didn't always agree with their publicity tactics. The media would be out in force reporting every move the authorities made, giving the bad guys a heads-up, providing them with time to counter with evasion into deeper cover. Frank knew the best way to deal with a sinister ego like Cezar Nicloai was to take him on one-to-one, so he would reveal himself. That FBI full assault crap wasn't going to fly in this situation.

Frank parked the cruiser in his driveway and stared out the windshield at the hibiscus-lined path to the back yard. After several moments he broke his semi-trance, stepped out of the car, and went to the rear of the vehicle. When he opened the trunk, a shadow on the driveway moved past him. He groped under his arm for his Browning and twisted around to face the source of the shadow. Frank felt his pulse race and a chill swept up his back as he locked eyes with Alasdair MacGowan.

"I did na come to kill ya," Alasdair said and smiled.

"Good to know," Frank said and released his grip on the Browning.

"Can we have a word?"

"Sure. How'd you know I was here?"

"It's your home. Figured you'd come here sometime."

"You still diving in Vero?"

"Yeah, we dive again tomorrow."

Frank led Alasdair to the back yard tiki bar where they sat across from each other on wicker stools. An uncomfortable moment passed before Alasdair spoke.

"Celine's gone."

"What do you mean 'gone?'" Frank asked.

"She's missing. I flew home yesterday to pick up more equipment. There's warm food in the microwave. The front door's wide open and her car's sitting in the driveway."

"Are you sure?" Frank said. "Maybe someone picked her up and they went to the store."

"And left her Gucci purse? She never goes anywhere without that purse."

"So what are you doing here?"

"There was a note," Alasdair said and took out a piece of paper from his back pocket and handed it to Frank.

Frank unfolded the paper and read its brief typewritten message:

**CALL THE POLICE AND WE KILL HER.
WE NEED TO ASK HER QUESTIONS.
WE GET ANSWERS, SHE GETS RETURNED
UNHARMED.**

"You call the cops?"

"You see what it says. They'll kill her."

"They always say that—"

"It's all my fault."

"It's not your fault."

"I should never have gotten into unauthorized police work. This could be all about the Omega film."

"It's about power," Frank said.

358

"I'm sorry I got mad at you."

"I'd've reacted the same way."

"Where do we go from here?" Alasdair said. "We need to stop these people."

"The same bunch may have Agent Braewyn Joyce."

"They can kidnap FBI agents?"

"Apparently, seems there's not much they can't do."

"Where are they?"

"Somewhere in Miami, last estimate."

"Can we find out if they're the ones who have Celine?"

"Don't know. This Cezar Nicolai guy, AKA Anton Chernac, has got Agent Joyce somewhere in south Florida. Maybe Celine too. Braewyn caught them working on an arms deal and got pictures of several of the bunch, but that's about all I know. Nicolai says he's going to call me to talk about resolving things, but I'm sure that means trading things I know for Braewyn."

"And then he'll kill you both. He's got nothing to lose."

"I'm not crazy about the FBI, but I'm not going to let him hurt her, or Celine, because of me."

"Then let me work as backup when the time comes."

"That would be the best news I've had in a long time."

"What did you say this guy's name is?"

"Cezar Nicolai."

"What do you know about him?"

"I'm pretty sure he killed my father," Frank said.

"What makes you think he'd spare Celine?"

Frank didn't have an answer for that.

"I've got to get back to Vero," Alasdair said.

"I'm sorry," Frank said and put his hand on Alasdair's shoulder.

Frank felt bad about upsetting Alasdair earlier by charging that Celine was involved in collusion with Anton Chernac. Now she'd been kidnapped and his friend was devastated. The situation was growing steadily worse by the hour.

Frank hated to think what new hell tomorrow would hold. Whatever it would be, he would go to Miami and face it head-on.

Giving up was not a term Frank Dugan was acquainted with.

Chapter 51

Frank decided to stay at home for the night, since rushing back to Miami wouldn't be of much help to Braewyn Joyce until Nicolai called, set up their meeting, and stated his demands. He checked in with Tom Gardner to get any updates, but, so far, things were *status quo.* Nothing new on Agent Joyce or her captors.

He stood in front of the dresser mirror and stared at his drawn face for a long moment, then cast his eyes down on a framed photograph. In the picture were three people. A pretty woman in her twenties, and two very young children, a girl and a boy. He touched the faces in the photo with gentle fingers, turned away, and undressed.

Later, Frank climbed into bed and watched a few minutes of the late TV news, a lot of which was about the kidnapping. He set his clock for six AM, rolled over, and tried to grab a few hours' sleep.

The clock showed five after midnight when he was jarred awake. His cell phone vibrated actively under the light of the lamp on the nightstand as it crept toward the table's edge. Frank snatched the phone before it fell and read the incoming number. It was the international number the mysterious Chernac had given Roland days ago.

"Hello," Frank said.

"Detective Dugan, good evening," said the familiar voice.

Frank got up and began to pace the room.

"What's up, Nicolai?"

"I'm calling to set up our meeting. Our summit talk, shall we say."

"I'm all ears."

"Good. Now I'm sure you'll want to meet somewhere you can feel safe, so I've chosen the Oceanside Marina's al fresco bar in Miami Beach. Do you know it?

"I'll find it."

"Excellent. Will nine this evening work for you?"

"Why so late?"

"I have appointments through the day, and the restaurant is far less busy after those cheap seniors get their early-bird meals and hobble back to their condos."

"All right, nine it is. Will Agent Joyce be there?"

"I'll make sure she attends."

"She'd better look healthy. I get cranky when things are given to me in rough condition."

"I certainly understand. I'm sure you'll be most pleased. Of course you know this meeting of ours will require that you come alone. No backup, as you say. And, of course, no weapons."

"Got it. See you later," Frank said.

The growing storm outside began to light up the darkened sky and rumble. Rain followed and continued through the night. Frank lay on his side and stared at the flashing lightning patterns dancing on the window and through the curtains and wondered if his personal storm would ever pass and peaceful sleep ever come.

*   *   *   *   *

Later that morning, Frank called Alasdair and told him about his call from Nicolai.

"You're going to go meet this bastard on his terms, at his place of bidding and by yourself?" Alasdair said. "I thought we were partners. And I thought you were smart."

"We are partners," Frank said. "But I can't jeopardize Braewyn Joyce by bringing in extra troops."

"If you don't tell your sheriff, I will."

"No you won't."

"To hell with the sheriff, I should call out the marines."

"Let me handle this," Frank said. "I'll be okay."

"Aye, like you were okay when he kidnapped you, and okay when those two goons nearly killed you?"

"'Bye, Al."

363

Frank hung up, but no sooner had the screen on his cell gone black, when something struck him as odd about the conversation. He couldn't put his finger on it, but something didn't have the right sound to it.

* * * * *

Cezar Nicolai waited in the Mercedes at the Oceanside Marina parking lot while Vlad Torok performed final cleaning chores and secured the Viking. Nicolai's first overnight on the new yacht was even more restful than his stays at the Tresor Penthouse. The gentle lapping of water against the hull and marina bulkhead, the smells of the sea, and the far-off squeals of the early morning gulls all contributed to the euphoria.

Late morning brought another sun-filled day in the mid-eighties. Breezes from the Atlantic carried the aroma of coconut oil lotion, mixed with the flavors of smoky burgers, French fries and hot dogs, wafting inland from the beachfront concessions.

The Viking was moored a few yards from where he had parked. He could see its graceful superstructure backed by the dark water of Biscayne Bay. Cezar was anxious to get his FBI agent and her attendant on board, but he knew that would have to wait until dark.

When Vlad finished up, they would return to the house in Coral Gables where two of his men held Agent Joyce. Later they would drive to the marina and have her sedated body brought aboard his new portable headquarters.

Then he would meet with Frank Dugan and complete the answer to the Omega puzzle.

Cezar smiled. Things were going well. Exquisitely well.

*　　*　　*　　*　　*

Frank settled into his modest motel room in South Miami and planned out his next moves for the meeting with Nicolai only hours away. Trouble was, there wasn't much he could plan. Things would happen with little predictability. And it would be at night. That was worrisome, but he had to go through with it. Meanwhile, he had time to gather his thoughts and continue to work on the loose ends that plagued his life. First in line was the Omega poem.

He started by going over the first verse to brainstorm its plausible meaning. He had barely whispered the first words of the poem when his cell pinged. He thumb-tapped his way to the text message.

Our appointment is at 9.
Don't be late.

365

Frank immediately recognized the call log ID as Anton Chernac's international phone number he'd traced to South America the day he received it from Roland. The origin was Venezuela. That was it. No other information was available. Frank knew Nicolai wasn't stupid enough to give him a traceable number, but he felt compelled to hunt down anything that might yield information about his number one Omega formula fan. Frank ran the trace again, and got the same disappointing results.

Frank knew trying to pin down a permanent location on Nicolai was, regrettably, like trying to pick up mercury with a boxing glove.

*   *   *   *   *

Frank watched the light rain which began around eight-thirty and, through his car's open window, felt the steamy mist rising from the hot parking lot. The air smelled like molten asphalt. Weather forecasts had predicted heavy rains and, at eight-forty-five, an eastern cloudburst bombarded the Oceanside Marina. Intermittent gusts kicked up at first. Then sustained, 30 MPH winds whipped the maritime pennants on their masts that lined the waterfront and made them snap and vibrate like triangular bullwhips.

Frank parked the cruiser in one of the few empty spaces in the back of the lot and shut off the motor. On Thursday nights, he'd learned that the Oceanside Restaurant offered their "early bird" specials, which brought out the retiree crowd in droves. He decided to wait out the torrent for a few minutes in the car since tropical downpours were typically brief. He checked the surrounding parked cars for any movement, but saw none.

"Do you need a ride to the restaurant?" a voice hollered, muffled by the rain and Frank's closed car windows.

Frank twisted almost backward and to his left to see who was yelling. Stopped behind his car was a young man in an oversized golf cart equipped with a roof and side curtains. Frank cracked his window a couple of inches.

"Beg your pardon?"

"Would you like a ride to the restaurant?" the young man asked.

"Sure. Give me a sec." Frank said and rolled up the window.

Frank jumped out of the cruiser, locked the car with his keyless remote, and dashed to the golf cart. He slid into the seat beside the young man, dripping and squeaking on the vinyl upholstery.

"Some nasty weather tonight," the young man said and gunned the golf cart down the row of parked cars.

"I was going to wait it out, but I've got to meet someone inside, and I'm almost late," Frank said with water draining off him in rivulets.

The golf cart weaved its way out of the parking area, but as it approached the restaurant's *porte-cochère*, the driver cut the wheel sharply to the left and aimed the cart directly toward the boat slips off the main pier.

"You missed the restaurant," Frank said and pointed to it.

"Got another pick-up. Only take a minute."

They stopped at a fifty-five-foot Viking sport fisher, a yacht regarded by boatmen as the ultimate in floating man caves, where the young man jumped out and hustled around to Frank's side of the cart. Frank looked at the driver and noticed he was staring hard at him. He noticed something else. The man was pointing a Walther automatic three feet from his head.

"Let's go aboard, sir. And no fast moves, please."

"Cezar didn't like the menu at the Coral Reef Room?" Frank said and obeyed his chauffeur.

"If you have any firearms, now would be a good time to hand them over."

"I didn't allow for a shoot-out, so I came unheeled."

"Good. Then you won't mind if I check myself in case you overlooked something." The young man

368

said and spun Frank around and patted down his soaking wet clothing. He pulled up Frank's left pant leg and removed a snub-nose revolver from its ankle holster.

"Happy?" Frank said.

"Delirious."

The young man nudged Frank up the gangplank and onto the boat's deck where Cezar Nicolai stood waiting under its canopy.

"This is so much more private than the restaurant with all those inconsolable pensioners, don't you agree?" Cezar said.

"Much more private," Frank said. "I bet those old folks probably couldn't even hear a gunshot from this distance."

The young man pulled up the rear of the tight group, led by Cezar, as they filed down steps into a spacious salon in the center of the yacht. The young man closed the door of the passageway from the outside, and Cezar stepped down into a luxurious lounge and pulled up a stool next to a red mahogany bar.

"Sit, please, detective," Cezar said and indicated a pub chair next to a round, walnut captain's table with an inlaid chessboard. Frank sat, took in the elegantly appointed room and laced his fingers on the tabletop.

"I don't see Agent Joyce," Frank said.

"I don't see my document," Cezar said looking down at Frank.

"I have it, and you may have it as soon as I see her."

"You're a difficult man to bargain with," Nicolai said and shifted his glance up toward the door.

Frank sensed movement behind him. Large hands clamped on his shoulders, followed by the smell of heavy garlic breath and an unpleasant, moist warmth on his neck.

"I'll give you an opportunity to hand over the document before I allow Vlad to search you for it," Cezar said. "Let me encourage you to comply. Vlad's not particularly dainty when he's hunting for something."

Vlad removed his hands from Frank and stepped back.

Frank pulled up his golf shirt and reached into the rear waistband of his khakis and pulled out an envelope and flipped it across the table toward Cezar. The damp envelope slid off the table and fell to the deck where Vlad darted over to it, picked it up and handed it to his boss. Cezar opened the unsealed envelope and read the blue handwritten words on the single, yellow-cast page. Frank looked on intently.

"I'm told what I want is *'sealed in a pipe all eyes can see.'* That's a line in your grandfather's poem, isn't it, detective?"

"I wouldn't know," Frank said. "What poem?"

"Really, detective?"

"You keep saying I'm holding something back from you, but, from where I sit, it looks like you're the one holding all the cards."

"'*A pipe all eyes can see,*'" Cezar said. "The fuselage of a B-29 could be construed as a pipe, albeit a rather large pipe."

"What else does your poem say?" Frank asked.

"This letter says I have to go to Washington. To a big air and space museum near Dulles. What I seek is hidden in an incredibly famous 'pipe' there: the *Enola Gay.*"

"The *Enola Gay*?" Vlad said.

"The airplane that dropped the first atomic bomb on Japan," Cezar said. "The one about as easy to get into and search as Fort Knox."

"My grandfather wouldn't lie about that." Frank said. "And he wouldn't've put it in a place with easy access."

"But I'm not entirely sure about you," Cezar said to Frank, then turned to Vlad. "I think we need time to consider what's before us, Vlad. Study our options. In the meantime, let's make our guest more comfortable."

"I'm plenty comfortable, and I've given you the document, as we agreed. You're not going to go back on our deal, are you?"

Frank looked on as Vlad removed a maroon case from his pocket and opened it to reveal a hypodermic syringe with several milliliters of a clear liquid. Vlad carefully positioned the needle in his right hand. Frank leapt to his feet, but Vlad grabbed him by the neck with one massive hand, forced him down, and jammed the needle into Frank's shoulder. He put the empty syringe in his teeth, adjusted Frank into his chair, and firmed his huge hands on his shoulders to keep him there. Frank struggled, but the 350-pound man couldn't be budged.

Frank stared helplessly at the recessed light over the captain's table. It got fuzzy, glowed.

Then went out.

Chapter 52

Cezar Nicolai and Vlad Torok stood at the entrance
of the Dulles Air and Space Museum, officially
named the Steven F. Udvar-Hazy Center, and paused
at the gang of chrome metal doors. Cezar hoped his
ploy to gain entrée inside the famous B-29 bomber
would work, and burned to know the secret the
Enola Gay held and protected in her historic "pipe".

He knew, even if he prevailed on the officials to
allow him a private tour, his time would be limited
on the plane. And, unless he took a commanding
stance once inside, he'd never be able to delve into
places on the aircraft where he hoped the solution to
Omega puzzle was cached.

Vlad patted his brow with a handkerchief and
opened one of the doors for Cezar as he stepped
inside. They smiled at the greeters at the information
desk and were checked for any items prohibited in
the museum. One of the officials acknowledged their
paid parking ticket, which doubled as their
admission to the facility.

Continuing on, they passed through enormous
rooms that were like great sound stages on major
motion picture lots. The enormous hangars could be
viewed from two levels which encircled the
museum. Airplanes of every historical vintage hung

above and posed below them as if in flight, their wings and fuselages polished like the day they rolled off their assembly lines.

Soon they were in a great arched cavern made of metal girders and glass windows, and at its center was the most renowned warplane in history, sitting with her lowered landing gear resting atop massive scissor lifts painted a bright school bus yellow. A ten-foot letter **R** in a circle adorned her vertical stabilizer, and her wide wing flaps were in the down, take-off position. The quartet of giant engines, with their 16-foot, four-blade propellers were all aligned like perfect, upright crucifixes. Had her props been spinning, one could imagine the aluminum and magnesium giant lifting from the earth and roaring upward to meet her destiny on the Island of Honshu.

A security official walked toward the *Enola Gay* on the wide crosswalk that nearly passed over the nose of the plane and noticed Cezar and Vlad rapt in study of the famous bomber's cockpit mere feet below.

"First time to see the *Enola Gay*?" the official asked.

"Yes," Cezar said. "Quite a moving sight."

"She's been here since 2003, and since then, our attendance has tripled." The official said.

"I can understand why," Cezar said. "Is it possible to speak to a person in charge of this facility?"

"That would be Mr. Fleming, the museum's director," the official said. "I take it you don't have an appointment."

"That's true," Cezar said. "I hadn't planned on getting the opportunity to visit the museum, but we have a two-day layover here, and I desperately wanted to see the *Enola Gay* before I left. I'm writing a history on the world's most famous planes and want to feature your museum in the book."

"I think we may be able to arrange something for you," the official said. "Right this way."

*   *   *   *   *

Cezar found Director Herschel Fleming to be a pleasant man with a ready smile; a man, on outward assessment, he guessed was used to making his visitors' experiences at his museum unforgettable. Fleming graciously accepted the impromptu audience with Cezar and Vlad with a kind enthusiasm, unexpectedly considerate and genuine. Cezar foresaw his request for a tour as being much more of a possibility since he had encountered the affable gentleman.

"A book, you say, Mr. Evans," Fleming said. "Featuring our facility."

"Indeed, and it comes with a request and a sizable contribution to the museum's foundation."

"Go on," Fleming said, smiling.

375

"I don't mean to sound stuffy, but I'd have no problem writing you a generous check if I can access certain places in the museum the public never sees."

"Oh, my," Fleming said and rocked back in his desk chair. "What places do you mean?"

"I'd like to headline my book with the *Enola Gay*," Cezar said, "the most famous warplane in the history of the world. Make it my cover and centerpiece. I want to go inside her and show her secret places. The selling point of the book would depend on this original and unique spin. Publishers will be bidding aggressively to get the rights to print a book with this new, fascinating angle. And, of course, the more money the book makes, the more I'll gladly add to my original donation, not to mention, a personal section devoted to the museum's farsighted director."

"Oh, my," Fleming said, beaming. "Uh, by 'inside her,' do you actually mean going into the plane's cockpit, fuselage, and such?"

"Precisely."

"When would you wish to do that?"

"How about tonight, after hours?"

"Oh, goodness, I don't know…Security will have to be notified…and the maintenance crews will have to stay late to lower the *Enola's* scissor jacks."

"Then how about tomorrow night? I can return then with my checkbook, if that will give you time to arrange things," Cezar said. "I'm only here for two days, and won't likely have another opportunity to visit for months, which will seriously delay the book's completion and breakout on the market."

"Take my card. I'll see what can be done. Call me around ten tomorrow morning," Fleming said and picked up his phone.

Outside the museum Cezar and Vlad climbed into their rented Mercedes-Benz CLA Class sedan and drove out of the complex.

"Mr. Evans?" Vlad said and looked over at Cezar who was checking his cell's screen.

"Having people in your pocket who can forge passports is a blessing beyond measure."

"Your checkbook says 'CNN Acquisitions.'"

"My financial company. They'll think I have interests in the news media. What's your concern?" Cezar said and scrolled through pages on his cell.

"You actually have several million attached to that account. What if they deposit your generous donation?"

"I'll stop it before it gets credited to their account. You worry too much," Cezar said.

"I always have your best interests at heart. What about the detective?"

"I think Frank Dugan may still be useful to us. If he actually knows anything he's stubbornly keeping it to himself, but he'll make a mistake, leave a trail, and I'll be there to profit by it when he does."

"We've gone to a lot of expense to keep him under our control," Vlad said.

"Money's only worth the power and pleasure it can buy."

"And the FBI agent?"

"I asked Celine to call me today, but no call. I thought she could be an asset to us, but I'm not so sure now. Women. Can't be trusted."

"Concerned about her?"

"I have reason to be," Cezar said. "That's why I take precautions. Like putting the transponder in Dugan's shoe. So I know where the enemy is at all times."

"But you know exactly where he is."

Cezar consulted his cell phone's GPS app.

"Yes, I most certainly do."

Chapter 53

Frank woke and immediately felt like his head was in a medieval torture device. His sinuses were killing him from the thick humidity he labored to breathe. It was dark; so dark, he imagined, the darkness had mass that one could actually weigh.

It's thick, dark, warm, and humid. Where the hell am I?

He tried to sit up from where he lay and abruptly struck his throbbing head on something hard only inches above him. He reached up and grasped the tubular object. it felt like a metal bar.

I'm in a jail cell?

He inched and felt his way by using his hands and his feet. Seeing in the blackness was hopeless. He draped a leg downward to one side and sensed he was on a shelf of some kind. He slid out and downward more and his foot touched something solid a few feet below, something that seemed firm enough to hold his weight. Reaching up, he grasped the round metal object he'd hit his head on and used it to steady his descent to the floor below. Now, ever so slowly, he could stand up to his full height.

The thick humid air was sickening warm and laced with the smell of musty gasoline, or something like gasoline. It was the odor like that in an auto service garage. He could even taste it. Thoughts of the past 24 hours began to seep back into his memory. Maybe he *was* in a gas station, probably an abandoned old gas station out in the middle of no-damn-where. That would certainly fit Cezar Nicolai's M. O.

Perspiration dribbled down from his hairline and ran into his eyes. Not that it would matter for visual acuity, but it stung, and added to his agitation. Frank wiped his sweaty face on the short sleeve of his tee shirt and realized he was only wearing an undershirt, briefs, and his shoes and socks, now soaked through from the ankle-deep water on the floor. Next, he noted that the floor had small openings or spaces between slats of solid pieces he could feel through his athletic shoes. Probably, he surmised, what the mechanics worked on to allow for drainage when they sprayed down the bays of the garage.

With his arms sweeping slowly in a face-high arc from side to side, he eventually came to a pipe running horizontally along the wall to his left. He decided to follow it. In the next ten steps he came upon nothing, but on the eleventh, he was stopped by something directly in his path. Frank felt a large, round knob on a handle like he'd seen on bank vault doors.

Am I locked in a bank vault?

His heart raced and he could feel his blood pressure spike. He held onto the knob and tried to compose himself. *Deal with one thing at a time. Complete the procedure at hand, then move on to the next.* It was how he was trained in the Marine Corps. *Adjust, adapt, invent, improvise...prevail.*

One thing was now certain and it calmed his nerves: he was not in a bank vault. Couldn't be. Bank vaults aren't wet and they don't smell of petroleum products. He felt his pulse. His heart rate had dropped to less than 100 beats.

Frank ran his hand down the handle and felt a center recess, a possible pivot point, and beyond that, more handle and another large knob like the first one. Even in the blackness his mind assembled a picture of the mechanism and he knew how it had to work. He tried to push the top knob to turn the handle, but it didn't budge. He felt around for somewhere to sit and rest a moment and regroup. A large, drum-like object rubbed against his knees a few feet to his right. It was smooth and solid when he pushed down on it to check if it would hold his weight. He carefully lowered himself onto it, leaned forward and buried his sweaty face in his hands.

After a minute, he re-wiped the flood of new perspiration from his brow and eyes. He sat up and leaned back and placed his hands on the drum on either side to steady himself. His right hand felt the edge of a vertical piece of flat, sharp metal. Frank's fingers examined the metal farther right and he slid his hand several inches to its end, then downward. It felt like a metal flange, maybe part of a car fender. *Yeah, that's what I'm sitting on, a car fender; an old racecar fender like in the movies in the 1940s. I'm in an old garage with old racecars.*

His hand investigated farther down. Frank's heart rate went off the charts as his fingertips came to the twin propellers.

He was sitting on a torpedo.

Chapter 54

Braewyn Joyce's duct tape restraints pulled at the hair on her forearms and chafed her ankles. She was forced to hop from one place to another in her bare feet. The jaunt from the forward stateroom to the galley this morning was exhausting. The A/C on the roomy Viking yacht was working well and she could draw a cool, coffee-scented breath as she sat on the end of the curved booth that complemented an oval mahogany table.

Celine MacGowan prepared two cups of coffee and brought them over to Braewyn and sat opposite her captive in a deck-mounted swivel stool. She looked at the display on her cell phone for a second and placed it on the table.

"I'll remove the tape from your hands, but remember, I'm the one with the gun," Celine said and patted the automatic on her hip.

"Thanks."

Celine pulled a snap-blade knife from a Gucci purse sitting on the counter next to the sink.

"Gucci," Braewyn said. "Nice. Cezar buy that for you?"

"Bought it in Washington. Years ago, with my own money."

Celine cut the tape on Braewyn's wrists so she could separate her hands. She closed the knife, placed it on the table, and picked up her coffee mug. The two women sipped their coffee in an uncomfortable silence. Braewyn focused on various parts of the galley without making eye contact with Celine who busily checked messages on her cell. The ship's clock on the wall behind Braewyn dinged off six bells.

"I know you hate me," Celine said, "but don't even think about that knife."

"I can't believe what you're doing with your life. You had it made."

Celine tossed her cell on the table.

"With Alasdair? Give me a break. He's the most boring man in boredomville."

"And Cezar Nicolai is exciting?"

"He's incredible. Cultured, rich and, yes, he is exciting."

"You just met the man."

"I've known Cezar for years. He's come back into my life. He's everything I ever wanted in a man."

"He's a thief, a kidnapper, and a murderer."

"He does what he has to. Who has he murdered?"

"You're priceless. What did he and his beeftrust sidekick do with Frank Dugan?"

"He didn't murder that cop. He's just detaining him on his new submarine."

Braewyn's jaw slackened.

"Submarine? He has a submarine."

"Yeah. Old Russian Whiskey Class from the '50s. Paid a couple hundred grand for it...*in cash.*"

"Detective Dugan is on a sub?"

"Just off Stuart, as a matter of fact. So he can feel like he's at home...almost," Celine said and giggled.

"Who's manning the sub?" Braewyn asked.

"That's the cool part ... No one."

"He's floating around in a submarine with no crew?"

"Well, not exactly floating," Celine said. "Cezar had a dive crew take it down about 180 feet and leave it on the bottom. He wants to make sure Frank doesn't go anywhere. The man's amazing."

"Jesus God," Braewyn said, raking her fingernails hard through her gnarled hair and pulling it back tight enough to have to re-set her silver barrette.

"Come on, let's forget about men. Hop with me up to the deck outside," Celine said, pocketed up the snap-blade knife, rose, and shambled off in her flip-flops toward the passageway. "Let's get some fresh air and a little warm morning sun."

Braewyn stayed in her seat for a few moments and rubbed her hands around her ankles where the duct tape chafed her. She eventually summoned what strength she had and followed Celine through the narrow passageway and hopped up the steps to the open stern deck. Celine pulled a couple of deck chairs together and dragged them out from under the stern canopy and into the pre-noon sunlight.

"Come, look over here," Celine said and moved to the transom and extended her arms out toward the panorama of the marina. Braewyn moved in behind her. "This is why I love Cezar. Yachts, expensive cars, penthouses. Alasdair has an old SUV, a mortgage, and he gets shitty when he has to pay for a room at a fleabag motel."

The period had just dotted her statement when Braewyn yanked out Celine's Glock and hit her from behind with a slamming elbow to the back of her head. Celine's head jolted forward and her body doubled over the transom. She sprang back upright with acrobatic agility and turned to face her attacker. Celine yanked out her snap-blade knife and whipped it open, menacing Braewyn with razor-sharp blade. Braewyn jumped backward and aimed the Glock at Celine's chest.

"You sneaking FBI bitch," Celine said. "I'll cut your goddamn heart out."

"Put the knife down, Celine. Do it now," Bracwyn said.

Celine kicked off her flip-flops and began circling Braewyn.

386

"I knew I shouldn't have cut your hands free," Celine said. "How'd you do the legs?"

"Put down the goddamned knife."

"What? Gonna shoot me with that big ole gun, Special Agent Joyce?"

Braewyn countered Celine's moves with her own, always keeping out of range of the knife's ever-moving blade. Celine grabbed a flotation cushion and hurled it at Braewyn who ducked, but lost her footing on the dew-covered deck. Celine leaped at her fallen adversary, the knife raised high, and swung it downward at Braewyn's neck. Braewyn blocked the wrist below the hand wielding the knife with her left forearm, and pulled the trigger of the Glock aimed at Celine's midsection. The gun was silent as the knife flew from Celine's hand and skittered across the deck.

Celine dashed for the knife and picked it up at the base of the transom. Braewyn struggled to her feet and cycled the slide on the Glock, chambering a round. Celine took a low, defensive stance brandishing the shiny blade back and forth in front of her body.

"Drop the knife, Celine," Braewyn said. "There's a live round in the chamber this time."

"You won't shoot, you FBI pussy," Celine said and charged at Braewyn, slashing at her wildly.

A shot boomed and broke the morning quiet of the marina. Celine clutched her chest and staggered backward until her thighs slammed into the transom. The momentum carried her overboard, her feet flipping skyward, their white bottoms lit briefly by the sun.

Braewyn reached the transom in time to see Celine's head suspended by the stern mooring line beneath her shoulders. The line dipped downward momentarily from her weight and held her upper body out of the water. The heavy boat then pulled back on the line, returning it to its original tautness, sliding Celine's body free and into the dark water. Braewyn stared down at Celine's blank gaze as she sank slowly into the darkness beneath the boat and out of sight.

Braewyn waited for several minutes and searched the water behind and around the stern looking for any sign of Celine, but she never surfaced. She returned to the galley to get Celine's cell phone. She keyed in a number and waited. Braewyn tugged off the pieces of severed duct tape clinging to her legs that she'd cut through with the sharp edges of her barrette before going above.

"Hello, Jack, it's Braewyn. I'm at the Oceanside Marina," she said into the voicemail inbox. "I'm okay. I'm coming to the North Miami office. Get the people together. We need to find a Russian submarine."

Chapter 55

Braewyn had the North Miami FBI office buzzing with the account of her recent ordeal in Miami Beach. Jack Ortiz, the special agent in charge, moderated a meeting with Tom Gardner and several other agents in a glassed-in conference room. Ortiz, a man in his forties, handed out photos of Cezar Nicolai and Vlad Torok from the cell phone shots Braewyn got at the church.

Braewyn stepped out of the conference room and made a call at one of the desk phones in the outer office.

"Sheriff Brand, this is Braewyn Joyce. Do you remember me?"

"I most certainly do," Roland said on the speakerphone.

"I called because Frank's in a lot of trouble…because of me. Cezar Nicolai has somehow got him trapped on a submerged submarine off your coast."

"What?"

"I know. It's bizarre, but I believe it's true. I got it from a reliable source."

"You have your source with you there?"

"She's dead."

"This keeps getting better."

"I need you to gather whatever resources you have to help us find that sub. It's in about 180 feet of water off Stuart, so I'd start there. I've called the Coast Guard and the navy, and they're on their way, but we may need some locals. Pro divers with dive boats equipped with deep water radar and we need them now."

"I'll muster who I can right away."

"If you know Alasdair MacGowan's number, call him. He's a diver and may still be in Vero Beach."

"Frank gave me his cell number. Anything else before I start this rolling?"

"Get a helicopter searching the area, and take Frank to a hospital if they can get him to the surface."

"I'm on it."

Braewyn ended the call and stepped back into the conference room and stood across the room from Jack Ortiz.

"That's the deal, folks," Ortiz said. "Let's go out there and save a man and put a couple of bad guys away."

The room came alive with four men and six women agents erupting noisily from their chairs and bustling out the door. Ortiz waited until everyone but Braewyn was gone and moved close to her,

"I want you to take a few days leave, Agent Joyce," Ortiz said. "Catch your breath from all you've been through this past week."

"I'm fine, Jack. I want in on this one."

"I know you do and you've worked hard to get these guys set up for arrest, but I know when someone's over-extending themselves."

"How long?"

"Take a couple of weeks. Go to the beach. Play in the sun."

"We don't have a couple of weeks," Braewyn said. "Let me put that vacation on hold for now."

"You're sure you're all right? A hundred percent?"

"I am."

"Okay, but I've got a doctor coming over to check you out. He says you're okay, I'm good with you staying on."

"Thanks, Jack."

"And you get some rest *today*. We'll catch up with these guys," Ortiz said. "Don't you worry about that."

Braewyn said, "Right now, I'm only worried about catching up with one guy."

*   *   *   *   *

Frank's question as to where he was no longer posed a mystery. The air in the submarine was thickening and becoming harder to breathe. The water level in the compartment had risen another foot and kept coming. The humid darkness was maddening. Frank slid off the torpedo and down to the deck and sank into the cool water. He took a few moments to compose himself and think how he could survive his steel prison.

He struggled to his feet and felt his way to the blocked hatchway on wobbly legs. He gripped one of the knobs on the hatch and stooped his shoulder beneath his hands to bring his legs into the effort. He hoped he was attempting to move the massive locking device in the correct direction. He would only have the mojo for maybe a single attempt. It would be just his luck for the mechanism to open clockwise instead of the opposite way. He decided on counterclockwise anyway. *Lefty-loosey, righty-tighty.*

He sucked in one big breath and he pushed upward on the knob with both hands. The quadriceps in his thighs ached. He felt the strain in his core as he put all his force upward. His legs started to cramp. He was about to concede failure when the knob moved from three o'clock to two, then to one, and then spun freely all the way around. A pull on the handle and the heavy door swung open revealing three amazing serendipities: a lighted compartment, fresher air, and cans of beer lying on the slatted deck.

Frank sloshed into the next compartment, dripping water that trickled gently back toward the torpedo room. Even though it was humid as a steam room, he was dying of thirst, so he bent down and grabbed one of the cans of beer and checked the label. The only two words he could read were Boktok and beer, but that was enough for him to pop the top and slug about half the can down. It wasn't water, and it was warm, but it was wet and strong. He felt the energy and mental boost it gave him surge through his body.

Moving forward, Frank passed through a section with a line of valves and gauges that extended to another hatch at its forward end.

The adjoining compartment was lit by dim overhead bulbs in protective cages and contained a long center passageway that contained the sub's engines. Frank trudged to another opening several feet farther away. He plodded through the hatchway and saw banks of long levers coming up from the floor, and farther on, he entered the control room of the sub. Frank took a long look at the numerous gauges, switches and what appeared to be two large steering wheels. The thought of knowing how to use even a small part of what he saw was overwhelming. He equated his situation with dropping a cab driver into the cockpit of a 747 at 35,000 feet, where the pilots were slumped over dead.

Frank studied the numerous dials in front of him. The labels of the indicators were written in Cyrillic, but the numbers were in Arabic. One dial had its pointer stopped at 55 meters, which he translated to be nearly 180 feet. He was pretty sure it was a depth gauge, although the assurance of that offered him little comfort.

Frank returned to the room with the banks of levers; They were next to one bulkhead and were all in the same position. Frank judged, with his vast knowledge of outdated submarine operation, limited to John Wayne and Burt Lancaster movies, that the levers had something to do with buoyancy. *What the hell, try something. It's not like you're going to sink the sonofabitch.* He switched the position on two of the levers and waited. Loud, gurgling noises came from a part of the boat forward of the control room. A moment later he felt the deck beneath his feet begin to pitch upward at a steep enough angle to reel him backward. He grabbed onto a railing enclosing the levers to steady himself. The noises and the boat's upward movement stopped. A gauge with a bubble level attached indicated the boat's upward angle to be at 15 degrees.

Frank crab-walked over to other levers and pulled two more near the first two he'd already thrown. The gurgling sounds this time were fainter and seemed to come from farther away toward the bow. This time the boat pitched upward at a much steeper angle and dumped him on his rump on the deck. His body slid backward and his head slammed into the compartment's aft bulkhead.

Frank's eyes went dim and he rolled over in a heap unable to move.

*　　*　　*　　*　　*

One eyelid slowly opened on the left side of Frank's face. The room began to come into focus, but it seemed to be swaying as Frank's body gently rolled from side to side. He snapped himself awake and struggled to sit up, gave up, and flopped onto his back. His upper body was toward the boat's stern, his head rested below his shoes by more than two feet. Frank scrambled to move forward and get his head toward the bow. He clambered up a nest of pipes and petcocks to stand on his feet, but to stay upright, his stance was severely pitched toward the bow. Holding his position was uncomfortable and slippery. Gravity was trying to force him toward the stern. Frank made a impulsive decision. He yanked all the remaining levers to match the four he'd pulled. Loud noises belched and gurgled beneath his feet. The sub rumbled and began to level.

Frank made his way to the control room on more even footing, although the boat was still angled slightly up at the bow. The depth gauge showed the needle moving to lower numbers. It showed 40

395

meters and moving steadily toward 35. The sub was heading for the surface and its lone occupant's heart was doing an Irish jig.

Moments passed as Frank eyed the depth gauge intently. As the needle hit 15 meters the sub bounced gently, the depth gauge froze, and Frank's ecstasy waned. *What the hell? Why aren't we on the surface? Why is the boat still at an up angle?*

Frank found the control for the periscope and activated it. The periscope viewer slid up into its overhead sheath and Frank pulled down the folded-up handles and pressed his eyes to the ocular cups.

The view in the scope was of clouds.

Chapter 56

Frank made his way back to the compartment where he'd found the beer. Seawater now filled the room to a foot deep. Cans of beer jostled below the surface. Frank scooped one from the water and returned forward. He sank to the deck of the control room, pulled the beer's zip tab, and sipped the tepid brew. His thoughts of *almost* escaping his iron maiden depressed him. He closed his eyes and tilted his head back against the bulkhead.

Soon Frank was stalking bears in the woods of Maryland with Erich, his faithful German shepherd. A trusty BB gun, cocked and at the ready, filled his young boy's hands.

*　*　*　*　*

Frank kept hearing banging and scraping on the outer hull, but couldn't seem to muster the energy to get up and see what was causing it. The banging stopped and was replaced by other metallic noises coming from a distance forward and above him, then he heard water pouring into the boat's interior and splashing in a forward compartment. He figured the old tub had sprung a major leak and was filling with water.

Who would've ever guessed. I'm going to drown on a submarine that's right at the surface pointing at the sky.

More clanking noises came from the adjoining passageway and then a dark presence filled the doorway, obscured by the brightness of a powerful light aimed directly at Frank.

"Still alive, detective?" a vaguely familiar voice said.

Frank lay on his side. Blurry eyes saw a black and yellow alien move to him and try to roll him onto his back. He was helpless to fight him off, although he managed to summon a couple of weak thrusts at him with a free fist. Exhausted and half-conscious, he surrendered to the big man's strength and let him position him face-up. The intruder removed a diver's mask and leaned over Frank, inches from his face. Frank recognized the man above him. It was the smiling mug of Alasdair MacGowan.

"Are you able to talk?" Alasdair said.

"Yeah, …I can talk," Frank said, reality returning.

"How the hell did this sub get to the surface?"

"I pulled the levers over there. Lots of 'em. Then all kinds of shit happened."

"You blew the ballast tanks. Good, but she's down at the stern. You must've opened the valves aft. You muck with the torpedo tubes?"

"All you ever do is bitch."

"Sit tight, I want to check out the situation astern."

Frank watched Alasdair clamber down the tilted passageway toward the aft compartment and watched the light of his lantern until it disappeared into the engine room. A minute later, Alasdair returned.

"Throwing those other levers may not have done you much good in the long haul," Alasdair said. "She's taking on water like the *Titanic* back there. Listen to me carefully. This sub's bow is above the surface, but her stern, 200 feet aft, is down over 20 meters and sinking. This boat is hovering above a ledge that drops off to more than 3,000 feet, where the pressure can crush this old hull like a soda can. She's waving in the currents like an underwater weathervane. We get a strong gush of current, and she dives into the abyss, there's no ascending to the top. We have to get out of here now."

"How?"

"Navy guys are outside and topside. I asked them to let me take the lead on this."

"So they're sending down a rescue vehicle?"

"I brought gear for you."

"Oh, Jesus."

"We're going to go surfacing, not diving, so get your ass up so I can get you rigged out."

Frank managed to pull himself to his feet and hold onto Alasdair's waist belt as they scaled the steep deck to the forward escape trunk and hatch that opened to the sea outside. Steadying himself against the bulkhead, Alasdair continued to talk as Frank removed his shoes and socks and stood in his briefs and tee shirt. Alasdair helped Frank put on his scuba tanks, mask and fins, adjusted his regulator and made sure he was breathing a proper flow of air from his tanks.

"Look, follow me in everything I do at the escape hatch. Outside we're going to latch on to the anchor line from the dive boat that runs near the sub and use it to get to the surface, about 40 feet above us. It'll feel a little cool to you out there at first, but you'll be able to take it. It's almost noon up there and we'll be in warm sunlight soon enough. You hang onto me. And take those shoes. You'll need them on the dive boat."

Frank tied the laces of the shoes together and hung them around his neck.

"Come on. We'll be topside before you know it," Alasdair said.

Frank tried to nod, but his head was shaking so badly from side to side it barely conveyed the assent he intended. The two men struggled their way forward, entered the air lock, and Alasdair dogged off the hatch to the sub's interior below them and opened the valves above them enough to let the cold seawater flood the small compartment gradually. Frank felt the rising water envelop him like a frigid death coming to claim him. He trembled and breathed hard to assure himself that he indeed was alive. After the compartment filled, the upper hatch was opened and the Alasdair drifted out into the darkness of the open sea like a weightless phantom.

Frank followed, his upper body emerging from the sub, but abruptly stopped. Alasdair turned back to see Frank wrestling with a tank strap that had fouled on the hatch, holding him in the opening. Frank gazed in fear as Alasdair swam down to help him when the sub jolted and her stern swung downward and away from the ledge where she had lain. In seconds the boat was perpendicular to the surface like a massive steel pendulum.

Alasdair reached Frank and grappled with the snagged tank strap. It was at that moment that Frank saw Alasdair's's hair shoot straight up. The shoes around Frank's neck rocketed upward and swirled away in the powerful wake of the crash-diving vessel.

The sub was plummeting toward the blackness of the abyss.

At a hundred feet down, Alasdair unsheathed his knife and cut Frank's stubborn tank strap, and freed him from the hatch. Their downward momentum took them to 130 feet before the two men could begin to ascend.

Alasdair led Frank to the line running from the anchor, embedded in the coral clusters far below, to the dive boat on the surface. Navy divers swam in to join them. In the beam from Alasdair's powerful light Frank saw the sub for a few moments, and watched as it disappeared into the deep.

The men moved up the line. Alasdair faced Frank and clutched Frank's loose scuba tank and kept it next to his body with his arm. Frank grabbed Alasdair's waist belt and held onto him until they broke the surface and swam to the stern shelf of the dive boat. There they removed their cumbersome diving gear and were helped aboard by several other members of Alasdair's dive team. The crew weighed anchor and dropped a floating marker over the sub's location as the Coast Guard and navy boats drew alongside.

"She's slipped into a deep chasm, maybe more than 3,000 feet," Alasdair said to the lieutenant on the rescue boat. "She's taking on lots of water that could equalize and save her from being completely crushed, but I doubt it. May need to get the navy back out here to try to crane her up, if it's even worth the trouble. Russian, Whiskey Class, maybe Cold War vintage."

The lieutenant nodded and gave Alasdair a thumbs up as the dive boat roared away toward shore. A man wrapped a blanket around Frank and hot coffee warmed the two men as they rested on seats along the boat's gunwale. A young woman brought a pair of diver's neoprene boots over to Frank and he caught her as she winked at Alasdair. A man with a camera grabbed a shot of the group around the two men. Another man gave Frank a pint of bottled water he slugged down in one shot, then reached for more coffee.

"God, I thought I'd never drink another cup of coffee," Frank said holding his shaking coffee mug with both hands. "Anything from Braewyn Joyce?"

"She's fine. In the FBI office in North Miami. She called your sheriff and he called me."

"How'd you get here so fast from Maryland?"

"I was still in Vero with the dive group. Lucky for you."

"Something about the Irish."

"They're going to get you to a hospital," Alasdair said.

"I don't need medical attention."

"You've hit a rough patch, lad. You're shaking like a paint mixer."

"I'm okay. It's a little chilly out here in the wind. How would I get to a hospital? We're in the middle of the ocean."

"On that," Alasdair said and pointed to the distinctive police helicopter approaching them in the distance.

"The state police?" Frank said.

"Again, Braewyn and your sheriff."

"Damn. Did they alert the president?"

"He was busy playing golf."

The boat slowed to a gentle drift as the helicopter hovered overhead and descended. A rescue harness was lowered from the helicopter's side door davit to the deck of the boat. The crew steadied the harness as best they could as the boat rolled and pitched in the choppy sea. One of the dive crew beckoned to Frank.

"Get checked out," Alasdair said. "I'll meet you later at the hospital."

Frank got up and wobbled unsteadily over to the harness on the rolling deck and secured himself in its straps. The crew gave the men above the okay sign and Frank headed skyward. About halfway up the hundred feet to the aircraft Frank noticed something about the person standing in the helicopter's open door.

"Good God, is that you Rumbaugh?"

Far below departing helicopter, a pair of Nike cross-training athletic shoes gently floated northward on the Gulf Stream current.

*   *   *   *   *

Frank had barely belted himself into his seat on the helicopter when he asked Carl Rumbaugh for his cell phone.

Frank dialed a number and yelled above the chopper's roar.

"When the dive boat puts in at the Vero Beach marina, *arrest* Alasdair MacGowan."

Chapter 57

Braewyn was not happy about nearly being pulled from the FBI team chasing Cezar Nicolai, but Ortiz was a stickler for the agency policy which precluded agents from participating in pursuits of criminals who had harmed or threatened them.

She stared out from her window at the Mershon Hotel and knew Jack had made the right call, even though he modified his decision to allow her back in the hunt. It *was* personal. She wanted to kill Cezar Nicolai for kidnapping her, trying to kill Frank, and for being an incredibly dangerous psychopath. She wanted to watch his beady eyes roll back in his head as he drew his final breath from having 15 nine millimeter slugs pumped into his black heart. Imagining those vicious scenarios was cathartic to her, but totally unprofessional, and profoundly not FBI. She was a professional and she would act like one.

The loud knocks on her door startled her. She gripped her Glock and faced the door.

"Who is it?" she said and moved to the wall next to the door.

"Candygram," said the familiar voice of Tom Gardner.

Braewyn looked through the peephole, then opened the door.

"Cezar Nicolai is in Washington," Tom said and stepped inside the room carrying a portfolio case. "We tracked him to Dulles."

"What tipped his hand?"

"Cell phone use and facial recognition videos at the airports."

"Hapburg's file?"

"Right here in the case, fresh off Nicolai's yacht. Copies are with Ortiz, and I made sets for us and Detective Dugan."

"Give the original file to Frank Dugan," Braewyn said. "He needs to see any ink colors and graphics exactly the way they came from Hapburg."

"Next?"

"Let's get to Stuart. I have a sick puppy to visit."

*　　*　　*　　*　　*

Cezar dialed Celine on his cell. The phone rang more than ten times. Frustration turned to anger as he jammed the phone into the breast pocket of his linen sport jacket. He stared out the side window of the Mercedes, pursed his lips, and buffed a tiny smudge on the glass with a tissue from the car's dispenser.

"Still not answering?" Vlad Torok said.

"Something's wrong," Cezar said. "Very wrong. As soon as we finish here, we need to get to the Viking."

Vlad drove to the rear of the *Enola Gay*'s pavilion and parked where Herschel Fleming instructed him to leave their car. Fleming was waiting at the back door of the building and smiled as they approached. The interior was illuminated by only a few of the overhead lights hanging directly over the B-29, which gave it the reverent atmosphere of being on display in a great cathedral. Every footstep clicked and echoed on the buffed tile floor.

The maintenance men had lowered the *Enola Gay* almost to floor level on her bright yellow scissor jacks so access could be gained into the fuselage. A special stair unit was placed directly under the open rear bomb bay doors.

"Access to the interior of the plane can be tricky for us old folks," Fleming said. "It's not like boarding a passenger jet."

"We'll manage," Cezar said. He looked at the entry set-up, then glanced at Vlad.

"I'll go first," Vlad said under his breath to Cezar. "Give you a hand, if you need it."

"One of our guides has stayed late to give you a tour of the aircraft," Fleming said. "He's an expert on the *Enola*. I'll send the maintenance men home and wait for you in my office in the next building. Enjoy your tour."

The guide went up first and stepped onto the floorboards that ran down the center of the giant. Vlad managed to join him with a determined effort and a little hard breathing. Cezar climbed straight up and in without any hesitation or visible difficulty.

"Us *old* folks?" Cezar said. "Who was Fleming talking about?"

"Welcome to the most celebrated warplane in the world, gentlemen," the guide said and gestured to a distant point forward of the bomb bay. "Up there is where the bombardier sat at his specially designed bomb sight installed in the nose. We'll begin our tour there. When the plane was on its final run to the target, this man took complete control of the plane. We've placed special walkways over the open bomb bays to make passage easier. Follow my steps, gentlemen."

The guard moved forward in the fuselage with Vlad and Cezar close behind. When the three passed beyond the bomb bay, the huge man subtly removed something from his jacket pocket.

It was a maroon clamshell case.

*   *   *   *   *

Braewyn pulled into the parking lot of Martin County General Hospital and parked. Carrying the Hapburg file in a portfolio, she went to the registration desk to find Frank's room number. Tom Gardner stayed with the car.

A few minutes later, Braewyn got off the elevator on the second floor. She peeked into Room 210 and saw Frank putting on his clothes. Two Florida State Troopers sat in chairs on each side of the room.

"Is this where they keep heroes?" she asked.

Frank turned to her voice and smiled.

"Maybe," Frank said, then glanced at the troopers. "She says you guys are heroes?"

The state cops looked at each other and grinned.

"I'm referring to the man who risked his life to save an extremely troublesome FBI agent."

"I got you into that mess. Figured I should pull you out."

"Why in the world do you do the things you do?"

"Well, there are two things cops hate: change, and whatever stays the same."

"Amazing," Braewyn said and stepped closer to Frank. "They letting you loose on the world again?"

"No reason to keep me," Frank said while buttoning his shirt. "I'm fine."

"Where'd you get the clean duds?"

"Roland sent them. After he broke into my house."

"Your sheriff's a good man."

"Gets grumpy a lot."

"I'm available for a thank-you dinner," Braewyn said. "On me."

"Where?"

"They tell me Langford's in Jensen Beach is top drawer."

"Langford's it is, then."

"Here is Simon Hapburg's file, the original," Braewyn said and handed Frank the portfolio.

"Make any sense of it?"

"Not much, but you're the guy who knows about Omega formulas."

"Couldn't hurt to look them over."

"I'm thinking grouper and a nice Liebfraumilch."

"Ah, grouper. A specialty at Langford's," Frank said.

"What about appetizers?"

"What about dessert?" Frank said and raised one eyebrow.

"Let's see how the entrée goes."

Frank turned to the two state policemen.

"The hospital is throwing me out. Many thanks, fellas. I'll be okay from here."

"I'll notify your sheriff," the taller officer said. "By the way, he sent you something. It's in the closet."

The two men rose and tipped their campaign hats at Braewyn as they left the room.

411

"Take care, detective," the other trooper said from the hallway.

Frank opened the closet and found a neatly-packed box containing a jacket, money, and his gun. He gathered up the items, went into the bathroom, and closed the door. After a few minutes, he emerged, wearing a light windbreaker with his pistol in his belt holster.

"Normally, I wouldn't pass on confidential FBI information to an individual involved in an ongoing case," Braewyn said, "but I think the circumstances allow for it in this situation."

Braewyn stepped to the hall door and closed it.

"We've done extensive background work on Mister Cezar Nicolai," Braewyn said.

"And?"

"We're up against an extraordinary character."

"Tell me something I don't know."

"Okay. But this is the CliffsNotes version: he came from a second generation family who emigrated to America from Romanian and Russian roots."

"Was Count Dracula in his ancestry?"

"He dropped out of college for lack of money. Med school. His father got caught skimming money from his company and lost his job. Family went from low middle class to near destitution. Cezar applied for the Navy's Officers' Candidate School. He scored high on their evaluation and, upon completion, they made him an ensign. Assigned to a sub fleet out of Groton, Connecticut. Six years later he was discharged with the rank of Lieutenant Commander. He dropped off the radar for the next few years."

Frank sat on the bed.

"He's good at that," Frank said.

"We pick him up again in Russia brokering low-tech arms deals. Mostly small stuff with third world countries in Africa and the Middle East."

"He didn't get filthy rich hawking AK-47s in Somalia."

"It gets better. A few years ago he catches the brass ring. Actually, the platinum ring. He hooks up a squad of ballsy Muslim fanatics with a couple of Saudi Arabia's richest militants and scores huge. He drops everything else to feed weapons to jihadists… the al-Qaeda variety. He moves up to heavyweight ordnance: tanks, ships, trucks, rockets, even low-grade nuclear stuff."

"Now he's got money," Frank said.

"Now he's on a first name basis with every banker in Zurich."

"So why's he chasing me?"

"He has an obsession with world history, especially warfare. He studies men like Darius, Napoleon,… Hitler."

"So he wants the Omega weapon because he thinks it can make him like them? Brutus said 'Caesar was ambitious.' The bastard's well-named."

"He doesn't want to be like any of those men," Braewyn said.

"Why not?"

"They were all losers."

"Who then?" Frank asked.

"He wants to be Alexander the Great."

"Who wept when there were no more worlds to conquer?"

"And you want to fight this man?" Braewyn asked. "A man who believes in his invincibility?"

"I'd rather fight a man who believes in Hell."

Braewyn said, "This is only the tip of the iceberg. We have much more to talk about."

Braewyn's cell rang. She checked the incoming display.

"Yes, Tom," Braewyn said and listened for almost a minute, then ended the call.

"Alasdair MacGowan is being held at the Martin County Detention Center. Roland had him picked up in Vero. We have agents heading there now to take him into custody."

"I need to talk to him," Frank said and rushed out the door.

*   *   *   *   *

Cezar watched the flight attendant in first class come down the aisle with their drinks. She handed a margarita to Cezar and a Heineken to Vlad. Both were seated in the plane's center. The Internet news was on one of the video screen consoles in front of them. Cezar tossed a fifty-dollar bill on her tray for which she nodded a deep thank-you, returned to the service galley near the plane's cockpit, and drew the privacy curtain.

"Why would Dugan send us on this wild goose chase?" Cezar said. "It makes no sense. He has to know if I don't find what I want, I'll be back."

"Maybe he wants us out of the picture for a while," Vlad said.

"Again, why? Did he think I'd dash up here and leave him loose in Florida?"

"Not *very* loose, anyway."

"I wish he hadn't found the bug in his phone. His conversations with his diver friend were priceless."

"The good news is, you didn't have to give Fleming a donation."

"He should never have allowed us to park in the back lot," Cezar said.

"I'd love to have seen the reaction when that guide woke up and Fleming realized we were long gone."

Both men surfed for news on their monitors.

"Think the detective is okay?" Vlad asked.

"Dugan? Let's have a look," Cezar said and took out his cell phone and flipped his thumb through a menu of apps and stopped at a GPS tracking program. He expanded the view of his screen and located the position of the planted transducer in Frank Dugan's shoe.

The phone's GPS still showed Frank's indicator dot as being in the Atlantic Ocean a few miles due east off the Florida coast. It was a comfort for Cezar to imagine Dugan's maddening thoughts, knowing he was in a tight spot he couldn't escape, a situation he knew the cocky detective feared greatly; a tight, dark place in deep water, exactly as he'd blurted out on the phone to Alasdair.

"It's an ill wind indeed that blows no one any good," Cezar said.

"Beg pardon, sir?"

"It's Detective Dugan's location indicator."

"Still on the boat?"

"Yes, but wait, …it seems to have moved somehow."

"Well, the transponder is in his shoe, isn't it? He could have moved around on the sub."

"More than thirty miles north?"

"He's moving the sub?" Vlad said, his eyes wide.

"Incredible. I was hoping to keep him in place so we could wheedle some genuine Omega data out of him. Especially after what we went through on the

416

Enola Gay. How did he do that?" Cezar said, punching each word.

"Do what, sir?"

"The indicator says he's managed to move the submarine to near Vero Beach," Cezar said and showed the phone's GPS screen to Vlad. "I want him alive and where I put him. Get the news on the monitor," Cezar said and nodded toward the computer screen in front of Vlad.

Vlad brought up a major browser and clicked on the news link. A list of headlined items appeared on the right side of the screen. One in particular drew his attention.

Daring rescue in Florida saves
man trapped in Russian submarine

Vlad clicked on the item's hyperlink and the full story came up, along with a picture. The picture was of the stern of the dive boat, a few crewmembers, and in the center was Alasdair MacGowan sitting next to Frank Dugan wrapped in a blanket.

"I guess that answers that question," Cezar said. "Looks like he's indeed alive and in good hands. No ordinary man, our uncanny Detective Dugan."

"Look at the picture, sir. Look at the feet."

"Dugan is not wearing the athletic shoes we put the transponder in."

"So who's driving the sub?" Vlad asked.

"That's as big a mystery as this Omega formula."

Cezar and Vlad were so rapt in the news picture on the monitor they never noticed the plane turning in a wide arc.

Chapter 58

Alasdair, dressed in an orange jump suit and cuffed wrists and ankles, was escorted into the visitors section of the detention center where Frank waited. The guards seated Alasdair at the long table across from Frank; a ten-inch high partition ran down the center of the table. Frank dismissed the guards with a nod and they withdrew to a position twenty feet behind their detainee.

"I know you want to kill me," Alasdair said. "And I deserve no less from you."

"Oh, I considered it. It was tough, at first. The betrayal of a most trusted friend, the total disregard for the sacred bond between cop partners, built up an anger in me that you've only witnessed when I applied it against the low life we often have to face on the job. But in time you step back and begin to maintain some sense of sanity."

"When I mess up, I do it proper," Alasdair said.

"Yeah, you do," Frank said and stared at his old friend. "Why, Al?"

"One day, when you love again, you'll find out what lengths you'll go to to preserve that love."

"All this is about Celine?"

"Eighty percent. The video company was failing. I looked into bankruptcy. Then Cezar Nicolai came along, renewing his relationship with Celine and throwing money at us. He wanted help with his quest for the Omega weapon. He had information from the Hapburgs in Michigan that your grandfather had all the answers he needed, but, since William was long passed, he wanted to question your father. I put him on to Dellarue. He said he just wanted to talk to him."

"Joe's death didn't give you a clue about Nicolai's ruthlessness?" Frank asked.

"I was told Joe died from natural causes. I never knew it was murder until you showed up. You took me into that fallout shelter and I thought we were home free. Nicolai gave us a small fortune to work you for the information he wanted. Celine could barely control her emotions when she got the Omega film. Cezar knew then he was on the right track to get the weapon. Everyone was ecstatic, and Celine stopped nagging me about money."

"She wasn't kidnapped, was she?"

"No. She left me for Nicolai. How'd you know?""

"The purse. You said she was kidnapped and left her Gucci purse, but Braewyn saw she had it on Nicolai's yacht."

"I slipped up," Alasdair said and dropped his eyes to his shackled hands.

"You slipped up all over the place. The bug you put on my lamp when I went out to get coffee and donuts I later found to be the exact same make and model bug in my cell phone in Vero. I traced their purchase to your company. You never put up those video cams at Elm Terrace. I'll write that off to lack of money, but maybe you didn't want me looking in on your activities there. And while I thank you for your ocean rescue, you sure knew your way around that Russian sub. Probably because you helped put my drugged body on it."

"My God, I got sloppy. Cezar swore to me he wouldn't harm you."

"He didn't figure on my incredible submariner skills."

"When I got the call from your sheriff, I knew what I had to do."

"The list goes on," Frank said. "Inspection of the Tresor Penthouse trash turned up an empty bottle of Laphroaig scotch, your brand of choice, I remembered. And the real topper: the 'two goons' who tried to kill me in Jensen Beach. I never mentioned them to you. How did you know about them?"

"They told me about the incident later. They were specifically ordered *not* to harm you. Even help you get back to your car. The last thing Nicolai wanted was for you to be dead. Who would lead him to the Omega weapon then?"

"In spite of that, Nicolai used them again?"

"Nicolai had them killed. Right in front of me. Wasn't pretty."

"I bet," Frank said.

"Then Nicolai got Celine killed, and I do fully blame him for her death, not Braewyn Joyce. After that I knew my life was over."

"Why did Nicolai allow Celine to let the feds see the film?"

"He needed proof that the weapon was real, and knew the government could fully explore that. Their verdict was positive. After that, the race was on to find it."

"How are you holding up?" Frank asked.

"I try to keep it together, but I know I'm going to do time. Maybe a long time."

"You'll get a fair trial. May not turn out as bad as you think."

"A cop in the joint? Might as well shoot me now."

"Braewyn can get you into a low security federal prison. You'll think you're at a country club."

"That's possible?" Alasdair asked.

"You have a big plus going for you. You never had anything to do directly with the killing and violence. And you even saved one life. Big points to keep you out of the max lock-ups."

"Will you visit me on Christmas?"

"Well, I've crossed going to prison off my bucket list, but ... No power on earth could keep me away. I'm your friend ... through the good times and the tough ones."

Alasdair's eyes filled and reddened, his manacled hands stretched across the table barrier. The guards rushed in, but Frank waved them off and clasped Alasdair's hand.

"Do you know how to tell if a person is truly a friend?" Frank asked.

"No."

"You're always glad to see him," Frank said. "Always."

Chapter 59

The pleasant voice of the pilot announced calmly over the plane's intercom:

"We've had to return to Washington-Dulles International because of an unsecured piece of baggage in our rear cargo bay. Nothing serious, but a bit noisy. Our apologies for the delay in getting you to Miami. We'll get it properly secured and be back in the air in a few minutes."

Cezar Nicolai didn't think the pilot's voice was pleasant. The announcement portended danger he could feel in his core. He cursed the luck that his usual method of flight, his Learjet, was in for routine maintenance. He hated commercial flying, and was certain the forced return was for an entirely different reason than a cargo problem. He was sure it was for a problem with his alias, Mr. Evans.

The Boeing 777 landed and taxied into its docking area and wound its whining engines down to a low murmur. The passengers in first class stayed in their seats and rubbernecked out the windows to look for the maintenance people dealing with the problem cargo bay. Three substantial men, all younger than forty, entered the first class section and filed down the aisle directly to the shoulder of Vlad Torok. Two other air marshals rose from their coach

424

seats and positioned themselves in the doorway separating first class from the rest of the passengers.

"I need you gentlemen to unfasten your seat belts and come with us," one of the trio of men in airport security windbreakers said, and displayed a wallet ID.

Cezar nodded to Vlad to do as they were instructed without incident. The seven men exited the plane through the docking tunnel where Cezar and Vlad were closely escorted down the empty passageway leading to the boarding corridor. They marched the short distance without speaking. The two air marshals ended their escort at the terminal side of the tunnel, closed its accordion curtain, and returned to the plane.

The jet engines of the 777 spooled up and the Boeing pulled away from the dock. Cezar took the noisy departure of the plane as a good backdrop for a little self-made drama. He exhaled a loud, rasping breath, clutched his left forearm and collapsed onto the corridor's carpeting. Two of the security officers followed him to the floor and knelt to offer him help. With the speed of a young Mohamed Ali, Vlad slammed his ham-size fist into the face of the standing marshal. The security man hit the floor hard, unable to respond with a defense.

Cezar shot a karate blow into the throat of one of his attending marshals who rolled onto his back, gasping to clear his collapsed airway. The remaining marshal attempted to get to his feet and draw his sidearm, but Vlad was directly behind him and yanked the pistol from his hand. Cezar removed the pistols from the two downed men, while Vlad held all three at bay with the gun he'd taken.

"Get your IDs and radios out and on the floor and take off your jackets," Cezar said, gesturing with the pistols.

"You won't get far," the standing marshal said.

"All of you get up and head back to the end of the dock," Cezar said as the two downed men recovered enough to stand.

"Your plane's gone," a marshal said.

"Move," Cezar said.

The men did as they were told and marched back to the accordion curtain that covered the tunnel doorway. Cezar ordered them to reopen the curtain, which they did without question. The retracted tunnel now only extended a few feet into open air and was nearly fifteen feet off the ground.

"Jump," Cezar said.

Two of the security officers jumped right away, the last one hesitated enough for Vlad to step in and shove him out with his foot and reclose the curtain.

Cezar and Vlad donned two of the security jackets and picked up the IDs that most closely fit their descriptions. Vlad struggled to get the largest of the jackets to fit around his massive shoulders. Engaging the zipper was impossible.

Cezar took two of the radios, and Vlad shoved the rest to the side. The pair stuck their newly-acquired weapons inside their pants and snugged them under their belts, hidden by the jackets. That done, they calmly walked out into the boarding area, through the passageways, and down the escalator and outside to a line of waiting cabs.

Vlad flagged the nearest cab and both men climbed in.

"Get us to Parking Lot C," Cezar said to the driver. "I'll direct you from there."

The cabbie drove the short distance to the C lot where Cezar led the driver to a row of parked cars on the back side of the lot.

"It's right there. The Blue Toyota Corolla," Cezar said.

The cabbie stopped the car and Cezar paid him with a twenty. He waited until the cab drove out of sight, then darted between parked cars to a space on the opposite side of the row.

Parked there was the rented Mercedes-Benz CLS sedan.

The two men climbed into the car and casually drove out of the airport without a single police encounter, which surprised Cezar and elated Vlad.

"No cops," Vlad said.

"When plans fail, embrace the luck," Cezar said.

*   *   *   *   *

The highway patterns of passing cities and quilted patches of farmland could be seen in the clear morning air 35,000 feet below the plane as it made its way to Maryland. The seat next to Frank was empty so he put his briefcase there and reviewed the copies in Simon Hapburg's file taken from Nicolai's yacht. Braewyn Joyce and Tom Gardner had looked over the file at the sheriff's station in Stuart, but had found nothing that revealed anything useful regarding an Omega weapon. A set of the file documents were also sent to FBI headquarters for further analysis.

The Tresor Penthouse trash turned up DNA and fingerprints, but nothing that told him anything he didn't already know about Cezar Nicolai. There was a second person's DNA and other prints that couldn't be matched to anyone in government files. All the trouble Frank went through to obtain the Tresor's trash was basically a bust, except for one item that confirmed a hunch he'd already classified as factual. It saddened Frank to find it. It was the empty Laphroaig scotch bottle he knew connected Alasdair to Nicolai.

The Hapburg file added only one new item to what Frank already knew. It had to do with the delivery explosive used to propel the Omega formula's unidentified pulse or shock wave that supposedly killed whatever was within its effective radius. According to the document, the explosive was unusual in that it had to be brewed and left to mature before it could be used. The maturation process took exactly 11 days and purportedly caused the propellant to activate and release the deadly invisible pulse. While all this new information was important, it still did nothing to reveal anything about the business end of the formula. How that delivery system could be incorporated into something as complex as Doctor Dekler's equation, Frank had no clue.

The trip to Maryland was partly to enlist the help of a reputable realtor and set up the sale of the house. Frank wanted to get the Reo back from Alasdair's and put it somewhere safe, especially since no one would be at the MacGowan home to watch it. Keeping his pursuers where he wanted them was most important now. Leaving Orlando and flying to Kansas would have them nipping at his heels, but diverting through Baltimore-Washington International would keep the hounds guessing.

He put the Hapburg papers back in their file jacket and spied a wadded paper stuck in the bottom of one of the other folders. He opened it and skimmed its brief message. It was a memo from William to Simon that Frank hadn't seen in the batch from the fallout shelter.

October 16, 1962

Simon,

Early intel has confirmed Russian missiles being installed in Cuba, which may necessitate the re-deployment of the Omega Formula to active duty. To be safe, start putting together the delivery components. I'll take care of the rest.

Pray that Kennedy can back down Khrushchev.

Best regards,

W

Frank reclined his seat back a few inches and closed his eyes. He now was certain the Omega weapon was real. That chilling thought ramped up the danger to the exosphere.

There also was a more terrestrial concern:
Who else knew what he now knew?

Chapter 60

The house on Elm Terrace was as Frank had left it
weeks ago, with the exception of its newly painted
white exterior and trimmed landscape that were
striking in the strong afternoon sun of mid-August.
Alasdair had brought in experts who had made the
old place sparkle.

Frank parked his rented Tahoe in the garage
space once occupied by the Reo and jumped out. He
wiped his hand across the shiny fender of the
Corvette in the next bay like a schoolboy caressing
his first car. He locked the garage and went directly
into the house without clearing the front porch of
flyers and free newspapers. He shot a glance toward
the mailbox back at the curb, and allowed that its
pile of junk mail could wait until he got settled.

The inside of the house was stifling hot and the
air smelled of baked walnut and mahogany, but the
odor of neglect and garbage was gratefully absent.

Frank immediately switched on the air
conditioning and turned on the overhead fans in
three downstairs rooms. He made himself a drink,
clicked on the television, and sprawled on the parlor
sofa. It had been a trying week and his brain begged
him to rest.

Frank surfed through several programs on the TV and stopped at a documentary on the Smithsonian Channel that caught his attention. The show was about the discovery of the Spanish ship *Atocha* and its bounty of gold, jewels, and other historical artifacts discovered off the west side of the Florida keys by long-time treasure hunter Mel Fisher. The narrator described the long legal battles Fisher had undergone with the state of Florida over the ownership of what he'd uncovered and brought to the surface.

When the documentary ended, he changed channels. A breaking news banner silently scrolled across the screen informing viewers of the recent security activity at Dulles International, but Frank paid little attention to it until a black and white video began to play. Frank recognized the men centered in the clip. Cezar Nicolai and Vlad Torok were two men one never forgot.

Frank was pleased that Nicolai had taken the bait and went to see the *Enola Gay*. From the looks of all the cops in video, it appeared he'd done considerably more.

*   *   *   *   *

Through a filthy window, Cezar scanned the area where Vlad had parked the Mercedes and noted that the car looked out of place sitting near the beat-up International pickup truck and the 1950 Oldsmobile rusting on cinder blocks in the back of the rundown farmhouse. The place had looked trashy the night before, but in the afternoon light it was hard to believe it was habitable. Cezar considered the fact that the lone octogenarian who had called the place home would no longer need to concern himself with any of its desperately needed improvements, even if he would've been so inclined.

Vlad Torok shoved his way through the sticking front door of the house and stepped onto the screened-in porch. Cezar followed and focused his gaze on the pot-holed dirt road that ran from the front yard to a secondary road almost a half a mile away.

"What do you think?" Cezar said.

"Quiet. Not a car out there."

"Good. We'll take that county road to the highway," Cezar said. "Where did you put Farmer Brown?"

"Buried him in the compost pit out back. He won't put out a noticeable smell there."

"You're a thoughtful man."

"Get the car?" Vlad asked.

"Not yet. Wait until nightfall," Cezar said. "Darkness can be a useful ally."

*   *   *   *   *

433

The sun had set more than an hour before Cezar directed Vlad to drive around the DC beltway and take 95 north toward Baltimore. Vlad kept the high beams off, maintained an acceptable speed, and stayed out of the fast lane where state police cruisers concentrated attention. Cezar studied the signs announcing the approaching exits to Columbia, Maryland and the Baltimore beltway beyond.

"I called the marina people and had them check the Viking for Celine," Cezar said. "They said the FBI has it cordoned off as a crime scene. They didn't get a lot of details from the agents. Celine's nowhere to be found. She may have had to dispose of Braewyn and run for it. Not good."

"Celine should've contacted you by now."

"True," Cezar said working the car's GPS system in the dashboard. "We need to get rid of this car. It has a LoJack system, and by now, they may have traced us through the rental agency."

"What's our plan, sir?"

"I know a place nearby where there may be an important document I could use. Take the 195 exit up ahead."

"Where will that take us?"

"To a tiny place I was told about. In Catonsville."

*　　*　　*　　*　　*

The ring of the cell phone startled Frank from his short nod-off. He grimaced and fumbled in his pocket to pull out the offending phone. He squinted to read the phone's display, but didn't recognize the number.

"Yes?"

"Detective Dugan, it's David Hapburg."

"Hey, guy," Frank said and rose from the sofa. "How are you doing?"

"Okay, I guess. I didn't get a chance to tell you everything when we talked before. I was beating it out of my house and just wanted to get away."

"Your place is a shithouse, by the way. Nicolai and his buddy, King Kong, tore it apart. And the sonofabitch beat me to Simon's file."

"Sorry to hear that. God, I hate knowing he got more information about the formula."

"I now have the file. No big deal. Nothing he can use, really."

"You got the file? You killed Nicolai?"

"No. Long story for later," Frank said and paced the room. "Right now, what's up?"

"I found something else in the basement and took it with me when I left the house. I didn't want to leave it behind. I think it may be important."

"What?"

"I'm not sure this phone connection is safe," David said in a whisper.

"Give me a hint, but don't be specific," Frank said. "What did you find?"

"Another film."

Chapter 61

It was well after 11 PM when the Mercedes arrived at the Dugan house on Elm Terrace. Cezar instructed Vlad to park across the street where they could take a good, long look at the place to see if there was any activity inside.

"There's a light on in the one of the front rooms," Vlad said.

"There may be someone staying there, but more likely the lights are on a timer," Cezar said. "Check the mailbox."

Vlad slipped out of the car and gently eased the driver's door shut to muffle any noise. He pretended to check a rear tire for a few moments, then casually strolled over to the curbside mailbox and opened it. It was full of letters and advertisements. He closed the box and returned to the car.

"Doesn't look like anyone's been here for a while," Vlad said through the open door.

"Get in," Cezar said. "I'm going to order a pizza."

*   *   *   *   *

The pizza delivery man had rung the bell several times, but no one was answering the door at 1505

Elm Terrace. He tried banging on the door with his fist. Still nothing. He set the insulated cover with the pizza down on the porch glider and made a call on his cell. After a short conversation, the man grabbed the pizza, marched back to his Honda Civic, and roared away, never noticing the two sets of eyes watching intently from the Mercedes across the street.

"Park the car in the back, out of sight," Cezar said.

The Mercedes slowly rolled up the driveway and idled in front of the garage. After a few seconds, the purr of the engine fell silent.

"Isn't this the house where we had our chat with Joe?" Vlad asked.

"The same."

"But you said Celine told you about this place."

"Not the house, a tiny hidden room. Something Alasdair told her about."

Cezar and Vlad exited the car and studied the windows of the house.

"Let's chance it," Cezar said.

A minute later the two men were in the garage. Wood from part of the door frame lay shattered on the floor.

"She said it was down those steps in the last bay under that truck." Cezar said and led Vlad to the mechanic's pit formerly covered by the Reo.

Vlad stooped by the open metal door to peer under the Tahoe.

"It looks like where you'd work on your car," Vlad said.

"Oh, it's much more than that," Cezar said and descended the concrete steps to the bottom of the pit with Vlad, bent low behind him.

"Is this place going to help us with the formula?" Vlad asked.

"Move that tool cart and push on the electric outlet behind it."

Vlad followed the directions and turned sharply toward the noise that came from the wall next to the steps.

"Follow me," Cezar said with a note of satisfaction in his tone.

Cezar felt his way down the dark, narrow tunnel and groped the interior walls of the shelter until he found the light switch. The room's single, austere bulb dimly lit the space. Cezar surveyed the room and smiled. He rifled through the desk and rapidly assessed its few papers for their value, and discarded them just as quickly.

"Anything good, sir?" Vlad said from the doorway, his body filling the tunnel.

"No. Nothing. The place has been ravaged."

"What is this room?"

"A safe room, old style. My God, we were right here, Vlad, and didn't find this. Joe Dugan knew it was here, and I'll wager it was full of useful information then."

Cezar gave the shelter a thorough look around, and spent a moment at the victory calendar on the wall over the desk. He leaned on the small utility table a few steps away and squinted at the back of the enclosure where the light trailed off. He stooped to see if there was anything under the kneehole of the desk, and let his eyes sweep the room from his low perspective. He rose and patted Vlad on his firm shoulder.

Cezar shot out of the room and up the steps. While he waited for Vlad to struggle his way back into the garage, Cezar stopped for a long moment to stare at the Chevy Tahoe. He peered inside and spotted a yellow paper protruding from under the visor. He took it down and studied it.

"Find something?" Vlad said, emerging from the pit.

"A car rental agreement. Made out to a Frank Dugan," Cezar said and returned the paper to the visor.

"Take the Tahoe?" Vlad asked.

"I'd like to change vehicles," Cezar said as he stepped to the front of the vehicle and placed his hand on the hood, "but this one may not be a good choice for us. Dugan's been here recently. This car's still warm. Besides, this one has OnStar."

"This is his ride and he's not in the house?" Vlad said. "What gives?"

"Celine said he keeps other cars here. Like that Explorer over there," Cezar said and pointed to the vehicle. "Dugan must be out. A car could've been here in this center bay. If he's here, I can't believe he wouldn't have answered the door for the pizza man, but let's not press our luck. He'll be back. And we don't have a hostage to bargain with now. If he catches us here, I guarantee you, bullets will fly."

"Why don't we snatch a couple of license plates off some other car and put them on the Mercedes?"

"You know, you're almost as clever as that charitable Mr. Evans."

"Take the plates off the Explorer?"

"Better not. Dugan might notice and call the police."

Cezar slid into the car and watched Vlad clamber into the driver's seat of the luxury rental like a fireman on an alarm call.

The Mercedes eased out of the driveway and slowly motored down the dark street. Cezar reminded Vlad to keep the urge to speed in check as they drove toward the interstate. Cezar consulted a map on the GPS monitor and directed a carefully orchestrated getaway to Route 140 west.

*　*　*　*　*

441

Frank saw David Hapburg waiting in the rest area on the Harrisburg Expressway near York, Pennsylvania. As he approached, he could see David's head jerking toward every set of headlights that pulled in or out of the parking area. Frank roared up next to Hapburg's familiar Jeep Cherokee, shut down the Corvette's throbbing engine and jumped out.

"We have to stop meeting like this," Frank said as he climbed into David's car with an envelope in his hand.

"You own a classic Corvette?" David said, his right knee dancing up and down spasmodically.

"I had a need for speed," Frank said. "You okay?"

"When will this mess be over?"

"Soon, I hope," Frank said. "You staying around here?"

"My sister's in Lancaster. She and her husband run our family furniture business there and they want me to come work for them. I think I will. Got no reason to stay in Detroit. My job's not that great, and I want to sell the house and get away from all this spy business."

"How'd you know I was in Maryland?"

"Your boss. Sheriff Brand, isn't it?"

"That'd be him."

"He said he was sure you'd want me to know. Told me if I wasn't on the level he'd personally put me in the county's wood chipper. Like in the movie *Fargo*."

"He's a hands-on kinda guy," Frank said and pulled a photocopy from the envelope and handed it to Hapburg. "Would you happen to know who the man is standing next to my grandfather?"

"That's Simon Hapburg, *my* grandfather," David said and placed his finger on the mystery man in the picture.

That was the confirmation Frank wanted to hear.

"What do you think they're doing in this picture?"

"Not sure," David said. "Maybe working on a type of space tool. Looks like a shovel... or a hoe."

"Yeah, what I thought too," Frank said.

"They both did work for NASA, so it fits."

Frank stuffed the picture back into the envelope.

"I've got something to show you," Frank said and took the silk map from his pocket and unfolded it for David to see. "My grandfather took pains to hide this. Know anything about it?"

"Yeah, I do. It's the kind of map they gave our flyboys going on missions into enemy territory. Silk could get wet and still be okay to read."

"I know that much, but is there anything about this particular map?"

David looked more intently at the map in the bluish light straying into the car windows.

"Oh, yeah. My dad had one like this. They crashed a plane on the coast of Japan. On purpose. That's where they planted the Omega film. The one like you have. The pilot of the plane was given this map in case the pick-up submarine couldn't hook up with him."

"Did he make it out alive?" Frank asked.

"Yeah. The sub got him. Japs thought he drowned in Tokyo Bay. Ballsy sucker, but he got back okay. My dad told me Simon went to see the guy in Oregon after the war. That's where we got the map."

"Okay, so what's up with this new footage?"

"I'm not sure, but I know it's not the same as the film you have."

"How do you know?"

"I looked at a few feet of it with a magnifying glass. Looks like it's about the making of a movie, like maybe horror or science fiction. Had all these movie slates popping up.

"You seem to like movies a lot."

"I do. I go to the movies every week, and I've got every movie channel on satellite TV."

"And where is this horror flick?"

David dug under his car seat and pulled out a paper bag and handed it to Frank.

"Feels about the same size as the first one," Frank said as he took the 16mm reel can out of the bag and opened it.

444

"Yeah, I thought it was that one until I read the label."

Frank looked closely at the label in the low ambient light.

On the metal reel can was a single phrase:

O. F. Takes

Chapter 62

Cezar watched Vlad screw the newly acquired Maryland plates on the Mercedes over the existing plate. They had pulled off the 695 Baltimore Beltway in Pikesville, Maryland and hunted for a car whose tags wouldn't be missed right away. They'd driven several miles west to Reisterstown before Cezar spotted an ideal candidate in the back of a closed used car lot on Route 140 and took its tags. He granted that the move was chancy, but driving around with the original rental agency license plates seemed much riskier.

"If we make it to Westminster tonight," Cezar said, "I'll feel like we're safe. I could use a night's sleep."

"Is that house safe?"

"I've paid well to make it so. It'll be safe, my worrisome friend."

"Should we take a flight out in the morning?" Vlad said.

"No. Detective Dugan is in Maryland. We need to track his every move while he's here," Cezar said.

"How?"

"His cell phone."

"We can get access to cell locations?"

"I know a high ranking cop who will help us with that."

Cezar switched to the Internet on the onboard computer and pulled up the latest NBC news. One of the lead stories concerned two men who had been taken into custody, but later overpowered three air marshals and were on the loose. A multi-state police search was in progress to find and apprehend the pair. And the authorities had something that strongly favored their success: video footage from numerous airport surveillance cameras.

"This is not how I want my 15 minutes of fame," Cezar said.

"Time to adjust the battle plan, sir?" Vlad said.

Cezar Nicolai's sullen face said it all.

A tense night lay ahead.

*   *   *   *   *

As soon as the Corvette pulled up to the garage it was immediately apparent someone had visited the Elm Terrace address. Frank saw the damaged wood of the garage's open door frame, and had his Browning drawn before the Corvette's engine came to a stop. He slipped out of the driver's seat and took a cautious peek into the garage. Seeing no one, he stepped inside. His eyes shot to the mechanic's pit and he darted down its steps to examine the space.

The opening to the fallout shelter was closed tight, but the tool cart had been moved.

Inside the shelter, he saw evidence of intrusion, files open and in disarray on the desk, and chairs moved from where he'd left them. He found a magnifying glass in the shelter desk and decided to carefully look at the new film a few frames at a time. Frank had to agree with David's assessment. It looked like someone was making a sci-fi or horror film. The thing that jolted his attention was the bombing of the prairie dog colony. Not only was it real-looking, but an actual location was cited on the movie slates. Road signs were filmed as well as prominent landmarks. It was filmed near Wichita, Kansas on a lonely stretch of dusty prairie. A place he hoped he could later find and examine.

Frank closed the shelter and did his best to nudge the garage's busted door into a closed position, even though he realized locking it again was going to require a carpenter. Right now he had a plane to catch and he knew getting a direct flight to a small town in Kansas was impossible. Kansas City, Missouri, the closest city with a big time airport, would have to do.

From Kansas City, he'd have to resort to a less traceable means than flying. Frank was prepared to take a horse if he had to.

* * * * *

The TV announcer's voice immediately caught the attention of Cezar Nicolai who stopped chewing his late breakfast. The graphic in the background showed a picture relating to the news topic. Vlad and Cezar both caught a glimpse of the brief shot of Frank Dugan as they sat at the dining table in Westminster, Maryland.

"…and now the FBI has extended its search for the Florida detective to all across the United States," the announcer said. "His latest location was in the Kansas City, Missouri area where he rented a car with no known direction or destination yet determined. Detective Dugan was recently rescued from being trapped in a sunken submarine. Authorities believe he may be under mental distress from the ordeal. If you see this man, do not approach him. You are asked to contact your local police or FBI office."

Contact phone numbers appeared on the screen for the FBI hotline and the police.

"We have to find him and follow him," Cezar said. "Everything hinges on time now and I'm certain our time's running quite short."

"Another plane trip, sir? The airports are crawling with people looking for us," Vlad said.

"The Lear's ready by now," Cezar said and handed his cell to Vlad. "Call Beckham and get him here. Tell him to meet us and file a flight plan for

Kansas City, Missouri. There's a small airfield here in Westminster. He knows it. We've used it before."

"Got it," Vlad said and hit a button on the phone.

"We need to move right now. Get a crew together. Maybe two or three more men. Call Yan Bantich to get them and meet us at Kansas City International."

Chapter 63

Scrambling an FBI Learjet in an emergency was a lot easier than Braewyn had imagined. Within hours they were in the air and hurtling toward the America's heartland at just under Mach 1. Braewyn Joyce consulted a map of the central United States. Roland, seated next to her up front, looked on as she traced routes with her fingers from Kansas City, Missouri into Kansas.

"Last count, he left Kansas City and headed southwest toward Topeka," Braewyn said. "We'll get updates when we land."

"Where are we landing?" Roland said.

"Wichita."

"That's a good piece ahead of where he is."

"By the time we arrive, I figure he'll be somewhere near that area," Braewyn said. "By the way, my superior suggested that I not get involved in this case. Wanted me to take vacation time."

"You obviously refused," Roland said.

"Yep."

"You're ignoring FBI protocol?" Roland said.

"They sent me out in the field to flush out the quarry, then want me to go back and stay in the barn when the real hunting starts. So screw protocol."

"You think we can catch him?"

451

"To tell you the God's truth," Braewyn said, "I think he wants to get caught."

*   *   *   *   *

The Learjet 31 touched down at Kansas City International and minutes later Cezar and Vlad were in one of the airport bars checking the news reports. No updates were forthcoming on their stray detective. They headed for the rental car kiosks on the concourse.

Vlad took a cell call as they hurried through the airport.

"The new men are here," Vlad said. "I told them to keep in touch with us until we need them."

"Good."

"How safe are we here in the open?" Vlad said adjusting his Nike baseball cap and sunglasses.

"The travelers in the crowds will never even notice us. We're back east news. We need to be on our toes around security personnel. The hats and shades should do the trick."

"And you look a lot different without your mustache," Vlad said. "*I* hardly recognize you."

Under the pretense that they were supposed to meet with Frank, they questioned all the major car rental agencies. They scored a hit at a small outfit called *Miles-For-Less*, but their company had already been visited by the police and the counterman there was reluctant to render any more information about their customers. The clerk's reservations eased and he became somewhat more informative after Cezar peeled off several hundred dollar bills on the counter. The bribe got him a peek at the computer screen where Frank Dugan's transaction was displayed. It showed that he'd rented a Chevy Impala earlier that day and he was using the rental "for pleasure," but little else.

Cezar and Vlad went back to the Learjet and sat at the lounge table on one side of the aircraft. Both men carefully examined William's poem as it lay on the before them. A map of Kansas was also opened to the area surrounding Kansas City.

"We have to figure this out and we have to do it now," Cezar said. "What do men in their seventies, boys on the moon, flying with eagles, brains on paper, and Martian men have do with a weapon of mass destruction?"

"Mars was a war god," Vlad said. "Obvious to me that it has to do with warfare, maybe military."

Cezar looked hard and long at Vlad, then back at the papers on the table.

"There was a reference to "the deep six," a naval term. What is related to the military around here?" Cezar said and checked the Kansas map for answers.

"Leavenworth?" Vlad said.

"Hardly a place with world class weapons. No navy installations are nearby. They're a bit short on coastline around here. There is an air force base in Wichita. They stockpile conventional bombs, but it's hardly a place you'd associate today with mass destruction weapons."

Cezar tapped his finger on the map on the word "Wichita."

"Wait," Cezar said. "Maybe we're not thinking in the right time frame. This could've been a strategically important place in the 1940s. Boeing had a plant there that built B-29s. There may be a connection between that base and the Omega weapon."

"This isn't going to be as easy as we thought," Vlad said, "even though we have all the clues."

"No, it's not going to be easy, and we *don't* have all the clues," Cezar said then leapt from his seat. "We're not using our heads. The answer's back in the terminal."

Ten minutes later, Cezar and Vlad stood before the *Miles-For-Less* counterman.

"Could you do us a big favor? We need to catch up with our friend. Would you be so kind as to determine where he is? The car he rented has OnStar, doesn't it?"

The clerk shook his head.

"I'm not sure I can—"

Cezar shoved another five hundreds over the counter onto the desk in front of the clerk who looked around cautiously and then pocketed them with the dexterity of a carnival magician.

We'll be back in a few minutes. We have to pick up our bags downstairs."

The clerk picked up the phone. Cezar smiled and nodded at Vlad as they walked down the corridor and disappeared among the crowd.

*   *   *   *   *

The Wichita tarmac was simmering with heat waves rising from the surface like desert mirages. The FBI jet docked up to the terminal and Braewyn and Roland rushed through the passageways to get to the car rental agency where a Ford Crown Victoria was waiting to take them a step closer to Frank Dugan. Braewyn signed the paperwork for the car, picked up the keys, and checked her cell phone.

"The Kansas City Police have him on Route 335 heading south for Emporia," Braewyn said. "They sent us the Impala's plate number as well."

"What's the plan?" Roland said.

"We head for Emporia," Braewyn said. "Ninety miles northeast of us. Let's go. The rental people are waiting for us outside with our Crown Vic."

"Then what?" Roland said as they quick-stepped to the rental lot.

455

"We could get the locals to pull him over when we relocate his position," Braewyn said as she spotted the Crown Vic and the rental attendants. "But that's not the plan. We're making sure we can follow Frank, but it can't look too easy."

Braewyn held out her paperwork to the rental attendant.

"I'm lost," Roland said, as they were escorted to the Ford sedan.

"If we can follow Frank, so can someone else," Braewyn said.

Braewyn and Roland jumped into the car and wheeled out of the parking lot.

"I knew it. I've known it all along," Roland said. "The sonofabitch is crazy as a drunk lab monkey."

*   *   *   *   *

Frank knew the police were aware of his last location and that their information was being forwarded to the FBI and likely other authorities. His attempt to tiptoe across the country in anonymity achieved all the success of the Ford Edsel. In fact, he hoped he wasn't making his itinerary too obvious.

Frank knew better than to use his cell. For a seasoned cop on the run, that would be a stupid thing to do. It was bad enough he'd used a rental car with OnStar, but at least that was excusable, since most

456

people didn't have the service, and it wasn't standard issue in every GM vehicle.

The sign ahead welcomed him to Emporia. From there he'd head south to Wichita.

Frank didn't know if he'd been tracked yet, and if he had been, how close were his pursuers. He remembered an old marine joke:

"Run as fast as you can from the enemy until you catch them."

*   *   *   *   *

When Cezar and Vlad returned to the *Miles-For-Less* agency the clerk they had bribed was gone. In his place was a young woman.

"Excuse me," Cezar said. "Where is the young man who was here a few minutes ago?"

"He's on his lunch break," she said. "May I help you?"

"He was trying to reach a customer of yours for us. A friend."

"There is a note here," she said.

Cezar took the note she handed him, walked away from the kiosk and unfolded it.

"Good news, sir?" Vlad said, watching Cezar read.

Cezar showed the note to Vlad. The paper contained a single word:

457

Emporia

Chapter 64

Emporia was 90 miles from Wichita and Frank estimated he was almost two hours away. But he was in no rush. Frank was hungry and hadn't eaten since munching on those lovely smoked almonds on the plane.

Frank parked the midnight blue Impala behind a box truck on a side street and got out. Stretching his legs felt good after all the sitting. A leisurely walk down 6th toward Merchant Street took him into the aromas of home-style summer cooking, like pit-charred barbeque and grilling burgers. His nose soon led him into the door of The Kansas Kookery where he stayed for 45 minutes and ate more baby back ribs than Nero after the Coliseum games. His stay there was not on his schedule, but he needed the food, and he had plenty of time to get to Wichita before late afternoon.

*   *   *   *   *

Braewyn drove the Ford rental inside the city limits of Emporia and searched for any sign of a dark blue Chevrolet Impala. She drove east on Route 50, which became 6th Avenue, and followed their last information regarding Frank's location. The intersection of 6th and Constitution was the target.

"Here's Constitution coming up," Roland said. "Slow down."

"I don't see any Impalas," Braewyn said, straining to look in all directions.

"I see a car rental place," Roland said. "*Miles-For-Less*. Isn't that the one where he got the car in Kansas City?"

"That's what Jack Ortiz said," Braewyn said. "You thinking what I'm thinking?"

"He has to know the cops are on to his location," Roland said.

Braewyn circled the block and found a parking space near the corner of 6th and Merchant.

"I'll go on foot from here," she said. "Take the wheel, sheriff. I'll make this quick."

*　　*　　*　　*　　*

Frank found the Lyon County Historical Museum east of Mechanic Street on 6th Avenue. He stepped to the information desk inside the door. A tall young fellow, with "Eddie" printed on a badge on his shirt pocket, looked up at Frank and smiled.

"Howdy, sir," the amiable man said with an accent like a country singer. "What can we do for you today?"

"Can you tell me the best way to get to Wichita?" Frank asked.

"You betcha. 'Bout an hour and a half hop south of here," the clerk said. "Now, me personally, I'd take I-35, the faster way, but they's others who'd argue against that and claim that U.S. 50 be'd the best way to go."

"I'll take your way."

"Well, a block west of here is Commercial Street," Eddie said, pointing with two bony fingers, "which becomes Route 99. You go right onto that and you'll hit old 35 just north of here and turn left. Follow the signs to Wichita from there and you'll do pretty fine."

*   *   *   *   *

The clerk at the *Miles-For-Less* agency confirmed to Braewyn that Frank Dugan had rented an Impala in Kansas City, Missouri and paid his bill with a Capital One MasterCard. Braewyn put a call in to Jack Ortiz to place an official FBI demand on Frank's credit card company to determine any new charges, especially ones at car rental agencies. She also inquired about nearby rental agencies and was given a list by the clerk.

Roland was waiting in the Crown Vic on Merchant Street when she returned with the latest on their friend and lawman.

461

"I think we've temporarily lost him," Braewyn said.

"How about checking with OnStar?" Roland asked.

"I could, but that would be cheating."

"Come again?"

"I shouldn't use means at my disposal to track Frank if a civilian wouldn't also have access to it."

"You're going to even the playing field with killers?"

"It's the way Frank wants it."

"So now his loonyness has rubbed off on you," Roland said.

Braewyn gazed out the windshield.

"Maybe."

*　*　*　*　*

Eddie Parks punched numbers on the phone at the Lyon County Museum desk and waited.

"Emporia Gazette," the pleasant woman's voice said.

"This is Eddie Parks from the museum."

"Yes, Eddie. Did you want to speak to someone about your ad?"

"No, but I do need to speak to someone about that detective fella that everyone is hunting for."

"The missing man from Florida? What about him?"

"He left my place not a minute ago. Said he was going to Wichita."

"I'll contact the AP and the police," the woman said. "Anything else?"

"Yeah. He's gonna take 35 south."

* * * * *

At 3 PM, Cezar Nicolai sat in the airport lounge at Kansas City International, northwest of Kansas City, Missouri, and sipped on a margarita as he pored over a map of Kansas. Vlad Torok, beside him, chugged on his Heinekin, and stared at a Royals baseball game on the wide screen TV above the bar.

"At last count," Cezar said, tracing routes on the map with a pen, "Dugan was going into Emporia. He's got to be going south or west from there."

"Maybe what he wants is in Emporia."

"If it is, he'll stay put, and we'll have to drive there. It's seven hours away."

"No airport there?"

"Nothing big enough for us," Cezar said, tracing roadways on the map. "If he moves, where can he go?"

Vlad studied the screen on his phone. "Wichita is 90 miles from there. Much bigger town."

"And Wichita has something that relates to World War Two."

463

"Should I tell the pilot to warm up the Lear?" Vlad asked.

"Give me a second…"

The baseball game was interrupted by a special news announcement.

"KTKA-TV has just learned that Frank Dugan, the Florida detective being sought by the FBI, has recently left Emporia and is heading southwest on the Kansas Turnpike toward El Dorado National Park."

A photo of Frank popped on the screen.

"He is driving a late model, dark blue Chevrolet Impala," the announcer continued. "The special agent in charge, Braewyn Joyce, has ordered all authorities to stand down any attempts to intercede at or stop the car. Detective Dugan was formerly regarded as missing, and is now being sought for questioning and is not wanted for any crime. Anyone observing him should immediately contact the FBI's hotline at 800-FEDBASE."

The baseball game resumed and Cezar looked at Vlad, the corners of his mouth slightly upturned.

"When plans fail, embrace the luck," Cezar said.

"Go after him?" Vlad said.

"If we follow the turnpike southwest we don't hit El Dorado Park," Cezar said using a swizzle stick to chart a southwestward course on the map on Route 35. "We end up somewhere south of there. I have a strong idea where our man is headed. It's the only place possible. According to Hapburg's memos, it's where they tested the Omega formula."

Cezar turned the map over where expanded insets of cities were printed and stuck the swizzle stick on a particular point as Vlad looked on.

"Warm up the Lear?" Vlad asked.

"Indeed, warm up the Lear. Gather the men and make the flight plan for Wichita, Kansas."

"We're going to visit the McConnell Air Force Base, sir?"

Cezar Nicolai smiled and nodded.

Chapter 65

Braewyn learned the latest on Frank from Jack Ortiz and sped west on Route 50. Her hopes of overtaking him were slim since he was driving a fast car and had a 45-minute jump on their Crown Vic.

"He can't speed on this road and risk being pulled over," Roland said.

Access signs to the Route 35 Kansas Turnpike approached on the right.

"Take the ramp," Braewyn said to Roland.

"That goes back to Wichita," Roland said.

"I know. Take it." Braewyn said.

"What are you doing?"

"Call it intuition," Braewyn said. "Just *do* it."

Roland turned onto the access ramp.

"Hang on, Victoria," Roland said, patting the dashboard. "We're riding with a psychic."

*   *   *   *   *

Darkness fell as Frank rolled into Wichita. The Prairie Inn Motel, on the east side of town, was no five-star Hilton, but it was clean and affordable. Frank paid for a room on the second floor that faced the parking lot, and went to the motel's lounge for a drink. Tomorrow he would know if he was right

466

about his decision to come to Kansas. Tomorrow…so near, and yet it seemed like a lifetime away.

Frank sat at the bar and smiled at the portly bartender who approached.

"Johnnie Black on the rocks," Frank said.

"Coming up," the bartender said. "Here for the air show?"

"Air show? No."

"It's not until next week, but a lot of folks get here early to get the best rooms."

"No, I'm here to see an old friend."

The bartender placed Frank's drink on a napkin in front of him.

"From out of town?"

"L.A."

"Ah, Hollywood, eh? Always wanted to go there."

"Weather's nice."

"Ever run into any of those big famous movie stars?"

"Occasionally. They look a lot different when they're not in the movies."

"In disguise, huh?"

"Sometimes. Like most folks, they'd rather not be bothered."

"Forgive my manners. I'm Elwood. Would you care to see a menu, sir?"

"No, thank you," Frank said. "Name's Jesse."

"Welcome to Wichita, Kansas, Jesse. You holler if you need anything," Elwood said and moved down the bar to wait on a couple seating themselves at the far end.

Frank sipped his drink and watched a few rounds of Roller Derby on one of the four bar televisions, and did the only thing he could do to pass the time.

He waited.

*　　*　　*　　*　　*

Cezar had no problem discovering where a Frank Dugan was staying, in a town with a limited number of accommodations close to the McConnell Air Force Base. In fact, he hit pay dirt on his third call to a row of motels on south Rock Road.

"What's next?" Vlad said.

"We watch him. Everywhere he goes, we go. Looks like he's got business with the air base."

"How'll we get inside?"

"There's a museum there. They welcome tourists."

"I hope they don't watch a lot of TV," Vlad said.

"It's Mr. Evans they want, not Colonel Chernac."

"Maybe we'll stay lucky," Vlad said.

"Maybe?" Cezar said. "They will try to defeat us, and they will always outnumber us, but I didn't get rich by being afraid of risks. This means too much to me. Frank Dugan will lead us to the Omega formula and we will take it, and control the balance of world power."

"Where can we live that's safe?"

"You'll love Dubai."

Vlad smiled at Cezar's words, but Cezar saw the reservation displayed on his friend's face. He had never known Vlad Torok to back down from anything or anyone. For the first time in their long relationship, he caught a whiff of faltering confidence in his partner. Cezar knew Vlad would follow him into Hell, but he sensed that he had given the Spartan that dwelled in Vlad a pre-battle pep talk before they marched to defend a latter-day Thermopylae. His friend would not disappoint him, even though Vlad might fear that the Persian army would be coming to meet them at the Gates to Hades.

Chapter 66

Frank looked at his watch. It was 10:13 PM The bar and lounge were almost filled to capacity. Elwood, the bartender, was having a busy night making drinks Frank had never heard of. *What's in a Redheaded Slut, a Slippery Nipple, and an Alabama Slammer?*

Words flowed to Frank's ear from a familiar voice.

"It'll be a comfort for you to know that I've left the entire Martin County law enforcement service in the hands of Carl Rumbaugh and Greg Martinez," Roland said, standing behind Frank.

"Elwood, a draft beer for my great uncle here," Frank said. "Cheapest you've got."

Roland wrapped an arm around Frank's shoulders and gave him a healthy shake.

"Good to see you too," Roland said. "Before you ask, Agent Joyce is with her real friends, the FBI task force surrounding the motel."

"She okay?" Frank asked.

"Shit no. She's half frazzled chasing some half-drowned dumbass halfway to Santa Catalina. Hasn't eaten since we left Stuart."

"Got Tom Gardner with her?"

"No. They left him in Miami with the Celine MacGowan case."

"She came here all alone?"

"She's fine," Roland said. "I was with her. Don't get your balls in an uproar."

"The feds called and let me in on their plan a couple of hours ago. Nice of them to tell me. So I get used as bait, eh?" Frank said.

The bartender set up Roland's draft beer on the bar.

"Don't play that phony victim crap with me. You wanted it to turn out this way. And everyone else agreed this was the best way to deal with this guy," Roland said. "Plant a few seeds and see what comes up. Looks like two weeds to me, but hell, at least they'll be here where we can spray a shot of *Round-Up* on 'em."

"Don't underestimate Cezar Nicolai," Frank said. "He's a resourceful maniac, and he'll think nothing of killing anyone in his way. And his sidekick Vlad Torok is no slouch either. Picks his teeth with a jackhammer."

"Braewyn said Nicolai is sure you'll lead him to the Omega weapon?"

"Can't think of any other reason he'd be here," Frank said. "You sure he's here?"

"Feds tailed him to the airport," Roland said. "Learjet 31. Bastard knows how to travel. Rented a new Cadillac to boot. Must be nice."

471

"Didn't do so well at Dulles," Frank said.

"Got away, didn't he?" Roland said.

"Told you he's resourceful."

"He's got eyes on you, and he's imported extra help," Roland said. "He'll follow your every move, we figure, so we want you to lead him out in the open."

"Great," Frank said. "Why not paint a big bull's eye on my chest?"

"He'd be a fool to shoot the person who's going to lead him to what he wants," Roland said. "No, he'll keep his Golden Goose in his sights until that moment, *then* he'll probably kill you."

"Where's 'out in the open?'" Frank asked.

"We want you to go to the air base tomorrow," Roland said. "Braewyn's got you cleared to get into areas where the public isn't allowed. He'll likely try to follow you somehow. Probably go tourist. Fake IDs, his usual brand of bullshit, who knows? But once he hits that base, we take him down."

"To luck," Frank said and raised his drink in a toast, and Roland did the same.

Frank mouthed the simple toast, but it was his grandfather's words that ran through his head.
"Every day I see the sunrise is a lucky day. But I'd be wise to prepare for tomorrow, and not leave it to luck."

Prepare? Frank thought. *How do I prepare for the unknown?*

472

The FBI saw tomorrow as an infallible steel trap leading to an easy victory. Frank saw himself as a man rolling in heavy seas enduring an anxious night. Tomorrow's dawn would find him jostling in a landing craft, motoring at flank speed toward his personal Omaha Beach. Tomorrow the gate would drop, and he would jump into unknown depths and clash with a great force bent on winning the day.

Frank hoped by noon the day hadn't killed him.

*   *   *   *   *

By midnight Roland and Braewyn had said their goodnights to Frank and turned in. Roland's room, a few doors down the hall from Frank's, was the closest he could get with the high influx of guests arriving for the upcoming air show in Wichita. The FBI agents were across the hall in three separate rooms and everyone was provided with special radios tuned to a single channel with multiple sub-frequencies, which identified each user in a call.

Frank propped himself up in bed and read the Wichita Eagle while *Bullitt* played on a late movie channel. Frank felt a distant kinship with Steve McQueen who was currently chasing two bad guys in a powerful Dodge Charger with his tricked-out Mustang through the roller coaster streets of San Francisco. Detective Bullitt steered the two hit men

473

in the Charger into a fireball crash into a gas station as Frank's radio signaled with a unique beep.

"Dugan," Frank said.

"Special Agent Waylans across the hall. You okay, detective?" a Southern-accented voice asked.

"I'm fine. Watching a movie. Everything okay?"

"Oh, yeah, jus' checkin' in. Did you know there's a bottle of whiskey in front of your door?"

"No, I didn't," Frank said. "You take it. I'm good."

Frank pulled his Browning from its holster hanging on the bedpost and crept over to the door to peek into the hall. The door lock clicked and was ram-forced open by an unseen power. Frank was knocked backward and tripped over his feet onto the floor. The Browning and his radio fell from his hands and hopped across the carpeted room. Vlad Torok filled the doorway and held a Beretta automatic aimed at Frank's supine body. Cezar Nicolai pushed past his large associate and entered the room. Vlad stepped inside and eased the door closed.

"So, how are y'all doin' now, detective?" said Cezar Nicolai in an exaggerated Southern drawl. The large caliber revolver in his hand pointed at Frank's midsection.

Vlad picked up the radio and switched it off.

"Where's agent Waylans?" Frank asked.

"In his room," Nicolai said. "Poor boy died."

"Jesus, why, Nicolai?" Frank said. "You don't have to kill people to get what you want."

"Well, we tried the non-violent approach at first," Cezar said. "But sometimes you just have to change the battle plan. Spent an ugly couple of days in Herndon, Virginia and Dulles airport. Getting tough seems to work better for me."

"What's your new strategy?" Frank said and scooted on his rear toward the bed where the Browning lay.

"Looks like your team has a trap planned," Cezar said and gestured to Vlad to step between Frank and the bed. "I see a lot of not-so-touristy cars around this motel. Dark, government issue, everywhere. Stinks of FBI, cops, and the like."

"If you want the formula, I need to get inside McConnell air base." Frank said.

"That's exactly my plan."

"How?" Frank said and stood.

"Catch you up in the morning," Cezar said. "For tonight, you come with us. Vlad, get the detective's jacket."

While Cezar kept the revolver trained on Frank, Vlad grabbed Frank's sport coat off its hanger and checked its pockets. Finding nothing, he tossed the coat to Frank.

"A car awaits us," Cezar said and carefully opened the door to the hall and peeked down the corridor in both directions.

The trio moved silently down the hall to the fire exit and descended the stairs.

"I'd like to know how you expect to get into a high security air force base with me in tow as a hostage without getting yourselves killed," Frank said.

"Trust me to know a way, detective."

Nicolai stopped the procession on the landing between the floors.

"I tracked my submarine moving up the Atlantic coast," Nicolai said. "How did you do that?"

"Your leaky sub's on the bottom," Frank said. "About half a mile down."

"Half a mile down? We tracked a transducer in your shoe. Did you leave your shoes on the sub?"

"Ah, the shoes," Frank said and smiled. "Probably off Cape Cod by now."

*   *   *   *   *

At 6 AM, Roland called Frank on the walkie-talkie, but got no answer. He called agent Waylans and got the same. Frustrated, and knowing something was wrong, he called the front desk phone and had them ring the two rooms. No responses. He stealthily moved down the hall toward Frank's room, gun drawn.

Frank's room was locked, so he knocked. No answer. He turned to agent Waylans room. His door was not latched fully and Roland carefully pushed it open. On the floor was agent Waylans, his throat cut and blood puddled on the carpeting under his body like a maroon lake.

"Jesus, Mary, and Joseph," Roland said.

Roland radioed Braewyn's room.

"I'm in Waylans' room," Roland said. "He's dead."

"Dear God, no," Braewyn said.

"He's got Frank and we don't have shit," Roland said.

"Frank warned he was resourceful."

"I want to put a .45 hollow point between his goddamned resourceful eyes."

Chapter 67

In the back seat of the Cadillac Cezar Nicolai made a final adjustment on the tubular device curled around Frank's neck. It resembled a fat gray sausage wrapped in

clear plastic and was cinched up snugly under his chin and locked in place by two, heavy duty nylon cable ties. A red detonator protruded from the gray mass.

"Comfy, detective?" Nicolai asked.

Frank glared at him.

"It's only a little bomb," Nicolai said. "You'll get used to it."

Vlad Torok pulled the car up to within twenty feet of the guard booth plaza at the entrance to the McConnell Air Base and stopped. Frank watched Cezar punch in a number on his cell phone.

"McConnell AFB. Sergeant Adkins," an official-sounding voice said over the phone's speaker.

"We are in the black Cadillac outside your booth," Cezar said.

"I see you, sir."

"I have a man here, a detective named Frank Dugan. You may have heard of him."

The sergeant didn't respond.

"He's the Florida detective in the news. You must have seen him."

The sergeant appeared to be checking something in the booth, then looked out toward Cezar's car.

"I have, sir. What can we do for you?"

"You can let us inside the base. By the way, he's wearing a rather cumbersome necklace made of C4 explosive. About three pounds of it. I hold a remote detonator in my hand with the spring-loaded switch in the off position. Should anything happen to me, I will release the remote and vaporize the detective and kill anyone near him. Are we clear so far, sergeant?"

"Completely, sir.

"Excellent. Here I was expecting that government red tape you folks are so famous for."

The crossing gate bar swung upward.

"You may enter, sir, and you may park to the right in the lot marked A-5 Visitor Parking," the sergeant said and directed them to pass through and enter the base.

Vlad inched the Cadillac between the guard booths. Cezar, directly behind the driver's seat, held up the remote for all personnel at the guard plaza to plainly see.

Vlad parked near a close-set group of military buildings and aircraft hangars. A sign directed visitors to various areas accessible to the public. One arrow pointed to the General Vernon Ritter Museum of Air History. Frank realized that it had been named in honor of a man who had worked with his grandfather on the Omega Project. It was Ritter who likely approved the secret Omega bomb tests at this specially designated base where Frank learned he'd been the commander of the top secret B-29 Silverplate training in 1945.

Many contended that the giant "R" installed on the *Enola Gay*'s tail section stood for the word "Revenge," but Frank believed it was actually an homage and tribute to Ritter's superfortress leadership

The three men exited the Cadillac.

"That's where we need to go," Frank said indicating the museum sign.

"Why would something pertaining to the Omega formula be here?" Cezar asked, and followed Frank toward the museum.

"They tested the weapon near here," Frank said. "Planes from this base dropped the first prototypes."

"And the weapon is here?"

"The *formula* is here. It's hidden in the museum."

"You know where *exactly*?" Cezar said.

"I do," Frank said and stopped in the walkway. "Are you willing to kill yourself if things go south in there?"

"If things go south, as you say, won't my life already be over?"

"You could surrender."

A staff sergeant approached the three men and held up a white-gloved hand to halt them.

"Stand down, sergeant," a major said, approaching from several feet away. "These men are cleared to view the museum without base passes. All military personnel are ordered to leave the building."

"Thank you, major," Cezar said and turned to Frank. "Where to?"

"Over there," Frank said and pointed to a B-29 superfortress in the center of the main gallery, the size of a modern sports dome.

"Ah, the historic B-29," Cezar said. "We meet again."

The three men filed to the huge plane and stood under its rear bomb bay at the foot of a specially designed stairway leading up into the fuselage.

"In the tail gunner's blister is a small leather seat," Frank said. "Under the cushion is a storage pocket near the back. It's where the gunner kept a special saw-toothed knife to cut his way out of the Plexiglas if he needed to bail out or escape. Under the knife is a black metal box. It looks like it's the bottom of the compartment, but it's actually false and removable. Beneath it is the formula. You'll need that survival knife to cut out the bottom."

"You got all that from an idiotic poem from your grandfather?" Cezar said.

"The poem and other things."

"You said he never lied. How about that *Enola Gay* scavenger hunt?"

"*He* never lied," Frank said. "*I* did. The document was forged for me by an expert."

"If that formula is not here you won't leave this place alive, putting an end to your puzzles and lying," Cezar said.

"I don't figure I'll live either way," Frank said, "but I'd cherish a few more moments."

"Vlad, you keep him right where he is," Cezar ordered as he climbed the stairway.

"Why not let Dugan go get it?" Vlad asked.

"And take a chance he'd destroy it? No thanks, I'll perform the autopsy," Cezar said.

"Autopsy?" Vlad said.

"It means to see oneself," Cezar said and disappeared into the plane.

The sound of loud voices carried across the cavernous room from the entrance. People moving into the museum were arguing with the staff sergeant who stayed at the door. It was Braewyn and Roland, staring at Frank and Vlad from a hundred feet away. The two new arrivals rushed toward the B-29, led by Braewyn.

"Uh-oh," Vlad said.

Frank observed that Vlad seemed undecided as to what to do about the approaching visitors. Vlad looked up the stairway into the plane trying to locate

Cezar, but he wasn't in sight, so he climbed the first few stairs.

"You know what happens if you move," Vlad called back to Frank.

Vlad climbed into the fuselage and looked toward the plane's tail section. Frank watched him disappear into the rear of the fuselage.

Frank took the unsupervised opportunity to punch his finger through the plastic wrapping covering the bomb around his neck. He quickly gouged off a sample of the pliable gray material and tasted it. Braewyn and Roland stopped moving closer. Frank spat on the floor.

"It's all right," Frank said. "It's modeling clay."

"There's no bomb," Roland yelled to the airman at the gallery entrance. "Get some men in here. *Now!*"

Braewyn rushed to Frank and hugged him.

"I'm so sorry, Frank," Braewyn said. "It wasn't supposed to go down this way."

Vlad appeared in the open bomb bay. A second later, he dropped the nine feet to the floor of the museum, folded like a jackknife, and immediately bounced back to upright. He glared at Frank and Braewyn and charged them. The impact knocked Braewyn to the floor. She cracked her head on the slick tiles and slid fifteen feet away. Vlad encircled Frank's midsection in a face-to-face bear hug and constricted his powerful arm muscles like a 350-

pound anaconda. Frank groaned in pain with an audible rush of exhaled breath.

Two armed airmen ran into the gallery.

"Get the one in the plane," Braewyn said to the airmen.

They sprinted for the stairway under the B-29, rifles aimed at the bomb bay.

Frank looked to Roland who dove into the fray and tried to force Vlad to release his hold, but the huge man violently whipped Frank's body around like a calf in a crocodile's jaws and knocked Roland onto the polished tile floor. One of Frank's shoes flew off his foot and skipped across the room.

The airmen ascended and disappeared into the fuselage of the huge bomber.

Frank managed to pull one of his hands free and get to his jacket's outer breast pocket and extract a thin round object that resembled a pen. He was unable to inhale because of the pressure Vlad was exerting on his rib cage. In seconds he'd be unconscious if he couldn't get out of Vlad's steel grip. He summoned the strength to jab and drive the harpoon-pointed lock needle deep into Vlad's throat. Vlad released his hold on Frank and dropped him to the floor.

Frank rolled onto his back and gasped for all the air he could draw. Vlad stumbled away moaning and tugged at the embedded lock needle. He gave it a ferocious yank and pulled it out, screaming. Blood spurted from his carotid artery. In seconds, he dropped to his knees, his blood pumping out with every heartbeat, spraying the floor red around his writhing body.

Frank gulped more air and scrambled to his feet. He lurched for Braewyn, her still body sprawled on the floor several feet away.

Shots boomed out from inside the B-29.

Frank's body jolted and his head snapped violently backward from the linebacker-like tackle from Vlad Torok. Both men hit the slick floor and slid for several feet. Vlad tried to strangle Frank, but the fake bomb necklace interfered with his attempt. Frank threw a flying elbow back at Vlad. Again and again he struck his giant head, crushing Vlad's nose. Vlad's chokehold on Frank lessened and the big man slid off him. His massive torso rolled onto the floor, his shaking hands trying in vain to stem the red torrent flowing from his neck.

Frank slowly rose and gazed at the pathetic eyes and dying hulk of Vlad Torok.

"There's a switch, someone giving *you* a needle," Frank said, between panting breaths. He stood over the enormous man as he exhaled a final blubbering rush of air and lay wide-eyed. The Goliath was, at last, deathly still.

A dozen more airmen rushed into the scene and surrounded the dead man and Frank's group. Several airmen clambered up into the plane. Frank helped

Braewyn to her feet, aided by a couple of airmen. Roland wobbled to a hunkered stance, looking like a rodeo cowboy whose bronc had hurled him to the arena dirt.

"Nicolai," Frank said. "Where's Cezar Nicolai?"

Everyone looked around the room in silence. Those who had seen him go up into the B-29 cast their eyes in that direction, but nothing stirred. Frank ran to the tail of the plane and looked up at the rear gunner's blister. Airmen appeared above the stairway under the plane, guns in hand.

"Get medics in here," one airman yelled from the bay. "We've got two down."

Moments later, several of the airmen returned to the floor. Their leader crossed to Frank and shook his head.

"Your man's gone, sir," he said and looked back at the bomber. "And so are two of mine."

Chapter 68

The Air Force command issued a base alert for the missing Cezar Nicolai, and the local police were called, but he'd vanished.

Frank gritted his teeth as an airman with bolt cutters removed the snug neck piece from his throat without taking out his voice box. Afterward, Frank and his entourage left the air base in the Crown Vic. As they pulled out of the visitors' parking area they noticed Cezar's rental Cadillac still parked on the lot.

"He's on foot?" Roland asked.

"Not for long," Frank said. "He's lost his main protector, but he has others who jump to his beck and call. I'll bet he's already plotting his next move."

"I've got every resource out hunting him," Braewyn said.

Frank stared at Braewyn.

"Where were all your resources when we were fighting for our lives in the museum?"

"The base commander thought it best to use his men and held ours back," Braewyn said.

"Yeah, they were a lot of help," Frank said, pressing on his sore ribs. "I didn't come here to tour the McConnell Air Base. I also didn't come here to visit Wichita, but they've each served their purpose. Tomorrow I want to finish what I started. There's one tiny condition I need you guys to agree to."

"Here we go," Roland said.

"No, no, don't be that way," Frank said. "It's only one tiny request."

"Let's hear it," Braewyn said.

"I'm going out of town for the day," Frank said. "I need to visit a place. Alone. It's personal."

"What's the condition?" Roland asked.

"You guys stay at the motel 'til I get back," Frank said, "then we all go home."

"I smell fish," Roland said.

"We can't go?" Braewyn said.

"Rotten fish," Roland said.

"It's important I go alone," Frank said. "End of discussion. Let's haul ass out of here. I could use a drink."

*   *   *   *   *

Cezar saw the black Hyundai Sonata as it slowed and stopped at the corner of South Rock Road and East 31st Street where he stood behind a thick tree. When the woman driver looked to her left for oncoming traffic, Cezar dashed out and jumped into the passenger seat with his pistol leveled at her ribs.

"Scream and you die right here," Cezar said.

"Please. Take the car. You can have it, just let me out," the woman said.

"Drive."

"Where?"

"Go left here, and turn left again at the next road."

"You live down there? It's a park," the woman said and turned onto the cross street.

"Go there. And stop shaking."

"I can't help it. Is it money you want?"

"What I want is for you to shut up, stop shaking, and drive."

The woman made a nervous turn toward the park and drove more than two miles into a wooded area that culminated in a dead end.

"Pull over up here on the right. Next to those trees."

The woman did as she was directed and stopped the car.

"Can I go now?" the woman said, her voice faltering and her hands shaking worse than ever.

"Put the car in park and get out."

The woman fumbled with the gearshift, then the door handle, and finally got the door open and stumbled out, clutching her purse. Cezar climbed out and directed her to the broadleaf trees nearby. He carefully searched for anyone around who might be able to see them. He saw no one.

"I have a husband and two children," the woman said as she wobbled in her high heels into the shade of the woods with Cezar directly behind her. "One's very sick. I was going to the drugstore to get him medicine. You can have my money. The druggist knows me and will give me the medicine on credit. He knows we're good pay. We've been customers of his for years and he—"

Cezar had wrapped the muzzle of the revolver with his jacket and fired a single shot into the back of the chattering woman's head.

He ambled leisurely back to the car, pleased that the woman at last had stopped her continuous blathering and incessant shaking. He knew his Lear would be under heavy surveillance, so going back to the Wichita airport would be suicidal. To pick up the trail on Frank he had to find him and follow him to the genuine Omega formula he was certain was nearby. Cezar called one of his acolytes who had flown in with him and told him to ready their forces.

Cezar was certain Frank would go straight to it, now that he would think he was safe from his unrelenting pursuers. He could feel an electric charge sweeping over his scalp and down his neck as he envisioned following his unruly detective right up to the answer to the mystery of the Omega device, and its recipe for world-changing power. Tomorrow he would place his hands on it.

Tomorrow he would be undefeatable.

Chapter 69

The Wichita FBI agents led the caravan of federal
and local law enforcement personnel from the air
base back to the Prairie Inn. Frank, Braewyn, and
Roland went to the motel bar to unwind from their
morning ordeal and to lay out their next move.

The plan was that Frank would file his statement
with the local authorities regarding the killing of
Vlad Torok. Then he would go on his lone mission
in the morning. When he returned, he would drive
the Impala to the rental agency in Wichita, while
Braewyn and Roland followed in the Crown Vic and
picked him up before they all flew out of town. That
was the plan until Braewyn came to Frank's room
after leaving the bar.

"They've found a woman's body in the park
near the air base," Braewyn said. "Shot once in the
back of the head. She'd been driving a late model,
black Hyundai Sonata, according to her family. The
car's missing."

"Sounds like Nicolai's handiwork," Frank said.
"God almighty, he kills people like you and I slap
mosquitoes. It means nothing to him."

"Tomorrow we'll follow you to the rental
agency over on…," Braewyn said and tapped some
screen links on her smart phone, "Air Cargo Road at

the Wichita airport. Looks like it's on the west side of town."

"I'll find it," Frank said and stared at Braewyn. "What?"

"The hug at the air base. Is that in the FBI manual?"

"You looked like you could use one," Braewyn said. "What? Not as cozy as the one Vlad Torok gave you?"

"That bastard's hug nearly crushed my rib cage."

"And mine?"

"That one hurt a lot less," Frank said. "So, do you now believe I've told you all I know?"

"Oh, I'm sure, now more than ever, that you're holding back. I think you believe what you're concealing is for the good of the country and not its detriment."

Frank stepped over to the window and panned his eyes across the motel parking lot.

"Did you say a black Hyundai?"

"Yes," Braewyn said and moved to the window.

"I see one sitting all by itself on the back row," Frank said. "What do you think the odds are of it being driven by a guest here?"

"Parked in the back row? I'm not sure," Braewyn said and quick-stepped to the door. "I'll scramble the guys."

"No. This is my thing."

Braewyn stopped.

"If that's Nicolai down there, he wants just me, and I only want him. You and your crew stay put. I'll take it from here."

"We have a dozen armed men in this building. Why should you march your macho butt out there alone and face him like a Dodge City cowboy?"

"Because cowboys and I know what has to be done," Frank said and checked his Hi-Power for a full magazine and a round in battery.

"I'm sending the troops," Braewyn said.

"Not until I'm finished with him," Frank said, his tone firm.

"Or he's finished with you." Braewyn said. "He's wanted by the FBI. And I'm sending in all I can to take him down."

"This isn't about surviving anymore," Frank said. "It's about stopping him from getting the Omega formula. The odds are two to one in our favor. I kill him, we win; we kill each other, we win; he kills me, you can have at him."

Frank brushed past her and strode out of the room.

*   *   *   *   *

Frank skirted the full rows of parked cars in the lot and made his way carefully to a point where he could see the Hyundai from thirty yards away. He

493

squinted in the bright morning sun to make out an occupant behind the harsh reflection of the windshield. A moment later, a short man dressed in a gray business suit got out of the car and went to the trunk and opened it. It was not Cezar Nicolai, but Frank watched him carefully as he pulled out a briefcase from the trunk and hiked over to the motel office.

Frank turned back toward the motel. As he approached the doorway leading to the rooms, Braewyn appeared with several agents behind her.

"I'm supposed to be taking time off for R&R," Braewyn said.

"Relax. No Nicolai. No shootout," Frank said as he stepped to within arm's length of her.

"Buy you a drink, Wyatt?"

* * * * *

Frank stared into his drink and stirred the ice cubes with his finger.

"Going on your solo trip tomorrow?" Braewyn asked.

"Maybe."

"I thought that was your big plan."

"Cezar Nicolai is out there watching my every move. He's watching me right now. I can feel him. He's going to follow wherever I go, and he's never going to give up 'til he gets what he wants."

494

"We'll get him first."

"Not before he figures out where the Omega formula is," Frank said. "He's got the same information I do, and he knows he's close as long as I'm close."

"So what are you going to do?"

"I have to lure him away from what he wants. He'll follow. He has to."

Frank watched Braewyn looking at herself in the large mirror mounted on the back of the bar.

"Jack Ortiz was right," Braewyn said. "I need a vacation. I look like twenty miles of bad road."

"Do it. Take a vacation. Get the hell outa here."

"I can't as long as you continue to bait this murdering bastard," Braewyn said, glaring at Frank. "I'm an FBI agent. I vowed to protect people like you from people like him."

"Here's a start— find out who owns the black Hyundai out there and ask the motel office about the man who just drove it here. Short, homely dude in a gray suit with a briefcase."

"That car just arrived here? Why didn't you mention that before?" Braewyn said and jumped off her barstool and rushed to the corridor off the lounge.

"It'll all be over soon," Frank said.

"Yeah, I know," Braewyn said and ran down the corridor.

495

*   *   *   *   *

When Braewyn reached the front desk of the motel, the alleged gray-suited man was gone. The clerk said the man was here to see the Wichita Air Show and wanted to see if there were any vacancies. The clerk told him the inn was fully booked and sent him on his way.

Braewyn charged out into the parking lot and searched for the Hyundai.

The gray man and his black Korean car were gone.

Chapter 70

The early morning air was warm and clear as Frank drove the Impala northwest on Route 90 leading out of Wichita. He passed a weapons testing laboratory on 33rd Street that had formerly been known as the United States Testing Laboratory. It was this facility that was cited in the second film David Hapburg had given him. The lab had worked secretly with William Dugan's covert team to test the Omega weapon. According to the film, that testing was done at an area approximately five miles away. Frank had transferred the geographic co-ordinates he'd seen on the movie slates to the car's GPS. After all these years, Frank didn't think he would find the exact spot looking as it appeared in the 1945 film, but he did have its basic location. He hoped the destination he desired didn't have a Walmart sitting on it.

A brief stop at a convenience store got Frank a cup of coffee and area information from a couple of the locals in the parking lot. He hated having to leave a message at the motel desk that he'd meet Braewyn and Roland for breakfast at 8 AM at the Prairie Inn's restaurant, but he needed to put distance between him and everyone else involved in this cross-country chase. This was a gig he had orchestrated, and he planned to be its soloist.

Frank turned onto a secondary road he'd been told went out onto the open prairie. The remaining distance to the long-ago test area passed under the powerful Impala's wheels in minutes, and Frank slowed to carefully pan the uninhabited terrain of the seemingly endless dry grassland. He was so absorbed in looking for an area that resembled the one he'd seen in the Omega films that he didn't notice the Kansas Highway Patrol cruiser closing fast behind the Impala. The whoop of the cruiser's siren startled Frank. He slammed on the brakes and gazed into the rear view mirror.

The police car, with its lights flashing, pulled up close behind Frank, and the trooper got out and headed for the driver's side of the Impala. Frank rolled down the window.

"Driver's license and registration, please," the officer said.

Frank noted his name plate which read: T. Hunter.

"This can't be for speeding," Frank said and dug for his ID.

"I didn't stop you for speeding," the trooper said.

Frank handed the trooper his license and the rental registration papers. The officer looked over Frank's credentials and stared at Frank through his dark aviator glasses.

"So?" Frank said.

"We got a bulletin about a Florida detective who's been missing. Looks like I found him."

"I'm not missing, officer."

"What are you doing out here?"

"Just on a historical visit. I'm looking for an old weapons testing site. It's supposed to be out here somewhere. My grandfather worked here during the war."

"I see," the trooper said. "You go on with your hunt. I'll file a report that you're okay and check on you later to make sure you don't get lost. This is a pretty lonely stretch of road. Not used much since they put in the interstate. Kinda like a desert out here. Gotta watch out for snakes and… other bad things."

The trooper returned Frank's papers.

"I'll be careful."

The trooper returned to his cruiser and climbed behind the wheel. The roof lights went out, and the cruiser pulled onto the road and drove past Frank. A minute later, it disappeared around a distant turn in the road.

Frank called the motel and rang Roland's room.

"It's 7 AM," Roland said. "This better be important."

"Seen Braewyn this morning?"

"I haven't seen my feet yet."

"I left you guys a message at the desk. When you see her, take her to breakfast and tell her I'll join you later."

"Why can't you tell her?"

"She'll ask me a lot of questions I don't want to answer right now."

"Where are you?" Roland asked.

"See? Like that one," Frank said and ended the call.

Frank slowly drove a mile farther down the road and stopped when something caught his attention. Prairie dogs, lots of them. They started popping up from small mounds spread out all over the parched ground and grassy patches a hundred yards to his left. He checked the GPS. He was within a mere yards of the location on the horror film slates.

He quietly slid out of the car and crept low toward the colony of prairie dogs. He made it unnoticed for about thirty yards and crouched behind a solitary boulder, large enough to hide him from the road. He moved to the prairie side of the rock, reached under his lightweight windbreaker, and pulled down his Browning 9mm. He rechecked its ammo. He felt his shoulder rig for its two extra mags, then snugged the pistol into the holster.

Frank stepped around to the roadside face of the rock and leaned against it. He took an old, Prince Albert tobacco tin from his jacket pocket, opened its rounded hinged top, and checked it for a folded piece of yellow paper. He took out the paper, unfolded it, and slowly went over the physics equation he got from Doctor Dekler. He flipped over the paper to see the back side, read more, then refolded it. Satisfied that all was in order, he carefully placed the paper back in the box, recapped it, and tucked the bright red tin into his jacket pocket.

Frank knew Nicolai was there. He could sense his evil presence. The Kansas State trooper didn't fool him either. No real cop pulls his cruiser butt up against the rear bumper of a pull-over unless he's trying to box it in. Nicolai's money could buy phony cops to run surveillance for him and report Frank's exact location. Nicolai was nearby, no doubt about it. He could feel his eyes. But Frank wanted Nicolai to see him; wanted him to see the tin box with its mysterious folded paper. Frank was certain Nicolai would keep his detective alive as long as he believed it would bring him closer to the Omega formula's whereabouts. But Frank hadn't come out here to tease Nicolai. He'd come to end their relationship.

Frank turned away from the road and looked over his surroundings for possible cover. There wasn't much to hide behind on a prairie, and even less that would stop bullets. Parallel to the road, an uncharacteristic ridge rose fifty yards away. It contained several boulders protruding from the dusty soil and offered an elevated position and cover. The glacier that had crept through this land all those millennia ago had planed the terrain flat, except for a few large rocks that stubbornly refused to be milled down, merely accepted a smoothing, and now stood alone like giant egg-pillars in a North American Stonehenge. Frank judged it to be the best location to retreat to, should the lone rock position where he stood prove untenable.

He expected any attack to come from the road. His eyes scanned that solitary byway, the only passage capable of carrying a large vehicle.

An hour passed. Then three more. The sun climbed high overhead and scorched the already baked land. The rock Frank rested against offered some shade, but what little it did provide forced him to constantly move around it to get protection from the blazing sun. As noon approached, the rock's shade was nearly non-existent. The jacket he wore to conceal his shoulder rig was soaked through. Frank hadn't thought it would take so long to draw Nicolai out.

Where the hell is he?

He wished he'd brought a bottle of water, and the more he thought about the oversight, the more his tongue stuck to the roof of his tacky mouth.

Where is that sonofabitch? Have the police or feds caught up with him?

Frank's cell phone vibrated.

"Yes," Frank said, perspiration dripping on the phone from his sweaty ear.

"Warm enough for you, detective?" the familiar voice of Cezar Nicolai said.

"Why do you ask that? I'm in the bar at the Wichita Country Club."

"Could've sworn you were sweating your life away behind a big rock."

"Can't keep anything from you, you clever guy."

"Been out there a long time. Get what you came for?"

"Naw, can't find it. Getting ready to pack it in and head out."

"What's in the little red box?"

"Red box?" Frank said and threw a handful of dirt at an approaching spider. "Oh, you must mean my tobacco case."

"Come now, detective. I know you don't smoke."

"Just took it up."

"Looked like a paper with perhaps a chemical formula on it."

Frank was amazed at the optical ability of Nicolai's spy equipment.

"No, it's only my Internet passwords. Never can remember them all."

"Got a deal for you," Nicolai said. "Leave the little red box, and all that's in it, by the rock where you are, and I'll let you drive back to your motel where you can get a cool drink and take nice dip in the pool. What do you say?"

"Why don't you come and take it?"

"I'll give you a couple of more hours to think it over."

The phone went dead.

"Shit," Frank said and looked upward at the merciless sun.

This is not turning out to be my best idea. Maybe Roland was right. I'm a knucklehead.

Frank expected Nicolai to be watching his every move. He was banking on it. Probably had a binocular position set up where he could take in the entire area. But he knew also, whatever advantage he thought he had was gone... all but one. Nicolai had spotted the tin box, as Frank wanted him to, and probably believed what he and Frank strove to find was at hand. Precious good that would do him if Nicolai killed him, but he still wouldn't have the Omega formula.

Two more hours in the Kansas summer sun was not a healthy option.

Hell, two more hours here and Nicolai could walk up and take the tin box off my heat-stroked dead body.

Frank had to get someplace where he could survive. One fact was sure. Where he was wasn't it. He knew his best chance was to get to his car and make a getaway, but that would only prolong the ordeal with Nicolai. And he might not even make it the sixty yards to the car without getting cut down by Nicolai with a rifle. The ridge with the boulders was his only chance. It wouldn't solve his need for water, but it would provide the cover he'd need, cover from bullets and the sun. Now all he had to do was get there...and it was 150 feet away across open, knee-high prairie grass and crusty dust bowl dirt.

The Marine Corps had taught Frank to crawl across such expanses without being seen. It involved sloth-like movement on one's belly, progressing at a rate of a few feet a minute, often only inches a minute. He would have to cross the distance in about thirty minutes or risk heat prostration. The grass would help hide him, and if he smeared his body and clothing with prairie soil, it could serve as a makeshift camouflage.

Frank dusted himself from head to foot with powdery dirt. He was sure Nicolai could observe him doing everything, including the ploy to disguise his appearance, but that was inevitable. Once he headed across the expanse he might get lucky and fall off Nicolai's radar and go invisible in the breeze-blown, shimmering grass.

It was time to go.

Slinking away from the rock, flat on the ground, Frank Dugan became a human snake in the grass. He hoped this tack would fool Nicolai, but, it wasn't fooling the wary prairie dogs. The entire surrounding colony made short, barking noises, then, in seconds, disappeared into countless burrows. He moved in a serpentine pattern at what seemed like the speed of a garden slug, but in fifteen minutes, he'd made it halfway. His eyes were burning from the sweat-soaked dust running into them. The dust also irritated his nose. Frank wasn't certain of how far away Cezar had positioned his spy nest, so he had to carefully muffle any sneezes which might reveal his whereabouts. Seventy-five feet to go. The goal line was in sight.

The growing sound of a vehicle drifted up from the road behind Frank. He raised his eyes a couple of inches above the grass and peeked behind him. A State Police cruiser was roaring down the road heading toward the Impala.

Another one of Nicolai's cops? The bastard brought his troops.

The cruiser came alongside the Impala and slowed to a creep. Frank dropped down low and stayed motionless. He could see activity at the road through open slits in the dry grass.

The cruiser turned toward Frank and started to drive in his direction, but immediately dove into a grass-covered drainage ditch, its tires losing traction and throwing up thick clouds of dust.

A gust of hot prairie wind blasted the side of the rise where Frank was hiding. The grass flattened and changed everything. Frank was in the open and visible.

"Oh, shit," Frank said and sprang to his feet running full-tilt for the boulders on the rise. Twenty feet short of the cover of the rocks, he pivoted toward the road.

The trooper scrambled out of the disabled cruiser and faced Frank. It was the trooper who had pulled him over. He drew his pistol, aimed at Frank, and started pumping bullets downrange as fast as a human could pull a trigger.

Chapter 71

Frank cursed his bum luck and sprinted for the boulders. The dirt around his feet exploded with bullets and chunks of caked soil. He zigzagged and finally dove between the two closest monoliths. A slug ricocheted off the one to his right and whirr-buzzed away into the air.

Frank found a narrow opening between two huge rocks where he could get a slotted view of the roadway and the cars below. He watched the trooper return to the disabled cruiser and open the trunk. He pulled out a large-barreled weapon that, from the distance, Frank couldn't readily identify. The trooper went to the driver's side of the car, opened the door and picked up a cell phone.

Frank watched the trooper talk briefly on his cell then fiddle with something on the strange device. A moment later, that same weapon was aimed at Frank's position and fired with a tremendous blast from its muzzle. *Good God, it's a grenade launcher!* A visible projectile came soaring toward the boulders in an arcing trajectory. In the split-second before it hit, Frank knew exactly what it was, and what it could do, and flattened himself to the ground behind the larger boulder.

The grenade hit twenty feet to the left of Frank and exploded into a hundred metal fragments, spewing in all directions at the speed of sound. The boulder saved Frank, but just when he thought he was safe, a second blast came from the road. Frank had one second to make a decision. He dove to the side of a boulder on the right of the ridge. The grenade went off near where he'd been two blinks ago. A jagged piece of shrapnel hit and embedded in Frank's left thigh and stung like he'd been lashed with a bullwhip.

Not knowing how many more grenade volleys he could survive, Frank decided to go on the offensive. He wriggled his way across to the far right of the ridge, out of sight of the highway. He clawed his way around the rock to get an eye on the road. He steadied his Browning on his grounded left palm and took aim downrange at the trooper as another grenade boomed his way.

The shot from the Browning left the barrel at the same moment the grenade was flying up at the ridge to the left of Frank. The trooper dropped the grenade launcher and reeled backward onto the hood of the cruiser. The grenade's deafening blast went off near enough to Frank to sting him with flying dirt. He was momentarily blinded by the barrage, but shook it off and wiped his dirty, sweat-covered face with the front of his shirt. Frank peered down toward the road as the trooper slowly slid down the hood of the cruiser and folded in a heap in front of the car's grille.

Frank's cell vibrated. He ripped the phone from his pocket.

"Why don't you come yourself, Nicky, instead of sending these incompetents?" Frank said.

"Soon enough, detective," Nicolai said. "Where'd you find the little red box?"

"Same place I'm going to put you. Under a rock."

"You know we could end all this on a win-win."

"Yeah, how so?"

"You and I go in together on this. We sell the weapon to the highest bidder and split the money."

"What kind of bids you think we'll get?"

"We'll start at two billion and work the auction from there. I figure it'll go to twenty billion or more. That's billion, with a 'b.'"

"Na, no deal. I got all the money I need."

There was a lengthy pause before Cezar spoke. "Thirsty?"

"I'm good. Got a six-pack cooling in a trout stream up here," Frank said and ended the call.

More vehicle sounds came from the road. Another Highway Patrol cruiser pulled up behind the one in the ditch. The trooper got out and rushed to the downed man at the front of the car. Frank leaned against a boulder and took aim at the second trooper as he stood and scanned the rise. Frank squeezed the trigger back one millimeter.

"Frank Dugan?" the trooper yelled. "Agent Braewyn Joyce sent me to find you."

Frank broke his aim and released the pressure on the trigger.

"How did you know where to find me?"

"She followed you out of town up 'til you went onto Route 90."

"Why'd she stop?"

"Radiator hose blew."

Frank found the explanation plausible, but he wasn't about to trot out and show himself.

"What's your name?"

"Sergeant Yancy Burgess."

"Sergeant, it's going to get jumpin' around here in a few minutes. You better watch yourself."

"Agent Joyce filled me in. You need backup?"

Frank didn't trust the trooper. He wouldn't put any deception past Nicolai's hired men.

"Take cover down there where I can see you. We'll be able to work the bad guys from two angles."

"Whatever you say. I can call for more help," Burgess said and sat back in his cruiser.

"No time. We're it, partner," Frank said, knowing the trooper would call it in, even if help would arrive too late.

Chapter 72

Frank Googled the Kansas Highway Patrol on his cell and checked up on Sergeant Burgess. He was legit, apparently, but Frank chose to err on the side of caution and keep his new ally at a distance, even though he would have risked a bullet to get one swig of water from him.

The area was creepily quiet, and Frank shifted his eyes alternately between Trooper Burgess and up and down the lonely road. The hot air was now dead still, not even a bird chirped or fluttered by. The silence was like that of the motionless grandfather clock at Elm Terrace. It was more noticeable when absolutely nothing was heard. He was tired and desperately thirsty, but he knew he had to stay vigilant. He knew Cezar Nicolai would be.

A distant gunshot pop came from the road below the boulders. Frank ran to check out its origin from a space between the huge rocks. He had barely reached the boulders when he heard the deafening blasts of three gunshots behind him and felt severe pains in his back, which pummeled him to the ground. The bullets had struck him below his shoulder blades. His eyes rolled back and it was all he could do to stay conscious. He soon felt strange hands tugging at his clothes and rolling him over onto his back, frisking him and going into his pockets. Frank's gun was ripped from fingers and the magazine was ejected and clinked on the rock-strewn ground. The Browning was tossed several feet away.

"So, this is goodbye, detective," Nicolai said, standing over Frank's supine body, holding a pistol.

Frank's eyes strained to focus, but he could see that a snub-nosed revolver was aimed directly at his head. He painfully struggled to get up on his elbows to face Nicolai, and spit the dirt and grass sticking to his mouth.

Nicolai tucked the revolver in his waistband, opened the Prince Albert tin, and took out the yellow paper inside.

"And this would be the answer to the Omega formula?" Nicolai said as he unfolded the paper.

"Don't ever use that, Nicolai," Frank said and winced. "The world doesn't need that kind of destructive power."

"This strange physics equation is the answer, eh?"

"Ha, it's a goddamn ruse like everything else connected to this Omega crap."

"I think, for once, you may have come up with something useful."

"What are you going to do with it?"

"Why, rule the world, detective."

Nicolai stepped several feet away and turned to Frank who labored to his feet.

"I know those three bullets are merely lodged in your Kevlar body armor, but I can't leave without concluding our memorable friendship."

"I think I know how this ends," Frank said.

"We could've been great partners."

"Ah, a chess master asks for a draw."

"I'm not sensing defeat," Nicolai said. "I know as much as I need to get the final answer."

Nicolai held up the tin box, then slipped it into the breast pocket of his shirt.

"What's another few million lives to a man with no conscience?" Frank said.

"Before you fire your service weapon, detective, you have to make careful judgments. I have no such moral constraints."

"You've got what you want. Take it and go."

"You'd continue to meddle in my work and cause me trouble, so, sadly no. Though I must admit, you've been a worthy adversary. I will miss dearly our little back-and-forths."

"As will I."

"You killed my dearest friend. And for that, there has to be repayment."

"He was trying to kill me. You killed my father. Where does that leave us?"

Nicolai walked away in the direction he'd come. Frank stood and rubbed his painful back. A second later, the short man in the gray suit appeared from behind the row of boulders on Frank's right. He was aiming a long-barreled, large caliber revolver directly at Frank's head from a car length away.

"Ah, the hired help arrives to do your dirty work, eh, Nicolai?" Frank said.

Gray Suit cocked the hammer and took dead aim at Frank's face.

"Oh, he's not here to do my office," Nicolai said. "No one's going to deprive me of this victorious moment. He's only here to be what you police call backup. Put down the gun, Mr. P. I'll take it from here."

Mr. P stuck his pistol in his belt and held his position. Nicolai withdrew his revolver from his waist and cocked its hammer. Frank put his thumb on his left wrist like he was checking his pulse.

"Time to go, detective. Your pulse rate won't matter now," Nicolai said and took aim at Frank's head. "Adieu."

Frank pressed a button on a small device under his watchband. Nicolai's breast pocket exploded, knocking him backward to the ground, his gun flung to the side. Mr. P made an attempt to pull out his belt-tangled pistol, but Frank was on him before he could clear the gun's long barrel. Frank hit him with a bone-shattering punch to his face. Mr. P's nose crushed under the blow and blood gushed from the damage. He stumbled backward, hit his head on a nearby boulder, and crumbled to the ground.

Thirty feet away, Nicolai recovered enough to crawl for his revolver. Frank had no time to grab Mr. P's pistol or get to his Browning. He did the only thing available to him. He snatched a round fist-size rock from the ground as Nicolai struggled to his feet and raised his gun toward Frank. Frank hurled the rock at Nicolai like a World Series pitcher. The 90-mile-an-hour stone smashed into Nicolai squarely in the abdomen with an audible thunk. He wailed, dropped his pistol, clutched his gut, and slumped over in agony.

Frank scrambled for the Browning as Nicolai stretched down to retrieve his revolver. Frank dove the last few feet for the Browning, grabbed it, and rolled on the ground. Nicolai managed to get his pistol up, aimed and fired three shots at Frank's head. Two of Nicolai's bullets whizzed past Frank's cheek, but the third one grazed the top of his right ear. Frank fired at Nicolai's body mass, certain he was wearing body armor, and struck him in the sternum. Nicolai faltered backward from the imparted shock that radiated throughout his middle.

"Dumnezeu, Dumnezeu," Cezar bellowed, facing straight up at the sky. "I emptied that gun."

"Not the one in the chamber," Frank said.

Frank had evened the fight. He knew both men were out of bullets.

Nicolai grimaced and thrust his hand into his pants pocket and retrieved a speedloader for his revolver. Frank knew the decision he made next would either save his life or kill him: go for the Browning's magazine, or go for Nicolai.

He charged at Nicolai as he dropped six fresh bullets into his revolver's cylinder from the loader. Frank hit him squarely in the side of his face with a prodigious punch. Nicolai staggered back, blood filling his left eye. Nicolai managed to hang onto his revolver, but the open cylinder spilled several bullets onto the ground. Frank stalked his enemy and swung again. The hammering blow snapped Nicolai's head violently backward. Nicolai reeled for two more steps, lost his legs, and fell onto his back, unconscious.

It was then that Frank heard two deafening blasts next to him.

Chapter 73

Frank grabbed at his aching ears, but quickly realized he wasn't hit. Mr. P lay bleeding from a huge hole in his forehead and another in his throat, his cocked revolver still in his hand.

Sergeant Burgess stepped out from behind Frank, his service pistol extended in his hand. He stared at the downed man. Frank looked over to Trooper Burgess who holstered his gun and leaned against a boulder. He pressed on his bloody shoulder with his palm, in obvious pain.

"He got me down at the road. Said he came to help, then plugged me."

"How bad are you hurt, sergeant?" Frank said.

"I'm good. A through and through. No sweat. Got first aid in the cruiser."

"Let me grab something and I'll help you back to the road."

Frank stooped next to Nicolai's body and picked up the remains of the tin box near his feet.

"I heard an explosion coming up here," Burgess said.

"This guy on the ground here likes to use fake explosives," Frank said. "I don't."

He put the shredded tin in his jacket pocket, picked up his 9mm magazine off the ground, jammed it into his Browning, and cycled a round into the chamber. He eased the hammer down and snicked on the safety.

"I'll need your cuffs to secure him. We'll need EMS to treat him before we take him into custody."

"I saw him trying to nail you with head shots," Burgess said. "I'd've gone for the body."

"He had to. Knew I wore a vest. He had three shots to get me."

"And he missed with all three."

"Well, not entirely," Frank said, wiping blood from his ear.

"Close, but a snub-nose isn't the most accurate piece," Burgess said.

Frank stepped toward the trooper who held out his handcuffs.

A metallic snapping sound came from behind Frank. He turned to face its origin. Nicolai was sitting upright with the closed revolver leveled at Frank. Frank raised the Browning.

Click, click, click came from Nicolai's pistol. Two booms echoed through the rocky ridge. Nicolai fell onto his back, his brow and right eye perforated by the 9mm slugs.

"Keep the cuffs, sergeant."

Frank examined Nicolai's body to confirm he was dead. He finally holstered his gun and exhaled a long breath.

"We come into this world either crying and hollering, or without so much as a whimper. We go out pretty much the same way."

Frank removed the revolver from Nicolai's hand and checked the cylinder.

"The next click would've been a winner," Frank said and gathered up Mr. P's gun.

Frank plodded over to the trooper, tore off a piece of his tee shirt, and dressed his wound to staunch the bleeding from his shoulder.

The two men trudged down toward the police cruisers. Two FBI cars and more highway patrol vehicles converged on the scene down on the road, lights flashing, sirens wailing and whooping.

"That other dead guy down at the road has on Trooper Tim Hunter's uniform," Burgess said. "Wonder where Tim is."

"Not in a good place, I suspect," Frank said.

"The dead guy took one right between his eyes. Looks like it came from that ridge where we were. Take a pretty damn good shooter to pull that shot off."

"Sometimes it takes a little luck."

"I hear a cop from Florida won the National Law Enforcement Association's marksmanship award for this year," Trooper Burgess said. "They say you're from Stuart. You ever run into him down there, detective?"

"Every morning," Frank said and grinned.

Chapter 74

The local police and the FBI interviewed and got statements from Frank and Sergeant Burgess at the local hospital where they were treated, and later turned the prairie crime scene over to their CSI units. Trooper Tim Hunter was found in the trunk of his cruiser, dead from a gunshot wound to the back of his head.

The following morning, Braewyn's FBI team and the rest of the local authorities worked on the wrap-up of the Cezar Nicolai case in Wichita. Frank ducked out of the intense questioning by mid-afternoon and went into the Prairie Inn bar in hopes of seeing Elwood to say goodbye. And to treat himself to a scotch.

*   *   *   *   *

Roland returned to the Stuart station with hopes that Carl Rumbaugh hadn't mortally wounded the reputation of the Martin County Sheriff's Department. He looked forward to having his top detective back, and to getting re-elected as sheriff in the fall. Farther ahead, he wanted to one day retire, maybe marry a nice lady and start a cattle ranch again.

Roland remembered Frank had put in his unsolicited two cents about that.

"You know, marrying at your age could put sex out of the relationship," Frank said.

To which Roland countered:

"I can still push up my glasses with my tongue."

Roland also noticed something new was added to the department's Wall of Commendations, a place where outstanding service awards were displayed in pictures and plaques of those who went above and beyond to protect the citizens of Martin County. A large trophy sat in front of the wall, inscribed with the name of Detective Frank B. Dugan, law enforcement's Top Gun and champion of the year's national marksmanship tournament held earlier in Beltsville, Maryland.

Roland ran his hand over the shiny brass eagle atop the trophy, smiled, and looked forward to the upcoming election.

Before he left, he squared up the photo of Frank that hung on the wall.

*　　*　　*　　*　　*

Frank talked Braewyn into flying back to Maryland with him to pick up the Corvette before driving it back home to Stuart. They had over three hours on the plane to talk. They talked about the dinner at Langford's that needed to be rescheduled.

They talked about Cezar Nicolai and people who want too much from life and the world. They talked about Alasdair. They talked a lot. Somewhere 30,000 feet over West Virginia they stopped talking and kissed.

*   *   *   *   *

Washington was quiet on the Thursday afternoon when Frank and Braewyn returned. He had offered to take her home from the BWI Thurgood Marshall airport after making a stop at Elm Terrace to get the 'Vette. The DC rotaries weren't as jammed up as usual and the traffic elsewhere around the nation's capital was merciful.

The route to Braewyn's apartment took the Corvette past the Iwo Jima Memorial at Meade Street and Marshall Drive in Arlington, Virginia. He parked the car across from the sunlight sparkling on the Potomac, and stopped to look at the famous statue by Felix de Weldon of the six brave men erecting the American flag atop Mount Suribachi in 1945. The flag had been raised on February 23rd, the birthday of Colonel Paul Tibbets, the man who flew the *Enola Gay* to Japan and dropped the world's first atomic bomb ever used in warfare.

Frank Dugan hoped the second one dropped on Nagasaki would be the last.

*   *   *   *   *

A 9-by-12 FedEx mailer arrived at Elm Terrace while Frank was arranging the estate auction for the saleable contents in the Maryland home. Frank opened the package and pulled out two letters and a large photograph.

The top letter was from a Nebraska law firm stating that their client, General Vernon Ritter, had requested that the enclosed documents be sent upon his death. The second letter was a handwritten one which read:

Frank,

I thought you should have this when I no longer would be around to possess it and reminisce about the "good old days." I'm sure it will find a permanent home in your collection of family memorabilia.

The event I photographed should be obvious, but the inclusion of a single civilian in the picture will make it a rarity. I believe you are acquainted with the civilian looking on the proceedings with justifiable pride.

The accompanying photo showed the Japanese signing the surrender on the battleship USS *Missouri* in 1945. In the scene, General Douglas MacArthur looks on as one of the Japanese representatives signs

524

a document at a table on the dreadnaught's deck. In the background, among the throng of military uniforms, stood the lone civilian that Ritter cited.

It was a young William Dugan dressed in a dark, double-breasted suit.

The letter continued:

General MacArthur signed the Japanese surrender with three different fountain pens, one for each of his title and two names: General... Douglas... MacArthur. One of the pens belonged to his wife. A second pen he donated to the U.S. Military Academy at West Point. The third pen he gave to William, a bright orange Parker called a "Big Red." I'm sure your grandfather kept it as a cherished memento. I hope it has found its way to his grandson, of whom he was so proud.

My very best wishes,

Vernon Ritter

Frank noted the postmark on the mailer. It was yesterday, August the 14th, a date he'd never forget. And today was the 15th, the day the Japanese surrendered. It was also Braewyn Joyce's birthday. Which exact birthday he had no clue, and dared not press to find out, but he would call her and ask her out to dinner for the occasion.

If his good luck continued to hold, she'd say yes.

* * * * *

On the first of September, Special Agent Braewyn Joyce of the FBI made a formal news announcement that, after a careful and diligent investigation, they concluded that the Omega Formula project was a complete and ingeniously successful ruse, formulated and carried out by a handful of dedicated and courageous American patriots. They further said the weapon depicted in the propaganda film, and used to persuade the Japanese to surrender, never existed and never actually could exist.

With that they closed their investigation on the entire affair.

On the same day, Frank received a text message from Dr. Edward Clement. It read:

A group representing the victims of Raymond Grandview's horrors has prevailed on the courts to re-evaluate his sanity. They found him sane and overturned his original sentencing. They take him tomorrow to a federal super-max in Arizona to serve out his life. 23 hours a day in a small cell. No color TV this time. Thought you'd like to know.

526

Chapter 75

In October, Frank sold the house at Elm Terrace, gave the Ford Explorer to charity, and had the Reo insured and shipped to his home in Stuart, Florida. He would drive the Corvette south when he returned from a trip he needed to make, now that Cezar Nicolai was dead and the Omega hubbub was, at last, over.

Frank flew into Wichita, Kansas, rented a car and aimed it northwest, out of Wichita.

In just over an hour he arrived in Hutchinson, Kansas. He motored down Plum Street toward 11th Avenue looking for a particular place.

His grandfather's poem played out, verse by verse, in his head, and he reviewed the solution he'd long held as to its meaning.

Men wish to swing in their seventies and fly with eagles,

His grandfather had been a near-pro golfer. He taught Frank to play as soon as he was big enough to drag a bag of clubs. William firmly believed there was no better way to assess character than to spend four hours on a golf course with someone. He often told Frank that a good golfer should be able to play near par, under 80 strokes, scoring in the *70s*.

like boys who dream of playing on the moon.

There actually was a boy-turned-man who played golf on the surface of the moon.

Find someone to recount the sheep,

Who counts sheep? A shepherd…or a *Shepard*. Like Apollo 14 astronaut Alan Shepard.

avoid the deep six that rusts plain iron,

Shepard was ex-navy, and knew the term "deep six" was a nautical reference to something disposed of, like a dead body or a scuttled decommissioned ship. He played his two historic shots on the moon's Fra Mauro highlands with a specially-made Wilson six iron constructed of a light aluminum-type alloy that could never rust. And, unlike many things abandoned on the moon, the club was never disposed of in that way. Thus, it would always "avoid the deep six."

and keep a tool as a rune.

Many items used on the moon never returned to Earth, but Shepard's special golf club-tool was brought back and *kept* with the astronaut. The club was attached and adapted to a moon sample recovery tool, which was ceremoniously donated by Alan Shepard to the United States Golf Association Museum in New Jersey, where it was preserved and displayed. But in 2007, the club was evaluated, and later purchased by its creator, and moved to Hutchinson, Kansas.

Frank pulled into the parking lot of the Kansas Cosmosphere and Space Center at 4:30 PM, a half-hour before closing time. He entered the museum and walked its gigantic halls where many important pieces of space history were displayed. He was looking for one particular piece.

In a cavernous hall with space capsules and gigantic rockets displayed in the walkway, close enough to touch, he found what he so fervently sought.

It was a large bulletproof glass cube. Inside the cube was Alan Shepard's unique golf club William had designed and fashioned from the original moon rock recovery tool. At its top was a handle; a long, sealed metal tube made of what appeared to be aluminum, or a magnesium alloy. Frank had always wondered why William had underlined the word "handle" in the closing of his letter, but now that became abundantly clear.

*You were always superb at solving puzzles, so
I'm certain you can <u>handle</u> this one.*

Your loving grandfather,

William

The cylinder had a diameter of perhaps two
inches and looked like a smooth 10-inch length of
silver pipe.

> *If need be loosed this awful power,
> it lies asleep until that hour.*

Frank knew that inside that closed cylinder was
a rolled piece of parchment, tied with a red ribbon,
which contained the instructions needed to make the
most frightening weapon the world would ever
know… or need to forget.

> *Sealed in a pipe all eyes can see,
> but blind to all, save you and me.*

This was the clue William wanted Frank to find,
think about, and decide upon.

After he first watched his grandfather's
propaganda film, he worried that his veneration of
his mentor would be destroyed by learning the tests

shown in the movie included the killing of humans, regardless whether they volunteered or not. Frank knew there were those who would sacrifice themselves, no differently than the Japanese kamikaze pilots, to ensure the victory of their beloved country, and to defend freedom in the world. American soldiers did that every day, but they are given a chance to defend themselves. Murdering those heroic, defenseless, and willing heroes would never preserve his love for the most important man in his life. Thankfully, the *O. F. Takes* film from David Hapburg showed that the humans were, in fact, only actors in what they thought was the making of a science fiction movie. No humans were ever killed.

Not so for the prairie dogs. They died, and they weren't acting. Cezar Nicolai had been correct on that count.

Now came the terrible onus of what Frank knew. The famous golf club, which was on loan to the Cosmosphere, and technically his by inheritance, would always be owned by him, regardless of what befell the museum where it was currently displayed.

Should his country ever be in peril of being conquered by bellicose fanatics from outside her borders, there was an awesome remedy in the center of his nation, waiting to be unleashed, but Frank believed political bureaucracies should never be given an option on that power. In addition, he pondered what was to happen when he neared his time of departing this mortal coil. The terrible burden, that one day, Frank, like William, would have to pass on the secret, pressed on his heart like the weight on the back of Atlas.

William spoke once more to him.

Powerful knowledge awaits, and awesome power requires huge responsibility.

The answer to the Omega formula's use would always have to rest in the hands of those who knew the meaning of *huge responsibility.*

Through a journey that had taken Frank into deep mysteries and up against seemingly unsolvable clues, Frank, the detective, had arrived at the truth. That same destination brought Frank, the grandson, to the assurance of one more undeniable fact:

Frank's grandfather never lied.

*   *   *   *   *

When Frank arrived back in Stuart at his home on Stafford Drive he dumped his luggage on the floor and tossed a fistful of mail on the leaving table. He poured himself a Johnny Walker Black and strolled around the living room. The long drive from Maryland in the Corvette had made his legs ache for exercise and the movement felt good. He took in the late afternoon sun beaming outside his picture window, sipped his drink, and wandered into foyer to flip through the mail.

A play program lay next to the pile of letters and ads. He had brought it home from a theatrical production of *Watch on the Rhine* he'd attended at the Stuart Playhouse. He picked it up and studied it for a moment.

Frank stepped over to a tall bookcase in the living room and stared at the framed photo of his father Joe in his Baltimore police uniform, and smiled.

He reached to an eye-level shelf and pulled out the first edition of *Les Miserables* his grandfather had given him. He opened the antique book and placed the theatre playbill in its splayed pages.

A framed photo of his grandfather, on the opposite side of the shelf, faced Joe's picture. William, dressed in a dark business suit, stood on the deck of the great battleship *Missouri*. The tableau of the two photos on the same shelf held his gaze for a full minute. Then...

Frank closed the book.

About the Author

Paul Sekulich was a Hollywood television writer and script doctor for several years and has now trained his sights on novel writing. He teaches television and movie scriptwriting on the college level, and holds degrees with majors in Theatre and Communications.

Detective Frank Dugan will be his lead character in a series of books he has planned for the near future. His new Frank Dugan crime thriller, *Resort Isle,* the prequel in the series, is currently available on Amazon. Another Frank Dugan thriller, *Murder Comes to Paradise*, will be making its debut this summer.

Another novel by the author is already out and titled, *A Killer Season*, a crime thriller about dangerous gambling and gunplay in Las Vegas that explodes into the European arena.

Paul and his wife Joyce live in Maryland.

If you'd care to email or share your thoughts about this book with Paul, or see upcoming works from the author, visit his website at:

http://mdnovelist.com

I can't adequately express, in these few lines, how important reviews are to authors. Please take a moment to leave me a review at Amazon.com.

It keeps writers writing. And it's appreciated beyond measure.

-- Paul Sekulich

Made in the USA
Middletown, DE
21 March 2017